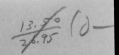

Beyond the Mask

Gordon Craig, Movement, and the Actor

Irène Eynat-Confino

Southern Illinois University Press
Carbondale and Edwardsville

Printed in the United States of America
Designed by *Cindy Small*
Production supervised by *Natalia Nadraga*

Library of Congress Cataloging-in-Publication Data

Eynat-Confino, Irène.
Beyond the mask.
Bibliography: p.
Includes index.
1. Craig, Edward Gordon, 1872–1966—Influence.
2. Theater—History—20th century. 3. Movement
(Acting). 4. Puppets and puppet plays. 5. Theatrical
producers and directors—Great Britain—Biography.
6. Stage design. I. Title.
PN2598.C85E9 1987 792'.0233'0924 86-31569
ISBN 0-8093-1372-3

The paper used in this publication meets the minimum requirements of American National Standard for Information Sciences–Permanence of Paper for Printed Library Materials, ANSI Z39.48-1984. ∞™

Contents

Contents

Illustrations

Preface

By the beginning of the century Edward Gordon Craig was regarded as one of the greatest innovators in theatre, and this is also how Stanislavsky greeted him when Craig came to produce *Hamlet* in 1908 at the Moscow Art Theatre. Today, Stanislavsky is one of the apparently indestructible pillars of the modern theatre and Craig one of its most controversial figures, a ghost that can neither be ignored nor appeased. His contribution to the modern mise en scène is indisputable, and his concept of the actor's role in the theatre has raised passionate debates. Craig was never a favorite with those who expect a prophet to be a lawgiver, an artist a theorist, a theorist a man of action: he was not a second Leonardo, though Leonardo was his hero. Craig's many-faceted work disturbs those who would rather see him either as a stage director or as a stage designer. Various studies have chronicled and discussed his concept of an architectural stage and his controversial idea to replace the actor by the über-marionette, an oversize puppet. Some students of Craig have taken his formal withdrawal from the über-marionette idea at its face value and accepted the über-marionette as a metaphor for the ideal actor; others ignored the retraction, viewing all of Craig's work as a futile attempt to banish the creative actor. The fact that the über-marionette was intended to be only an instrument for an entirely new art of movement was often overlooked. Indeed, in 1964, in his essay "Gordon Craig's Concept of the Actor," Charles R. Lyons established that for Craig "the essence of the art is symbolic movement," showing that Craig's "concentration is upon movement as the primary source and the primary means of expression of the art."[1] In 1968, in his study of Craig's concept of the mise en scène, Dietrich Kreidt emphasized Craig's quest for "pure movement."[2] In 1970, in his Gordon Craig Memorial Lecture, "'After the Practise the Theory': Gordon Craig and Movement," Arnold Rood called attention to "the very soul of Craig's theory about the art of the theatre: Movement."[3] And, in 1979, Harry C. Payne defined Craig's ideal theatre as a theatre of "pure movement."[4] Nonetheless, the role of movement in Craig's work and thought has not yet been systematically explored. It is true that his retractions and his ambivalent attitude toward the actor in his published writings, together with the vast number of unpublished diaries, notebooks, designs, and letters that are scattered all over the world, do not facilitate the task of the scholar in quest of "truth."

It is beyond the scope of this study to give life again to the forms, colors, and sounds that surrounded Craig, to revive the multitude of voices past and present that spoke to him, or to re-create the flux of private, artistic, social, and political events in order to comprehend the scope of his work. Ours is the task of the critic: not the reconstruction of experience but its evaluation, based on the understanding and interpretation of its most significant elements. Since a compliance with the method and tools of a specific school of thought can restrict as well as illuminate, I have preferred to be eclectic in my choice of method and tools for interpretation.

The main purpose of this study is to define the nature and development of Craig's concept of movement. The unpublished documents that I have examined add new information about Craig's sources of influence and provide additional arguments and insights into his theory as it has been formulated in his published writings at various stages. His concept of the art of the theatre received its final shape during the years 1905 and 1906, when he traveled throughout Europe and came in close contact with poets and writers, painters and musicians, architects, dancers, and theatre people. During these years and until World War I, Craig's dedication to his task—the renaissance of the theatre—was motivated not only by his love for the theatre but also by an almost secret yearning: "to bring Belief to the world." His concept of movement is closely related to this goal, as are also the über-marionette and the kinetic stage that he invented.

The book is divided into three parts, following both a chronological and a topical order. The first part is not a partial biography but an attempt to delineate certain decisive factors in Craig's formative years and in his development as an artist. The second part is devoted to the invention of the instruments for movement and covers a span of approximately three years: from 1904 to 1906, by the end of which Craig's theory of theatre was already shaped. This part relies extensively on unpublished documents, among them the "Uber-Marions" notebooks (1905–6), which have been fully deciphered for the first time by this author. The third part examines the concept of movement in Craig's writings, productions, and experiments and discusses his various attempts to implement his ideas on an international scale. Models of the instruments were built, *The Mask* was being published, *Hamlet* was produced at the Moscow Art Theatre, and the School for the Art of the Theatre opened in Florence in 1913. This part deals also with Craig's debacle after the war, when the vast artistic project intended by him to benefit the whole world became merely a private vision. The Afterword provides insights into the tortuous sets of psychological, aesthetic, and circumstantial factors that led to Craig's failure to complete his theory of movement.

The material used consists mainly of unpublished notebooks, daybooks, letters, designs, and photographs but also includes annotated books, newspaper clippings, puppets, masks, and stage models, all of which belong to different Gordon Craig Collections, notably those of the Bibliothèque Nationale, Paris; the Victoria and Albert Museum, London; the Austrian National Library, Vienna; the University of California at Los Angeles; Harvard University, Cambridge, Massachusetts; the University of Texas at Austin; the collection of Mr. Edward A. Craig at Long Crendon, England, the collection of Professor Arnold Rood in New York, and the collection of Professor Norman Philbrick as exhibited at Stanford University in October 1985.

Acknowledgments

I wish first to thank H. E. Robert Craig, Administrator of the Edward Gordon Craig, C. H., Estate for the permission to quote and reproduce from the works of Edward Gordon Craig.

I owe a special debt of gratitude to Mr. Edward A. Craig, whose unfailing interest and enthusiasm encouraged me in my research and whose suggestions and advice have been of invaluable help. I would like to thank Professor André Veinstein for the stimulus and support he provided. Miss Cécile Giteau, Conservateur-en-chef des Collections Théâtrales at the Bibliothèque Nationale, brought to my attention various unpublished writings of Craig and to her I owe my special thanks. To Professor Arnold Rood, who allowed me to consult writings and drawings from his collection, I am grateful for his warm hospitality and advice. I wish to thank Dr. Christine Gruber at the Austrian National Library, Dr. Jeanne Newlin and Miss Martha Mahard at the Theatre Collection of Harvard University, Dr. David Farmer and Miss Ellen Dunlap at the Humanities Research Center of the University of Texas at Austin, and Dr. Brooke Whiting at the University Library of the University of California at Los Angeles, as well as Mrs. Sabine Coron at the Bibliothèque de l'Arsénal and Mrs. Nicole Laillet at the Bibliothèque Nationale in Paris, for their kind assistance.

I also wish to thank the Centre National de la Recherche Scientifique, Paris, and the Israel Academy of Sciences and Humanities for their grants in support of this research.

≻ *Part I* ≺

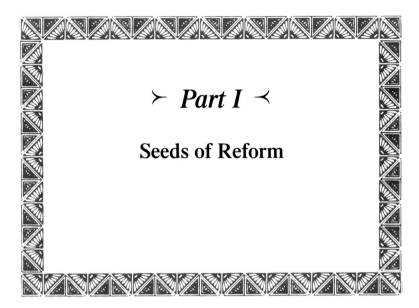

Seeds of Reform

≻ I ≺

Father and Master

Edward Gordon Craig was born in 1872 at Stevenage in Hertfordshire. His mother, Ellen Terry, was later to become the most famous actress of Victorian times. His father, Edward William Godwin, was already a well-known architect.

Ellen Terry, born into a family of actors, went on the stage at an early age and acted for several years in the shadow of her elder sister Kate, who was a favorite with the public. In 1864, when Ellen was only sixteen, she married the celebrated painter George Frederic Watts, who was thirty years her senior. It was during her short marriage to Watts that she first met Gladstone and Disraeli, Browning and Tennyson. After the marriage failed, she returned to the theatre for three years, and then in 1868, she again left the stage and retired to the country with Godwin. Two children were born: Edith, or Edy, in 1869 and Edward, or Teddy, in 1872.

Godwin, who began his architectural career in Bristol, was first an enthusiastic supporter of the Gothic revival launched in England in the early 1850s by Pugin. Ruskin's *Stones of Venice* led to a significant change in Godwin's conception of his art until it was modified again, this time under the impact of Japanese art. Among his contemporaries, Godwin was considered a remarkable draftsman and artist, though controversial; his younger colleagues regarded him as their true leader. He took a deep interest in English history and archaeology and also became an authority on Japanese art. Godwin had the same approach to art and architecture as the Morris circle, designing not only buildings but also entire interiors, furniture, wallpaper, and clothes. His designs became known for their simplicity and elegance and won him a number of important competitions and commissions. His concern for high standards in planning and execution made him among the first who sought to institutionalize his profession in England, thus preparing the way for a school that would give the architectural student proper knowledge and adequate training. Godwin propounded his views in lectures and articles and through active participation in the debates of the various professional organizations to which he belonged. In time, he began to devote more and more of his efforts to the theatre, to which he had always been attracted: he had been writing theatre criticism for journals and newspapers in Bristol and London since early 1857. He began his active participation in theatrical productions by designing, first, costumes and, then, the sets and properties. Next he assisted producers with the mise en scène, and finally in 1884, he produced his first play alone. He advocated historical accuracy but often subordinated it to artistic effect.

Godwin believed in the power of environment to shape personality and proposed that the notion of beauty be extended from art and architecture to each object that served man in his everyday life. At Fallows Green, the house he built at Harpenden in 1872, and later on in London, his children were surrounded by the furniture he designed and walls hung with Japanese prints. Their toys and picture books were carefully chosen, as were their clothes, and music filled the house, for Godwin played the organ and Ellen Terry the piano. Shakespeare was a household word, as both parents loved his plays and used to read them together. Their friends, among them William Burges, Whistler, Burne-Jones, and Oscar Wilde, belonged to the Pre-Raphaelite and the Aesthete circles. At Fallows Green, far from the city and close to a rural community, the two artists were forging a new way of life, unbent by social conventions and surrounded by works of art and the beauty of nature. In this idyllic haven, the architect retained his professional and artistic occupations, and the actress took care of the children, the household, the goat, the ducks, and the chicken. The purse was soon completely empty.

In 1873, a year after Craig was born, Ellen Terry returned to the stage and the young family moved to London. She played in Charles Reade's *Wandering Heir,* which opened on 20 February 1874. When she was offered the role of Portia by the Bancroft company, Godwin was given the artistic direction of *The Merchant of Venice*. Godwin did not limit himself to the role of designer, he also advised Ellen Terry on her acting, and indeed this role brought her quickly to an outstanding position among the famous actresses. Beside his work on this production, Godwin also began now what was to become a long series of articles on "The Architecture and Costume of Shakespeare's plays," in which he discussed the problem of achieving historical and archaeological accuracy in settings, costumes, props, and manners.[1] But the partnership between the two artists did not last, and in 1875, shortly before the opening of *The Merchant of Venice,* they separated. Godwin married soon afterward. Two years later, in 1877, after she got a divorce from Watts, Ellen Terry married Charles Wardell, an actor whose stage name was Charles Kelly. Three years after she married, Ellen Terry separated from her new husband. That year, she became the leading lady at the Lyceum, Henry Irving's theatre.

On each of the two prominent figures of his childhood—Ellen Terry and Henry Irving—Craig wrote a book. Not on Godwin. This, however, should not deceive us about the extent of Godwin's influence on Craig during his formative years. On the contrary. The publication of *Henry Irving* in 1930 and of *Ellen Terry and Her Secret Self* (which he dedicated to his father!) in 1931, both written during a relatively short span of time, was for Craig a symbolic act, an emotional release. This writing was an attempt to reshape past experience by an act that was both public—through the printing and publication—and repetitive, with each reading, an act that was also a ceremony of investiture; in this ceremony the invested was supposed to become the character whose symbols he wore—the investiture being done through the magic of the word. In his private drama, in which Craig identified with Hamlet, both Ellen Terry and Henry Irving were active participants: through the writing, Irving (the King) became Craig's (Hamlet's) "master" and Ellen Terry (the Queen) became "Nelly," the loving mother who had been overshadowed by the actress. This was also an act of exoneration and a tribute to these figures. No such ceremony was necessary for Godwin, because Godwin was from the very beginning an idealized image, an emotional refuge, a ghost. Craig had paid his tribute to Godwin long before he wrote his books on Ellen Terry and Henry Irving, and his mind was at rest: he had never betrayed the image, nor could the image ever betray him.

Godwin's influence on Craig is not explained by Dudley Harbron in his biography of Godwin, *The Conscious Stone* (1949). John Stokes, whose essay "An Aesthetic Theatre: The Career of E. W. Godwin" in *Resistible Theatres* (1972) is the first serious attempt to evaluate Godwin's contribution to modern theatre, affirms that Godwin's teachings were passed on to Craig through Henry Irving. Speaking of Craig's first and only viewing of a production to which Godwin contributed, *Claudian,* seen by Craig at the age of twelve, Stokes suggests that Craig must have been both moved and inspired by Godwin's classical conception of space and color and also by the blocking of the actors, though there is no evidence that Godwin and not Wilson Barrett, the producer, took care of the latter. Stokes also singles out the tendency of both father and son to assume control of the production and to impose a unifying view on all its different stages. Enid Rose, one of Craig's early critics, claimed that he was "predestined" to continue his father's reform of the theatre, though why he should have taken up his father's and not his mother's task she does not explain.[2] Her book, which appeared in 1931, was written under the strong impact of Craig's personality and reflects Craig's own view of the matter. He was by then persuaded not only that he was pursuing Godwin's task but also that their fate as artists was similar. Denis Bablet, on the other hand, does not detect any notable influence of Godwin, though he concedes the existence of inherited inclinations, such as a special sensitivity to architectonic forms.[3] Paul M. Talley suggests that "Craig's career received its initial impetus from the need to prove himself Godwin's son and to secure for Godwin's unpopular ideas the honor they deserved."[4] The attitude of Craig's biographer, his son Edward Craig, is much more circumspect. In his captivating book *Gordon Craig: The Story of His Life,* Edward Craig contends that it was Henry Irving who came to represent, for Craig, the father figure and not Godwin, who had left when Craig was a child of three. The emotional vacuum created by Godwin's departure was filled for only a short time by Ellen Terry's second husband, Edward Craig says, and from the age of eight on, Craig had Irving as the dominant male figure in his life. Michael Peter Loeffler completely dismisses the possibility of Godwin's influence on Craig, on the grounds that Craig barely knew his father. He nevertheless follows Bablet's lead and affirms that Craig inherited his father's sense of space as well as his unconditional devotion to theatre.[5] However, this devotion came to Godwin relatively late in his life. It seems much more likely that Craig was inspired by the examples of Ellen Terry and Henry Irving, whose devotion to theatre was enormous, if perhaps different from Godwin's. Finally, Harry C. Payne asserts that "Godwin did, at a distance, become a model," while he hastens to add that "still, as a deserter, Godwin remained a ghost, more than amply replaced by 'the master' Claudius, Henry Irving."[6]

Thus, if Godwin's influence on Craig is acknowledged, it is perceived mainly in Craig's approach to space organization and attributed to heredity. If no influence is recognized, this is explained by Godwin's absence from Craig's immediate surroundings. Both attitudes are unequivocally deterministic, overlooking a major psychological fact, namely, that very often the impact of an image can be much more powerful and longer lasting than the impact of an apparently overwhelming physical presence.

Images are born, bred, stimulated, nourished, or repressed by real or imaginary actions, by concrete objects or abstract ideas. They loom up, develop, expand, contract, deterioriate, embellish, collapse, decompose, fade away, or spring back to life fresher than ever. Images never die. They lie in unknown shelters of the mind, waiting to be summoned to the surface by a sudden flicker of memory; then they burst forth, whole or distorted, vivid or muted, in dreams or wakefulness. What were those acts, memories, or mementos that nourished Craig's image of his father? The firsthand published sources—Craig's writings, Ellen Terry's memoirs, and Edward Craig's biography—offer many interesting details that can certainly be completed by the study of unpublished documents, within the framework of a separate research. Ellen Terry's memoirs are a model of Victorian discretion and reveal nothing about private matters. Moreover, these memoirs underwent the censorship of Edith Craig, whose attitude to her father was far from tolerant. In fact, the memoirs do not even mention Godwin's name as the father of Ellen Terry's children, and Godwin's role in her life is only vaguely alluded to. What these memoirs do help us with is a description of the atmosphere in which the young Craig grew up. Few but illuminating details concerning the relationship between Godwin and his children are provided by Edward Craig's biography.

As for the *Index to the Story of My Days,* a work of Craig's old age, not only does it reveal significant moments in a long process of discovery and retrieval of the father, but it also enlightens us as to Craig's attitude to Godwin across a haze of many years. Craig's view of Godwin is colored by sentiment, but it at least has shed many of the former inhibitions about both parents. Selecting from his many daybooks, notebooks, letters, and other mementos (such as books and programs) the dates and events he considered most relevant to his story as an artist, Craig created in the *Index* a sort of compendium in which one finds incisive notes about events in Godwin's career that had been at the time totally unknown to Craig. These entries on Godwin are short and informative, but they grow in scope as Teddy the child becomes a youth. The entries are followed by comments that disclose little by little an image of the father that Craig created out of scattered pieces, collecting whatever scraps of knowledge about Godwin he could get hold of. The father he discovered was a product of his own imagination and served as an emotional support when he needed him most. His mother was dedicated to her work and had little time to spend with the child. Irving, for her sake, bestowed on the young Teddy much care and attention, but their relations never attained the same degree of affectionate familiarity as those between Charles Kelly and the young boy. Partly because of Irving's nature and his devotion to his work, partly because of social conventions, theirs was more of a guardian and ward relationship. It seems as if professional and private circumstances had cast Irving in the role of a surrogate father and he applied himself to the task as best he knew. But a physical presence could never win the battle against a persistent ghost. The *Index* does *not* convey the picture of a happy young boy, surrounded by a household of indulgent, adoring females.

One incident touched on by Edward Craig perhaps suggests Godwin's attitude toward his little son at the time he left Ellen Terry.[7] Soon after their separation, which occurred some time before March 1875, Ellen Terry left the house on Taviton Street where she and Godwin had been living and moved to Camden Road. On Tuesday, 3 March, Godwin went to the house on Camden Road while Ellen was absent and tried to take Edy away. Members of the household prevented his doing so.[8] A day or so after this, Godwin, apparently suffering from one of his frequent spells of depression, got a friend (Mr. Wilson) to try and arrange a reconciliation with Ellen. Wilson wrote to her, but instead of waiting for her answer, and probably urged by Godwin's distress, he went to her house on Friday evening. He did not meet her, but his letter arrived soon after he left. Ellen Terry's reply to Mr. Wilson's letter, written the following evening, made it clear that no reconciliation with Godwin was at all possible—after Tuesday's incident—nor would she hold any further communication with him. She had, she said, offered to let Godwin "have the boy," and he tried "by unfair means" to get the little girl. Since it seems unlikely that Godwin actually tried to take the child by force, the word "unfair" is to be taken as meaning underhanded, done while Ellen was absent from the house. (Immediately thereafter the children were sent away to the country with their nurse.) Who else, besides Mr. Wilson, knew about Ellen Terry's original offer and about Godwin's refusal? Did Craig ever learn about it? If he did, he certainly refused to believe that Godwin did not want him: in a household where Godwin's name was taboo and was associated with unpleasant memories for the mother, even the truth about him could be interpreted by an adoring child as pure slander.

Ellen Terry's reaction after Godwin left was certainly that of an injured woman. Later, in her memoirs, Ellen Terry resented her difficult financial position in the early 1870s but without mentioning that this was also the period of her liaison with Godwin.[9] How much Godwin's lack of money contributed to the separation is not known, but Godwin had few commissions in those years, and after the brokers took possession of the furniture at Fallows Green in 1873, Ellen Terry returned to the stage, primarily, it seems, for money to help the household. Godwin's income did not improve much during 1874, and Ellen Terry had to go on tour, only to find on her return that the brokers had paid them a new visit. It was also at that time that Godwin, living up to his much publicized opinion that the profession of architecture should be open to women, took in a young female pupil soon to become his wife. Moreover, Godwin's chronic "ill health," which manifested itself in periodic (nervous?) breakdowns, the cause of which was not determined, no doubt added to the strained relations in the household. Their common interest in the new production of *The Merchant of Venice,* which was scheduled to open in April 1875, apparently did nothing to relieve the tension; it may even have made matters worse. The long retreat in the country had quieted much of the stir that Ellen Terry's elopement with Godwin had caused, but she was still legally married to Watts, and for years she had been ostracized by her own family and by their close friend the Reverend Dodgson (Lewis Carroll). Now that she had returned to the stage, she wanted her separation from Godwin to be made under the best possible conditions—that is, quietly and discreetly, for she hated scandal.[10] Her second marriage, in 1877, brought her back to "respectability"; henceforth, she would take the greatest care to keep up appearances. Godwin's name was forbidden in her house—though she herself could not always obey this rule.[11]

Some of Craig's childhood memories connected with his father's absence are evoked in the *Index:* no specific events are recalled, only a state of mind. So, for example, Craig remembered the atmosphere of conspiracy around him, which was due—as he later came to realize—to his being an illegitimate child whose father was in some inexplicable way the villain of the piece.[12] As a young boy, he felt and was made to feel different from other children, and he was constantly full of anxiety. He could never forget the discomfort and the sense of being in the wrong that were so much a part of him throughout his childhood. He used to feel near him the omnipresent (absent) father and waited for him in vain to materialize before his eyes; instead, he was left with an image, "a spectre and a reality."[13] The pages in the *Index* describing the young boy's painful quest for his father are distressing in their sincerity. Craig's rare gift as a writer compels the reader to share the pain, the sense of loss, and the hopeless longing of the young boy for a beloved ghost. Years later, the reading of Heine or Montaigne would bring him a sense of consolation that he associated with his father.

The *Index* enumerates the Godwin mementos of Craig's childhood as cherished items of the past. In January 1884, while Ellen Terry was on tour in America with Irving, the young Teddy saw *Claudian,* whose settings and costumes were designed by Godwin, at the Princess's Theatre. (Years afterward he would still remember a crowd scene, an earthquake scene, and the melodramatic acting of an actor whom he had known at the Lyceum.)[14] There was also a visit to Harpenden with his mother in January 1890, a few days before his eighteenth birthday. That August, he saw the town hall in Northampton, built in 1861 from designs by his father, chosen in competition. Craig had been on the stage for one year and touring with the Haviland and Harvey company during the summer when he received a letter from his mother, asking him to go and see the town hall and make some sketches of it for her. Her letter discusses Godwin's faults—his carelessness about money and his impracticality—but also recognizes his merit as an artist whose ideas were too advanced for his own time.[15] Her request for sketches seems to have been a sincere, if tardy, effort to bring her son into some touch with his father's work. By now, Ellen Terry, it appears, considered her children strong enough to face social pressure and mature enough to understand the past and accept its heritage. A year later, the three of them together paid a visit to Fallows Green.[16]

The next important entry in the *Index* is connected with Hamlet, the role Craig played for the first time in 1894, when he was twenty-two. He identified with Hamlet because, as he wrote, he too had lost a father. This was to become almost an obsession.[16] Another entry, from 22 October 1895, when Craig, a promising young actor, was married and himself the father of two little children, mentions having written the music to two songs, one of them "My father is dead, I do not know how"; Godwin had died nine years before, on 6 October 1886.[17]

Another entry from 1896 refers to Craig's acting the role of Edward IV to Irving's Richard III. In this entry, Craig tells of obtaining a photograph of Godwin and matching his makeup to that image.[18] If this is indeed what Craig did—and no other source confirms this detail—the challenge was only too obvious. This act, in a way bold and insolent yet known only to himself and muted by the mask of the role, allowed him to make a dramatic statement and point out the similarities between the two Edwards, the Shakespearean king and his own father. For the space of one evening, the three Edwards (character, father, and son) merged, in order to challenge evil. And evil was personified by Irving, under the mask of his role as Richard III. The entry in the *Index* tells how Irving fell ill immediately after the performance; Craig and Edy went to visit him the next day.[19] The first night of *Richard III* took place on Saturday, 19 December 1896. After the performance, at his home, Irving fell down the stairs and injured his knee so badly that the theatre was closed for more than a month. When it reopened, on 25 January, it was with *Cymbeline* and *Olivia,* both starring Ellen Terry.[20] *Richard III* was put on again on 27 February 1897. Craig says that he was replaced in the role of Edward IV and whimsically ponders why.[21] According to the chronology earlier provided by Craig for Janet Leeper and printed in her small book *Edward Gordon Craig: Designs for the Theatre,* Craig did continue in the role from 27 February till 7 April 1897. Be that as it may, one must never forget that the entries of the *Index* were carefully put together by a very skilled writer who was still emotionally bound up in those occurrences.

The unfortunate chain of events that followed the first night of *Richard III* must have convinced Craig that his act reached its goal. Irving's acting did indeed look bizarre that night—"but no more than usual," his enemies would say. Bernard Shaw, who attended the performance, wrote in the *Saturday Review* that Irving "was occasionally a little out of temper with his own nervous condition."[22] If Irving was really drunk onstage, as some people claimed, then Craig's makeup may have disturbed him, or the point of it may have been totally lost on him; even if he grasped the resemblance to Godwin, he may not have understood Craig's intentions. At any rate, Irving's performance was startlingly inept. Ellen Terry, who was in the audience that night, wrote Bernard Shaw a week later from Monte Carlo, "H. I. is always 'out of temper' when I dont act with him." As for herself, she said, "I was ghastly ill all the evening in the box."[23] One assumes the remark to mean that she was embarrassed for Irving's sake. Craig's private little drama, a play within a play, needed no audience. If the king (Richard) saw the point—and Craig remained convinced that he did—that was sufficient. Fancying himself Hamlet, Craig cast Irving as Claudius, or fancying Irving Claudius, in love with Hamlet's mother, he was Hamlet. Craig never abandoned the conviction that Irving's fondness for Ellen Terry had got in the way of a possible reconciliation between Ellen and Godwin while there was still time—Godwin was estranged from his second wife when he died—and somehow prompted his father's death.[24] This belief became a lifelong obsession. He recognized in Irving a friend, but also an enemy: an enemy because he had been responsible for keeping Ellen from reconciling with Godwin, the only man to whom she was ever deeply attached. He blamed his mother for not, so he judged, supporting his father when he needed her most. As his own passion for the theatre grew, he dreamed of the theatre they had dreamed of and was convinced that they could one day have built it together.

Although he never ceased to admire Irving as an actor, as Craig developed intellectually and artistically, he came more and more to reject the values Irving stood for. Not only was this reaction part of the self-assertion process of the young man—a reaction that would justify the assumption that Irving was indeed Craig's father figure—but it also went hand in hand with the building up of the image of the real father. He shared with Godwin the same attitude toward the role of the artist in the theatre, but he rejected his belief in the importance of archaeological accuracy in the mise en scène. From his associations with various aesthetes in the nineties, and his friendship with young artists like James Pryde, William Nicholson, William Rothenstein, Max Beerbohm, and others in the New English Art Club, Craig learned new media and techniques of artistic expression and new ways of looking at the theatre. And when he examined Irving's teachings in the light of aesthetic principles that were, not unexpectedly, akin to those held by his father, the contrast added to the already glowing image he had of his father. Along with this aspect of the unrecognized and romantic-tragic artist image, Craig also conceived an image of a spiritual guide and sage, drawn, rather unexpectedly, from Montaigne. After Craig bought the three volumes of Montaigne's *Essays* in 1893, he began to hear in Montaigne's voice the voice of his dead father.[25] In Montaigne, Craig found wisdom coupled with a keen *joie de vivre* and a craving for independence as fierce as his own. In addition, he shared with Montaigne a heritage of brick and stone. One of Montaigne's main occupations was the upkeep of the estate he inherited from his father—whose very name, Pierre, was symbolic of solidity. Again and again in the *Essays,* "stone" recurs in metaphorical usage.[26] Craig's father, who had left a legacy of numerous buildings in stone and brick, was an obvious parallel; Craig, like Montaigne, was moved to "care for" the father's legacy in stone. Godwin was, of course, *the* Artist par excellence, a fallen angel (fallen because in Craig's private mythology he did not get the support of Ellen Terry), an ambiguous model of success and failure, a prophet exalted by his mission but nevertheless an isolated man, unrecognized and betrayed. This prophet's experience with men—and this is the link between the two aspects of the image—provided Craig (via Montaigne) with solace and advice. This composite image of the father as Artist and Sage challenged the image of the "master," Henry Irving.

The young Craig began to collect Godwin's essays as well as other mementos connected with him, such as an opuscule on *Helena in Troas* that Godwin had produced in 1886 at Hengler's Circus. Shortly after the *Richard III* incident, Craig bought excerpts from *The Architect* that included Godwin's essays on "The Architecture and Costume of Shakespeare's Plays" and bound them together with Godwin's other articles on theatre. In 1900, on his birthday, he was overjoyed when he came across the Vecellio costume book that Godwin had shown to Ellen Terry while they were working on *The Merchant of Venice*. He bought it at once.[27]

Craig was twenty-nine when he had a vivid dream about his father that seems to symbolize his own birth as an artist. He recorded the dream in detail in one of his many notebooks.[28] The dream was an expression of Craig's awareness of his artistic "coming of age"; his growing interest in his father and the building up of his image were concurrent with Craig's artistic apprenticeship, and the dream marks the end of the quest and the finding of the self. Craig the artist came into being, as the dream showed, with the blessing of both parents but under the guidance of the father. By now, Craig had identified with the role of the Artist, one of the two faces of his father's image. Later on, in 1904, when Craig arrived in Berlin, he was proud to find that Godwin's name was not unknown. In a letter he wrote on 6 September 1904 to his close friend Martin Shaw, Craig described his joy at discovering that Godwin's work in architecture and theatre was well known in the artistic circles in Germany. But he also confessed to his friend his hesitation and embarrassment at talking openly about his father's ideas because of the awkward situation that an article in the press had created. It appears that this article had identified Craig as Godwin's son, a position that only Godwin's son from his second marriage could legitimately claim.[29] Craig's position as an illegitimate son still bothered him.

Several years later, when he started his journal *The Mask,* Craig began to publish Godwin's articles on theatre, but without mentioning that Godwin was his own father. These articles appeared in *The Mask* from 1908 to 1913; in 1914, Godwin's article on dress was printed. Such was Craig's tribute to his father. In this journal, dedicated to the art of the theatre, Godwin was placed among such authorities as Serlio, Goethe, and Nietzsche; as Craig's interest in the history of the theatre became deeper and deeper, he also became more and more convinced of the importance of Godwin's contribution to modern theatre. In his *Henry Irving* he did not fail to emphasize Irving's debt to Godwin.[30] Craig even dedicated his book *Ellen Terry and Her Secret Self* to his father. And in his *Fourteen Notes,* printed in 1931, he listed Godwin together with Antoine, Appia, Fortuny, Bakst, Reinhardt, Stanislavsky, and himself as reformers of the modern theatre. This publication contains several comparative tables, and the one artist—besides Craig himself, of course—who stands out among all others by his many abilities is Godwin. Craig wants the reader to know that Godwin, unlike Antoine, Appia, Fortuny, Bakst, and Stanislavsky, was not only a designer and a director but also a theorist and a writer, an architect and a craftsman.

Consciously or unconsciously, Craig tried to be equally versatile. He did not attempt to assert his father's views on theatre, nor to adapt them for his own use, since they were, as he well understood, the product of a specific moment in the history of the theatre and of the past. However, like Godwin, he also believed in the unity of conception in art and considered the director not as an overseer but as an artist who imposes *his* interpretation and controls all stages of the production. Moreover, it was the Artist as such that he tried to vindicate, not only because Craig considered the Artist's dilemma an ever recurring evil, but also because he identified, in this respect, with Godwin. As Craig saw it, although Godwin's views and works were stimulating and influential, he nevertheless did not receive the support he deserved and even Ellen Terry, the woman and artist he loved, failed him. Craig would feel that like his father he too was a misunderstood artist whom everyone plundered. Like him, he would also feel betrayed by his beloved woman and artist (Isadora Duncan). He could understand Godwin and would never condemn him, whereas Irving was always there, open to scrutiny, analysis, and criticism. Craig created an idealized image of the absent father partly by a long process of search but also partly by intuition. This is why, on reading Harbron's biography of Godwin in 1949, he could feel that although many of its details were new to him, he had long known the truth "through [his] blood and bones."[31]

In a sense, Craig's whole work can be considered a work of vindication, for he restored Godwin to his rightful place among the leading artists of the theatre, while at the same time and by his own achievements he legitimized his position as Godwin's son. He did in fact continue his father's task. His book *Towards a New Theatre,* published in 1913, opens with a passage from *Hamlet,* act I, scene 5, that ends with the Ghost's order: "Revenge his foul and most unnatural murder." This he did.[32]

But Craig could never deny the affection he felt for Irving. He praised his merits as an actor and recognized his debt to him as a teacher. His was a love-hate attachment to Irving. Of course, his rebellion against Irving could well reinforce the thesis that he did regard Irving as the father figure, were it not for the fact that Irving was, after all, only a substitute for the real father whose existence could not be denied. Curiously enough, Craig's rebellion against Irving was not only an act of self-assertion but also an act of self-oblivion and identification with an idealized image of the biological father. But this contradiction is only one of many in the complex web of ambiguities that constituted Craig's personality. His emotional attachment to Irving and Godwin finds its corollary in Craig's approach to acting and movement. All his life, Craig oscillated between his fascination with the compelling, brilliant acting of a few artists and his vision of an ideal, abstract style of movement that could benefit many people. This was in fact an intellectual and an emotional fluctuation between two sorts of movement—not between a representational and an abstract movement but between two levels of expression, which come at different moments to fulfill different functions.

≻ 2 ≺

Setting the Stage

After Ellen Terry separated from Godwin, she continued to raise her children as before, surrounded by music and works of art. Craig later assumed that she did so out of respect for Godwin, but certainly the love for the arts that she instilled in her children was her own quite as much as it was Godwin's.[1] Young Teddy was first sent to a boarding school at Southfield Park, Southborough, then to Bradfield College, a public school, and then to an English school in Heidelberg. At this stage, he not only interpreted the term "escapade" literally but also carried it out with such gusto that he was soon expelled from school. He now was a few months short of seventeen, and the stage being more exciting than any academic life, school was abandoned. Back home, he did not escape schooling entirely, for he had lessons under private tutors. He also studied drawing and played the piano, all the while waiting for his first role.

Ellen Terry's dedication to her work did not fail to inspire Craig's own way in the theatre, once he had decided that this was his vocation. Everything at home was centered on Ellen Terry: the daily life was scheduled to fit her needs, and not even her brief marriage to Charles Kelly could disturb the rules of the household. Though her career was her stronghold and brought her both financial security and a respectable social position, she never ceased to waver between her emotional inclinations and the need to obey social conventions. As a respected mother of two illegitimate children, she was a paradox in Victorian society, falling somewhere between the not quite proper and the proper. Her sister Kate, after a successful career in the theatre, left the stage, married in the haute bourgeoisie, and devoted the rest of her life to her family. But Ellen Terry's two early incursions into domesticity, first with Watts, then with Godwin, took her away from the stage and taught her the value of self-sufficiency. Moreover, they also enriched her emotionally, and when she returned to the stage in 1873, her art was ripe. Like his mother, Craig would also spend several years away from the stage, trying his hand as a wood engraver, a writer, and an editor, an experience that would prove beneficent, for it would help his vision of the theatre to crystallize.

Picture books of Caldecott, George du Maurier, Blake, and Walter Crane were Craig's childhood companions, and Japanese prints decorated his nursery walls. This environment so shaped his aesthetic inclinations that Craig, as a young child, naturally preferred pictures to books. Only Howard Pyle's powerful illustrations to *Robin Hood* could tempt him into reading the book.[2] When he was thirteen, he started taking drawing lessons. By 1890, when he was eighteen and had already been on the stage for almost a year, the National Gallery was still his favorite place. Though his taste was not always identical to that of Ellen Terry, they used to visit art galleries together. So, for example, in July 1890, they went to Agnew's to see the *Briar Rose* series of Burne-Jones; Ellen Terry was very much moved by the paintings, while Craig remained totally indifferent.[3]

It was not only the aesthetic experience itself that appealed to Craig but also the potential use of the visual arts as a source of inspiration to the theatre artist. He was eighteen when he discovered the drawings of Edwin A. Abbey, Louis Loeb, and Oliver Merson.[4] Three years later, in 1893, he became a close friend of James Pryde and William Nicholson, and they introduced him to modern painting. If we listen to his *Index,* his preference was mostly for the painters of the Italian Renaissance—Bellini, Crivelli, Piero di Cosimo, Ghirlandajo, Uccello, Piero della Francesca, Mantegna (but not Botticelli). He also admired the early Michelangelo, Raphael, Leonardo da Vinci, Van Eyck, Callot, Rembrandt, Canaletto, and among contemporary painters Turner (but not Constable or Gainsborough), Blake, Rossetti, Ruskin and Morris, Bonnard, Lautrec, and Maurice Denis. This list probably includes the artists whom Craig still cherished by the time he was writing the *Index* but is incomplete, and Edward Craig adds to it Whistler and Monet. Bablet mentions Japanese art as another source of inspiration.

Very often in his writings Craig liked to bring forward his "masters"—and they were indeed very many. In *Towards a New Theatre,* he wistfully acknowledged his debt to no less than thirty-six artists, among them his own son Teddy, who was at that time only eight years old. It seems that Craig rather preferred not to leave the task of compiling the list of his "sources" to his critics, and whenever the occasion arose, he fell to the task with ironic pedantry. But to declare oneself the follower of a long and dignified line of established authorities in art—and little Teddy's merits must indeed have been great—is a well-known tactical device among innovators in general and among aesthetic rebels in particular. To its user, it seems a trustworthy means to persuade the skeptical into accepting what at a glance looks to be (and often is) an iconoclastic approach. An amusing example of this strategy is Hugo's defense of the grotesque in his preface to *Cromwell;* another is found in Zola's essay "Naturalism on the Stage," where he attempts to prove that his is a literary school "as old as the world."[5] Or, closer to Craig's time, there is Wilde's refutation of naturalism in "The Decay of Lying," where he brings in Herodotus, Cicero, Tacitus, Pliny, Hanno, *The Lives of the Saints,* and Casanova, among others, in order to support his own truth. Though they certainly are informative, Craig's long lists of "masters" impress us as the sign of his too-eager wish to create for the reader an image of a serious, studious, and discerning artist, well informed about contemporary trends in arts, literature, philosophy, and aesthetics and also having a sound background in the history of the fine arts. In the *Index,* he indicates that at eighteen he was reading Bacon's *Essays,* Shakespeare, Marlowe's *Dr. Faustus* and Goethe's *Faust, Part One,* G. H. Lewes' *Life of Goethe,* Tolstoy's *Kreutzer Sonata,* the biographies of Edmund Kean and Mrs. Siddons, two historical novels by Kingsley, as well as Heine, Shelley, Rossetti, and Buchanan—and what is puzzling is that he still had time for acting and elocution lessons. Later on came Alexandre Dumas and Walter Scott, Balzac and Dickens, Lamb and Coleridge, Walt Whitman, Montaigne, Flaubert, Wagner, Nietzsche, and also Ibsen, Strindberg, and Dante's *La Vita Nuova.*[6] These were the "masters" that Craig knew by the time he started his London productions. By then, his love for reading had taken over his love for "pictures," and four authors were his favorite: Dumas, whose novels Craig read and reread with amused affection; Montaigne, who became a lifelong companion; Wagner, whose innovations in drama and theatre architecture kindled his imagination; and Walt Whitman, for a reason that Craig would be aware of only years later, namely, his mysticism.

Painting, literature, and theatre. Theatre too (or should we say mostly) was part of Craig's life, from the day he was born. As mentioned earlier, his parents used to read and study Shakespeare together. A little later, watching his mother rehearsing her roles—often Shakespearean—became a daily occurrence. Being the son of a celebrated actress he was approached at school by both fellow students and teachers as an authority on theatrical matters. Thus, to become an actor seemed the natural course for him to follow. With Ellen Terry's and Irving's help, he went on the stage when he was seventeen, and the Lyceum became his second home for several years. Ellen Terry chose Walter Lacy, an older actor, to teach him diction, but Craig would always maintain that his real teacher was in fact his mother. He got acting lessons on the spot, by watching Irving, like all the other young actors at the Lyceum. The young Craig played in melodramas and in Shakespeare, and Hamlet was one of his most successful roles. His work with different touring companies put him in touch with different styles of acting and directing, various types of audiences, and a versatile repertoire. He also gave private performances in order to increase his earnings. All this was part of the normal apprenticeship of a fledgling actor, and as Craig's technique improved, he became more and more appreciated on his own merits and not merely as the son of the famous Ellen Terry.[7]

The proximity to Irving, who devoted so much thought to the faithful reproduction of historical settings, and his own interest in Godwin's work, gave Craig a much more comprehensive view of the theatre than an ordinary young actor of his age might have. His interest was not limited to acting only but also included play production. From the moment he entered the profession, he began to collect material such as Edwin A. Abbey's designs for Shakespeare's plays, and he soon also discovered Herbert von Herkomer. Herkomer was a flamboyant artist whose theatrical events were quite in another vein than Irving's but attracted fashionable society and theatre people alike. Craig went to a Herkomer production almost as soon as he began acting at the Lyceum, in 1889. In September 1890, with Irving and Ellen Terry, he went to Herkomer's theatre at Bushey to see *An Idyl.* A year later, Craig was one of the few people who attended Herkomer's lecture on "Scenic Art" at the Avenue Theatre in London. He kept a copy of this lecture, which expounded Herkomer's ideas about a new architecture of the theatre, the abolition of the footlights, an adaptable proscenium, and a new way of using light for atmosphere. As Edward Craig showed in his paper "Gordon Craig and Hubert von Herkomer," Herkomer found an eager pupil in Craig.[8] Craig produced his first play in 1893, after he had been on the stage for only four years. This was *No Trifling with Love,* prepared during October and November, and performed on 13 and 14 December 1893, at Uxbridge. Craig himself played Perdican.

In 1893, Craig learned wood engraving from two of his friends, James Pryde and William Nicholson, and began spending much of his time in their company, working at wood engraving. That same year he legally adopted his stage name, Gordon Craig, and married.

It is very likely that in spite of his talent and his growing reputation as a good actor, Craig's many activities outside the theatre after 1893, as well as his friendship with young painters belonging to the New English Art Club, were enough reason for the managers of the London stage to hesitate to employ him, and the roles he deserved were not offered him. Irving, too, no longer seemed to have roles for him at the Lyceum, nor were there many roles for Ellen Terry any more either. The Lyceum still gravitated around Irving, but not for long: by the end of 1897, his career was definitely on the decline, and in 1899 the Lyceum passed into the hands of a financial company.

Craig took up his newfound love, wood engraving, with enthusiasm, however, and with good prospects of making a decent living by it. He liked being independent. Throughout his life, he proved again and again that he was not a person who could easily live or work under constraints or as just another member of a team. By 1897, at the age of twenty-five, he had already mastered his recently acquired art. To work as he pleased, far from a wife and children from whom he had become estranged, free from the tyranny of a manager, free from the discomforts of a life on the road with a touring company, and free to create in a medium close to his father's—this is what he now chose. What had seemed only a natural course at the age of seventeen had become by now not disappointing but insufficient. He had tried for several years to combine the two activities, acting and wood engraving. Ellen Terry's son and Irving's pupil, handsome and gifted, he had all the attributes for becoming a very successful actor, but the artistic circle to which he belonged opened new vistas. Here he found an echo to Godwin's preoccupations, which were now his own, and here he met with an enriching artistic stimulus. Here, among his talented friends, there was an adventurous spirit of experimentation in art and an aesthetic outlook that appealed to him. Craig's connection with this artistic circle sealed his fate as an actor. As his friend Rothenstein would later affirm, Craig's gifts were "too varied to allow of his acting and nothing more."[9] Craig possessed the agility and flexibility of mind that enabled him—now that he had mastered different techniques in art—to pass from a two-dimensional, graphic medium to a three-dimensional, kinetic one, and then again to a written code of semantic signs, always finding the right vehicle for his idea. This facility of transposing expressive content from one medium to another also explains Craig's claim that his designs were never anything more than an expressive equivalent to what he actually intended to do on the stage.

If Craig believed he had found in wood engraving his own mode of expression, in the long run it only brought him closer to the theatre. Like his friends and teachers James Pryde and William Nicholson—the Beggarstaff Brothers—who put their art to commercial use, Craig thought that it might bring him, too, financial independence. In this he was mistaken, and it was Jess Dorynne, the young actress who was his companion before he met Elena Meo, who gave him help and support. The years 1898–1900, which were spent with Jess, were marked by a rich artistic output and extensive reading, such as Lamb, Coleridge, Ruskin, Tolstoy, Goethe, Wagner, and Nietzsche.[10] Craig started his own art journal, *The Page,* in 1898 and a year later published *Gordon Craig's Book of Penny Toys* and *Henry Irving and Ellen Terry,* a book of sketches. His *Bookplates* appeared in 1900. These years were also a period of reflection and maturation, and Craig became interested in what people of the profession he had left behind wrote about it (among his many readings we find, for example, Charles Reade's scrapbook, which he bought in 1899). His concept of a new breed of artists, artists of the theatre, was slowly taking shape, and he came to realize that he belonged not to the New Art but to the New Movement in theatre. And for him, the New Movement was definitely Symbolist.

≻ 3 ≺

The Symbolist Theatre

At the end of the nineteenth century the Symbolist theatre was the product of the Idealistic belief that art, and with it the theatre, was not only an aesthetic experience for its makers and beholders but also an opportunity for metaphysical quest and spiritual discovery. This belief entailed a fundamental change in the use of the stage materials. The mise en scène was not limited to expressive means and techniques; it also implied the arousing of an emotional and intellectual response from the audience. Two trends in the mise en scène were slowly taking shape, the one establishing a strict hierarchy of the theatrical materials, the other requiring their synthesis. The cleavage between the two trends became institutionalized long after the Symbolist theatres ceased to exist: this occurred with the founding of the Vieux Colombier by Copeau in Paris in 1913. By the end of the 1880s quite a number of art theatres had been formed in the wake of the Idealistic movement in Paris. They were mostly run by amateurs, with few financial resources, and their life was very short. The most successful and famous among them was the Théâtre d'Art, founded in 1890 by Paul Fort, a sixteen-year-old poet; its successor, the Théâtre de l'Oeuvre, was founded in 1893 by Aurélien-Marie Lugné-Poe, a young actor who had started his career at Antoine's Théâtre Libre. At the Théâtre d'Art and the Théâtre de l'Oeuvre two groups of young artists joined powers: the Nabis painters and the Symbolist poets. The productions were explicitly experimental and often rather crudely mounted because of lack of money, but for a period of seven years (1890–97) the

Symbolist theatre thrived. Its survival for such a relatively long period is a paradox, for it presents us with a case where practice followed theory and not vice versa.

Inspired by Wagner and Mallarmé, not a few contradictory versions of a somewhat confused doctrine on the nature of the ideal theatre found their way into the French artistic world. Wagner's theory on theatre filtered through mainly in the articles of *La Revue Wagnerienne;* Mallarmé's views were known from the source and exerted a strong influence on the poets and painters who founded the Symbolist theatre. Mallarmé himself attributed his theory to his emotional response to Wagner's music.[1] He believed that dance was the only theatrical element capable of expressing "the transient and the unexpected," the Idea, and he thought movement in theatre should achieve the same lightness and allusiveness as dance. The theatrical performance should be a harmonious synthesis of words, gestures, scenery, ballet, and music; the scenery should be allusive, not simulative, and music and movement should together serve as stimuli to bring the spectator to a transcendental state. The most important themes for the theatre were those of Schopenhauer and Swedenborg—the mystery of life, the futility of human will, the belief in the redeeming power of art, and the workings of chance. A play should deal, however, with one subject only, which should be treated on an abstract level from the very beginning. This conception is in fact a projection of Mallarmé's approach to his own medium, poetry; in theatre, as in poetry, he considered latent meaningfulness superior to the literal or the explicit. As Haskell M. Block has pointed out, Mallarmé wanted a "dematerialization" of the stage.[2]

During the first years of the 1890s, Symbolist journals like *La Plume, La Revue blanche,* and the short-lived *Théâtre d'Art,* also the more general *La Revue d'Art dramatique, La Revue indépendante* and *L'Ermitage,* were full of articles on theatre. Pierre Valin, in an article entitled "Le Symbole au Théâtre," discussed the "materialization" of the ideal world by means of scenery and costumes and made a clear distinction between stage symbolism, intended to intensify feeling, and verbal ("poetic") symbolism, which purports to convey meaning and thereby aims at the intellect.[3] François Coulon went back to the classicist formulae, demanding for the Symbolist drama clarity and concision, coherence and brevity, and the discarding of picturesque, diverting elements. The Symbolist playwright, he advised, should choose simple subjects, limit the play to three acts, keep the unity of action, and carry the plot through swiftly and with no digressions. The scenery must fit the subject, but it should *suggest* the leading theme and intensify the impression created by the sense and sound of the words.[4]

The mise en scène became subordinate to expression, and theatrical means or stage materials became means of expression—*moyens d'expression* and not merely *moyens de mise en scène*. Another Symbolist writer, Camille Mauclair, distinguished between three major approaches to drama: the psychological and analytical; the metaphysical, which he ascribed to Maeterlinck; and the Idealistic, meaning Racine, Shelley, Villiers de l'Isle-Adam, and Wagner. Mauclair considered the Idealistic approach best suited to bring to the stage "intellectual and philosophical entities" incarnated by superhuman figures that would symbolize ideas and feelings while offering to the ignorant crowd or to the second-rate minds a story. It was under the cover of the narrative that the enlightened spirit was supposed to perceive "the splendour of the pure idea." And because the Idea is "eternal, unchanging and universally resplendent," Mauclair maintained that faithful adherence to historical time and place is restrictive and detrimental, as is adherence to the unities of time and place. The poet-playwright must, however, respect the unity of action in order to enhance the expressive power of the drama. The drama must be built on two levels: the narrative (aiming at a bigger audience) and the abstract (intended for the "artist-spectator"). Similarly, Mauclair would have the chief characters represent the spirit, leaving the secondary characters to represent the material. In Mauclair's own words, the theatre should be a synthesis where, in a setting composed of visual and acoustic sensations and as costly and lavish as desired, the great and sublime heroes would speak in a magnificent language: free of terrestrial bonds, they would express eternal ideas. Close to them and "bedazzled" by their brilliance, "beings of an inferior order" would pay them their "human tribute." In this way poetry and psychology, scenery, passion, dream, and the quintessence of reality could be integrated into a symphonic whole, with all extraneous elements pared away. It goes without saying that Mauclair also advised a harmonious coordination of scenery and text and the use of symbols.[5] Villiers de l'Isle-Adam's *Axel* fits this theory perfectly and may have served as model.

In 1891, Jules Huret's *Enquête sur l'évolution littéraire* appeared first as a series of sixty-four interviews of artistic and intellectual personalities in *Echo de Paris* and then in book form. It established Symbolism as a growing, dynamic movement in art and a successor to Romanticism, and—for the Symbolists and others—it also served to focus attention on the quest for transcendence. Under the impact of Schopenhauer and Swedenborg, the intellectual and artistic effort to abolish the boundaries between sense and intellect, to grasp a dimly perceived truth beneath illusory appearances, transformed art into both a means and a goal. And the polysemy of the symbol made art a particularly expressive medium for the quest. As Charles Morice declared, the symbol alone had the power to sweep the spirit farther and farther; it alone could condense and suggest intensive life; it alone sought to unveil not the "immediate Truth of the vulgar sincerity of the oath before the judge" but a vital truth, "the food and glory of Art."[6]

The Symbolists approached theatre not as a ramification of literature but as an art in itself, which may use elements also utilized in other arts. The theatrical creation is alternately viewed as a synthesis of such artistic elements or as a synthesis of different arts. For the Symbolists, the synthesis is not merely a technique but a Weltanschauung. In Morice's words, it "renders the spirit its homeland, unifies the heritage, brings back Art to Truth and Beauty. The synthesis in art is THE JOYOUS DREAM OF THE BEAUTIFUL TRUTH."[7] He advocated a synesthetic art of the theatre. In the art of painting, the symbol also became the essential condition of art, first under the influence of Sérusier, who toward 1890 propagated among the Nabis a theory inspired by Gauguin, Plotinus, Schopenhauer, and Swedenborg, asking the artist to elevate himself above the physical bonds of daily life and discover the great symbols of the language of the universe. For Mallarmé and Maeterlinck, however, the exploration and expression of experience through verbal symbols were soon exhausted, language seeming to lose its mediating power, and they were among the first to make a nonuse of language for symbolic purposes. Mallarmé, in his last poems, broke off the verse and used the blank page to indicate silence, which thus became a dramatic and symbolic means of expression. Maeterlinck made a similar use of silence in his plays, creating an atmosphere heavy with obscure allusions. The synthesis of arts—among them painting and poetry—in theatre offered new possibilities both for metaphysical exploration and for technical experiments to achieve a greater expressivity. In theatre, not only could each material or element—actors, scenery, costumes, props, light, sound effects—serve as signifiers, but the interplay of various of these elements used simultaneously could create composite symbols with new and unsuspected meanings. Universal symbols could be used along with private ones, iconic symbols along with the dynamic. Thus, the term "expression," used in a restricted sense as denoting the real and the understood, worked at one level, while "suggestion" worked at another, subtler level. "Suggestion," Morice wrote, "has in its power all that expression lacks. Suggestion is the language of the correspondences and the affinities between the soul and nature. Instead of *expressing* the reflection of things, it penetrates them and becomes their own voice. Suggestion is never indifferent and, in essence, is always new because it speaks of the hidden, the unexplained, and the *inexpressible* in things."[8] This is also the meaning ascribed by Craig to "suggestion" (unlike Adolphe Appia, who endowed "expression" with a rich connotative power). "Suggestion" was needed to create the atmosphere of mystery that was considered most conducive to the perception and revelation of Truth and Beauty. "Suggestion"—a convenient term that like "expression" covers *both* the process and its contents—used symbols. The different levels of reality uncovered by the symbol were variously referred to as the "Beyond," the "Implicit," "Truth," the "Eternal"—terms that denote on the part of their users a mystical inclination, a desire for transcendence and sometimes a spiritual discovery. Yet the symbol served but a happy few, a small elite who had common intellectual and artistic attitudes and, furthermore, did not disdain other possible means of reaching the Beyond, including drugs and occultism.

The two Symbolist theatres, in their quest for spirituality, often chose pieces whose language was obscure if not hermetic. And when the play or poem seemed insufficiently obscure, that necessary quality was supplied by other means such as mysterious allusions in intonation, a sophisticated use of pauses or acting without sound, and melodramatic devices, the idea being that the phenomenon is never what it seems to be and all is but an appearance that needs to be decoded. Often, following Mauclair's precepts about the sublime, the characters were closer to the heroes of the French classical tragedy than to those of the Théâtre Libre: gods and demigods, kings and princes, heroes and knights, high dignitaries, supernatural figures, conventional characters or archetypes. A second group included extraordinary figures, doomed by fate or enslaved by a forbidden passion but still belonging to the nobility. Another distinct group consisted of ordinary people who belonged, unfortunately, to realistic foreign plays, like Ibsen's, but had undergone Symbolist surgery, becoming symbolic in spite of themselves and in spite of their begetter.

There was, of course, the problem of interpretation: should the Symbolist actor interpret the character realistically and emphasize its symbolic aspect (a technique that would have a glorious comeback under the name of "distancing" or "alienation"), or should he let the Idea come forth in speech by using a flat voice and a minimum of movement? The latter view, the depersonalization of the actor, is best expressed in Jarry's *Ubu Roi* and his writings on aesthetics. In general, the actors at both the Théâtre d'Art and the Théâtre de l'Oeuvre used stylized movements, with a few slow and majestic gestures. All movement was supposed to be symbolic, and the fewer movements there were, the greater their impact. (Malicious gossip would have it that it was all the doing of Lugné-Poe, who was such a bad actor!) Sometimes, the actor sought to become simply anonymous, even unnoticeable, limiting his movements to a few very stylized, unrealistic gestures. Often the movements imitated those of the puppet.

The predominant tendency was to depersonalize the actor and to avoid details—not only in acting but also in costume and props—that would give the character too much consistency, too much "flesh." In the experiment for a Symbolist theatre, the actor was but one item. Acting was broken into its components and each was experimented with, in order to achieve either more expression in the acting itself or to enhance an idea by speech alone. An interesting instance of this sort of unity was the production of Paul Napoléon Roinard's *Song of Songs* on 11 December 1891 at the Théâtre d'Art. Roinard, who also directed the play, had his actors stress certain vowels not simply for meaning but in coordination with music, movement, colored light, and even scent, which was sprayed in the audience. In *La Fille aux mains coupées,* written and directed by Pierre Quillard and performed at the Théâtre d'Art on 19 and 20 March 1891, verbal signs were conveyed by two spatially distinct bodies of actors. The narrator stood alone on the forestage and recited those passages in the text that were written in prose; the actors recited those in verse, behind a gauze scrim. The scrim, as well as the verse, placed them in the realm of the Beyond. Elsewhere, in a production of Henri de Régnier's *La Gardienne* at the Théâtre de l'Oeuvre on 21 June 1894, several actors mimed the action onstage while others, hidden in the orchestra pit, spoke the roles: voice was thus separated from movement. Another attempt to depersonalize the actor was through the use of the threnody, the final purpose being the creation of a state of perceptiveness in the audience not unlike the one effected in ritual by incantation. The rhythm of the threnody and the slowness of movement together created an atmosphere of bewitchment—some called it bewilderment—and mystery, which fascinated the spectator.[9] By the use of stylized movement and threnody, the structure and the rhythm originally intended by the playwright could be varied so that each performance brought out new shades of meaning. No attempt was made to use rhythm systematically to enhance or efface objects, actions, or events and to expand duration. Whether intentionally or not, the modification of duration led to a distortion of events and characters and reinforced the gap between empirical reality and theatrical fiction. Anything and nothing could occur in such a world, where nothing was measured by the "normal," empirical scale of time—a lesson that has been rediscovered rather recently by the American director Robert Wilson.

In this theatre, production and theory were never very far apart. Discussing a production either before or after was customary. Not long after the performance of *La Fille aux mains coupées,* Quillard published an article in *La Revue d'Art dramatique* in which he explained the principles that guided his mise en scène:

> The mise en scène necessarily depends on the dramatic system adopted, and since this dramatic system contains symbols, the mise en scène is its very sign and symbol. . . . The speech creates the scenery as well as anything else. . . . *The scenery must be a pure ornamental fiction that makes up the illusion by analogies of color and lines with the drama.* . . . A backcloth and several movable curtains will very often be enough in order to give an impression of a boundless multiplicity of time and place. . . . [Thus] the theatre will be what it ought to be: a *pretext for dreaming.*[10]

Quillard's approach was typical of those artists who, under the influence of the Symbolist poets, emphasized text over the other stage materials. This was the dominant approach, but the Nabis also had their say. Bonnard, Maurice Denis, Dethomas, Sérusier and Munch, Ranson and Vuillard, and also Gauguin and Toulouse-Lautrec took part in the various productions, by designing and painting settings, programs, or posters. An impressive lithograph by Gauguin was printed in *Théâtre d'Art,* the organ of the young theatre, for Rachilde's *Madame la Mort,* produced on 19 and 20 March 1891. This showed a gray skull on a dark and misty background and below it a blurred human form emerging from a swirl of thick smoke, its head touching the skull, conveying an almost dizzying sense of phantom. It is a splendid example of the way in which the aesthetics of the Symbolist painters inspired a new direction in mise en scène, where, for the first time, the artist was free to create, not simply reproduce, reality by the use of symbolic forms and colors. It was mainly under the influence of the painters—even when priority was given to speech—that the stage became a separate, independent realm, a group of materials to be shaped together by the director, working with scenery, costumes, light, sound effects, and actors and using them to convey, in a symbolic fashion, the main ideas of the piece. The director could choose painted scenery or realistic settings and could use symbolic forms and colors in light, scenery, and costumes, as well as symbolic sound effects (often out of context), and he could use light. Light became an important means of expression, creating mood, accompanying movement, and serving as a leitmotiv. (One of the many important discoveries that grew out of the synesthetic approach in the mise en scène was the ability of light to structure time and place; in *Song of Songs,* for example, colored light was used to express the correspondences, and the rhythm of the changing light modified that of the action.) Traditional visual and acoustic symbols were not so much displayed as suggested—reproducing an Indian landscape, for example, by playing a few notes of an Indian melody.

The action unfolding on the stage ceased to be a spectacle intended to entertain or instruct; instead, it was an experience that brought together the creators and the audience for the purpose of uncovering, in a common pursuit, the hidden significance of phenomena. The stage, fraught with metaphysical significance, was the land of the dream, the myth, the legend. The audience, no longer mere spectators, entered into a universe, one that was not only fictitious but also supernatural. In the illusory and often very mysterious realm created by the whole mise en scène, the spectator was an indispensable partner. He was invited to know—expected to know—as much about the performance as possible. To this end, besides articles about forthcoming productions, informing the potential public about the aims, means, and procedures of the theatre in a specific production, often a preliminary address was delivered before the performance, and a defense was printed in the program.[11]

The change in the traditional use of stage materials and techniques that the two Symbolist theatres introduced was the basis from which both Craig and Appia proceeded to reform the modern theatre. The Théâtre d'Art was a theatre of poets and painters for whom it offered mainly an ephemeral experiment; when they were satisfied that they had answered certain questions and discovered certain things, the theatre ceased to be. The Théâtre de l'Oeuvre, briefly its successor, deserted the Symbolist movement in 1897, when Lugné-Poe turned to more eclectic and remunerative enterprises. It required a visionary like Craig, or a theorist like Appia, to turn the Symbolist experiments into a dominant force in the modern mise en scène.

Although young Craig seems not to have read the French Symbolist essays on theatre, in the early nineties his friends often crossed the channel and he heard the echo of the Symbolist productions in Paris. Innovative, if sometimes pretentious, shocking, or simply boring, the Symbolist theatre was a stimulating and fruitful experience for all artists who came to the French capital. No one could plead indifference. At Mallarmé's "Tuesdays" the groups were international: Whistler, Wilde, Symons, Yeats, George Moore, mingling with such artists as Huysmans and Henri de Régnier, Moréas and Pierre Louÿs, André Gide and Paul Valéry, Debussy, Redon, Gauguin, Vuillard. Craig read Oscar Wilde's works in particular, for Wilde had been Godwin's friend and disciple, and Craig also knew Yeats, who would be the first to use Craig's screens, and

Symons, who was the most ardent disseminator of French Symbolism in England.

The main vehicle for the New Movement in theatre in England was the Independent Theatre, founded in 1891 by J. T. Grein after an energetic campaign led by George Moore in favor of an English "free theatre." Largely because of Irving's efforts and artistic achievements, the theatre in England had become a recognized cultural institution and had been undergoing subtle changes under the influence of the artistic movements. By the end of the 1880s, two main tendencies, the historicist and the Aesthete, were taking shape. The former was oriented toward an elaborated mise en scène, the latter toward a stylization. Lady Archibald Campbell's open-air performances and Godwin's stylized productions took place side by side with magnificent spectacles at the Lyceum, which were known for their meticulous reconstruction of historical settings and costumes, and William Poel's so-called reformed Shakespearean productions, which were "more true than true" to Shakespeare. In 1889 Antoine and the Théâtre Libre came to London, demonstrating a new acting style (inspired by the already well known Meininger company) and presenting a new, controversial subject matter. The Independent Theatre, unlike its French model the Théâtre Libre, did not limit itself solely to the gospel of naturalism but introduced to the English public Maeterlinck and the French Symbolists as well as Ibsen and Shaw. Although it attracted a great number of artists, intellectuals, and fashionable society, the Independent Theatre did not succeed in fostering a new generation of playwrights, nor was it bold enough to commit itself and produce all the plays that Shaw had to offer.

The Independent Theatre disappeared in 1898, after only seven years, but it made a distinct contribution to the English stage. One of its most successful undertakings was the visit of the Théâtre de l'Oeuvre to London in 1895. On this occasion, Lugné-Poe brought to the English public not only the Symbolist innovations in matters of drama and mise en scène but also its production of Maeterlinck's *L'Intruse,* which had been given a single performance by Beerbohm-Tree at the Haymarket Theatre three years earlier, and *Pelléas et Mélisande*. Maeterlinck had a great reputation in the Symbolist circles in London. Besides the performance of *L'Intruse* (27 January 1892), William Archer's article on him, "A Pessimist Playwright," had appeared in the *Fortnightly Review* as early as September 1891. Four of Maeterlinck's plays were published in English translation in 1892: *La Princesse Maleine,* translated by Gerard Levy, and *Pelléas et Mélisande, Les Aveugles,* and *L'Intruse,* translated by Laurence Alma-Tadema. Other French Symbolist poets were not only read and translated but also came to England to lecture. Verlaine was brought over in 1893 by John Lane, Symons, and Rothenstein for lectures in London and at Oxford. That same year *Harper's New Monthly Magazine* published a long article by Symons entitled "The Decadent Movement in Literature." In 1894, at an international exhibition of posters held at the Aquarium of Westminster, works of French Symbolists aroused great interest. (Craig would remember vividly two posters, one of Bonnard for the French Symbolist magazine *La Revue blanche,* and another by Maurice Denis.)[12] The same year, Mallarmé came to lecture at Oxford and Cambridge. The *Yellow Book* dedicated much of its space to the French Symbolists, and through articles that frequently appeared in the press, Symons kept the English well informed about the latest events in the Symbolist circles in Paris.

On its 1895 visit, the Théâtre de l'Oeuvre played at the Opéra Comique for one week, from Monday, 25 March, to Saturday, 30 March. The engagement included two performances of *Pelléas et Mélisande,* three of *L'Intruse,* two of *Rosmersholm,* and two of *Solness le constructeur.* The style of the mise en scène was not uniform. *Pelléas et Mélisande* used a single setting, a backdrop painted to look like an old tapestry. All the indoor scenes were played in front of the tapestry. For the outdoor scenes, the tapestry split in the middle, showing another painted backdrop. Props were few, and lighting was used mainly to create a mood of mystery; the costumes were copied after Memling. The acting was studied; movements were few, slow, and symbolic. The text was delivered in a monotonous chant, occasionally interrupted by long, suggestive pauses. Meaning was less important than sound, in keeping with the desire to emphasize mood. Lugné-Poe, in close collaboration with Maeterlinck, had integrated all the stage materials—voice, movement, sounds, forms and colors, acting, settings, costumes, props, and incidental music—in a stylized production that made the play a series of symbolic occurrences in a remote and legendary past. The same style of mise en scène was used for *L'Intruse,* but for *Solness le constructeur* and *Rosmersholm* Lugné-Poe used a "stylized" realism, the realism of the poor, on an almost empty stage. Reviews appeared in the *Daily Telegraph,* the *Stage,* the *Times,* the *Illustrated London News,* the *Morning Post,* the *New Budget,* the *Athenaeum, Pall Mall Budget,* and the *Saturday Review.* Some were flattering or enthusiastic, some disapproving or indignant, but all pointed out the unusual atmosphere created by special effects.

There is no record that Craig saw any of the performances of the Théâtre de l'Oeuvre in London or that he attended any of Verlaine's or Mallarmé's lectures. He certaily knew about Verlaine's visit, since his friend William Rothenstein arranged it. Craig probably was prevented from seeing the Théâtre de l'Oeuvre while it was in London because he was on tour with Hubert Evelyn's company; on 31 March 1895, the day after Lugné-Poe's last performance in London, Craig was acting in *La Tosca* at Eastbourne. It is of interest, however, that of the four plays performed by the French theatre, *L'Intruse* was later included by Craig in the repertoire of the über-marionette theatre in Dresden, and *Rosmersholm* was the play for which, at Duse's request, he designed the scenery in 1906. One can safely assume that Craig knew about Lugné-Poe's visit, if not from the newspapers then from his friends' account. For the artistic circle to which he belonged, these were hectic days indeed: Lugné-Poe's visit took place not long after Max Nordau's violent diatribe *Entartung (Degeneration)* appeared in London in its English translation; only a few days after Lugné-Poe left, on 5 April, Oscar Wilde was arrested.

If Craig did not see any of the performances of the Théâtre de l'Oeuvre, he did attend Forbes-Robertson's production of *Pelléas and Mélisande* three years later, on 25 June 1898, at the Prince of Wales Theatre. The role of Mélisande was played by Mrs. Patrick Campbell, Golaud by Forbes-Robertson, and Pelléas by Martin Harvey, who had been Craig's understudy at the Lyceum. Maeterlinck was already an influential figure among young artists in England as well as in France. His *Treasure of the Humble,* with its famous chapter on theatre, "The Tragic in Daily Life," had been published in English the year before, not long after it appeared in French. Max Beerbohm covered the performance for the *Saturday Review* and gave a flattering account, but years later, in 1906, Craig would remember the acting of Mrs. Campbell and Martin Harvey as a "drivelling insipid manner," "poses without sense—and sounds without reason."[13] If Craig shared his friends' admiration for Maeterlinck, he had his own ideas of what a Maeterlinck production should be like—not, apparently as in Forbes-Robertson's production, an imitation of Lugné-Poe. Beerbohm, in "More from Maeterlinck," an article published on 2 March 1899 in the *Saturday Review,* defended Maeterlinck's drama and poetry with genuine insight. He stressed the emotional value of Maeterlinck's static play and contended that his characters were not flat, as his detractors claimed, but real, simple, and human figures that should never be represented on the stage by mere puppets; he also praised the mystery that the playwright so masterfully wove round his heroes, a mystery that made them look real and full of pathos. Beerbohm implies that the characters lack consistency, for he notes quite rightly that they should not be played by puppets, because only a living actor could round them out; moreover, he perceived that it was the technique of "strangeness," the mystery, the web of ambiguities, that prevented the characters—such as they were, represented by puppets or not—from falling completely flat. The same year, in June 1899, the first book in English on the French Symbolist movement appeared—Arthur Symons' *The Symbolist Movement in Literature,* dedicated to Yeats. A whole chapter of this important study was devoted to Maeterlinck and discussed the use of *puppets* instead of actors.

Puppets were favorites with the Symbolist artists. The belief that the puppet was best suited to convey an idea was widespread among these artists in London as well as in Paris, and the puppet theatre became a model of concise, symbolic expression. The first versions of Jarry's *Ubu Roi* had been produced by him at Rennes in 1888, 1889, and 1890 with his own puppet theatre, the Théâtre des Phynances. In 1889, Maeterlinck introduced his play *La Princesse Maleine* as a "puppet drama," and in 1894 he presented his volume of three plays published in Brussels as "little dramas for puppets" (the volume included *Alladine et Palomides, Intérieur,* and *La Mort de Tintagiles*). In Paris, the Petit Théâtre de Marionnettes was founded in 1888 by Henri Signoret, and his repertoire included such old masterpieces from the world drama as *L'Anneau de Sakountala* and *Dr. Faustus*. Signoret's puppets were about eighty centimeters tall and were manipulated by levers from below. Jacques Robichez, in his study of the French Symbolist theatre, explains that this mechanism made the movements of the puppets slow and rigid and thus limited the choice of plays to those that did not require movement of the feet. Realistic plays were plainly impossible. Robichez says that this, rather than aesthetic bias, was the main reason for the choice of the specific plays. Thus, necessity gave birth to a particular acting style.[14] Whether this is true or not, it is clear that the style of the Petit Théâtre coincided with Symbolist views, attracted the young artists, and was looked on as a Symbolist theatre. After Maurice Boucher became director of the theatre in 1889, the repertoire became largely one of old, mystic tales. The theatre survived until 1894. Another puppet theatre that was popular with the Symbolists belonged to Paul Ranson, the Nabi painter. He put it up in his own studio in Montparnasse, wrote plays for it, mainly farces, and produced them for his friends, with their help. The heads of the puppets were sculpted by Georges Lacombe—who had his own puppet theatre at L'Ermitage, his country estate, where the Nabis used to come and paint—and by Maurice Denis. Scenery and costumes were designed and painted by Maurice Denis, Vuillard, and Sérusier; France Ranson, the painter's wife, was the costumière, helped sometimes by Vuillard's sister, Mme. K.-X. Roussel. Ranson himself manipulated the puppets, sometimes with his wife's help, and spoke all the parts. In 1891, Ranson produced Maeterlinck's *Les Sept Princesses* at the home of State Counsellor Jean-Claude Coulin at an evening that was to be long remembered by the Nabis and their friends.[15]

The poets believed that the puppet could supersede the actor because it did not obstruct speech and therefore allowed the text to reach the audience in its pure form; the painters were captivated by the puppet's docility. All were fascinated by its expressivity and visible emotional impact on the audience. In London, the attraction was primarily among painters. Rothenstein mentions in his memoirs that he once hired a "particularly good" Punch and Judy show to perform in his studio at Glebe Place in Chelsea; among those invited to attend were William Archer and Bernard Shaw. Another time, apparently in the mid-1890s, he had a small street puppet theatre come to his studio so that he could make pastel studies of the puppets and of some of the scenes; he showed these studies to Craig, who was "amused" by them.[16]

Another theatrical genre that attracted the young artists was the music hall, with its vivid, colorful spectacle standing in sharp contrast to what Rothenstein would call "the drabness of ordinary life."[17] Craig, who knew a good actor when he encountered one, admired the artists of the music hall, especially Albert Chevalier and Dan Leno, and would remember them in the *Index* in long, nostalgic pages.

Young artists favored the Symbolist theatre, the puppets, and the music hall. The larger public was moving away from the Lyceum and applauding Beerbohm-Tree at Her Majesty's Theatre, while the proponents of the new drama, headed again by J. T. Grein, in 1899 founded the Stage Society. New technical improvements were being introduced in the theatre machinery—like the electric bridges, for example. The time was ripe for a systematic reform of the theatre.

4

The London Productions

Craig had tried his hand at producing a play when he was only twenty-one. Three years later, in 1896, he produced *Hamlet* and *Romeo and Juliet* at the Parkhurst Theatre. In 1897 he produced two other plays with a company of his own, *François Villon, Poet and Cut-throat,* by S. X. Courte, and *The New Magdalen,* by Wilkie Collins, performed at the Croydon Theatre Royal (Craig had already played in these pieces two years before). Then followed almost three years dedicated to wood engraving, writing, and editing. Symbolist art and glimpses of Symbolist theatre, puppets, and the school of spectacle of which the music hall was only one of the many exponents in London—all this was part of Craig's life during his years of apprenticeship, from the moment he went on the stage until his first major production in 1900. By 1900 Craig had already published an art journal of his own and three books of designs. He had learned in the previous several years to organize space: he knew the value of line, volume, and color; the power of bold simplification; and the use of the interplay of light and dark. As a wood engraver, he was free by now from the influence of Pryde, Nicholson, and Japanese art. He was an artist in his own right.

Yet Craig missed the theatre, as he confessed to Martin Shaw in one of his letters from 1899.[1] Craig met Shaw, a young musician, in 1897, and they became close friends. Shaw introduced Craig to Bach's *St. Matthew Passion,* which was to obsess him for many years to come—he would again and again plan a spectacular performance for it in a specially built edifice. When Shaw founded the Purcell Operatic Society, the two young artists joined hands in its first production, Purcell's *Dido and Aeneas*.

Though Craig's first consequential production was an operatic work most obviously because of his friendship with Shaw, with whom he shared common attitudes to theatre and music, Craig was still very excited about the possibilities. Not only was it a chance to work with Shaw to create a piece of art in a theatrical genre that was still deeply embedded in an obsolete Realism and, at the same time, to revive old English music; it was also a chance to test some of the ideas he had been interested in—Wagner's, and also Herkomer's, which included changing the shape of the stage and the auditorium, replacing the footlights with a whole system of projectors and spotlights, and using a domed sky.[2]

Craig designed the scenery and the costumes for *Dido and Aeneas* and directed the actor-singers in their movements; Shaw took care of the music. The production was an artistic success, and the receipts were bigger than the expenses. More operatic productions followed. *The Masque of Love* (from Purcell's opera *Dioclesian,* with text by Phineas Fletcher) was produced in 1901, and *Acis and Galatea* (by Handel and John Gay) and *Bethlehem* (by Laurence Housman, with incidental music by Martin Shaw) in 1902. These productions imposed not the coordination but the subservience of all the stage elements, including the actors, to music, since Craig, like the Symbolists, considered music the highest form of art. The actor-singers were amateurs—only two were professionals—and since they were only too willing to partake in the artistic adventure, the risk of conflicts or of clashes of temperament was almost nonexistent. In 1903, Craig prepared designs for several scenes of *For Sword or Song* (by R. G. Legge), which his uncle Fred Terry produced, and he designed and produced Ibsen's *The Vikings at Helgeland* and *Much Ado about Nothing* for Ellen Terry's company. Craig's work was based on a thorough knowledge of stage business, acquired through long years of apprenticeship and practice as an actor and as a young director, and also as a wood engraver, writer, and editor. It was also based on his experience as a spectator and his readings on theatre. A poetic theatre emerged, made of space and movement, movement and music, music and space. A self-consistent aesthetic approach was at work in all the productions: these were no mere Symbolist experiments but the persevering realization of a coherent aesthetic conception.

Although these productions had a noteworthy *succès d'estime,* they had but a very short run—the longer run was that of *Much Ado,* which Ellen Terry took with her on tour. For Craig they were an end in both senses: they were a final step taken after a long search for theatrical means in accordance with Symbolist tenets, and a goal successfully attained. During his work of preparation, however, it became clear to Craig that these productions were also the end of the road: they could serve him mainly as a working basis from which a totally new art of the theatre should emerge, for he was preoccupied by movement and its relation to space.[3] Visions of a new art could already be seen in Craig's early stage designs dating from 1899, such as the design for *Hamlet,* act 3, scene 4, with its big, empty surfaces of architectural shapes.[4] Such as they were, these productions were superior to anything that had been achieved before on the Symbolist stage. Edward Craig, Denis Bablet, Michael P. Loeffler, and Christopher Innes have given detailed accounts of these productions; therefore I shall dwell here very briefly only on those features that pertain to what Craig considered in 1904 a still unsolved problem, movement.

Craig offered an Aesthetic theatre that carried the Symbolist stylization one step closer to abstraction. Like the Symbolists, he believed in the primacy of formal values in art, and he sought to convey the central idea of a play in powerful images, through suggestive movement, line, color, light, voice, stage effects. (He would later describe this method in his essay "On the Ghosts in the Tragedies of Shakespeare" published in *The Mask* in 1910.) The touchstone was the suggestiveness of form, and in order to achieve it Craig had recourse to conventional symbols as well as to impressionistic techniques. Means and techniques were selected for their connotative value, and their use was calculated in such a way as to cause a spectator to sever all links with his immediate physical reality.

Like Gauguin, Craig's aesthetic choice was guided by two constants: by a tendency to *simplification,* which led to the limiting of props and scenery to bare essentials, and by the search for *suggestiveness.* Beerbohm was the first to point out the relationship between the two in his review of *Much Ado about Nothing:* "By the elimination of details which in a real scene would be unnoticed, but which become salient on the stage, Craig gives to the persons of the play a salience never given to them before. Even when he dwarfed them, they were midgets clearly defined by reason of the simplicity surrounding them. Now that he gives them their full size, they are more definitely men and women (and therefore more dramatic) than they could be under any other system."[5]

Craig adopted the synesthetic, Symbolist approach in the mise en scène, and all his productions were excellent demonstrations of its effectiveness. Each of the sparsely used details had to evoke, reflect, or enhance the idea, the feeling, or the state of mind that the director was interested in. Each detail had to work in concentrating attention on the central idea. *Acis and Galatea* used a single theme—Arthur Symons called it a "pattern"—in costume, scenery, and movement. The illusion created and the orchestration of the various moods plunged the audience into an avowedly make-believe world that strongly appealed to the senses and the imagination; the spectator was supposed to be left with the feeling that he had been living through an extraordinary, intense experience. Rothenstein specifically mentioned this effect on the audience in a letter to Ellen Terry about *The Vikings,* in which he also praised the scenery, the delivery of speech, the movement, and the blocking of the actors.[6]

One of the important techniques by which Craig brought masks, costumes, and scenery into a single comprehensive, all-sweeping movement, was his sophisticated use of electric lights. Instead of using footlights, he used light and color to turn actors and settings into an organic whole, a living body in motion. The visual composition was harmonious and dynamic at the same time—as can be readily seen today in photographs of the various performances. In *Dido and Aeneas* (1900), Craig used symbolic colors for props, scenery, and light; the costumes were in contrasting, unusual colors according to the press reviews. Movement was carefully coordinated to enhance music, either by complementing it or by contrasting it. Craig's notebook for the production shows that he worked with the actors on a slow and easy walk to follow or counter the music, on actions, and on "head actions." In other words, he worked on body exercises for flexibility, coordination, and control of movement; synchronization of movement with sounds—i.e., music—and performance of movement unsynchronized with music (these two exercises are staples of modern eurythmics); actions; performance of series of movements; head actions, or mime. Altogether a serious program for any beginning actor.[7]

A sample of the acting Craig wanted is provided in his introductory note to the "Design for the First Movement" for the prologue of the *Masque of Hunger,* written in 1903. As Craig indicates, the movements of the actor—who is wearing a mask—are "slow and deliberate." Sounds are to be used for evocation and so is the human voice: the actor is breathing heavily, his snorts have to recall the bull's when it is separated by force from his mate—Craig seems to have believed that his audience would be familiar with such a scene from "nature." Then the actor should emit a series of sounds that would echo a "restrained bellowing" and finally resolve into a lament: "Pain . . . Pain . . . and Sorrow." The suggestive, auditory signs are obviously inspired by observation of nature. Visually, the actor, the costume, and the scenery are blended into a harmonious whole: the actor is standing on a little heap of mud, his costume in rags, and he is holding up to the audience the dead body of his little son. The "scene" (here, the stage effects) reflects the actor's movements and enhances their significance by creating an atmosphere of despair and inevitable doom: the figure of the mourning father slowly disappears into a developing storm of black rain that together with the sounds suddenly comes to a stop.[8]

A different stylized movement was devised for *Acis and Galatea* (1902), where Craig used the geometric form of the square as a kind of visual leitmotiv not only in the scenery and the costumes but also in acting. Unlike his *Masque of Love,* where he used dance elements, all movement was stylized here into straight lines and right angles, resulting in a puppetlike rigidity where no "curves" were allowed. Symons, who witnessed the performance, was especially intrigued by the sudden leaps from kneeling positions.[9] As for the chorus, Craig integrated it into the setting and turned the whole into a writhing, living body. An instance of this method is caught in a photograph of the chorus, published by Edward Craig.[10] The photograph shows the *merging* of scenery, costumes and actors, not only through the visual leitmotiv of the square but also through movement: narrow strips of cloth, hanging down from the flies, mix with the strips hanging from the sleeves and the headdress of the actors. Thus, the chorus became technically part of the scenery and the two together formed a living, moving universe. For the strips belonging to the scenery shifted at the slightest movement of the actors, making the actor part of, and reflected in, a larger body. This technique would recur in the famous golden cloak scene, the court scene, of the Moscow *Hamlet* (act I, scene 2); here, the actor became an undifferentiated element of the chorus that was, in its turn, part of the scenery.

The interaction between movement and space was one of Craig's preoccupations, and he used to study it with Elena Meo's help. Together they would go to various multi-level areas in London, where Craig closely watched her movements to see how different phases of light and darkness affected these movements, and the effect the environment had on her shaping and duration of movement. His impressions were put down later, in 1905, in the famous series of four designs, *The Steps.*

Two things should be emphasized here. First—and this can certainly provide a partial answer to those who claim that Craig's ideas on acting were vague—for each new play, Craig devised a new set of movements in accordance with the spirit of the play. And most important: this was always a *stylized, symbolic movement,* whether the movement itself was symbolic, like the straight-line movement in *Acis and Galatea,* or whether it was movement and voice used in a symbolic way, like the movement of the chorus in *Acis and Galatea* or the nature-inspired use of voice in the *Masque of Hunger.* Second, in order to enhance the symbolic character of the dramatis personae, Craig proceeded to *depersonalize* the actor, by using masks, stylized movement—such as the puppetlike movements—or a costume that turned the actor into a living element of the scenery. The movements followed the lead of the French Symbolists when they were "slow and deliberate," or puppetlike, or used symbols from nature. However, as Symons quickly perceived, in all Craig's various and varied productions there was an underlying aesthetic method. He never allowed himself mere flights of fancy—though fancy played a great role. His productions were works of art that possessed, in Symons' words, "breadth and dignity."[11]

The spectator (practically speaking, this meant a handful of faithful artistic friends) was now an almost equal partner in a game for two, the other partner being of course the artist, the maker of rules and the initiator of the game. Actors, scenery, light, and sound were manipulated pieces in a game of subtlety in which, if the game had initially been well prepared, both sides won: the spectator responded, and his prize was enjoyment and a sense of transcendence; the artist was gratified both by the spectator's response—in itself an affirmation of the artist's successful enterprise—and by a personal sense of fulfillment, having created an aesthetic whole and conveyed significance.

The favorable acclaim of Craig's productions came mostly from the artistic circles to which Craig belonged and where, in a sense, Godwin had preceded him. Godwin was an Aesthete, and so was Wilde, his friend and disciple and a spokesman for the English Symbolists in the early nineties. In one way or another, all Craig's friends were associated with the New Movement—James Pryde, William Nicholson, Paul Cooper, William Rothenstein, Max Beerbohm, and Haldane MacFall, as well as Yeats, Symons—the list is long. Beerbohm, Symons, and Yeats were all contributors to the *Yellow Book.* There were also Graham Robertson, Laurence Housman (whose miracle play Craig produced), Walter Crane, and Swinburne. *The Studio,* the influential Symbolist magazine that had launched Beardsley in 1893, printed in May 1899 Craig's woodcut of Irving as Louis XI; it was also here that Haldane MacFall's flattering article on *Dido and Aeneas* was published in September 1901. The final recognition of Craig as an artist of the New Movement came with his election in May 1903 to the Society of Twelve. As a member, Craig could participate in exhibitions along with such famous draftsmen, etchers, wood engravers, and lithographers as Augustus John, Charles Shannon, Charles Ricketts, William Nicholson, William Rothenstein, William Strang, Thomas Sturge Moore, Muirhead Bone, and Lucien Pissarro.

Craig was still engaged in drawing and wood engraving while producing his plays. Indeed, this activity offered him a medium for ideas originally intended for the stage, while it also provided a most welcome income. As a matter of fact, it was slowly becoming a very tempting substitute. The year of *The Vikings* and *Much Ado* was also the time of a frustrating professional collaboration with Ellen Terry and his sister, Edith, and a disappointing experience with the professional actors of Ellen Terry's company.

The need for a theatre of his own, with a new breed of actor, became more and more urgent for Craig. He took three simultaneous steps, which he expected to be immediately effective: he decided to open a school for the art of the theatre, he made a direct appeal for support to the larger public, and he published several articles meant to win over the established theatre and its enlightened sponsors to his ideas. In May 1903 Craig confidently announced the opening of a School for the Art of the Theatre. Though Craig was now a famous figure among artists and an "enfant terrible" among theatre people, his announcement fell flat. (A year later, Herbert Beerbohm-Tree founded at His Majesty's Theatre a school of drama that Craig was quick to denounce as a mere actors' agency: this was to become the Royal Academy of Dramatic Art.) Another abortive attempt was Craig's plan to found a Society of the Theatre that would have provided him with the necessary financial support. At the same time, between February 1903 and January 1904, Craig succeeded in having six articles, five letters to the editor, and a talk published by various newspapers: "Stage Management," "The New Theatre," "National Opera," "On Theatres and Actors," "The Modern Stage," "On Stage Scenery," "The Theatrical Art," "The Theatre: Trade or Art?" and "A State Subsidized Theatre." These articles brought Craig's ideas on the present and future state of the theatre to at least some public attention. In 1900 Craig considered himself the only representative of the New Movement in theatre in England. In 1903, he expected to win over the commercial theatre. But his recent productions were, it appeared, no more than trial balloons that too soon went up in smoke. Nonetheless, the smoke was a glorious smoke. If nothing else, critics and artists alike remarked on the innovative aspect of Craig's creations. Though the "ultra-modern aestheticism" of *The Masque of Love* was condemned by the *Pilot,* artists like Walter Crane and Yeats wrote enthusiastically about *Dido and Aeneas,* Haldane MacFall and Arthur Symons praised *Acis and Galatea,* and James Huneker *The Vikings.*[12] Even Bernard Shaw had to confess that nothing quite like Craig's *Much Ado* had been done before.[13] Only Craig was not content with being merely a fashionable prophet; he was not going to be satisfied with directing a small "théâtre d'art" in London or elsewhere. Whenever Craig spoke about "his theatre," he meant a well-established institution, enjoying a big budget, with a solid social, financial, and cultural backing and active on an international scale. He meant, in fact, the sort of thing he planned, later on, for the Uber-Marionette International Theatre in Dresden.

≻ 5 ≺

Foundations

Whatever the reason—whether to give a continuity and consistency to his body of work or to make his ideas more acceptable to a greater reading public—Craig's critics often oversimplified his views. Clarity was enhanced at the sacrifice of complexity: quotations from early issues of *The Mask* were coupled with quotations from *Henry Irving, The Art of the Theater,* or *The Theatre Advancing;* early productions were explained in terms of later publications; and late achievements were highlighted by early pronouncements. Craig himself justified this procedure by issuing from time to time very convenient denials, retractions, or rectifications. This is why, in order to better understand the background of the controversial über-marionette and Craig's concept of movement, one must first look at his attitude toward his art before he left for Germany in 1904 and before he wrote his manifesto, *The Art of the Theatre*—that is, during the period of his London productions. We shall turn later to the reasons for, and the verisimilitude of, Craig's retractions.

Craig cannot be considered the disciple of a specific artist or of a specific thinker, and as we saw earlier, his readings were rather eclectic. As shown, Craig's listings of "masters" have to be approached very cautiously, for they tend to serve his public image rather than point out artistic debts. He used to count his masters as one counts one's assets. Pater's ideas, as well as Symbolist views on art, reached him through the writings of Oscar Wilde. Wilde is mentioned in an interesting passage in the *Index,* in which Craig wonders about the motives behind his artistic activities in his youth and the artists—another list of masters—who inspired him.[1] His "urging" power when he started his London productions in 1900 was not ambition, he says, or gain but love for his work and the theatre. He recalls his "affection and admiration" for Irving (this is a mellowed, post-1930 assertion) and for architecture and painting: Italian painting, the ancients, Pryde, Nicholson and Rothenstein, and from 1906 to 1909, Serlio. Third in his "affection and admiration" come four writers, Wilde, Beerbohm, Shakespeare, and Montaigne, then Isadora Duncan's dance. Of course, his retrospective glance embraces a much longer period than that of his London productions. But what is surprising in this context is the reference to Wilde, because this is the only place in Craig's published writings where he acknowledges such an "affection and admiration" for him. Neither Ruskin nor Goethe, Wagner or Nietzsche provoked such a response. Elsewhere, Craig's comments on Wilde are patronizing. So, for example, in *The Mask* (1908), Craig described Wilde as "merely a very remarkable intelligence and a man whom some considered a great artist."[2] A very guarded comment. Neither did he include Wilde's name among his many acknowledged masters in *Towards a New Theatre* (1913); age seems to have allowed Craig to shed some of his inhibitions. The younger Craig refused to be identified as one of Wilde's disciples, just as he had refused to direct Wilde's *Salome* in 1903, although the play kindled his imagination so much that he prepared several designs for it. During the period of his London productions, Craig shared Wilde's attitude toward the artist, even though he differed about the function of art in society. Moreover, the form of Craig's first long essay, the Socratic dialogue, was the same form that Wilde preferred because of the many possibilities of argumentation that it offered. Wilde used this rhetorical technique in "The Critic as Artist," where he also commented on its merits, and in "The Decay of Lying" and "The Portrait of Mr. W. H." as well. Craig used it in *The Art of the Theatre,* the manifesto he wrote and published in Germany in 1905. Besides, when he came to Germany, Craig was greeted as an Aesthete and he felt flattered to be so.[3] Far from the social and moral conventions of England, he was then pleased to see that Wilde and also Beardsley were admired by the artists he met.[4] Perhaps, in his old age, Craig felt that in his early writings he had done less than justice to Wilde and sought to amend the error when he wrote the *Index.* Or was it sentiment? Wilde had been one of his parents' close friends, and one of those who recognized Godwin's originality as a thinker, referring to him in 1885 in "Shakespeare and the Stage Costume" (an essay later reprinted under the title "The Truth of Masks" in

Intentions) as the "most artistic spirit of the century in England." Craig found in Wilde the confirmation of his own belief in his father's excellence. Brilliant wit, bold exuberance, and an insistent enthusiasm made Wilde the most spectacular exponent of English Symbolism. Craig had been familiar with this colorful figure since he was a child, for even after Ellen Terry's separation from Godwin, Wilde still remained one of her "three particular friends" and "devoted admirers" (the other two, mentioned by Craig, were Alfred Gilbert and Burne-Jones).[5] Though Ellen Terry judged it prudent to put a distance between her young and handsome son and Wilde's intimate circle, Craig read Wilde. It is of little relevance here—though Craig may have been aware of it—that Wilde was only a brilliant translator of theories that had originated with Théophile Gautier, Baudelaire, Pater, or Godwin. Wilde, unlike Craig, never liked to talk about his sources and his masters. But Wilde did have the talent for giving old ideas such new gusto that they made him glitter in their splendor.

Like Wilde, Craig believed in the artist as a creator in more than one field of art; this was the credo of the Pre-Raphaelites, as well as of Ruskin, Morris, the Symbolists and the Art Nouveau movement. Ruskin, Morris, and Godwin engaged in a variety of arts and crafts; Wilde wrote poems, plays, novels; and Craig's many talents had led him to acting, directing, drawing, wood engraving, writing. When Craig devoted himself to directing only, he brought to his task a new conception of the director as an arts and crafts man. Whereas the traditional director was no more than a stage manager (though a multifaceted one, who might also serve as prompter, doorkeeper, costumier, billsticker, theatrical agent, and performer or as star actor, producer, and administrator), Craig's director was an *artist* of the theatre, a creator in his own right. He alone was entitled to decide, select, and organize his materials and choose the proper methods and procedures. He directed the cast, designed the costumes and scenery, chose the incidental music, planned the lighting. The success of the production depended entirely on his ability to convey meaning in a beautiful form; the director, not the star actor, became the most important factor in the play production, and the functions of the star actor and the director became differentiated and distinct. If Irving's eminence as an actor helped to elevate the actors' social status, Craig's achievements would help the director's rise as an artist.

Both Wilde and Craig conceived the aesthetic experience, that of the creator as well as that of the beholder/reader, as a superior form of activity, involving both intellect and emotion. Art, according to Craig, was an independent realm, far and above what was commonly referred to as "reality"—an outlook similar to that of Wilde, as expressed in his

"Decay of Lying." (Later on, in 1913, Craig would echo Wilde almost word for word when he wrote in *Towards a New Theatre* that "art creates life, it doesn't imitate it." Was Wilde's being too good a master the real reason that he was not mentioned among the other masters referred to in this publication?) The task of the artist, according to Wilde, was primarily to create beauty, by reshaping the "rough material" provided by nature: beauty being perceived both as a spiritual symbol and as the source of sensual delight.[6] But while Wilde was attracted, for example, by the sensual appeal of Ruskin's musical prose, as Godwin had been too, Ruskin held an additional allure for Craig: the intellectual validation of this appeal. Craig went somewhat deeper into Ruskin, into the Platonist idea that both beauty and truth—a moral perception—are high-ranking Ideas that should be embodied in art. Whereas Wilde professed a disdainful disparagement of moral values, Craig, like Ruskin, believed in the moral and religious value of art. Moreover, as Ellen Terry had written to Bernard Shaw, Craig had "caught socialism long ago."[7] His was not an art for art's sake. The artist's task or, as he defined it, the "Deed of the Artist," was *Expression,* which thought he inscribed on the flyleaf of the copy of Roget's *Thesaurus* that was Ellen Terry's gift to him on his birthday in 1903.[8]

Like the Symbolists, Craig understood reality to be not the imprint of the senses, not empirical experience, but the intuitive perception of an underlying idea belonging to a different level of the real, the "beyond." Only art could reveal the "beyond." Craig's emphatic antagonism to Realism was better demonstrated in his productions than in his well-argued articles of this period. Thus, he could ironically declare in the program of *Dido and Aeneas* that such "particular care" had been taken by the stage director regarding the scenery and the costumes that they were "entirely incorrect in all matters of detail." This was a far cry from Godwin's or Irving's meticulous antiquarian concern but very close indeed to Jarry and his *Ubu Roi.* As Yeats wrote in the *Spectator* on 11 May 1903, Craig created in *Dido and Aeneas* "an ideal country, where everything was possible, even speaking in music, or the expression of the whole life in a dance." Symons wrote about *Acis and Galatea* in the *Monthly Review* in June 1902: "The imagination has been caught, a suggestion has been given which strikes straight to the nerves of delight, and be sure those nerves, that imagination will do the rest, better, more effectually, than the deliberate assent of the eyes to an imitation of natural appearances." James Huneker described the special atmosphere created for *The Vikings* in similar terms.[9]

In the "Minute Book" of the Society of the Theatre that he tried to set up during these years, Craig emphasized that the stage production should appeal through the senses to the imagination rather than to the intellect.[10] Though the "Minute Book" was written well after the productions, contemporary critics agreed that this is what he succeeded in doing on the stage. For example, Christopher St. John wrote about *Bethlehem* in the *Critic* in January 1903: "What is the scenery like, do you ask? It consists of a plain backcloth, but, subtly lit, it appeals to the imagination as the boundless sky of God." To grasp the deep impact of Craig's mise en scène, one must again refer to Symons' review of *Acis and Galatea:* "Mr. Craig aims at taking us beyond reality," he wrote. Symons explained the secret of Craig's method: "He replaces the pattern of the thing itself by the pattern which that thing evokes in his mind," a pattern arrived at by conceptualization. Like the French Symbolists, Craig translated a lived-through experience into an *aesthetic equivalent,* through a process of *simplification* and *implication* in which, by discarding superfluous details, he reached a certain decorative intensity that was evocative as well. Form, color, and movement created an intricate, harmonious, symbolic pattern that pleased the eyes and the mind. Craig's mise en scène, so innovative against the English theatre background, could easily lead Ellen Terry to think that he considered the "pictorial" aspects before the dramatic significance.[11] But, as Christopher Innes so aptly showed, this highly symbolic "pictorial" side was also a good vehicle for the dramatic significance. For Craig, a simplified, symbolic "pictorial" element was one of the means by which he could achieve the same high quality of spiritual experience in theatre as was to be found in music. Unlike Wilde, who considered life and literature "the two supreme and highest arts," Craig adopted Pater's credo that "all art constantly aspires towards the condition of music."

The molding of the hardest material of the stage, *movement,* intrigued Craig, as it intrigued the Impressionists, the Symbolists, and Wilde himself. Wilde was convinced that movement could best be rendered by the word, affirming that the word could prefectly suggest movement and the imagination re-create it.[12] Moreover, Wilde believed in the power of the spoken word to stir imagination and proposed to revive the old art of recitation that was at the root of literature, in order to revitalize literature itself. "We must return to the voice," he wrote. "That must be our test, and perhaps then we shall be able to appreciate some of the subtleties of Greek art criticism."[13] The tales he wrote were such a "return to the voice," and so were his plays. Acting he considered to be a mode of creative interpretation, and he compared the actor to the critic: "Each of the arts has a critic, as it were assigned to it. The actor is a critic of the drama. He shows the poet's work under new conditions, and by a method special to himself. He takes the written word, and *action, gesture* and *voice* become the media of revelation."[14]

Craig went a step further. To Wilde's "*action, gesture* and *voice,*" he added *scene.* In his productions, scene itself was involved in movement, and new patterns of movement were designed for the actors. As Craig's notebooks and sketchbooks from this period show, he was slowly forging the concept of a new theatre, more dynamic and more spectacular in its symbolism. The London productions were only transition pieces in his quest for the ideal theatre. He became interested in the English masques, where the verbal signs give way to the visual and the dynamic. But instead of trying to adapt or revive the old pieces, Craig chose to write new ones, which bear the stamp not only of his aesthetic outlook but also of his socialistic ideas. So, for example, the scenario for the *Masque of London* was written in 1901, the drafts for the *Masque of Lunatics,* the *Masque of Hunger,* and *Harvest Home* in 1902, and Craig continued to revise them during the next few years.

He also prepared numerous drawings, with an eye toward producing these masques. Several of his designs for the "mimo-dramas," as he called these scenarios, were later published in *Towards a New Theatre,* in 1913. Lacking a theatre of his own, Craig took advantage of the one medium available to him at all times, drawing. He tried to convey his ideas on movement in theatre in "stage visions." These "stage visions" had begun to fill his sketchbooks since 1896, like the color drawing for the Ophelia scene in *Hamlet,* where the features that would later become characteristic of his style are already discernible, and where the influence of architecture is quite clear.[15] Craig's artistic output from 1897 to 1900 included some two hundred engravings. In 1900, he also designed scenes for *Hamlet* and *Peer Gynt,* along with "stage visions" like *Enter the Army.* In 1901, there were, among others, scenes for *Henry V (The Tents), The Lights of London,* and *The Arrival* (a "stage direction"). The stage setting for *The Merchant of Venice* was designed in 1902. During these few years Craig also made a great number of studies of movement in addition to many drawings, mostly in pen and wash (landscapes and sketches of actors), that were published in various art magazines. In 1904 he prepared more designs for his masques and also scenes for *Venice Preserved, Hamlet, Julius Caesar,* and *Macbeth.* At the same time, he was searching for a theatre of his own and a school of his own.

The reign of Edward VII brought a liberation of the arts and gave free rein to a hitherto stifled craving for new entertainments. Nonetheless, artistic endeavors like those initiated by the young director of the Purcell

Operatic Society or those patronized by a celebrated actress like Ellen Terry were favored only by a small group of artists and connoisseurs who could lend them but sporadic and limited support. These aesthetic enterprises were applauded by fashionable society as long as they provided a fresh and stimulating diversion, but the larger public rushed elsewhere. The stage was realistic in style and in interest, and it belonged to Granville-Barker at the Royal Court Theatre and to Beerbohm-Tree at His Majesty's Theatre. It became more and more clear that there was no prospect for Craig in London. He left in 1904 for Germany where, if he did not obtain his own theatre or his own school, he did work out his theory of the ideal theatre.

≻ *Part II* ≺

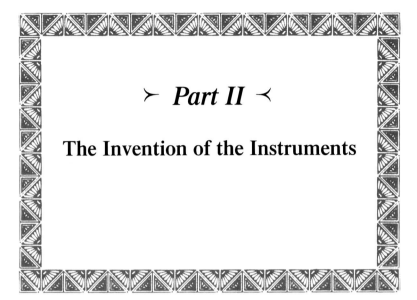

The Invention of the Instruments

6

Assertions and Self-Assertion

In June 1903, at the invitation of Count Harry Kessler, a well-known German patron of the arts, Craig crossed the channel and visited Weimar and Berlin.[1] A second visit followed a year later, in August 1904—again at Kessler's invitation, this time with a definite production project in view, Hofmannsthal's adaptation of Otway's *Venice Preserved.* Now Craig settled down in Berlin, a central meeting place for artists from all over Europe, as well as from smaller German cultural centers like Munich, Dresden, Hamburg, and Leipzig. Craig was very impressed by Berlin, with its monumental buildings and the latest addition to the Wertheim department store in Leipziger Platz unanimously praised as an example of modern aesthetic functionalism. Isadora Duncan described in her memoirs her long walks with Craig through the streets of Berlin and Craig's admiration for the "*neuer kunst praktisch*" buildings.[2] Alfred Messel, who was responsible for the Wertheim addition, was the architect whom Craig had in mind for the Uber-Marionette International Theatre in Dresden.

When he arrived in Berlin, Craig was under the impression that his production of *Venice Preserved* at the Lessing Theater was already settled.[3] Craig had brought with him from England some bitter memories of his work with professional actors under another management than his own. Now he expected to have at his disposal a theatre, a company, and the necessary means—and free hand—to produce a piece of art similar to what he had created in London. Many years later (in *Henry Irving,*

1930), Craig would claim credit for having introduced in 1904 the New Movement in theatre in Germany, France, Holland, Russia, Scandinavia, and Italy. Though he recognized the contributions of Adolphe Appia and of Isadora Duncan, he scorned Stanislavsky, Reinhardt, Meyerhold, Fortuny, Roller, Linnebach, Diaghilev, Copeau, Pitoeff, Tairov, Komissarjevsky, Piscator, Jouvet, Baty, and "others"—in this order—as mere "doers." Nonetheless, when Craig went to Berlin in 1904, all he wished for was a theatre and a school. Unfortunately for him, the situation was very different from what he had been given to expect.

By the turn of the century, theatre was an important part of the social and cultural life in Germany. Having one's plays produced not only satisfied the aesthetic urge to see one's creative work come to life on the illusory stage but also represented a much-prized sign of social recognition and acceptance. The press reflected this attitude, prominently reviewing current productions; as a result theatre critics themselves became celebrities. (A good example is the case of Dr. Otto Brahm, who, though Jewish and in spite of the big wave of anti-Semitism that swept Germany and Austria during the 1890s, attained an important position as a theatre critic and became the director of the Lessing Theatre.) There was a clear-cut distinction between two types of theatre—popular entertainment, such as the music hall and the variety theatre, and "art" theatres. The latter reflected the social structure, each class lending its support to its own theatre. The Freie Bühne was supported by rich merchants, industrialists, and art collectors, such as James Simon, Eduard Arnold and Franz von Mendelssohn.[4] In the early 1900s, Max Reinhardt's theatre, the Deutsches Theater, was supported by the haute bourgeoisie, the Royal Opera was financed by the imperial court, and the Freie Volksbühne by the industrial workers. A system of organized membership enabled theatres to free themselves from depending totally on patrons, and so, for example, the Freie Volksbühne could count in 1905 up to 11,000 members. The Lessing Theater, where Craig expected to produce a play, was supported by rich patrons (Count Kessler was one of them) and by the bourgeoisie.

As it was, artists in Germany formed if not a special social class then a distinct caste. Roy Pascal affirms that between 1880 and 1918 artists evolved into a distinct social class that regardless of any professed views embodied bourgeois values in their ways of living and in their work. A common denominator was their claim to the role of the modern prophet and redeemer, as well as the claim to a uniqueness that was supposed to free them from conventional moral and social obligations—two claims that both Craig and Isadora Duncan made their own. What Pascal calls "the worship of *Geist,*" together with a widespread elitist conception of culture, gave the artists a much-needed legitimacy and secured their role as high priests of the *Geist*.[5] Few of the artists were financially independent, however. Some had a profession, like Richard Dehmel who was a clerk in an insurance office, and others enjoyed a private income, like Stefan George; but many depended on the good will of a patron, who was usually a rich industrialist or a banker, if not the intendant of a princely court or a rich aristocrat. The imperial court supported its own group of artists, of whom it demanded allegiance not only to the established, official aesthetic norms but to moral ones as well—it is known that when news of Isadora Duncan's pregnancy reached the aristocratic sponsors of her school, some of these who were close to the Kaiserin withdrew their support. Only a handful of artists were able to subsist on their earnings alone.

No doubt, given the system of patronage of artists and theatres and the privileged status of the artist in Germany by 1904, some sort of financial support, which would automatically bring also social and cultural support, was indispensable to Craig, a foreign artist. Indeed, this support was to be expected, especially since the initiative for Craig's coming had been taken by the well-known Count Kessler, who introduced Craig as an artist of genius and an innovator in theatre. Ten years later, after Craig's influence in Germany had become visible in the work of other directors, Sheldon Cheney would refer to him as "the best known secessionist from the regular theatre."[6] But Craig was greeted as such from the very first moment of his arrival in Germany in 1904.

Besides his artistic achievements, what launched Craig now was the name of his patron, who had become famous for his support of outstanding artists such as Henry van de Velde. Craig perceived his situation as a privileged one that entitled him to certain prerogatives, and the prevailing attitude toward the artist only reinforced his conviction. It is quite possible that Craig perceived his rights even more readily than his duties, and this certainly did not help his dealings with other theatre directors who also regarded themselves as artists. But again, this attitude was not at all uncommon or unexpected in the artistic milieu. Therefore one cannot but wonder at the enthusiastic but unwise step taken by Count Kessler when he brought the young director to Germany but did not lend him all the aid he needed. As an amateur and patron of the arts—and a patron of the Lessing Theater—Count Kessler must have known that just as the painter needs his brush, his paints, and his studio, so must a director have his theatre—an instrument and materials that are so much more difficult to obtain. As it was, the theatre itself could not exist in Germany without the support of patrons, of an organized body of amateurs, or (even more rare) of an enthusiastic and faithful general public. Craig did not get the proper backing and means that would have enabled him to integrate into the German theatrical system. Perhaps the reason lay in Kessler's impression—made clear in the correspondence between Kessler and Hofmannsthal—that Craig was primarily a stage designer and illustrator.[7] Kessler's main help to Craig was obtaining a commission for him to design Hofmannsthal's *Electra* for a possible production by Duse and also to illustrate Hofmannsthal's *White Fan* and *Death and the Fool.*

The first obstacle that Craig encountered in Berlin was the uncordial attitude of Dr. Otto Brahm, the director of the Lessing Theater, with whom he was supposed to work. Craig must not have been cordial himself, since Brahm had won his name as a theatre critic and Craig could rightly consider him a representative of literature and not a man of the profession; moreover, Brahm's fame as a director was based on the naturalistic style of his productions. Brahm was distrustful from the very start. He considered Craig not only an outsider who was being imposed on him by one of the most influential patrons of his theatre but also an artist of divergent views and therefore dangerous. At first he was merely indifferent—Craig's first contacts were with Emil Heilbut, the editor of *Kunst und Kunstler,* who acted as a mediator and translator between the two—then aloof, arrogant, and condescending. Kessler's role in trying to force Craig on Brahm showed an astonishing lack of human understanding. It was not long before Brahm took advantage of a technical difficulty to cancel the collaboration.

This matter could have been considered a minor incident, had it not been for its disproportionate and disastrous influence on Craig's career as a director. Left alone in the territory of the "enemy," Craig tried to find a business manager who would launch him on an international scale, the way it had happened to Isadora Duncan. He entrusted Maurice Magnus, a young journalist, with this task, but their cooperation did not lead to anything, either in Germany or anywhere else.

Craig's flamboyant personality, his unusual views on theatre, his London productions, and his exhibitions in Germany, Holland, and Austria, along with his missionary fervor, made him a celebrity in his own right. This satisfied his desires to some extent, but not entirely. If he left London with the intention of finding a theatre for himself, the situation after the Brahm affair made it clear to him that he had to work alone and bring his work not to a limited audience but to an international one. His scene was now the international scene, and Germany was only the entrance. Projects were plentiful, among them a theatre in Holland, but they led to nothing. In truth, Craig was no longer interested in doing more productions in the regular theatre: his thoughts were all on an international über-marionette theatre.

Craig's frequent travels during 1905 and 1906 obviously interfered with any sustained artistic and professional commitments. His frequent comings and goings in and out of Berlin during these years look at first glance like purposeless perambulations; but if he joined Isadora Duncan on many of her tours, he was moved not only by his feelings for her but also by an insatiable curiosity for places, people, and art and, most important, by his sense of mission as an artist. While he was traveling he continued to do his engraving and drawing, promoting his ideas wherever he went. Whether to justify his presence near Isadora or to help her by his experience, he also took on the role of her manager, several months after they first met. They were together on tour very soon after their first meeting—in early January 1905 in Cologne, then, on the fifteenth, in Dresden, two days later in Leipzig, and from the twenty-fourth to the thirty-first in Hamburg. In February Craig was in St. Petersburg, Moscow, Frankfurt, and Wiesbaden, and during March he traveled back and forth from Berlin to Breslau, Frankfurt, Düsseldorf, Brussels, and Villers-la-Ville in Belgium. In April he was in Antwerp, Amsterdam, and Cologne, then back in Berlin. In May he visited Dresden twice, then went to Bonn and Freiburg. In June he was again in Moscow, and by the end of the month he was in Heidelberg. In July he visited London, went to Weimar, then returned to Berlin. He was still there by the beginning of August, later to go to The Hague, Tutzing, and Zurich. During most of September he stayed in Berlin, but at the end of the month he went to Frankfurt and Hallé. If the "Uber-Marions" notebooks are correct, he attended the opening of his exhibition in Vienna on 1 October, then joined Isadora on her tour in Amsterdam, Utrecht, Amsterdam again, Leyden, and The Hague. He was in Berlin at the beginning of November, then spent a fortnight in Dresden. In December he went to Amsterdam.

This listing, based mostly on published material, is far from complete, but it gives a good idea of Craig's hectic activities during 1905. By the beginning of 1906 Craig was again with Isadora on a tour, and Martin Shaw joined them as Isadora's conductor. The tour took them to Nuremberg, Augsburg, Munich, Amsterdam, The Hague, Copenhagen, Stockholm, and Göteborg. From June to October 1906, Craig divided his time between Berlin and Amsterdam, Rotterdam and Noordwijsk (where Isadora was in seclusion, awaiting the birth of their baby), with a short visit to his family in London in July. In October, Eleonora Duse's production of *Rosmersholm* took him to Florence, but during most of December and January he stayed in Berlin. At the beginning of February 1907 he left for Nice to meet Duse, but by the end of the month he was back in Florence, where he decided to stay and work on his experiments. However, he again joined Isadora in Amsterdam in March. In May they were together in Stockholm and Heidelberg, then Craig returned alone to Florence, which was to be his headquarters for the next ten years. His own exhibitions had taken him in 1905 to Düsseldorf, Cologne, Weimar, and Vienna, and in 1906 to Rotterdam. In 1906, the printing of the Isadora Portfolio also took him to Leipzig several times.[8] Considering the amount of time spent on these travels—made by train—one is astonished at Craig's rich artistic output during these years.

In Germany as well as in Belgium, Holland, Denmark, Sweden, Russia, France, and Italy, Craig met a great number of leading artists. Among the writers he met, his most important encounter was with Hugo von Hofmannsthal, who had translated and adapted *Venice Preserved* for the Lessing Theater. Craig prepared a series of designs for Hofmannsthal's *Electra* for a possible production with Duse, and he made several designs for the publication of his *Death and the Fool* and *The White Fan*.[9] Craig also met Gerhart Hauptmann, whose son Ivo, a painter, became very interested in Craig's work with the über-marionette. Craig knew Detlev von Liliencron, Hermann Sudermann, Richard Dehmel, and Hermann Bahr. When he visited Stockholm in 1906, he met Strindberg. Among the painters there was Marcus Behmer, the Jugendstil etcher and draftsman, Ludwig von Hofmann, a member of the Berlin Sezession and a good friend of William Rothenstein, and Max Klinger, who, like Ludwig von Hofmann, had contributed to the famous review *Pan* (which was supported among others by Count Kessler). Through Kessler, Craig met the Belgian architect Henry van de Velde, the leader of the abstract trend in the Jugendstil movement, and the Austrian Sezessionist architect Josef Hoffmann, who in 1905 built the famous Palais Stoclet in Brussels. In Holland, Craig met the painter Marius Bauer and the painter and novelist Jacobus van Looy, who became his friends. Craig apparently had no contact with the young painters of *Die Brücke* in Dresden, although he held two exhibitions in this city and also planned to build his über-marionette theatre there. In the musical world, Craig met Josef Joachim, Frederic Lamond, and Siegfried Wagner, the son of the composer whose dramatic theories he admired. (Craig also had met Cosima Wagner at a lunch with the Von Nostitz family in Dresden.) The two outstanding theatre people whom Craig came to know were, of course, Eleonora Duse and Max Reinhardt. He planned to collaborate with both of them, but in the end, he designed only the settings for Duse's production of *Rosmersholm*. Reinhardt, perhaps more than anyone else, helped publicize Craig's ideas, because he put them to brilliant use in his own productions. For example, his settings for *Winter Tale* (1906) and *King Lear* (1908) could easily be mistaken for Craig's, and those for *Jedermann* (1923) looked similar to Craig's settings for *Bethlehem*. J. L. Styan detects Craig's influence also in the Expressionist acting style that Reinhardt used for *Das junge Deutschland* (1928) and in Reinhardt's overall use of shafts of light in space.[10]

Craig was hopeful that published writings could not only spread his ideas but also, by reaching a larger audience, gain him supporters. Shortly after he arrived in Germany he began work on a book on theatre, focusing on the visuality of movement and on the superiority of the marionette as an instrument for movement. The title of the book was to be "Theatre—Shows and Motions." The most important part, the fourth chapter, was to be devoted to "the actor and attack," commenting on "the actor-manager as artist, craftsman and public man" and centering on Antoine, Irving, and Reinhardt. The fifth and last chapter was to provide the "philosophy" and assert "the Puppet and the Art of the Theatre and spectacle." Craig drew up an outline in 1904 and made notes on the various chapters in 1905, 1908, and 1909 but never finished the book.[11]

Craig did, however, complete and publish in 1905 the famous essay *The Art of the Theatre*. Craig began dictating the essay in Berlin on 22 April 1905, interrupted work in order to attend the opening of his exhibition in Dresden on 1 May, and finished on 4 May. The essay was immediately translated into German by Maurice Magnus and printed in booklet form. Kessler, who had written the preface to the catalogue of Craig's exhibition in Berlin in December 1904, agreed to let his preface also be used for *The Art of the Theatre*. An English edition appeared in London in June 1905; it was translated into Dutch and published in Amsterdam in 1906, and an unauthorized Russian translation appeared in Moscow the same year. Craig wrote two other essays in 1907, "The Artists of the Theatre of the Future" and "The Actor and the Uber-Marionette." They were published in *The Mask* in 1908. Together, the three essays form Craig's artistic manifesto.

The Art of the Theatre stated the main elements of Craig's theory. For this essay, Craig adopted the elegant literary form of the Socratic dialogue, which was also used by Wilde.[12] This form allowed Craig to make a case and discuss a hypothetical situation, a way of persuading by indirection, without openly attacking the existing theatre and its ruler, the star actor. Craig could thus pose counterarguments and refute them in logical succession, in such a way as to build up his thesis and make it not only plausible but convincing. The tone of the essay was subdued and even slightly humorous. In the next two essays, the tone would become much more assertive. In May 1905 the über-marionette was still reposing in the wings, waiting to be brought out at the propitious moment. For the time being, the area had to be cleared of all extraneous matters that might obstruct the future message, public opinion had to be gently prepared for the coming of the über-marionette and the new art of the theatre.

But if the tone of this essay was subdued, its contents were subversive. The essay became Craig's first important salvo in his long battle against Realism in the theatre. For the first time, Craig was attempting to show a larger reading public—not just the readers of art and theatre magazines, who probably were already convinced—what was wrong with present-day theatre. Craig wanted more than just converts: he wanted supporters for his special theatre and school by which he could proceed to reform the theatre. The essay was received with mixed feelings. Artists and writers such as Hauptmann or Sudermann were, naturally, enthusiastic; others accused Craig of being an Aesthete—"as if it were something I oughtn't to be," he remarked in a letter to Ellen Terry from Zurich in August 1905. In this letter he quoted, in free translation, from an article printed in a Munich newspaper shortly after the opening of his exhibition there on 1 June 1905 and the publication of the booklet. The indignant, chauvinist author of the article, who happened to be the producer of the Wagner Festspiel that year at the Prinz Regenten Theater in Munich, attacked Craig not only for his aesthetic views but also for being a foreigner, an outsider, and an English Aesthete who presumed to show the Germans what good taste really was. Craig quoted him as saying: "We do not want aesthetic or tasteful English art in our theatre, we want manly German art."[13] Not all Craig's detractors were so polite; some actually accused him of being a charlatan.[14]

The thesis of the essay is that the director is the sole creative artist in the theatre, which should be considered an instrument in the hands of the artist. The role of the performer is limited, and Suggestion—not Reproduction—should be the guiding principle for the mise en scène. At present, Craig says in the essay, the theatre is in an interpretative phase--following the criteria of his own achievements—but it is moving to a creative phase in which action (movement and dancing), scene (scenery, costume, and lighting), and voice (spoken or sung word) will make the play as such unnecessary. It will be a primarily visual theatre, on the order of the masques and pageants of old, which offered as their main attraction a fabulous spectacle, but with the difference that along with amusement it will offer "full intellectual exercise."[15] Not that Craig abandoned the appeal through the senses to the imagination, but he was now approaching his new audience with new tools: logic and the appeal to the sacrosanct "intellect." For Craig, writing was an instrument to woo, convince, attack, destroy, or hold up to ridicule. He could very well impose on himself the rigid structure of the Socratic dialogue in order to advance his plea in a logical way, but he was unprepared to enter into a philosophical discussion on intellect and imagination. And these notions are used interchangeably in his writings. As he well knew, the viability of his theatre could be demonstrated in one way only: by having him build it. To this end he needed supporters, and he was now appealing to what they prized most: their "intellect."

In the essay, Craig rooted the origins of theatre in dance. As Ferruccio Marotti has pointed out, the idea had already been advanced by Georg Fuchs the year before, in 1904, in *Die Schaubühne der Zukunft*. Craig's approach to acting—influenced by the Symbolist experiments in Paris and now based on his own work with his actors in London—denoted his propensity to consider theatre, a spatial but also a temporal art, as essentially spatial. Craig treats materials used by the theatre in a manner similar to the inert matter used by the painter or the architect. By breaking down acting into its components, he transforms it from an individual creation of the actor into a combination of elements easily manipulated by the director. Movement and voice are treated as materials to be shaped by the artist. When the stage director in the essay is asked by the playgoer whether he expects the "intelligent actors almost to become puppets," he evades the issue: "A puppet is *at present* only a doll, delightful enough for a puppet show. But for a theatre we need more than a doll," he says.[16] The actor having been thus dismissed as the dominating element in the theatrical creation, the director takes over as the main dynamic force.

This conception of the director's role was not totally new, but Craig was supplying it for the first time an aesthetic foundation; the director was now given the dignified rank of an artist. Throughout Europe, the director had been slowly gaining power in the theatre, though he was still often also a performer. There had been the Duke of Saxe-Meiningen in Germany; there were Granville-Barker and Beerbohm-Tree in London, Stanislavsky in Moscow, Otto Brahm and Reinhardt in Berlin, as well as the two French pioneers Antoine and Lugné-Poe in Paris. And there was also, of course, Craig himself, who based his theory on his own practice as a director. The director should possess, according to Craig—and he had himself in mind—an "intuitive apprehension," "great intellect," and "aesthetic refinement." Only that sort of creative genius could restore the art of the theatre "to its home."[17] The director is the artist of the theatre, who creates with action ("the very spirit of acting"), words (the "body of the play"), line and color ("the very heart of the scene"), and rhythm ("the very essence of dance").[18] The selection and use of these materials depend on the director's interpretation of the play (speaking of the current interpretative stage of the theatre). In the same way that the beholder of a painting must look for similarity not between the painting and its model but rather, as Maurice Denis maintained, between the painting and the artist's feelings, so the spectator no longer must search for the production's adherence to reality but should consider the production as the expression of the director's interpretation, of the artist's feelings. As Craig explained in a letter to Martin Shaw written in May 1905, the director's *present* task—and this would include Craig's own work with the Purcell Operatic Society or with Ellen Terry's company in London—was one of *interpretation:*

> I don't hold that [*Bethlehem* and *The Masque of Love*] were examples of theatrical art. I brought my craft and you yours to the INTERPRETATION of another's art. As alas always is with the theatre today. We may have "*interpreted*" better or worse but we *created* not a jot. On the other hand I am now at work creating a work of theatrical art. . . . I shall make its shape and colour, its sound and sense, its movement and tone. I shall not employ actors nor pantomimists but what I shall call "figures" (über-marionettes is too complicated).[19]

Meanwhile, Craig was busy with other writing. An article by him entitled "Etwas über den Regisseur und die Bühnenausstattung" appeared in the July 1905 issue of *Deutsche Kunst und Dekoration.* Another article, "Uber Bühnenausstattung," on the mise en scène, had already appeared in *Kunst und Kunstler,* and two letters to the editor, concerning the Otto Brahm affair, had been printed by the liberal newspaper *Berliner Tageblatt,* a national publication, on 10 and 26 January 1905 (similar letters were sent to eleven more newspapers all over Germany). But Craig was beginning to think about changing his tactics. He wrote to Ellen Terry in August 1905: "But I begin to see what is against the easier and more speedy success of the idea in Munich, it is that I have developed the idea too swiftly, thinking of little else, whereas all the world is thinking of a good deal else and not of my idea. I must return and speak of the *fringe* of the idea" (my emphasis).[20]

Since Realism was the stronghold of his "enemy," Craig's attack must become more and more sustained. The explanatory note Craig wrote for the program of *Rosmersholm* in December 1906 was defiant, not subdued as before. By then his project for an über-marionette theatre had already suffered a serious setback, but the production of *Rosmersholm* with Duse gave him renewed hope. In this explanatory note, Craig contrasted Realism and Art, Exposure and Revelation, and the photographer and the artist. This production was for him the forerunner of the new creative art of the theatre, though he had only contributed the scenery to it. The new aesthetic experience of *Rosmersholm* was a ceremony at which the spectator might comprehend "the *value of the spirit* which moves before [him] as Rebecca West" (my emphasis). He offered the audience, as he said, a "vision." In a letter to the editor of the *Saturday Review* in November 1906 he had declared that the new theatre would be "a theatre of visions, not of sermons nor a theatre of epigrams."[21]

By the beginning of 1907, although there was no other production with Duse in view, Craig was again full of confidence. Isadora had promised to give recitals concurrently with the über-marionette theatre performances, and Craig was sure of the success of their joint enterprise. Together they would create, he believed, the new art of movement.

≻ 7 ≺

Movement

Isadora Duncan

Encounters with strong artistic personalities and confrontations with new ways of thinking and with new means and techniques of expression proved to be most fruitful incentives to Craig. The meeting with Pryde and Nicholson led Craig to discover wood engraving, enriching his vision of theatrical space. Jess Dorynne introduced him to aesthetics, and his readings in the field developed his critical attitude to theatre. His friendship with Martin Shaw brought him to a deeper understanding of music not only from the listener's but also from the performer's and the composer's point of view. Thus, his approach to theatre had been illuminated by the wood engraver's sensitive glance, by the thinker's knowing discernment, and by the musician's logical scrutiny and refined perception. The über-marionette idea materialized very soon after Craig met Isadora Duncan: this meant a radical change of means and techniques for movement in theatre and the replacement of the actor by a manipulated figure, the über-marionette.

Isadora was involved in the über-marionette project from the outset. Most of Craig's letters to her are unfortunately lost, but those of Isadora that are available show beyond any doubt that he wrote her constantly on the project and that she helped him as much as she could. For example, when she was on tour in Brussels in March 1905, he wrote to her about his decision to make wooden marionettes and asked her to look for "dollies."[1] In her letters, especially those of 1905 and early 1906, she often used the terms "puppet," "doll," and "marionette" as metaphors, and one senses that the über-marionette occupied an important place in their day-to-day relations to the point of also becoming part of Isadora's preoccupations.[2] In a moment of moral and physical distress, apparently discouraged at having to work with her body as an instrument, she even echoes Craig's views on the human performer.[3]

Today it is not easy to know what Isadora's dance was really like. Modern dance has long since incorporated these once revolutionary innovations, so it is difficult to evaluate their impact on the contemporary audience. Nor can Craig's reports, in diaries, notebooks, talks, and articles over a period of fifty years, give an accurate account of the 1904 aesthetic experience. At best, they can only reveal how this experience was lived and relived through the film of memory and the mist of emotion. To get a clearer view, one must turn to Isadora's own writings from that period, to the evidence of those who saw her dance, and to the photographs and drawings that captured some moments of motion in her dance during the years 1904–7.

Isadora Duncan was twenty-six when she met Craig. She was pretty, ambitious, and already a master of public relations. She had a tremendous confidence in her powers and in her goal, and an unequaled showmanship. She had recently achieved fame and riches, a barefoot Cinderella who was only too glad to lose her slippers in order to conquer the world. She was born in 1878 in San Francisco and got her training, such as it was, at an early age. She was still in her teens when she began to give dancing lessons in order to help her family subsist. In 1896, at eighteen, she danced for a short time in a vaudeville show at the Masonic Roof Garden in Chicago, then joined Augustin Daly's company in New York. The next year she took dancing lessons from Ketti Lenner in London and from Marie Bonfanti in New York. Her first concerts took place in New York in 1898, with the composer Ethelbert Nevin at the piano. By 1900 she was in London (with her mother, sister, and brothers), dancing at private concerts, reading, studying the art of ancient Greece at the British Museum, and trying to discover the exact nature of the movements that are caught in the frozen poses on Greek vases. In London, too, she saw performances of Ellen Terry and Eleonora Duse, and in Paris, at the Exposition Universelle, she saw the Japanese dancer Sada Yacco. By the end of 1901, Isadora was doing solo performances with Loïe Fuller's company, on tour from Berlin to Vienna, through Leipzig and Munich. In April 1902 she was in Budapest, having found the right impresario, and well launched on her career as an international star dancer. She was in Munich again in November 1902, and in Paris in May 1903, after which she went to Greece. By May 1904, the year that Craig moved to Berlin, she had been adopted by German society and the artistic world and had danced at Bayreuth in *Tannhauser*'s Bacchanale at the invitation of Cosima Wagner. German aristocracy honored her as an artist, and with the help of her sister Elizabeth, she opened a school for dance in Berlin, in the fashionable Grünewald. When Craig met her, she was already popular, admired, gossiped about: a celebrity.

Although at the beginning of her career in Europe, Isadora riveted the attention of the audience mainly by her chiton and her Greek poses, she never claimed to revive the old Greek dancing art—though this is what many believed she was doing—but the art of Dance itself, as only the Greek could understand it. She dispensed with the standardized movements of classical ballet and with its traditional costume and also rejected the music of ballet, dancing to composers of her own choice. Above all, she claimed to be American. America was looked on as the land of dreams and of unlimited possibilities, the symbol of freedom, the country where a new and ever-larger democratic society was growing. (Indeed, the number of immigrants to the United States between 1900 and 1910 was a staggering 7.75 million, the highest ever in a single decade, higher than the peak number, 5.24 million, reached between 1880 and 1890.)[4] Isadora possessed all the qualities that popular imagination attributed to the American: energy, audacity, and an independent mind. "Liberation" was her password. She considered dance an art of liberation for the individual as such and for women as a hitherto dominated class. For her, dance was both self-expression and the means toward the liberation of the female body, but never a legitimization of eroticism. She desired to make dance not only supreme among all the arts but also a vehicle for "what is the most moral, healthful and beautiful in art."[5]

Isadora read literature, philosophy, history. She kept informed about the latest events in the artistic and intellectuals circles in London, Paris, Berlin, or anywhere her tours took her, being everywhere fêted by artists and writers. Her outspoken views astonished some of those who were attracted by her art, embarrassed others: though a dancer, she believed in the magic of words, and throughout her career she gave speeches, before, after, or between concerts. From speeches defending her views she soon moved on to sermons about the importance of Truth in matters of aesthetics, morals, and politics. She was devoted to the feminist cause and made it part of her artistic revolution. One of her earliest lectures, *Der Tanz der Zukunft* (The Dance of the Future), published as a pamphlet in Leipzig in 1903, asserts the main points of her aesthetic credo: (*a*) nature as a model of harmony; (*b*) the human body as a microcosm; (*c*) the individual—more specifically, woman—and her right to self-assertion and self-expression;

(*d*) movement and dance as self-expression. The essay is imbued with a yearning for freedom, a cosmic sense, and a pantheistic vision—all of which echo her favorite poet, Walt Whitman, and show how deeply immersed she was in her role of artist-redeemer. She outlined at great length the idea of freedom inherent in dance and claimed that natural and beautiful movement could be performed only if the body were allowed to move freely, unhindered by the conventional ballet costume.

Although Isadora was never explicit about her training and rather preferred to leave this part of her artistic background in the dark, her criticism of ballet techniques was not naïve. It is of course of little relevance whether her great art was generated by her rebellion against the physical and emotional constraints imposed by ballet, whether it took shape because she was unable to perform great feats of skill but was too ambitious, or too full of spirit, to stop dancing on that account, or simply because she possessed vision and genius. In her view, ballet had not changed since Balthasar de Beaujoyeulx defined it, three hundred years earlier, as a "geometrical arrangement of several persons dancing together to the diverse harmonies of numerous instruments." Comparing it to "natural" (performative) movement, she repeatedly criticized its overstressed movements and affected poses, its exaggerated steps and the pain-inflicting tight bodice and pointed shoes, and deplored its puppetlike performers.[6] She appreciated technical virtuosity but denied any expressive value to what she considered to be a codified, fossilized, and rigid system. She condemned the sensual appeal of the ballet, based—as she believed—on sensational feats of skill and spectacular scenery; she attacked its artificial, contrived movement. She was convinced that ballet movement went against the natural laws of gravitation as well as against the will of its performer and was therefore sterile and expressionless. The ideal movement that she had in mind was to be a chant to the beauty of the human body, as created by nature and as forever embodied by the ideal of classical Greece. Isadora, with her idealistic concept of nature, looked to nature for the images she sought to express in the movement of her dance. She believed that the codified ballet deformed the body and corrupted the intellect, and she could never understand how, if ever, ballet could express any ideal at all. But rather than trying to reform ballet, she wanted to get hold of the source itself—plain and "natural" movement—and shape it into a work of art that belonged to a tradition long lost in the dark ages.

Isadora had read Haeckel's *Riddle of the Universe* while she was studying ancient Greek vases at the British Museum, and she was still one of his disciples during her association with Craig. Approaching the task of reconstructing the art of dance in ancient Greece under Haeckel's influence, she placed the captured movements on the vases in what seemed to her, rather simplistically, their most natural context, daily life, with its "normal," routine, functional, and imitative gestures and movements. It did not occur to her that the Greek dance might also have been codified, as ritual dances often are. "Nature" and the Greek (idealized) movement seemed to her equivalent. She was convinced that she was rediscovering the beauty of the human body and of movement, such as it should have been carried on through the ages, unspoiled by codifications. On these vases she also discovered the undulating line that she identified with different sorts of waves in nature.[7]

Following Delsarte, Isadora considered the body an instrument for the expression of feelings and believed that every emotion had its corresponding movement, easily understood by all. Early in 1901 the French critic André Levinson defined Isadora's dance as a mimic art that used imitative gestures. Indeed, it was this aspect of her dance that made her so popular with the larger public, and her famous *Blue Danube,* with its wavelike movements, is a good example of how she put to use not only Delsarte's method but also her past experience with Daly's company.

By 1904, however, Isadora's style had been effectively refined to "natural" movement, a few lights, and music. Movement involved the whole body, head, limbs, spine, and back. Undulating movements grew out of one another in harmonious sequences, no longer seeking to be imitative. Isadora discovered a totally new and unsuspected range of expressive movements and built her method on the concentration of movement in the solar plexus, as Martha Graham would later do. (The solar plexus as the starting point of movement explains the upward direction of movement that is so striking in the many drawings of Isadora done by Rodin, Fritz von Kaulbach, Jean-Paul Lafitte, Maurice Denis, José Clara, Bourdelle, Abraham Walkowitz, Dunoyer de Segonzac, Grandjouan, John Sloan, Robert Henry, and Craig.) Francis Steegmuller, who edited her correspondence with Craig, quotes various press reports from her tour in Russia in December 1904 where they praised her "marvellous plastic sensibility" and the expressivity of her hands and bare legs.[8]

In a literal as well as in a metaphorical sense, Isadora was "moved" by music; emotion was filtered and conveyed by controlled, stylized movements that astonished professional ballet people by their effective simplicity. She stylized the "natural" movements performed in everyday tasks and arranged them, together with newly invented movements, into flowing, expressive patterns. She devised her own method for training the body toward greater flexibility and strength. Her own training consisted of everyday movements like leaping, walking, running, or skipping, following the rule of the least effort. She dismissed the Dalcroze system as rather "killing" and "paralyzing," and the Swedish gymnastics as unfit for a flowing movement.[9]

In July 1905, while Isadora was between tours, she drew up her own "precepts for the teaching of the school" and composed a series of five hundred training exercises, going from simple to complex movements, which were to be taught to the pupils at her school. Not for a moment did she believe that her art could not be perpetuated and passed on to a younger generation. Again and again she affirmed that she never regarded herself as a soloist—a statement belied by her entire career. What she could and did convey to her pupils was a fervent search for beauty and expression in movement, but what she herself defined as "the role of imagination" in the creative process was not in her power to teach.[10] Craig was quick to perceive that her art was highly individualized. On the other hand, John Martin—who never saw her dance—was apparently sure that if the principles of her style had been clearly defined and presented in a systemized way, her art could have been kept alive.[11]

Isadora's dances were in a sense based on psychological themes, but like Loïe Fuller's, they were plotless. They expressed the emotional, intellectual, and physical impact of music, music that for Isadora represented the very quintessence of life. To what extent she actually conveyed her response to the audience depends partly on whether one thinks that *any* interpretive experience can be shared. As Susan Langer showed in her essay *Feeling and Form,* there is a universal confusion between self-expression and dance expression, as between feeling shown and feeling represented, or as between symptom and symbol.[12] The slight time lag between the musical momentum and the dance expression only adds to this confusion. A dancer may develop a phrase that although initially propelled by the music grows into a totally independent expressive entity, which certainly does not help the beholder understand the stage symbol. Indeed, the translation into discursive terms of the symbol that is perceived during the interaction of sound, movement, and space is a very complex matter of semiotics. But if it is impossible to say *what* exactly was conveyed, the *expressivity* of Isadora's dance has certainly never been disputed: she did convey significance, and her interpretive experience was indeed shared by the audience.

Carl van Vechten, who followed her career over the years, considered her dance in 1909 "poetical"; in a review written in 1911 he noted her "expressive poses and movements," pointing out that she *portrayed* and *indicated* feelings and ideas. In 1917 he wrote that her dance was always "pure" and "sexless," adding that "always abstract emotion has guided her interpretations." On the development of her art throughout the many years of her career he observed that it progressively gained in strength, and he detected a growing inclination for concrete images rather than the earlier abstract ones. With the years, her body lost its grace and flexibility but gained in expressivity; she now used rhythmic gesture and expressive *stasis.*[13] Elie Faure, who saw Isadora dance not long before she died, said that she "demonstrated while dancing."[14]

However, we are concerned here with the earlier part of her career, when she used "abstract images," or pure movement. Her dances were carefully composed under the stimulation of music, when the "motor" in her soul was stirred to life.[15] Sometimes the impulse came from movement itself, as she wrote to Craig from Warsaw in December 1906.[16] She explored new combinations of movement and, using music not originally intended for dance, discovered new rules of harmony from which she created whole patterns. Years later, in "Terpsichore," an essay written probably in the early 1920s, she would explain that her intention was to recover "the natural cadences of human movement" and that only great composers "combined with absolute perfection terrestrial and human rhythm."[17] She considered the rhythm of Bach, Gluck, Beethoven, Chopin, Schubert, Wagner, and Schumann more appropriate to the rhythm of the human body than the rhythm of ballet music, which was restricted to only one line of movement. Her dance expressed the theme of the music and generally followed its rhythmic structure, but she often used the rubato and she also danced without music. (She would claim that Beethoven taught her rhythm, Nietzsche—spirit, and Wagner—sculptural form.)[18]

During her liaison with Craig, Isadora was still exploring the nature of movement and the components of dance, and her letters to Craig bear witness to her search. In a letter to Craig written in March 1905, for example, she explained that she was studying the relation of dance to nature and how to convert the magnetic forces of nature and their wave-like movements into aesthetic form.[19] Three other letters to Craig, all written in December 1906, show her devoting her time to the study of the "different relations" of music to dancing.[20] She believed in the unity of music and dance as being "natural" and thought that dance was generated by music. No doubt, the music she chose contributed in a great measure to establishing her as a serious artist, for it attracted an elite audience that appreciated refinement and stylization in art. This music removed her dance from any erotic context and aroused in her audience a feeling of spiritual elevation. Intellectuals could delight in this new art of dance without condescension, as could lovers of classical music, and their recognition reinforced the value of this dance as a serious, artistic endeavor—despite its unmistakable sensual appeal. The sensual element was enhanced by the bare legs and the transparent fabric of her tunic or draped robes, but this was a subliminal eroticism. Isadora's recitals beautifully belonged in the early twentieth-century atmosphere of artistic renewal, between the last sighs of the Art Nouveau and the first cries of Expressionism. Martin Shaw, who was her conductor in 1906 and 1907, wrote in his memoirs that Isadora used to leave her audience in a state of ecstatic delight.[21] But there were art amateurs who disapproved of her dancing, and Count Kessler, as well as Hugo von Hofmannsthal, were among them: Kessler thought she was "awkward, amateurish and uncultured."[22]

What astonished and fascinated Craig was the beauty and the expressivity of Isadora's dance, for this was achieved not by a skillful combination of light, costume, and movement, as in Loïe Fuller's dance, but mainly by movement alone: this was "pure" movement, with no story line. The interests of Craig and Isadora were converging: she was exploring movement as the main element of dance, and he was studying it as the main element of a stylized art of the theatre. Both aimed at restoring their art to its original high rank. They used to discuss their readings and share their doubts and their discoveries, finding support and stimulation in each other's work; it was only after their estrangement that each of them sought refuge in his own work and excluded the other. One example of this artistic communion is Isadora's letter to Craig, written in Göttingen probably in March 1905, where she draws his attention to Goethe's theory of color, which might be of interest to him (she was then reading Goethe's *Conversations with Eckermann*).[23]

Neither Craig nor Isadora found in nature simply a model for imitation. It was a source of inspiration. Isadora was convinced that she was restoring dance to its "natural" state by eliminating the stylization introduced by the ballet. For Craig, however, the regeneration of the theatre passed through stylization—the stylization of what was already, but not in Craig's view, a stylized movement. For Isadora, whose instrument and material was the human body, nature had to be taken into consideration in the process of shaping movement—that is, the physiological limitations of the human body determined in large part its molding into an aesthetic form. Craig rejected these limitations altogether. Whereas Isadora was a fervent admirer of Haeckel, Craig used Haeckel's teachings to his own end to help him define his own position. He rebelled against the positivist outlook, and after attending one of Haeckel's lectures in Berlin, on 17 April 1905, with Isadora, he jotted down his seven-point aesthetic credo in his private notebook, under the double title "The Belief. My reaction to Haeckel. 1905."[24] The entry begins with a firm assertion of belief in make-believe, proceeds to attack the star system, declaring it on the decline—but why attack it if it was dying anyway?—and ends by announcing that the theatre is on the eve of a renaissance. How was this renaissance to take place? By turning the theatre into an art—and furthermore, Craig implies in the second and the sixth points of the credo, the artist is more suitable than the star actor to bring about the change (this idea is of course also at the core of *The Art of the Theatre*). Both Craig and Isadora believed that in order to create a new, viable art one must go back to the sources, to the study of the use of materials in art before it reached its present, corrupted state. Both Craig and Isadora went back to the past, but each of them turned to his own mythical golden age: Isadora sought inspiration in ancient Greece; Craig turned to ancient Egypt and the Far East. Isadora molded the past to fit her own aesthetic inclinations and kinetic potential, and if we are to judge by her career only, myth did indeed serve her well, surrounding her with a romantic aura not untainted by scientistic pretense. But if the myth of the "natural" ancient Greek civilization served her at the beginning of her career, she knew how to shed this heavy burden as soon as she achieved fame.

Isadora was convinced that she embodied the ideal movement that Craig had seen in imagination only, and Craig's comments on her art seem to agree on this point. The letters he wrote during this period to his friends Martin Shaw and Haldane MacFall bear proof of his overwhelming enthusiasm. Craig never denied the deep emotional and aesthetic impact of her art and recognized her vital, revolutionary contribution to modern dance. It was a revelation for him to discover when he met her that she had been composing her dances by following two basic principles in which he also believed, simplicity and functionalism. These principles also inspired other great artists, like Henry van de Velde and Josef Hoffmann and also Adolphe Appia, who was then totally unknown to Craig (or so he maintained). For Isadora, these principles meant purposeful movement, purified of any superfluous or decorative detail, movement completely mastered and controlled in order to achieve concise expressivity. For Craig, these principles meant a new stage, a new performer, and one omnipotent artist who should use his materials in a simple, concise, and expressive way.

Craig was particularly struck by Isadora's use of *stasis*—Isadora later affirmed that she had learned the value of immobility from Ellen Terry and Eleonora Duse—a condition ("stillness") that he believed was the chief virtue of the marionette. But Craig was also impressed by the expressivity of Isadora's "pure" movement when she danced without music. He wrote to Shaw on 29 May 1905: "Miss D.'s most amazing dance is without music at all—and so wonderful are her rhythms that one does not miss the music." And he added: "I consider her by far the most wonderful woman artist who has appeared. Duse—very nice—and the rest of 'em very fascinating—but this dancing depends on nothing except itself and is most amazing in its technical qualities."[25] What Gauguin, Maurice Denis, and the Nabis did in their medium, Isadora accomplished when she danced without music: she treated dance as an independent medium and attributed an intrinsic value to movement, so that movement ceased to be an element in a texture of music and sound and became *texture* itself. It was this expressive movement, wholly independent of sound, that Craig wished to achieve in theatre. Moreover, he wanted to ensure its continued perfection, performance after performance. And since he was aware of the uniqueness of Isadora as an artist, the ideal performer had to be found or invented.

"The Actor & Attack"

Deeply rooted aesthetic traditions are no more easily destroyed than other traditions. It would take Craig a lifetime to notice that the tradition of theatre as a mimetic art was as strong and as full of vitality as ever, in spite of his long and sustained efforts to uproot it.

"The Actor & Attack" was the title of the fourth chapter in "Theatre—Shows & Motions," the book that Craig planned to write when he arrived in Germany but never completed. His articles on theatre and the actor had appeared in the press since 1903, first in England and then in Germany. As we have seen, for each of his productions in London, Craig devised a new set of movements, a new style of acting, the aim of which was to depersonalize the actor and contribute to the beauty, harmony, and expression of the whole. This was not an easy task, working with actors of Ellen Terry's company whose training was in the realistic stage tradition. Craig's encounter with Isadora Duncan convinced him that the human being, and especially that special breed, the actor, was not a suitable instrument for movement in theatre. He wrote to Shaw from Berlin: "My dear old theatre was never meant for actors to play games in."[26] The "Uber-Marions" notebooks, with their careful planning of the über-marionette and the Uber-Marionette International Theatre that was to open in Dresden, prove beyond doubt that the über-marionette, despite Craig's later ingenious retraction, was not a metaphor or an ephemeral vision but a palpable instrument for movement. The über-marionette was as concrete as the kinetic stage, the second instrument for movement that Craig invented and experimented with at the Arena Goldoni in Florence.

In March 1907, from Florence, Craig sent Isadora the two essays, "The Artists of the Theatre of the Future" and "The Actor and the Uber-Marionette." Both essays were printed the following year in the first and second issues, respectively, of Craig's new journal, *The Mask*. The third issue started the publication of an inquiry—an international symposium—Realism and the Actor. In the first essay, movement was viewed as a metaphysical power, the essence of life itself. But the human body was judged unfit to serve as an instrument for artistic movement. The second essay revealed Craig's invention, his instrument for performing such movement—the über-marionette—and challenged the conventional attitude toward the actor's role in the theatre. It begins with a so-called debate on the nature of acting and Craig's conclusion seems simple: since art arrives only by design, acting is not an art—he was not speaking about the exceptional actor, of course. Then, abandoning the "fringe of the idea," he launched an open attack, announcing the über-marionette project, long planned in detail and now about to have its second chance with Isadora's financial support. Well before the publication of the two essays in *The Mask,* the "Letter to Eleonora Duse from Gordon Craig" (written after the two essays) appeared in the *Washington Post,* on 1 December 1907, together with Craig's interview with Francis Cotton. Craig quoted Duse's famous remark—"To save the Theatre, the Theatre must be destroyed, the actors and actresses must all die of the plague. They poison the air, they make art impossible"—but he added: "Those who have the spirit would live," and furthermore, "one must show what is to take their place." The interview showed just what was going to take their place, the über-marionette, and gave a general account of Craig's experiments with this instrument in Florence along with Craig's views on the actor.[27]

With the publication of the two essays in *The Mask,* the war on the actor was declared: acting was not an art, it was not teachable, and the actor had to become an artist of the theatre in order that the theatre become an art. To this end, Craig said, it was necessary for the theatre to evolve from its present stage of imitation and impersonation to that of symbolic expression and finally to the use of man-made instruments in order to create a real work of art and reveal, not depict. "Revelation" was also the term used by Wilde to describe the actor's task in the theatre. In this last stage, the actor-become-artist would find the perfect instrument for expressive, nonmimetic movement. It is clear that Craig, in discussing the "perfect instrument" for this movement, is not referring to the human body but has in mind the über-marionette or another man-made instrument. Craig saw the development of the actor into an artist as analogous to his own; Craig had now reached the final phase, when he was indeed creating suitable instruments for his ideal movement. In fact, the dialogue in "The Artists of the Theatre of the Future" is not between an artist (Craig) and an imaginary, open-minded, young actor but, like the dialogue in *The Art of the Theatre,* between Craig and his alter ego.

The task assigned to the future artist of the future theatre is in reality the one that Craig had assigned to himself. Craig had passed through the first two stages and he was now, by his own set of standards, a creative artist. Since the instruments of movement were already invented—though Craig was still to discover the rules for the ideal movement—Craig had in fact no need for creative actors-become-artists-of-the-theatre but, rather, disciples. And he needed the actor as an innocent, unsuspecting soldier.

Whatever the psychological reasons for Craig's rejection of the actor, his arguments never lost their validity. Too often his critics are inclined to forget that Craig's first concern was not to put an end to theatre but to perfect it, so that it could become a work of art; this work of art would, in turn, serve a loftier purpose. Craig wrote in "The Artists of the Theatre of the Future": "I believe also in the necessity of daily work under the conditions which are today offered us."[28] In the future, there might well be a theatre without a written text and without actors, but—and this was part of Craig's long-term strategy—he did not believe in sudden upheavals: it was still necessary to work in the present, with the actors and with the playwright as they were. It is essential to the understanding of Craig's theory that he did not suggest the eclipse of the actor; rather, only his emergence as an "artist": an artist of the theatre who would be enlightened enough to choose a better instrument for movement than the human body. It was therefore imperative to bring the actor to this final stage by helping him to detach himself from impersonation or mimetic acting, reach "representation and interpretation," then create expressive, nonmimetic movement. Craig described this evolution as a liberating step for the actor, since he considered impersonation as a state of bondage: bondage to the playwright and bondage to the rules of imitation. Craig never realized that the actor's second stage might be looked on as a new and intolerable bondage, a bondage to the director whose role is here that of the supreme—and sole—artistic judge.

Craig's attack on the actor was based on the assumption that the actor (barring only a few) had an inborn incapacity of expression. Craig debunked the myth of the actor's creative powers and explained that the strong impact made by exceptional actors is due to the skillful projection of their personality. Craig thought that only a few very outstanding actors, Irving being one of them, had complete control over their physical expression and their emotions. Moreover, even when the actor had full control, there was still the element of chance to be taken into account, and this element could destroy *design,* which was the characteristic feature of a work of art. The ordinary actor, as a fallible human being, depended on his memory, feelings, and physical shape, not to mention whims, desires, or aspirations; from an artistic point of view, he was unreliable as an instrument for expression. To trust him was to put one's faith in chance, and this was precisely what a work of art had to avoid at all cost. A living creature, no matter how perfect his self-control, was always prone to unforeseen changes, a "mechanical perfection" of the "facial and bodily expression" being practically impossible. The task of the actor was to suggest and evoke, and to this end Craig used him in his London productions—until the professional actor spoiled his design.

Craig made it quite clear that he loved the actor as a human being but mistrusted him as an artist:

> When I set out to captain and pilot my ship I will not risk taking actors on board. Where actors are—there can be no successful or long captaincy.
>
> I will not risk taking actresses aboard.
>
> Both actors and actresses have the most generous natures in the world—they often endear themselves to who they come in contact with. There are few people in the world who have such natures as actors and actresses, but for all that it is dangerous to have them on board. They have too much temperament.
>
> The duties do not all fall on one man.[29]

Actors have not only "temperament" but also vanity and a dislike of authority. The actor's behavior backstage is the subject of an entertaining vignette in "The Artists of the Theatre of the Future" depicting the trials of the stage manager. Another vignette in the "Uber-Marions" notebooks relates the "Monday morning" of the stage director who finds on his desk some twelve letters, nine of which Craig bothers to detail in a telegram-like style. The first letter, concerning "dressing rooms," is signed by an actress, one Lucy Jones. The second, "Posters and Paper," comes from Mary Phips, who is upset about her position in the billing notices and in the advertisements in the press, all the worse "together with the bad notices I recd etc." The third letter, "Whistling man. birds," from the Honorable Mrs. Henton, is apparently complaining about a whistling man in the audience, imitating a bird, or did birds fly into the theatre? The fourth is plain enough, concise, and to the point: "Salary £100." The fifth enumerates the injustice done to its (unnamed) sender: "Parts not good enough. Mr. I. gets in the way of the limelight."[30] The sixth complains, "The costumes designed by Mrs. C. do not suit me." The seventh attacks the whole scheme of the production, offering instead "My conception of the part etc." and also tacks on, "The stage manager is most rude to me etc." The eighth is a not so subtle attempt at pressure: "I have recd a most nice letter from Mr. Zodiac of the Theatre Zodiac offering me more money, better parts—what am I to do." As for the last letter disclosed, it is the protest of a superior being who cannot afford to work with such a bunch of—but let us hear him in person: "We have been waiting at rehearsals for a parcel of nonentities—these mere supers etc." They all sign "Faithful and obedient servant."[31] The vignette stops here. What is the besieged stage director to do? Should he demolish or just remodel the dressing rooms? Bribe the critics and get better notices for Mary Phips? Should he ask the whistling man—in case he is a recidivist—to turn to hissing, a much more traditional weapon? Are £100 enough, more than enough, or barely enough for the claimant? Should he fire Mrs. C. (the costume designer) or the plaintiff? Should he recast the entire production or just change the actor's part? Or perhaps take the understudy instead (which would make two persons happy instead of one: the understudy and the "rude" stage manager)? Should he bribe the one seduced by Mr. Zodiac's offer and make him (or her) stay, or seize the opportunity and get rid of him (or her)? Craig does not say. Among the senders of the letters the proportion of the ladies to the gentlemen is three to one, and we must trust Craig's experience as an actor and as a director that this was "true to life." The vignette appears under the heading of "Affairs of the Theatre" but its purport was by no means administrative only.

Still another reason for Craig's not "having them aboard" was financial. While he was working on his project for the Uber-Marionette International Theatre in Dresden, Craig wrote to Ellen Terry about the "insufferable difficulty" that comes from having actors in the theatre, pointing out the expense; he was convinced that with über-marionettes instead, "this time" he would have "final success."[32]

Nonetheless, if Craig wanted to see his idea conquer the world, he had to prepare his army, and the actor was still his soldier. Since he believed that the improvement of the existing theatre would inevitably lead to the ideal art of the theatre, Craig had to fight and work, as he said, "under the conditions which are today offered us." Craig had no patience with any of the prevailing acting styles. He disliked realistic as well as naturalistic acting because they were based on man's innate mimetic tendency and were not the product of a deliberate design. He loathed vulgar imitation, impersonation, and exaggerated theatricality. If being "true to nature" was sometimes effective, he argued, it was owing either to accident or to the projection of personality. He agreed with Irving that "to appear to be natural, you must in reality be much broader than nature"—but Irving, unlike Craig, saw nothing wrong in the beneficent "electric force of a strong personality."[33] Neither did Craig approve of the Symbolist acting, although the movement he devised for his own London productions had been inspired by it. In the "Uber-Marions" notebooks he condemned the "drivelling, insipid manner" of delivery used in Forbes-Robertson's production of *Pelléas and Mélisande* in 1898 and the "poses without sense—and sounds without reason" (fig. 1).[34]

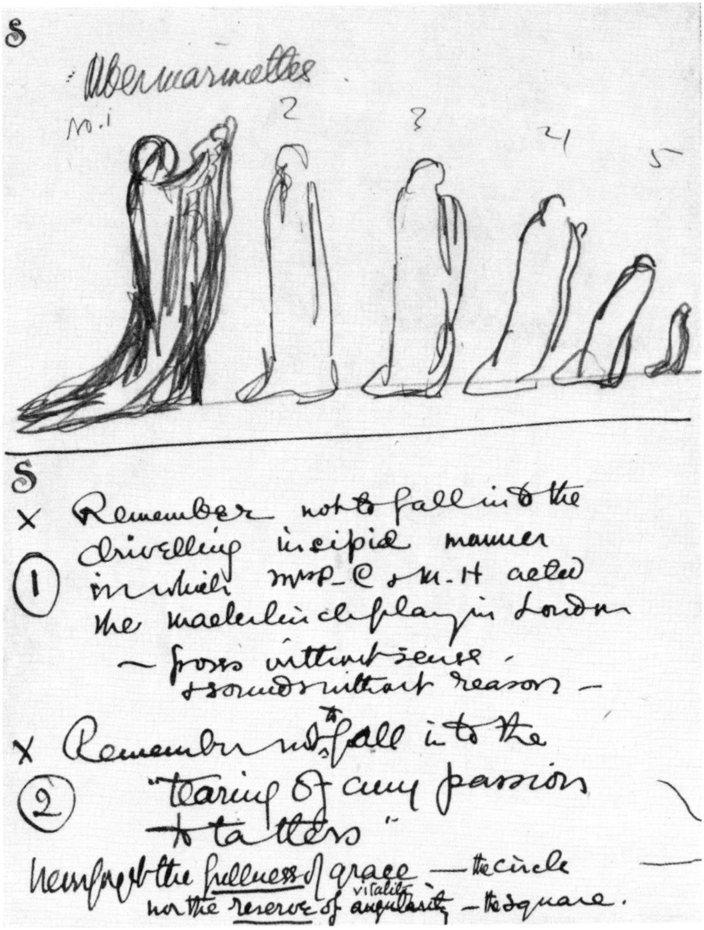

1. A page from the "Uber-Marions" notebooks. Edward Gordon Craig Estate and Bibliothèque Nationale, Paris.

What, then, was the acting style Craig proposed? Symbolic acting, one of whose promoters was none other than George Henry Lewes. Lewes, who had introduced Hegel's aesthetics in England before Pater, regarded all art as symbolic and theatre as representation, not illusion. For him, "true to nature" did not mean plain imitation of external symptoms but the selection of the typical and its representation through symbols that were stylized natural expressions. Physical qualifications and perfect diction were the actor's indispensable basic assets. He asserted that the very separation of art from nature involves calculation, and therefore in acting everything had to be deliberate. Simplicity and a sense of proportion should guide the actor in his choice of gestures; exaggeration was an "untruth." Impersonation or the identification of the actor with the character was not to be allowed, and the actor should choose significant gestures, symbols of emotions. These symbols, in order to be recognized as such, have to "follow nature"—follow, but not *reproduce* it; they are "idealized expressions," used by the actor in order to represent. Craig bought Lewes' *On Actors and the Art of Acting* (1875) on 9 October 1906, but it is quite possible that he had read the book before. Like Lewes, Craig proposed an acting style consisting mostly of symbolic gestures (he conceded that it was practically impossible to create a style made solely of symbolic gestures). Acting must be the physical expression of a mental process, the product of invention and selection. He wrote in the "Uber-Marions" notebooks under the heading "Notes on acting":

> To indicate actions by what not to do.
> The dictates of taste—
> The Kiss: the lips not to meet
> the faces not to touch
> the hands not to touch
> Why not?
> For this reason: that two veriest fools can show the audience that they are supposed to be in love by kissing—just as a boy of 5 years old by drawing so on the wall [follows a rudimentary sketch of a donkey] can show other schoolboys that he intended to draw a donkey, and just as an older boy can by drawing show his fellows.

And he explained:

> Our business in the theatre is first to find what we wish to show the audience. Let us say it is Love. Then to refuse the usual, common, external poses of Love but to search the imagination for symbols—beautified signs—that will almost bring the very spirit of Love. This Spirit of Love we must then seize and retain and while it remains with us *we must invent some pattern of symbols by which this spirit can be summoned before the eyes of the spectator.* We all know what the majority of the pantomimists have arrived at and use to indicate the passion. They place their hands one upon the other over their hearts and move their body sideways in a movement indicative of physical pleasure. That means "my heart is filled with Love for you." Now, is not this the equivalent of the donkey drawn by the boy on the wall? Is it more intelligent? Is there any art in it? In plainer terms, is it not the invention of a not very clever creature, whereas a work of art is in very plain terms nothing more than the invention of an exceedingly clever creature, can only be invented by a very clever creature, a complete being.

> Or take a simpler thing than Love. Let us suggest a thief running away—a man passing swiftly across the stage in [a] poor kind of shape, a figure conveying the thought of escaping villainy—by means of symbolic action. This is fine stuff, this is—art.[35]

If today the "symbolic action" or the "pattern of symbols" may seem no more than vague indications about an undefined field of acting, it is because we have lost some of the innocence that is the key to understanding the aesthetic approach of a whole generation of artists and art amateurs, whether Symbolists or not. For us, post–Freudians, post–Jungians, and poststructuralists, with our distrust of the media, with our perception of every sign as polyvalent, and with years and years of realistic theatre behind us, Craig's terms are meaningless. We have lost the belief in the efficiency of "symbolic action" and a "pattern of symbols" in acting, and we tend to welcome them in anthropological studies rather than in theatre. Does Craig's theory then have only a temporal and local value? Rather than jumping to that conclusion, we should remember that Craig was dealing with two enduring techniques in art, namely, stylization and symbolization, which are expressed differently at different moments in the history of art. Craig suggested that the idea of a fleeing criminal could be shown by "a figure conveying the thought of escaping villainy," first by having the figure "in a poor kind of shape," that is, by its appearance (costume, mask or makeup, posture of the body), then by the action performed: "passing swiftly across the stage." These indications of visual signs were more than sufficient for Craig's contemporary director or playgoer to express or understand the *idea* of the experience in question. Other signs could be found today.

Craig proposed that a code, a pattern of symbols, be created by the actors themselves.[36] The pattern must embody aesthetic value: these have to be "beautified signs" (Craig's confusion with signs and symbols is easily understandable because the symbols become now signs in a given pattern). The invention of the symbolic movement therefore depends not on the mimetic abilities of the actor, nor on his physical qualifications (on this point Craig disagrees with Lewes, having before his eyes the example given by Irving), but on his imagination and intellect. Again, the actor's progress from Impersonation to Representation and Interpretation and then to Creation and Revelation, marks also the gradual development of his artistic abilities. If Craig would not accord the actor the rank of an artist during the second stage, it is because the actor's "invention" did not follow yet any definite rules, that is, it was not the product of design but of "uncontrolled" mental powers. Craig expected to find such rules by experimenting with actors and with puppets or über-marionettes.

However, although Craig did not establish the elements of the ideal acting style but temporarily assigned the task to the actor, he did lay down the guidelines. The first was to *avoid mimetic movement:* instead of simulation, the actor had to use suggestion. The second—*restraint.* The third—good taste, that is, the acceptance of *conventional norms in morals and aesthetics.* The few, calculated, significant gestures had to "give suggestions of certain emotions."[37] "The Perfect actor would be he whose brain could conceive and could show the perfect symbols of all which his nature contains," he wrote in "The Artists of the Theatre of the Future."[38] All this was epitomized in Irving, who claimed that self-control and self-awareness alone distinguished between nature and art in acting. Perhaps Craig was only justifying his fascination with Irving's acting, but he created an image of Irving as the perfect actor, who took his inspiration from nature and forged symbols that conveyed the *idea* of a feeling without using outworn clichés, plain imitation, or exaggeration—an actor whose slightest movement was calculated, whose timing was perfect. Until the right method of training was found, Craig believed that the traditional one might still serve as an expedient, as it took care of the actor's instruments—his body and his voice. Finally, it was the director's task to select among the symbolic movements invented by the actor, coordinate and harmonize them with the rest of the elements—scene and voice—and the spirit of the play. In his instructions to the director, Craig recommends to him the use of "noble" artificiality (again the "dictates of taste") and the restriction of action to the indispensable and significant.[39] He affirms that only by a refined sense of proportion can the director reach that state of balance where beauty is created.[40]

Ideally, Craig foresaw that the actor, who would spend up to five years in the second stage, would learn for one or two years all the different jobs related to play production and would become the ideal stage manager, the director he described in *The Art of the Theatre* and "The Artists of the Theatre of the Future." It is only after six to ten years in this capacity that the director would be ready to "create," namely, he would use or invent a man-made instrument for movement, he would become an artist.

The purpose of Craig's experiments was not only to find the perfect instrument for movement but also—and this showed the influence of positivist thought—the rules of movement. Craig assumed that there must be logical, *universal* patterns of expressive nonmimetic movement, which had yet to be discovered. He searched for the basic elements of symbolic acting, the rules by which it could be worked out (thereby easing the actor's task), but by 1907 he had only found the guidelines for his search. If Craig failed in his search it was also because of the difficulty inherent in his subject matter, the universal symbol. It was not that there is no common ground on which to build such a system of symbolic action—Darwin discovered similarities in the expression of basic feelings in various civilizations and Craig, via Haeckel and Isadora, must have heard of them—it was simply that Craig definitely wanted to avoid the use of mimetic elements and clichés, and this made his task almost impossible. Transparent simplicity in a universal, symbolic pattern of movement, this would also be the goal of the journey of Peter Brook and his company in Africa some seventy years later.[41] The search goes on.

The *mask* was an essential tool for the symbolic acting that Craig proposed. He considered it "the only right medium of portraying the expressions of the soul as shown through the expressions of the face."[42] Besides, the mask was a proper means for reducing expression and thereby intensifying it. As a director, he had already used masks in his London productions and was aware of their dramatic immediacy.[43] Furthermore, he mistrusted man's innate mimetic tendency, and the mask was one means by which the director's control on expressive movement could be enhanced. But the mask is also closely related to Craig's conception of the ideal art of the theatre as a ceremony in praise of Creation and linked to the restoration of Belief to the world. Its ritualistic, sacred origin and the dualism of life and death embodied in it make it a symbolic means par excellence.

The mask is, however, a deceptive vehicle: it enhances illusion while it destroys it, and by doing so it enforces the symbolic aspect of the performance; in other words, the mask is both the cover and the sign of empirical reality. It is part of the aesthetic game, while it is also a constant aside to the audience, an essential factor of distancing. For the actor, the mask is the sign of the identity of the Other, designed to prevent him from impersonation or identification; on the other hand, it may also provide for him the proper cover under which he does merge himself with the character. One effect is certain: the mask calls attention to the expressivity of body movement, endowing it with a salience not possible otherwise. This is why a different body training is needed for the actor (the coordination of the body movement with the mobility of the head and the spirit of the mask), along with a psychological state of readiness, of acceptance of the other self imposed and emphasized by the mask—a state that may lead the actor either to identification or to distancing. Craig did not propose such a training; furthermore, he suggested using not one but several masks for one character during the performance (figs. 2 and 3).

The "Uber-Marions" notebooks describe the innovative use of two masks simultaneously. One such double mask consists of a half-mask worn all through the performance, with a second, full mask, attached to

2. An actor. From the "Uber-Marions" notebooks. Edward Gordon Craig Estate and Bibliothèque Nationale, Paris.

3. The changing of masks. From the "Uber-Marions" notebooks. Edward Gordon Craig Estate and Bibliothèque Nationale, Paris.

the half-mask by gauze, that can be held up in front of it. Another possibility for a double mask is the alternate use of masks: while the half-mask is kept constantly on, the performer holds an unattached mask in front of his face, and two other full masks are fastened to his cloak, ready to be used at the right moment. The half-mask is neutral but does not depersonalize the performer completely, since the lower part of the face is uncovered (as in the commedia dell'arte); but the effect of depersonalization is achieved by the full mask held or attached in front of the half-mask. The changing of masks during performance is still another technique proposed by Craig and bears a symbolic significance.

For models, Craig thought of using heads of Greek terra cotta statuettes and ancient Egyptian figures or some of those from his collection of Japanese, Javanese, and African masks. A brief notation in the "Uber-Marions" notebooks indicates Whitman's poem *Faces* as a possible source of inspiration. For the masks used by actors (Craig also proposed masks for the über-marionette), he suggested using elastic and cloth; the materials should be thin in order to emphasize expressive lines.[44]

Although the use of masks was audacious enough, it did not meet the same passionate opposition as the über-marionette, perhaps because to the actor it was not a threat but rather an aid that he could easily discard. In fact, Craig's masked actor would have been a very creative depersonalized performer. In the existing theatre, masks were not yet considered another weapon in the hands of the tyrannical director bent on depersonalizing the actor, only a specific theatrical device meant to enhance theatricality in certain genres like masques, pageants, or commedia dell'arte. At most, Craig's claim could be viewed as "aesthetic," the equivalent—for the larger public—of "extravagant." However, Craig demanded a depersonalized actor, the mask, and symbolic movement, because he believed, like the Symbolists, that artistic—and artificial—means and techniques could best create a spiritual, aesthetic experience for the audience.

The question of what effect symbolic action might have on the audience is an intriguing one. The effect of acting is inseparable from what the spectator perceives as "truth," and the perception of "truth" depends as much on the clarity of the message and the lack of interfering noises as on the spectator's ability to decipher the message. Craig assumed that the spectator would speculate on what was conveyed to him. As we have seen, he used different techniques of distancing, long before Brecht made them his personal assets; the über-marionette was also a means of distancing. As a result of the distancing techniques, the "truth" perceived was what Paul Ricoeur calls a *vérité tensionnelle*—a tensional truth.[45] The spectator's emotional involvement (which both Craig's and Brecht's productions led to, whatever their intention) provided him with a sense of belonging, while he underwent at the same time the effect of the distancing techniques that were meant to lead him to speculative thinking. The truth perceived was thus created by the dialectics between these two poles, emotion and intellect, metaphor and concept. In a letter written to Ellen Terry in September or October 1905, he said:

> I saw Sarah B[ernhardt] the other day walking all over the stage in a play—dancing—making pictures—singing—flying—leaping—cooing—crowing—hypnotising—laughing—in fact enjoying herself. And I saw again as clear as clear how she wasn't acting at all. I don't know what name could be given to it to express all she did and all she suggested—it wasn't art because it excited whereas a Rembrandt, a Mozart, a Pyramid soothes—brings peace, not excitement and restlessness. No, it was some unnameable thing—a piece of life—maybe greater than any art—but NOT art anyhow. Perhaps it was a confession. I cheered and shouted and thought I could have made a speech to the audience as to how wonderful it was—I was carried away by Sarah—but not by art.
>
> Yet must there be something which shall be a piece of theatre art. The thing is to discover it.[46]

Nothing suggests that Bernhardt's acting was not the product of a successfully carried-out design—and Irving certainly "enjoyed himself" as much in *The Bells*. Perhaps it was part of Bernhardt's special gifts that she could create the impression not of acting but of simply being. Craig's comments are typical of his ambiguous attitude toward the actor: he was sensitive to the physical impact of the actor's presence on the stage and derived pleasure from it, but at the same time he also resented its emotional impact. Craig came to Bernhardt's performance with definite views not only on what acting should be but also on its effect on the audience. Not that he denied that Bernhardt's acting was effective in rousing emotion. But the affective impact he was interested in should have led to a more enduring intellectual experience. In other words, not the enjoyable entertainment, not the pleasurable, ephemeral catharsis but a transcendental experience, induced by the aesthetic experience—this is what Craig strived for. While he continued to enjoy the good old theatre—melodramas, comedians like Dan Leno, or Sarah Bernhardt—he searched for the definition and creation of a refined, dematerialized art of the theatre, something that was, in his own words, "beyond theatre." He was already growing closer to the concept of theatre as a religious ceremony that links the sacred with the profane, solves on a mythical level the conflicts of life, comforts the spirit, and inspires to a "new endeavour."

But the theatre is a Rembrandt *and* a Goya, a Mozart *and* a Wagner, a Maya pyramid *and* an Egyptian pyramid—a reflection, stylized or not, of the complexity of life. Was Craig's task of symbolization and sublimation possible at all? He had been nurtured in a theatre that thrived on emotion. Now the emotion that he had in mind was of a different nature, a state of feeling evoked not by a "piece of life" but by symbols—the product of artistic design—related to a metaphysical subject matter (like "Creation," or "Life"), a state of acute perceptiveness, of self-effacement and self-oblivion, of tender acceptance, a state that "soothes"—a state akin to the mystical trance. This was a theatre that "could extract," as Payne says, "emotional balance."[47]

And since, after all, Craig mistrusted the actor's ability to achieve this glorious end, he assigned the task to man-made instruments for non-mimetic movement, the über-marionette and the kinetic stage.

The Uber-Marionette

"The Actor and the Uber-Marionette" and the "Uber-Marions" notebooks are the main sources on the über-marionette. The über-marionette is not mentioned in *The Art of the Theatre* or in "The Artists of the Theatre of the Future," but all three essays borrow from the "Uber-Marions" notebooks. These notebooks were completed during 1905 and 1906 and contain several additions made in 1912, 1921, and 1934; their entries do not follow any chronological or topical order, and few of them are dated. Craig's choice of material for the three essays was dictated mainly by protective, cautionary considerations. And since he could assume that the historical and aesthetic background of his newly invented instrument would be more interesting and illuminating to the reader than technical data, secrecy was that much easier. When he wrote *The Art of the Theatre,* the project of the Uber-Marionette International Theatre in Dresden was only in its initial stage, and Craig had good reasons for not making the details of the project public; by the time he wrote the two other essays, in 1907, he had started work on his experiments in Florence, so secrecy was even more necessary, especially as Reinhardt and others had seemed so eager to borrow his ideas. The "Uber-Marions" notebooks provide additional information on the über-marionette as well as on its theatre. Moreover, they offer a new insight into the role of the über-marionette not only in Craig's theory but also in his mental makeup.

Craig's writings contain only the vaguest of clues on the question of when he got the idea of the über-marionette. In his notebook "Confessions," completed during the years 1901–3, when he was working on his productions in London, he mentions a "being" that was to come instead of the actor, but it is not clear whether it was intended to be another human performer or something else.[48] For a long time the marionette had been the favorite of the Symbolists and the Impressionists, and also a favorite with Craig and his aesthetic circle. As early as 1890 Maeterlinck had proposed to banish the actor and replace him with the marionette (Maeterlinck, admired by Craig, was also the only contemporary playwright Craig included in the repertoire of the Uber-Marionette International Theatre). In 1902, a small book on the origins of the puppet play appeared in London and quickly became popular in the aesthetic circles. This was *The Home of the Puppet-Play,* a translation of an address delivered by Professor Richard Pischel at his investiture as rector of the Friedrich University in Hallé-Wittenberg in 1900. This book, as Jean Jacquot shows, was read by Craig too.[49] Although we do not know if he read it shortly after its publication in London or just before writing his essay, he made use of it in "The Actor and the Uber-Marionette." Much of Pischel's work is a historical survey of the puppet, in which he traces its origins in India and its subsequent appearance in Java. He contends that the actor and the drama were late imitations of the puppet and the puppet play. It was here that Craig learned about the Javanese puppet-jester Semar, whose name he later took as one of his many pseudonyms (John Semar was supposed to be the editor of *The Mask*). Here Craig also discovered that the popular Indian plays had no written text but used instead a given storyline and improvisation.

Soon after this publication, an "Apology for Puppets" was included in Arthur Symons' *Plays, Acting, and Music: A Book of Theory* (1903):

> The living actor, even when he condescends to subordinate himself to the requirements of pantomime, has always what he is proud to call his temperament; in other words so much personal caprice, which for the most part means wilful misunderstanding; and in seeing his acting you have to consider this intrusive little personality of his as well as the author's. The marionette may be relied upon. He will respond to an indication without reserve or revolt. . . . he can be trained to perfection. . . . [The illusion of the puppet theatre] is nothing less than a fantastic, yet a direct, return to the masks of the Greeks: that learned artifice by which tragedy and comedy were assisted in speaking to the world with the universal voice, by this deliberate generalising of emotion. . . . In our marionettes, then, we get personified gesture, and the gesture, like all other forms of emotion, generalised. . . . I find my puppets, where the extremes meet, ready to interpret not only the "Agamemnon," but "La Mort de Tintagiles"; for the soul, which is to make, we may suppose, the drama of the future, is content with as simple a mouthpiece as Fate and the great passions, which were the classic drama.[50]

In Germany, Craig found the same interest in the marionette among the artists. The stage was set for the advent of the über-marionette.

The über-marionette was a newcomer, an invention. This "beyond puppet," as Craig called it in the "Uber-Marions" notebooks, was named to echo Nietzsche's *übermensch.* No other term could better have designated the new functions and new attire of the fallen idol who had become a Punch and a Judy. Big marions were not an innovation, but their specific use in Craig's new art of the theatre was. Jarry had proposed in 1896 using big marions as part of the cast for the production of *Ubu Roi* at the Théâtre de l'Oeuvre, but in that case they would have been no more than caricatures, used in the same way as grotesque figures in a carnival. The big figure has always had a stronger physical and emotional impact on its beholder than the smaller figure, and the myth of the artificial man is very old—as old as the myth of Galatea, the statue that was brought to life by Aphrodite to please Pygmalion, the sculptor who had created it. Other legends tell of the Golem from Prague or about Don Juan and the statue of the Commendatore; one also thinks of Frankenstein. In most of these there is a certain element of malevolence: the big man-made figures are powerful and, often, a blasphemy to God. Not so the über-marionette, Craig's big figure, which was destined by its inventor to be an instrument of salvation, capable of expressing better than any living creature the "unseen forces" and reviving the "ancient ceremony" to which Craig aspired, for example, in his work for Duse's *Rosmersholm.*[51] The über-marionette was one tool by which the third stage, the Revelation, could be accomplished.

Edward Craig says that the idea of the über-marionette as a super-puppet was inspired by one of Richard Teschner's puppets.[52] Richard Teschner, a Sezessionist Austrian painter and sculptor, had studied in Vienna in 1900 and 1901. He settled in Prague in 1902 and began to take an active interest in marionettes in 1903. In 1906, after more than a year of preparation, he produced Hofmannsthal's *Death and the Fool* with his marionettes. During 1906 he visited Vienna twice and held an exhibition of his works in Karlsbad and Reichenberg, also showing his marionettes. He made beautiful, rounded marionettes of wood, with long limbs and delicate features; their average height was about one and a half feet. Teschner moved to Vienna in 1909, and in 1911 he created the exotic figures of his soon famous *Goldenen Schrein,* taking his inspiration from the Javanese Wayang. Circumstantial evidence allows one to suggest the possibility of Craig's having seen one of Teschner's puppets, possibly even having met Teschner through Hofmannsthal or perhaps through Arthur Roessler. Craig was associated with both these men during 1905 and 1906, and in 1905 prepared a series of drawings for Hofmannsthal's *Death and the Fool,* which was "in work" at Teschner's marionette theatre in Prague. Roessler, who wrote the introduction to the catalogue of Craig's exhibition that opened in Vienna on 1 October 1905, was to devote a whole book to Teschner and his work many years later.[53]

Other models for the über-marionette—especially if we keep in mind its unusual size—were available in the literature and art of the ancient world. In ancient Egypt, statues with movable limbs were used in ceremonial rites; besides, the Egyptian funeral statue, like the mummy, was in a sense, as Erwin Panofsky pointed out, "a body waiting to be resuscitated," existing in a world of magic reality.[54] Since the über-marionette was closely linked with the Belief that Craig wanted to bring to the world, it is certainly possible that the idea of the "beyond puppet" was suggested to him by the reading on ancient Egypt that he did soon after meeting Isadora (fig. 4).[55] Craig may also have read about the mechanical statues described by Hero of Alexandria in his *De Automatis;* these statues could march and dance and were used in ancient Greece in various religious ceremonies. Perhaps, too, Craig's partiality to manipulated instruments dated from his first years of wood engraving when he collected the charming carved penny toys made by gypsies and drew them on wood blocks. All these diverse sources, in some unknown measure, may have fused into the inspiration for the über-marionette—an outsize marionette, with a new range and style of movement and new functions as a performer.

Craig began collecting marionettes in 1905, with hopes either of finding one that would fit his purpose or of copying some of the existing techniques and working out a design of his own. With the aid of Isadora and other friends such as William Rothenstein, who brought him marionettes from their travels, he acquired a considerable collection, including examples from Java and Burma. After studying the various types, he settled on the articulated marionette as best for his purposes: it had a range of movement and yet could be controlled by one person. In 1907 he started designing his own marionettes and having them made for him.

One thing that Craig especially liked about the über-marionette, besides its technical suitability, was that it had a glorious past as a ceremonial object. In his projected book, "Theatre—Shows and Motions," he intended to review the historical background that had led to the present degeneration of the theatre and demonstrate that its renaissance could be brought about only by reviving the use of the puppet in place of the actor. Consequently, the "Uber-Marions" notebooks contain two incomplete tables in which Craig outlined the development of the theatre in the East and the West from the years 1 to 1905, with various geographical and cultural subdivisions. Having decided that the actor must go, Craig let his imagination leap from the substitute, the puppet of modern times, to the ancient idol. The idea of restoring the ancient idol to its high rank in art and in ceremonial rites carried with it all the splendor usually connected with the mythical Golden Age. In his enthusiasm, Craig believed that the advent of the über-marionette could bring about a magical, radical change in the human soul.[56]

Craig's belief in the power of the über-marionette went hand in hand with his belief in his own power to materialize his vision of the theatre in a lasting and durable artistic form and to restore Belief to the world. Craig knew that in order to make the über-marionette into a successful instrument for movement, he had to start at the beginning and take it beyond the limitations of the conventional puppet. In a letter to Ellen Terry of August 1905 from Zurich, he specifies that he is not using marionettes, for "the marionette is only a doll."[57] The expressivity of the new instrument had to be much greater. In another letter that same month, to Martin Shaw, he said: "Expect to receive wonderful news within 3 months. I may then have my own theatre and my own company. NOT ACTORS but a CREATURE of my own invention—a blessed marvel my BOY!"[58]

In the "Uber-Marions" notebooks Craig gives several reasons for inventing the über-marionette. One is the element of chance in acting. To counter it, he searched for a "pliable" material, "which takes the impression of the artist but does not change after the impression is given," offering an everlasting "solidity" similar to the materials used by the painter, the sculptor, or the architect.[59] Since Craig intended to provide carefully worked-out plans for all the movements of the über-marionettes onstage, the human failings of the manipulator were of no consequence. A second reason for the invention of the über-marionette was the actor's innate inability—or so Craig believed—to control physical expression of feeling: "Instead of an actor who speaks, moves and feels all sorts of emotions, I have something which stands for a man or a woman, which moves, and something else which speaks and the only emotions *felt* are those felt by the audience."[60] Still another reason was to bring back mystery to the theatre. Using the puppet's power to fascinate, Craig dreamed of turning the whole theatrical performance into a magic operation.[61] And last but not least, Craig wanted the instrument of movement to be a work of art in itself.[62]

Craig used the terms puppet, marionette, and figure interchangeably in discussing the technical aspects of the über-marionette. When he prepared the plans for the Uber-Marionette International Theatre, he decided to have three main groups of figures, ranged according to size and social class. The first group included the average "person," four and a half to five feet high. The second group, "heroes," "remarkable persons," and high dignitaries, would be five to six feet. The third group included the gods, all six and a half feet at least. An average height of four and a half to five feet is given in the list of the "staff" of the über-marionette theatre. The conventional puppet, like the ones used by Signoret, was about two and a half feet, but the Burmese puppets were human size. Puppets

4. Colossal figures in the principal hall of the Great Temple at Ipsamboul. From *A History of Art in Ancient Egypt* (1883), by Georges Perrot and Charles Chipiez.

(usually grotesque figures) as large as the über-marionette heroes or gods were traditionally used only in carnivals. The special large size of the über-marionette is very important because of its immediate physical and emotional impact: the modern spectator has only to remember the famous Bread and Puppet Theatre in order to understand the effectiveness of the über-marionette. Only slightly smaller than the human being (a small reduction in size being an element of distancing), this new alter ego was now a far more serious threat to the actor than the lilliputian traditional puppet.

The über-marionette was round, made of wood, and padded. A flat figure was to be used only for crowd scenes (staged like the Javanese Wayang Kulit). The über-marionette theatre was to have twenty-five to thirty figures and they were to use masks. The masks, as well as the figures and the different costumes, were all designed by Craig.

Craig intended the range of movement of the über-marionette to be greater than that of the conventional articulated puppet. This is how he described the movements of one figure: "[It] *revolves, ducks, hides face with mantle,* etc. (and in this revolving the uberm. shows his or her dexterity)."[63] Its manipulator was called a "mover." The technical solution to the manipulation of the über-marionette was worked out later on in Florence.

The movement performed by the über-marionette is a selected movement, consisting of rare and suggestive gestures. The "Uber-Marions" notebooks contain movement notations and patterns designed on the stage floor to serve as a guide for the über-marionette—that is, for its manipulator—in the same way that choreographers use marked floors and notation for ballet. The notebooks give the first elements of a system of movement notation based on the square and the circle, or on straight lines and curved lines (fig. 5). The straight lines indicate an angular and direct, strong movement, while the curved lines demand a "sinuous, delicate bearing."[64] This system could indicate not only the form, force, and pace of movement (e.g., strong versus delicate, hops versus steps) but direction as well. One floor pattern is like a mandala, another like a maze.

The impersonality of the über-marionette and its stylized movement, Craig suggested, would make possible the treatment of certain topics that had been banished from the stage by what Craig called "the dictates of taste," or if dealt with at all, were treated vulgarly: "That which you may express by means of über-marionettes you may not express by means of live beings. Birth. A woman in child. Death. Suicide. Love. R[omeo] & J[uliet]."[65] The über-marionette, as the metaphor for man, imposes a schematic analysis of reality on the artist/director, thereby easing the task of treating such subjects as childbirth or suicide. Its impersonality creates

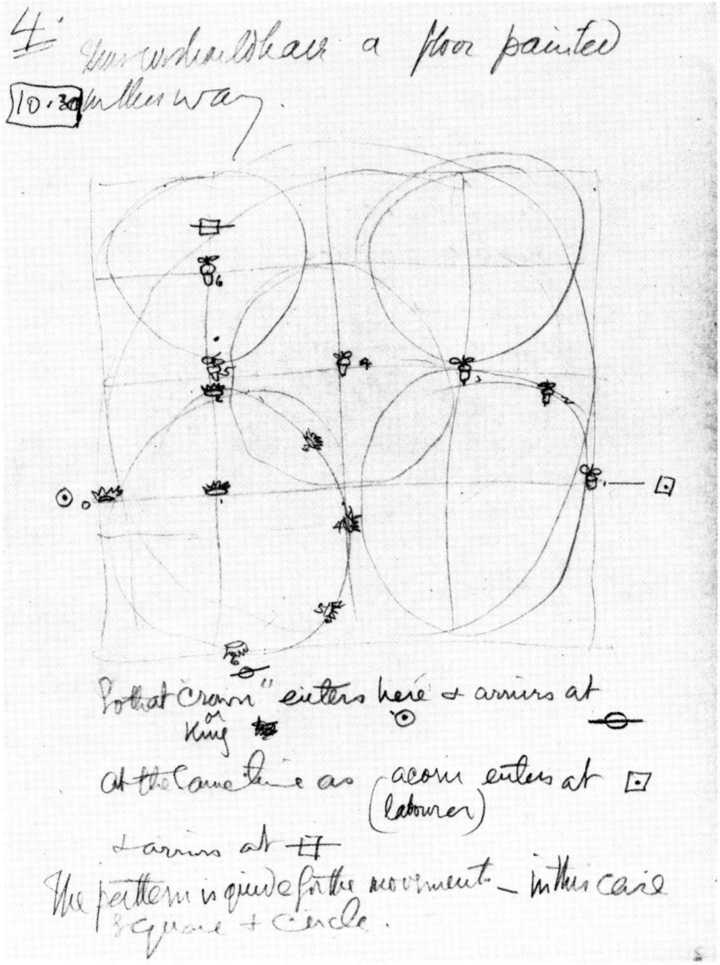

5. A patterned floor for the über-marionette. From the "Uber-Marions" notebooks. Edward Gordon Craig Estate and Bibliothèque Nationale, Paris.

a distancing that may hold back the emotional involvement of the audience and facilitates the process of communication within the "dictates of taste," that is, commonly accepted norms—moral, religious, or aesthetic. Like the puppet, the über-marionette is an indicator of transcendence, and as such it is an excellent vehicle for spiritual values. But the ultimate theme that the new art of movement would express and celebrate was Belief.[66]

Craig's main reason for inventing the über-marionette was therefore twofold: it was a metaphor for man, and it offered him an instrument that was easy to control. But if his purpose was expressive movement, why choose a tool whose dominant feature was stillness or immobility?

The stillness of the über-marionette was easier to defend in practice, on a stage (leading the audience to a suspension of disbelief), than in a pamphlet, and therefore Craig had to turn this liability into an asset. Moreover, he knew that the instrument was far from perfect: as he affirmed in his interview with Francis Cotton in December 1907, the über-marionette was only a temporary substitute—not until the actor would become a creative artist but until a better man-made instrument for movement was found.[67]

In his essay "The Actor and the Uber-marionette," Craig took pains to explain the paradox of the stillness of his instrument, choosing to fight his battle on philosophical grounds but without sharing with his "enemy" the same basic notions—which were in any event not totally clear to Craig himself. Opposing Aestheticism to Realism in the theatre, he found stillness to be a sign of artistic refinement as opposed to common life-like, or imitative, exuberance. His notions of Life and Death were based on an Idealistic approach: Life symbolized the unseen forces that animated the living; Death symbolized not the annihilation of matter but its transformation, the unseen force that inspired ancient civilizations to highly artistic achievements that defeated time and acquired an everlasting life. Therefore, in this essay, Craig associated stillness, or immobility, with the "calm motion" found in death and proceeded to what is very close to being a glorification of death itself. Thus, Stillness and Death became symbols of spiritual achievement.

The "Uber-Marions" notebooks offer a different justification for stillness:

> Let me say a word as to the stillness of my marionettes.
>
> That is not being unnatural, far from it. It is in fact being more like life. All those things which it is needful we should select from the Life theatre and place before the audience in our Art theatre, all those things I say possess this immobility.
>
> *Much* movement does not *represent* Life any more than *much* colour represents Life or [much] sound: only a certain *selected* movement, as only a selected colour or sound. And just as a bad painter will cover a canvas with all the colours at once because he thinks that will obtain the rich glowing colours of life, so have bad artists in the theatre believed that exuberant action—*unconsidered* action in short, would suggest the move-

> ment of Life. Whereas a good painter knows that by the use of but a very little but *well selected* colour, he can create the impression of intense gaiety. So does a good theatre artist also know that by the use of etc etc movement. Hence the stillness of my marionettes.[68]

Craig's arguments can be graphically summed up as follows:

1. In the "Uber-Marions" notebooks:		stillness	= selected movement
		selected movement	= Life (in art)
	∴	stillness	= Life (in art)
2. In "The Actor and the Uber-Marionette":		stillness	= calm motion
		Death	= calm motion
	∴	Death	= stillness = Life (in art)

All of this may appear to be logical, if we treat the notions of death, stillness, art, or life as mathematical signs, which they are not. But the argument in "The Actor and the Uber-Marionette" is only deceptively logical, because symbols and correspondences have a weird way of association. The argument of the "Uber-Marions" notebooks, based on a clear aesthetic choice ("selected" means of expression), was not used in the essay and this was rather unfortunate. It would have been easily accepted, since many of Craig's readers believed they knew the meaning of symbolic gesture, well-calculated movement, expressive immobility, and restraint. After all, such a movement had also been designated as the ideal expressive movement in *The Art of the Theatre*—where there was not the slightest hint that Craig had in mind not the actor but the über-marionette. Why, then, did Craig decide in the essay to glorify Death and the stillness that comes with it? The draft was perhaps too "technical," but that was probably only a minor reservation. Evidence shows that Craig was carried away by his vision of a ceremony theatre, a vision nourished by his readings on ancient Egypt whose civilization he regarded as death-oriented. He had a vision of monumental artistic achievements, similar to those inspired by death in ancient Egypt. He had a concept of death similar to Philippe Ariès' "tamed death"—death that inspires serenity and peace and calmness, harmony, and even joy—some of the same feelings that Craig had experienced while watching Isadora dance, celebrating the triumph of life. Craig's notion of death was not accompanied by an obsessive morbidity, as was the case with such artists as Odilon Redon, Gustave Moreau, Jan Toorop, Bocklin, or Max Klinger. Theirs was a notion of death nourished by an apocalyptic feeling, or by an affectation of this feeling, whereas Craig's notion was an intellectual fabrication. Like Hofmannsthal, he saw the artist as a reconciler, and as such, he wanted to impart his vision: his was now a vision of Death that was as inspiring and creative as Life, a vision of Death that *was* Life and creation! A vision that only the über-marionette, through its stillness, could impart. Craig was apparently quite oblivious of the fact that his readers did not have this same vision and could hardly share the creative euphoria that had enabled him to overlook the usual negative connotations of death. His unwise selection of material for this major essay betrays a naïve overconfidence; his cause certainly did not gain much by it.

Craig's overconfidence in the über-marionette in 1905, as well as in 1907, was based on the real prospect of having an über-marionette international theatre. He wrote on 15 July 1905:

> There will be many of those who will ask "But what Life will you be able to get in your stage shows, what life is there in a Puppet? For a few moments it may be interesting to watch dolls with their awkward actions, but for an hour it would be intolerable." To such, there is no answer. The entire world is made up of so many large cliques—each of which is in its turn divided into many other smaller cliques. Each of these cliques finds the Faith, Manners, Arts, Governments, amusements, of the others *intolerable.* Only on one point are they all agreed, and that is to be intolerant. And on my theatre I shall show the intolerance of these cliques to the special clique who finds it *delightful,* not wearisome, to watch my puppets.
>
> The day of the actor is about to close.
> & all night will the earth
> travail, & at the break
> of the next day comes
> the über-marionette.[69]

In 1905 Craig had a promise of support from Kessler and a committee of businessmen in Dresden. At the beginning of 1907 he had the promise of Isadora's support, and as soon as he finished writing "The Artists of the Theatre of the Future" and "The Actor and the Uber-Marionette," he sent them to her to read. The articles paved the way for the advent of the über-marionette.

In a period of creative ebullience in the plastic arts (Cézanne, Rousseau, Matisse, Picasso, Klimt, "Die Brücke," Klinger), in music (Schoenberg, Sibelius, Debussy), architecture (Van de Velde, Josef Hoffmann), drama and theatre (Shaw, Maeterlinck, Hofmannsthal, Stanislavsky, Reinhardt), dance (Isadora Duncan), psychology (Freud's *Three Contributions to the Theory of Sex*), in a period of turmoil in politics (the "Bloody Sunday" in St. Petersburg, where Craig went at the beginning of 1905) and of Einstein's revolutionary scientific discoveries—Craig was working on his newly invented über-marionette. What were his motivations for this "discovery" and what were its implications?

The invention of the über-marionette may have come as a subconscious reaction to the intrusion in his life of all those dominant personalities like Ellen Terry, Isadora, or Duse. This is the opinion of Craig's son and biographer, Edward Craig. If so, the über-marionette is the outcome of a magical, shamanistic operation: the making of a doll in the image of the enemy, an act of exorcism, a therapeutic act. And if indeed Craig resented the female domination in his life so much, the über-marionette would be another proof of the validity of Nina Auerbach's thesis about the extent of the demonization of woman during the Victorian period and the "transcendent power of angelic-demoniac womanhood."[70] That the über-marionette was the response to a basic inner need to manipulate instead of being manipulated there seems to be no doubt; that it also exorcised old demons and transfixed enemies—perhaps. But most certainly it was a conscious invention of a "very clever creature" (Craig's words), the invention of a man of the theatre who was wholly familiar with the tools of plastic arts and knew from experience the feeling, the course, and the outcome of a controlled operation. The strongest inspiration, most probably, was ancient Egypt, with its huge, moving statues, its huge architectural creations, and its ceremonies of Belief.

The über-marionette came at a time when it alone offered Craig the possibility of creating a theatre of his own. This was a theatre where he could be the only artist, with everything under his control, a dream come true. The über-marionette was the exclusive creation of the artist, of an artist who "perceives more than his fellows and records more than he has seen."[71] It was an *extension* of the artist. By using the über-marionette, Craig was building an ivory tower, severing his emotional ties with his fellow human beings. Like the architect, whose isolation is imposed by his medium, so the artist of the über-marionette theatre is proceeding alone, planning his project and building his theatrical performance brick by brick. He has helpers not partners, manipulators and readers not fellow artists. Like the architect—and Craig's father was one—he assumes total responsibility for the edifice and has complete control over it; he employs inert matter and gives it shape. Then he designs the movement and—like his mother, the actress, or Isadora, the dancer—performs it, not through his body but through its extension, the über-marionette. And here we touch on another aspect of the über-marionette: the über-marionette not only as a mask made by the artist but as a mask *for* the artist, a mask that Craig identifies with, the symbol of ideal movement.

Inasmuch as the über-marionette is a physical extension of the artist, it cannot be said to be a machine, a mechanical device; it is a tool. It is worked by hand and is meant to assist in a process of expression: it helps to bring about this process and to execute it. It does not perform regularly in a predetermined way like a machine but depends on the manipulator's will. Moreover, as a symbolic vehicle in a process of communication, it not only carries a message but constitutes an integral and decisive part of the message while it also conditions it. In inventing this tool, Craig followed the same procedure by which he had created the scenery or the movement in his London productions. There, as Arthur Symons remarked, "Mr. Craig aims at taking us beyond reality; he replaces the pattern of the thing itself by the pattern which that thing evokes in his mind, the symbol of the thing."[72] What we get is a man-sized anthropomorphous object that epitomizes at once man *and* marionette. The über-marionette, as a beautiful *objet d'art,* was in a paradoxical way a conscious attempt to deny the temporal nature of the theatrical creation, to overcome the immediacy of death by taming it, by holding it in bondage, freezing life in a manipulated statue. At the same time, this was also a conscious, symbolic attempt to subdue the chaotic, living nature of man by confining it within an inert, manipulated figure—an escape from truth as well as its revelation. The über-marionette was Craig's answer to Blake's symbolic figures, a symbol, an object, and an interpreter.

To invent a new symbol, one has to risk its being obscure. To reshape an old symbol, one has to risk introducing new, hidden, perhaps unwanted meanings and disrupting some of its most recognizable ones. This is what happened to the "invention" of the über-marionette. The new symbol was shaped out of an ancient fallen idol that carried with it a rich stock of pagan myths—one of them being the myth of the man-made monster. Thus, the über-marionette was seen as another Frankenstein, the first in a series of catastrophes: it rejected the actor, that age-old outcast who had only recently been elevated to respectability in the person of Craig's own master, Henry Irving. A theatre of moving statues? The age-old complicity between the servants of institutionalized culture, the entertaining minstrels, on one hand, and their masters and patrons on the other, could not allow this to happen even in the name of a sacrosanct Art. There is a bond of sweat and tears, of laughter and terror, of hope and joy, love and hate, between the actor and his audience, a bond of mutual dependence that will last as long as there are two men alive on this planet. The über-marionette turned into a physical threat for the actors, and this was decidedly not what Craig had intended, for the actor could still be of use to him. In fact, according to his theory, the victory of the über-marionette or of any other instrument for movement could be brought about *only* through the actor's transformation into an artist of the theatre (à la Craig). In his letter to the editor of the *Saturday Review* of 3 November 1906, Craig called the actors to join him in his efforts to build the theatre of the future, to create an art of movement simple enough to have an emotional appeal for all.[73] Incidentally, the Actors' Union had been established in England only the year before. It is interesting that Craig's ultimate purpose—the third and last phase, the phase of Revelation—was also the only one that held the attention of his critics. They judged, with some justification, that the phase of Interpretation was only an intermediate step toward the assertion of the man-made instrument for movement, forgetting that Craig did not consider it superfluous but mandatory. Indeed, Craig did not propose the über-marionette as a possibility but as the *only choice* for the theatre if it were to become a work of art. Craig's option meant that the actor as such was denied any participation in the artistic act—which was worse than considering him a mere instrument. As an instrument, the depersonalized actor could still take part in the artistic creation; but with the advent of the über-marionette, if he did not become the artist using a man-made instrument for movement, he was doomed to vanish. This was the only way by which the theatre could become a work of art, *a pure and perfect simulacrum: a make-believe* (this was Craig's word) *performed by a make-believe.* In Craig's ideal ceremony theatre the über-marionette becomes the go-between, the sacred object that replaces the human officiant in the ceremony of the artist/director/initiator's mystic union with the "unseen forces."

A discordant note in this harmonious theory is struck by Craig's self-defeating sensitivity to dramatic effects: thus he planned to use for the über-marionette theatre not only figures but also athletes, dancers, gymnasts, and models—all of whom possessed various physical skills and complete control over the body—together with extras. If Craig had been free to produce "Duse's play," *Rosmersholm,* this is the kind of performance that he had in mind.[74] This effect of contrasting juxtaposition was meant to enhance the significance of the piece to be staged but, no doubt, would have destroyed the aesthetic purity of the spectacle.

The codified movement with its rare, symbolic gestures, together with the special use of voices (chosen by their tonal range), the mask or the masklike face, and the unusual scene, offers an extraordinary spectacle—a spectacle of arresting beauty, remote yet within reach, solemn yet expressive of human passions. Craig had seen a Noh performance in 1900, in London. Yet the very survival of the Noh theatre is a sign of belief, of an undying belief in undying values such as beauty, purity, and truth, a belief in the everlasting power of the human spirit. Those who have been touched by the Noh and have been conquered by its magic have also shared—if even for the shortest moment—the belief that goodness does exist, that beauty and spiritual elevation are not vain words. And this is what Craig wanted to achieve in his theatre.

≻ 8 ≺

Scene and the Kinetic Stage

Craig's distinction between the several phases in the development of the theatre to a supreme art is manifest also in his approach to scene, that is, settings and lighting, costumes and props. For the second phase, that of Interpretation, he used a scene whose main purpose was to serve the movement of the performer. For the third phase, that of Revelation, he invented a scene to *perform* movement: this was *the Scene,* or the kinetic stage. From 1904 to 1907, the period under examination, Craig's work, as documented by his notes and designs, displays the shift from the representational to the abstract or cubist stage.

Craig's first thoughts on changing the architecture of the theatre were inspired by reading Wagner's work on theatre in 1897. At that time Craig had in mind a new kind of stage and an auditorium built on a slope, with the director's supervising box at the rear. When he came to mount his several productions in London, Craig did not fail to introduce changes in the architecture of the stages he worked on, all the while dreaming of a new theatre.[1] Nothing came of that hope, but his screens are part of today's theatre.

Craig believed that the scene should express the ideas of the play, create the mood, and serve the acting and movement. In his London productions, he eliminated not only all the merely decorative elements but the whole notion of a realistic representation of place and time. Instead, by the use of a few painted curtains and a few symbolic props, as well as various ingenious lighting techniques including backlighting and colored lights (he abolished footlights), he *suggested* time and place, ideas and moods, and created the illusion of a distinct level of reality that was "more true than true." Settings of huge dimensions began to appear in his stage designs as early as in 1896. Arthur Symons, who followed Craig's work from his first production, was quick to perceive the distinctive quality of Craig's scene. In his *Studies in Seven Arts,* published in 1906, he pointed out Craig's use of line in *Acis and Galatea:*

> Mr. Craig . . . has a genius for line, for novel effects of line. His line is entirely his own; he works in squares and straight lines, hardly ever in curves. He drapes the stage into a square with cloths; he divides these cloths by vertical lines, carrying the eye straight up to an immense height, fixing it into a rigid attention. He sets squares of pattern and structure on the stage; he forms his groups into irregular squares, and sets them moving in straight lines, which double on themselves like the two arms of a compass; he puts square patterns on the dresses, and drapes the arms with ribbons that hang to the ground, and make almost a square of the body when the arms are held out at right angles. . . . This severe treatment of line gives breadth and dignity to what might otherwise be merely fantastic.[2]

Describing the pastoral atmosphere in this production, Symons wrote:

> The tent is there with its square walls, not a glimpse of meadow or sky comes into the severe design, and yet, as the nymphs in their straight dresses and straight ribbons lie back laughing on the ground, and the children . . . toss paper roses among them, and the coloured balloons . . . are tossed into the air, carrying the eye upward, as if it saw the wind chasing the clouds, you feel the actual sensation of a pastoral scene, of . . . the spring and the open air, as no trickle of real water in a trough, no . . . imitation of a flushed sky on canvas, could trick you into feeling it. The imagination has been caught; a suggestion has been given which strikes straight to the "nerves of delight": and be sure those nerves, that imagination, will do the rest, better, more effectually, than the deliberate assent of the eyes to an imitation of natural appearances.[3]

This was, indeed, a Symbolist "pretext for dreaming," if not a "joyous dream of the beautiful truth." The mood was created not by conventional settings for the pastoral but mainly by movement and acting (the laughing of the nymphs, the tossing of paper roses and balloons), suggestive props, and lighting. Craig used the stage materials in terms of their inherent properties. Instead of realistic settings, he took the huge curtains and brought them to light in full size, and using a cyclorama on an almost bare stage, he achieved an impression of vast space, impossible to do by cluttering the stage and using lower curtains. In fact, he applied to the stage the teachings of the Symbolist and Impressionist painters, treating the stage as pure material and exploiting its specific properties. This is also how he treated light, using it to paint the settings, to indicate time, and to create mood. The London productions were the first phase in Craig's reform of the stage, when the elongated, geometrical forms he used could be viewed by his contemporaries as a reaction to the embellishments of Art Nouveau, although he retained its long, flowing lines.

The uncommon form of Craig's scene, with its vast spatial dimensions and huge architectural shapes or bodies that we have come to know mainly by the designs he made after 1904, has led his critics to different speculations on the possible sources of influence. Craig was aware that the most striking feature of the bodies was not so much their architectural form as their colossal size. In the *Index,* he mentions the tall beds at Hampton Court, first seen when he was a child, which left an indelible impression on him. He also mentions Louis Loeb's drawing of a performance in the Roman theatre at Orange, where huge doors stood out among all the settings. Servandoni's designs, where only the lower parts of the huge buildings were painted on the frame (the rest apparently rising high into the flies), were also a parallel. Another source of influence was Ruskin; Paul M. Talley presents a good case for the impact of Ruskin's *Seven Lamps of Architecture* on Craig's concept of space.[4] Both Catherine Valogne and Denis Bablet mention the possibility of the medieval towers at San Gimignano in Italy as a model, while Bablet also suggests that Craig's work was inspired by the architects Henry van de Velde and Josef Hoffmann, whom Craig knew during his stay in Germany.[5]
As Craig wrote in "The Artists of the Theatre of the Future," the artist of the theatre had three sources of inspiration: nature (for acting and movement), music (for light and staging), and architecture (for scene). He was highly receptive to new trends as well as to newly rediscovered old masters or monuments. Isadora Duncan particularly noted his enthusiasm for the functional modern architecture of Berlin.

Ancient Egypt, in which Craig took a particular interest in 1905 and 1906, was another source of influence. The architectural bodies that are so striking in his designs from 1905 on bear a strong resemblance to some of the monuments of ancient Egypt, pictures of which are reproduced in one of the books Craig read, *A History of Art in Ancient Egypt* (1883), by Georges Perrot and Charles Chipiez. This book contains numerous plates, including the "Interior of the Temple of the Sphinx," the "Principal Hall in the Great Temple" with statues along the wall representing the high priests, and the "Interior of the Hypostyle Hall" at Karnak—a reconstruction showing rows of colossal columns where the proportion of the column to the human figure is 20:1. One figure, labeled "Egyptian construction, epitomized by Ch. Chipiez" (fig. 6), is an

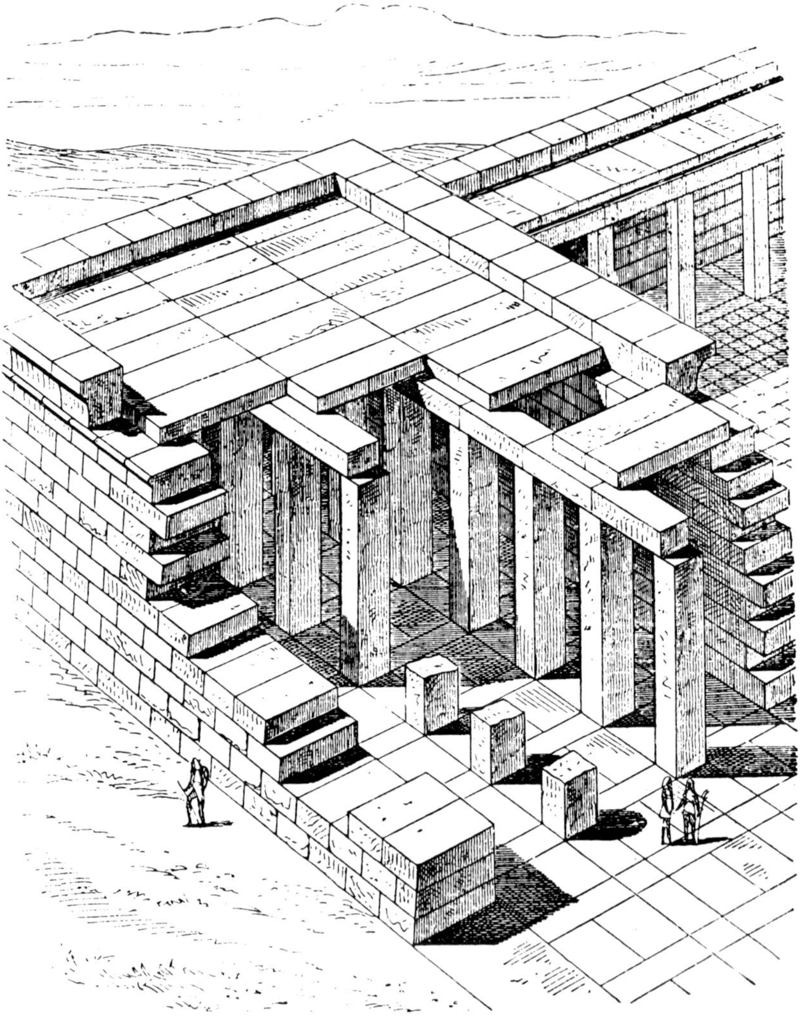

6. Egyptian construction. From *A History of Art in Ancient Egypt* (1883), by Georges Perrot and Charles Chipiez.

architectural rendering of the stages of building, showing the supporting columns, the wall constructions of huge dressed stone, the massive roof, and interior spatial arrangement, including the patterned floor. Another illustration, the "Interior of the Temple of the Sphinx" (fig. 7), bears a distinct resemblance to some models made in Florence, in which the opening of the stage was wider and lower than that in his designs. The text accompanying the figure says: "The pillars are plain rectangular monoliths; the walls are without either bas-reliefs or paintings, and there is not a trace of any inscription on any part of the building. The external walls are constructed of the largest limestone blocks which are to be found in Egypt."[6]

The architectural bodies may well have been inspired by all these various sources, but in the formation of Craig's concept of scene, his fascination with theatrical effects, achieved by the use of *contrasting juxtapositions,* played a major role. This fascination began at a very early age and was certainly due to the place theatre occupied in his life. From the age of six when he had his first walk-on role in *Olivia* at the Lyceum—and perhaps even before—he knew the world of make-believe as part of daily life. The tall beds at Hampton Court impressed Craig as a child not only because they offered such a menacing contrast to his own littleness but because they had astonishingly been intended for everyday use: their marvelously unexpected size illuminated their immediate surroundings in a new light, challenging the notions of right and wrong, of common and uncommon, and turning reality itself into a stage open for debate. Later on, melodrama taught him the value of such contrasting juxtapositions and their effect on the audience: he had himself played in melodramas and his master was no other than the best living actor of melodrama, Henry Irving. As a wood engraver, Craig learned to use contrasts between light and dark and between empty space and mass and line, a lesson learned also from Japanese art. And according to Edward Craig, among all the illustrators the one Craig admired most was Howard Pyle, who used impressionistic effects of line, mass, and light to show the movement of his heroes and villains, cowboys and Indians, in battle.

In all Craig's stage designs of the earlier period, even in those he did for *Hamlet* in 1896, and later, bold three-dimensional architectural shapes seem to expand the limits of the conventional stage. The delightful drawing for the "Ophelia scene" (1896) has two light green cubelike shapes on each side of the otherwise bare stage. A blue stage floor indicates water.[7] The straight lines and flat surfaces of the setting enhance the roundness of the human body and bring out the actor's presence and movements (Appia turned this same technique into a principle of the mise

7. Interior of the Temple of the Sphinx. From *A History of Art in Ancient Egypt* (1883), by Georges Perrot and Charles Chipiez.

en scène, *le principe du repoussoir*). The Ophelia drawing was done in watercolor, as was the design for *Hamlet,* act 3, scene 4, in 1899: the latter is similar in feature, having enormous architectural bodies and dwarfed human figures.[8] Craig used the dynamics of contrasting volumes very effectively in his London productions. So, for example, the design that inspired the mise en scène for *Acis and Galatea,* act 2, scene 1, "The Shadow," done in 1901, shows the pair of lovers cuddled together on an almost bare stage, dwarfed by the threatening, gigantic shadow of Polyphemus—an effect Craig achieved by the use of light projection.[9] In another design, prepared in 1904 for the *Masque of London,* "The Wapping Old Stairs," two dominant groups of monolithic, fantastic bodies and a zigzag of steeply climbing levels create an almost eerie sense of mass that not merely dwarfs the two figures on the stairs but nearly swallows them up. In a design for *Electra* (fig. 8), made in 1905 and reproduced in the *Index,* the impression of vast space is given by the use of very high painted curtains and by light. Light is also used to create mood and expression: a shaft of light falls on the central dark figure of Electra, and light casts two shadows of her figure, making her larger than life and also giving her expressive attitude two other dimensions.

The use of massive architectural shapes—high arcades or walls, painted for the London productions as for other projects on curtains or backdrops—and one or two dominant figures became, in a sense, Craig's trademark. He applied the technique very skillfully in *Much Ado about Nothing* (1903), which Ellen Terry took on tour to the provinces, and in the designs he prepared in 1904 for *Venice Preserved.* In Germany, Craig was commissioned to do a series of drawings for Hofmannsthal's *Death and the Fool, The White Fan,* and *Electra.* Many of his drawings and sketches in his notebooks toy with these same contrasting elements of design. In a drawing for *Death and the Fool* (fig. 9) in the "Uber-Marions" notebooks, the fool, holding a mask in front of his face, is half kneeling behind the bigger, overpowering figure of Death. The fool's pose is static, while that of Death is dynamic. The fool's figure is outlined by curves, that of Death by smooth, long lines. The contrast is further emphasized by light and dark in the costumes. Rather curiously, the influence of Howard Pyle is still evident in the melodramatic poses as well as in the suggestion of swift movement.

Intention is only one part of the picture, of course. What looks to be high and soaring in a drawing, for a stage set or a building let us say, may not turn out to be high and soaring at all. According to Marotti, Craig deliberately falsified elements in his drawings because of his "persecution mania."[10] The suggestion is not unfounded if we remember that in 1905 Reinhardt's assistants came to Craig's exhibition and copied some of his

8. *Electra* (1905). From *Towards a New Theatre* (1913). Edward Gordon Craig Estate and Bibliothèque Nationale, Paris.

designs; it was also in 1905 that Craig first started to fear his "enemy," as the "Uber-Marions" notebooks show. Whether or not the falsification followed in consequence is arguable. But in any case, it was finally on the basis of his set designs as shown in public exhibitions that Craig's work came to be appreciated or rejected. Craig would have liked the idea of teasing his so-called enemies—even by intentionally spreading the

9. Drawing for *Death and the Fool*. From the "Uber-Marions" notebooks. Edward Gordon Craig Estate and Bibliothèque Nationale, Paris.

rumor of the falsification, "revealing" its existence only to "close" friends and expecting the rumor to reach the "enemy" and scare him off. There is no dispute that a literal reconstruction of any project, based only on notes or drawings, is unreliable and incomplete, and one must keep this in mind when examining Craig's designs. It must also be remembered that the comments that accompany the designs published in *Towards a New Theatre* (1913), in *Scene* (1923), and in the catalogues of his many exhibitions were written well after the actual composition of the designs, long after the vision and ideas had worn off. Therefore, and until the key to the falsification—if such a key ever existed—is found, revealed, and used to illustrate the designs, and although our interpretation may be impressionistic, we probably have no other choice but to accept the designs as they are.

It is the post-1905 drawings that are most strikingly three-dimensional. The stonelike appearance of the huge rectangular blocks—the "cubes"—is due to the techniques employed, that is, wood engraving and, from 1907 on, etching, which Craig learned from Stephen Haweis. Craig uses the square and the circle to indicate volumes. Unlike Appia's designs, which suggest lightness and airiness by the use of a multiple-leveled open space, Craig's designs have a looming and threatening solidity, enhanced by the proliferation of the "frozen" masses. Sometimes he indicates shafts of light, but on the whole the renderings are dark. One misses the light, the color, and the movement that would be used on the real stage (in this sense they are indeed falsified). Like the earlier designs, made before 1905, these designs are constructed on the juxtaposition of opposites: dark and bright areas, empty spaces and solids, the suggestion of immobility and movement (by the oblique lines of light). This was a new, concrete environment, no longer a make-believe but an aesthetic end in itself. A harmonious, though "artificial," stage was created. The designs show arrested motion, an instant in an imaginary performance or in an imaginary occurrence. As such, they were intended to be an illustration of a potential scene, true only to the spirit of the event. As pictorial signs, indicators of an intention, they must be approached with caution. According to Willard F. Bellman and Paul M. Talley, these are "interim symbols," as well as a sort of "intellectual guide" between Craig and other artists.[11] They include visual suggestions for the mise en scène—setting, lighting, blocking of characters, movement (gestures and movement suggested by the interplay of light and darkness), outline of costume, and, most important, mood. They also suggest the director's symbolic interpretation, in terms of forms, colors or shades of colors, movement and pose, light and volumes. In the famous series of four designs from 1905, *The Steps,* for example, the tension is established in the first design, the first "mood," by opposing two massive walls that frame the multiple-leveled space in between. This space, the steps, inspires a feeling of imminent danger, of imminent fall in the direction of the proscenium; the proscenium is the only "place of rest," but it is also a place of confrontation. The steps impose the rhythm of movement, and the swifter it is the greater the feeling of danger. The difference in light between the various designs in the series indicates the change in mood and the dynamic or static pose of the figures, the event.

What could not be rendered in these designs is the whole *range of movement* that Craig had in mind, from the movement of the actor to that of the über-marionette, the *interplay of voices* chosen by their tonal range, and the *mobility of the stage*. Serlio's *Five Books of Architecture* and a study of Manfred Semper's *Handbuch der Architectur,* especially the fourth part dealing with theatre construction and the Asphaleia system of hydraulic lifts, led Craig in 1906 to the creation of the second instrument for movement, the kinetic stage. The vision was of a new stage resembling a musical instrument, with a keyboard to control the up-and-down movement of the architectural elements and the lighting. The long ribbons of the setting, which in *Acis and Galatea* merged with the ribbons of the chorus's costumes and reverberated their movements, have now been transformed into solids, put in motion not by the human performer but by the artist at the keyboard. The "cubes," as Craig called these tall, boxlike shapes (parallelipipeds), were born. This new instrument was invented by Craig while he was still working on the über-marionette project, and in his excitement at the multiple possibilities of motion it could offer, he wrote in "The Artists of the Theatre of the Future" that the human *form* as an instrument for movement had to be banished.[12] But he did not stop his work on the über-marionette, and the two projects ran simultaneously. Both instruments were far from being workable: while the über-marionette had at least a visible forerunner, the puppet, whose technique it could eventually borrow, the new instrument was as yet only a vision embodied in several drawings. The first drawing for the kinetic theatre—made in 1906—was directly inspired by one of Serlio's designs of a floor geometrically divided into squares. But the turning point had actually been 1905: designs made during this year include three-dimensional bodies like colossal columns, high arcades, endless stairs—resembling the monolithic works of the ancient Egyptians. From 1906 on, the designs show "cubes," sometimes grounded, sometimes suspended—the kinetic stage. The proportion of the human figure to these "cubes" is approximately 1:6 (fig. 10). Several designs do include an oversize figure, the über-marionette, and in this case the proportion of the figure to the cubes is about 1:2 (fig. 11).

The kinetic stage marks the break with the traditional concept of theatre, going beyond the Aristotelian aesthetic principles. What had been for Serlio a technical device for representation, and for the users of the Asphaleia system a plain mechanical vehicle, has now become an aesthetic object creating another aesthetic object (movement). The mimetic

10. Actors or human-size figures on the kinetic stage (1907). From *Scene* (1923). Edward Gordon Craig Estate and Bibliothèque Nationale, Paris.

element is no longer present, and what we have is a new, heretofore nonexistent level of reality. Space has been reordered. Instead of the familiar or conventional settings serving as a locale for the unfolding of movement, Craig created a space that was itself generating movement, accompanied by light and sound. The instrument was to create new forms in

11. An über-marionette on the kinetic stage (1907). From *Scene* (1923). Edward Gordon Craig Estate and Bibliothèque Nationale, Paris.

space, affecting the beholder the way music affects its listener. As movement possesses a hypnotic influence and can rivet its beholder, so the instrument possessed a compelling power of attraction. Is this "new art" contemplative, as Craig wished ideal art to be? To the extent that it creates a spectacle of pure motion and light, it is; the moment it includes the human figure—actor or über-marionette—with its distinct connotative power, it may, in Craig's own words, "excite," but it is doubtful whether Craig thought of this unexpected effect. The instrument was both solid and pliable, offering precision and clarity in performance. It could have created new configurations in space in a language whose elements and rules Craig had yet to discover—as he had yet to discover how to put his ideas in practice and operate the instrument. But in spite of its mobility, this would still have been a uniform, abstract world.

This dialectic of voids and solids, of darkness and light, was Craig's counterpart to Mallarmé's use of the blank page or to Maeterlinck's use of silence: a refusal of verbal signs, human voice, human presence, and human artifacts; a retreat from everyday reality; an ascetic and aseptic retreat. It was the symbol of a metaphysical void, not unlike that created by De Chirico, Paul Delvaux, and Magritte. There is a suggestion of monumentality both in the kinetic stage and in De Chirico's *pittura metafisica,* a monumentality that, as the term itself denotes, perpetuates memory—the memory not of life but of a lost purity, a lost greatness—and for Craig, paradoxically (for he created motion, symbol of life), a memory of Death. For the purity of form of De Chirico, as well as of Delvaux, Magritte, and Mondrian, is only pure appearance, a symbol of loss, absence, and sterility. On the kinetic stage, geometry or pure simplified lines, the model of which is classic architecture, replaced complexity and intricacy, rejected spontaneity, and introduced a sterile order in a seemingly chaotic world. As Marotti pointed out, the relationship between the white and black in Craig's designs recalls that of a Mondrian.[13] Indeed, like Mondrian, Craig created a world apart, using mobile volumes on the stage instead of static planes. But if the beholder of a Mondrian work has to contribute movement, by allowing his eyes to travel from line to line and space to space in an attempt to apprehend the work—and by doing so, he gives it life and meaning—not so the beholder of the kinetic stage who is in a constant state of receptivity that Craig refers to as "contemplation."

Craig's intention was that motion performed by the instrument should affect the beholder like music ("a Mozart"). Indeed, motion provides "produced representations" as music does, and both possess a nonmaterial "being-in."[14] If we follow Victor Zuckerhandl's lead, we do find in the new art the particularities of music. (1) Movement is governed by dynamic laws, which had yet to be explored by Craig. (2) Movement manifests itself through bodies—the "cubes"—like music. (3) The new art offers three simultaneous experiences: motion, time, and space. (4) The immaterial character of the work is a genuine element of nature. (5) The distinction between inner and outer world disappears—this was achieved by Appia through music and movement in his utopian Living Art, where the performer and the spectator are one and the same. (6) The movement of the "cubes," as it is nonmimetic and immaterial, expresses the nonphysical, the spiritual. (7) The contents cannot be translated into discursive terms. (8) Like music, movement (of the kinetic stage) is pregnant with nonphysical forces. Like tones, that have a direct physical impact—whether their source is man or a man-made instrument—movement exerts a hypnotic power on its beholder. Finally, tones have a visceral impact that has (inadvertently?) led Zuckerhandl to the ninth point, which is not missing in the kinetic motion: (9) there is a similarity between the motional (and musical) concept of the external world and the magical and mythical ideas of primitive or prehistoric peoples.[15] Craig did not reflect on these common features, but he was convinced that he had invented a supreme art that could compete with music in conveying a spiritual experience.

The movement of the architectonic kinetic stage would have been, however, limited in range of expression by the very *form* of the "cubes," much like the kaleidoscope, and in spite of the support of lighting effects or sound (music). This was an artistic expression of a mental makeup, in what Craig viewed as a new art but was in fact a new medium. The kinetic stage was only the first manifestation of the multimedia performance, which combined architecture, mechanics, light, movement, and sound, with or without the performer; in spite of the various elements it used, its polysemy would not only have been different but also poorer than that of Craig's "interpretative" theatre.

Craig was baffled by the technical problems posed by the invention of the kinetic stage, and it was only years later, in 1923, with the help of his son Edward Craig and a specialized engineer, that he found a solution.[16] As seen later, what Craig came upon in 1907, while experimenting with his stage model, was another mobile stage using *screens,* destined to serve the mise en scène of poetic drama during the phase of Interpretation.

Still, it was the kinetic stage that stimulated Craig, stirring up a vision of pure motion, of a new genesis—a vision that he later revealed in *Motion* (1907) and in new designs.[17] The "cubes" designs are glimpses of this vision, a graphic visualization. According to his wish, Craig's design is an *objet d'art,* similar in this respect to the über-marionette, the mask, the costume, props, or settings that the artist created. Offered to the view, the design displays still another *objet d'art,* the kinetic "cubes"; and the kinetic "cubes," frozen in a design or active on a real stage, are an integral part of still another *objet d'art,* the spectacle. Through this complex aesthetic experience, Craig obtains the emotional and intellectual involvement of the beholder.

Thus, the "cubes" can never be viewed as mere vehicles in a process of communication. They possess a too-powerful presence of their own. T. S. Eliot wrote of them as being "aggressive" and "calling attention to themselves."[18] The symbolic form, size, and material—and, on the stage, the direction, speed, and duration of the movement—of the "cubes" have an immediate impact on the beholder. Moreover, the connotations related to the elongated form, the huge size, and the stone, blend together and change with every shift of the "cubes" in space. Stone seems to be the material the "cubes" are made of in the designs, though the lighting or paint adding color to them may change this onstage. The huge stone (the menhir, the megalithic monument) has a magic function in many religious rites and it is, according to Mircea Eliade, an instrument of sacredness; moreover, the crystal is a Jungian symbol of wholeness. Phallic connotations are also introduced by this elongated form. The huge size brings in other religious connotations, because of the association of hugeness with gigantism; the symbolism of gigantism is closely related to the perception of divinity.[19] On another level, the juxtaposition of the "cubes" and the human figure (actor or über-marionette) emphasizes the ontological aspect of Craig's vision. Here again we have a contrasting juxtaposition, when the curved lines of the figure are surrounded by the high and massive parallelepipeds. Appia used the principle of *repoussoir* in order to enhance the presence of the human performer against the architectural elements of the stage (steps, platforms, and bodies). On Craig's stage, the human figure (actor or über-marionette) is belittled, almost annihilated by the huge bodies. The menacing aspect of these architectural elements is enhanced by the up-and-down movement of the "cubes" on the stage, a movement not unlike the grinding teeth of a ruthless machine—a Romantic symbol of the destructive power of industrialization. Moreover, this sort of movement dispels the sense of orientation—that of the beholder as well as that of the figure/character—in space; up and down become equivalent, and so do all other directions. The stage becomes a kaleidoscope manipulated by hostile powers, where the forlorn figure of man would be but another toy, an object, a prey to the blind forces of matter. Let alone the fact that to the Freudian psychoanalyst, the kinetic stage, a cave of stalactites and stalagmites suddenly put in motion, presents yet another image of the castrating female figure.

For the beholder, the kinetic stage—and the screens, for that matter—

serves as a canvas for imagination to draw on. But the moment the human figure is introduced, it transforms the dialectics between this stage and the audience, since it belongs to a different semantic field. A new dialectics, that between the figure and its environment, comes into existence, affecting that between the stage and the audience. Whereas the relation between the über-marionette and the kinetic stage is complementary (both being manipulated instruments), that between the actor and this stage is one of contrasting juxtaposition, as we have seen. The purpose of Craig's experiments in Florence was to explore these complex relations while working toward the perfection of the invented instruments.

9

Voice and Drama

Craig's belief in the dominance of movement over all other elements of the production is also substantiated by his attitude toward voice and drama. His experience as a director had proved that by deliberately omitting one of the three elements of theatre—movement, scene, and voice—he could enhance the expressivity of the other two, and his experience as an actor had taught him the value of the correct use of voice. At the Lyceum, productions of Shakespeare as well as melodramas owed their success not only to the astonishingly accurate representations of period and locale but also to Henry Irving's and Ellen Terry's masterful use of voice and movement, as Craig's reconstruction of Irving's acting in *The Bells* amply shows.[1] The music hall was another example of effective diction and intonation, and so was the puppet theatre in which the voice, separated from movement, was a major means of characterization. A different path was shown by Maeterlinck through his melodramatic non-use of voice—or the frequent use of pauses in speech—which invested his plays with mystery and rich metaphysical undertones. Finally, out of Craig's six productions in London, three were operatic works and voice was their major expressive means: *Dido and Aeneas* (Purcell), *The Masque of Love* (from Purcell's opera *Dioclesian*), and *Acis and Galatea* (Handel). In these productions, the choice of the tonal range of the voice as well as the duration of movement was imposed by music, the regulating force, and this ensured the exactitude of the performance. Craig did not forget this lesson when he came to plan the über-marionette theatre, where the voices of the readers were to be chosen by their *tonal range*. Four to six voices were required (bass, baritone, tenor, alto, contralto, and soprano), using *musical notes* for the delivery of speech. Thus, Craig not only ensured the musicality of speech but also controlled pitch, rhythm, and, indirectly, movement. "Pace, fire and vitality," this is what he demanded of the right delivery.[2] There is, however, no indication whether in the regular theatre the actors should also be chosen according to the tonal range of their voices.

Although in *The Art of the Theatre* voice was invested with the same value as movement and scene, this programmatic assertion is not, however, a faithful reflection of Craig's position concerning voice. The element of voice was never equal to that of movement and scene in the rest of his London productions, which emphasized scene and movement, nor in the dramatic pieces he composed for his theatre. In all his work on the London productions, the formal aspect, the spectacle, dominated. This emphasis followed naturally from Craig's belief that theatre was first and foremost a visual art that originated with the dancer and not with the poet. Nevertheless, he thought that many plays (Shakespeare's among them) were better read than performed, since words could sometimes better express ideas and feelings and better stir the imagination than any action on the stage. But like Irving, Craig did not hesitate, on the other hand, to cut the text of a play for purposes of dramatic staging.

Another influence on Craig's attitude to voice and drama was his interest in the masque. He began collecting material on the masque in 1899, after seeing *Beauty's Awakening,* a masque produced by the Art Workers Guild. Soon after *Dido and Aeneas* he produced *The Masque of Love,* which he later included in the repertoire of the über-marionette theatre. Since the masque made little use of speech, his imagination could have free rein. He was also attracted to the possibilities of movement in the mimo-drama, the short dumb show that used to be given in England until the early 1820s before and after the main play. This had developed into an independent genre that was quite popular in the 1890s.[3] The vitality of the masque and the mimo-drama reinforced Craig's belief in a theatre based mainly on movement and using little text, that is, little voice. He entertained the idea of new dramatic pieces that would allow the artist to design movement and scene, unencumbered by the demands of the playwright. These pieces would be subject only to a story line and a theme, using or not using speech. In 1901 Craig began to compose his own masques. In Germany, Craig discovered the same interest in mimo-dramas—Reinhardt was to produce several, and Hofmannsthal had produced his first ballet libretto, *Der Triumph der Zeit,* in 1900—and in the revival of pageantry. In a letter to Martin Shaw in May 1905, Craig stated: "I hold that *the theatre* should exist without its modern support of poet, musician and the rest and my belief is entirely in the stage manager of the future."[4] He had made the same assertion in *The Art of the Theatre,* written shortly before. About the pieces that were to replace the conventional drama, he explained to Shaw: "My first attempts and failures are put away in boxes—perhaps to be revived. 'Hunger.' 'Lunatics.' 'London.' 'A Mystery.' 'Dance of Death.' (How gloomy I was, Martin.) But now I begin to shape anew an old story. I shall make its shape and colour, its sound and sense, its movement and tone. I shall not employ actors nor pantomimists but what I shall call Figures. ('Ubermarionettes' is too complicated.)"[5]

Of these "attempts"—called masques and mimo-dramas interchangeably—we have numerous drafts, fragments, and designs, among them the *Masque of London,* which in *Towards a New Theatre* he calls a "mimodrama"; Craig started work on this in 1901. Most of the (unfinished) masques use almost no speech and are accompanied by designs. For the *Masque of Hunger,* started in 1903, Craig had in mind two versions, one with speech and one a dumb show. Other pieces were "silent dramas" and have remained in an embryonic stage, like the famous series of four designs made in 1905, *The Steps.* During the years 1905 and 1906, Craig wrote and designed many such pieces, including *Meetings and Partings, The Tale of Troy, Death of Socrates, Tale of Jason, Life of a Princess,* and a ballet, *Cupid and Psyche.*

The brief scenario *Meetings and Partings* gives us a hint of the kind of dramatic pieces Craig intended to use instead of the regular drama written by a playwright. It has three separate movements, in the musical sense, defined by three different locales: the Street, the Fields, and the Seashore. Speech is limited to a few words only. Since Craig uses the length of the written line and spaces for the dramatic emphasis of an idea—as L. M. Newman has already pointed out—it is best to quote here his own notes:

The Street – The Street woman—
The 300 other street women—shades. general movement
drones.
She a light
The men—beetles
The man—a light
The meeting—*3 words*—
The love—*one word*—
The Parting—*silence*

The Fields – The fields men & women
The girl—all chatter dying away.
The older man—silence.
meeting parting
The Seashore – The miserable woman—moans
meets the sea—
behind her comes death
& holding her as the
father holds the child takes her in—

Theme and plot are condensed in one phrase:

The woman meets Ugliness & takes it for Beauty
When she parts from it
it is Beauty but she
takes it for ugliness.[6]

What Craig envisioned, as this schematic outline well illustrates, was a theatre made of movement, scene, and voice, but with voice definitely not the main conveyor of meaning. Voice (or, for that matter, sound) creates the atmosphere (the drones, the chatter), but its use to express feelings is limited to two verbal exchanges and a moan. Instead, meaning is conveyed by silence and movement. The characters are depersonalized, defined only in a generic way; development is episodic—no climactic scene, rather a succession of short scenes. The technique is Expressionist, though that term was not yet in use. Craig intended to use the (round) über-marionette for the central characters, while for the rest he wanted to use flat figures, projected on a screen ("shades").

The masque *Hell and Paradise,* a scenario written in 1905, is also an allegory of Life, with psychological overtones. The first scene is a conventional exposition, an outdoor scene showing the six gates of Hell on one side of the stage and the gate of Paradise on the other, recalling the Hellmouth and the Paradise of the medieval morality play. Descriptions of the settings are mixed with explanatory comments:

Hell	Paradise
The Gates 6 and paths to them on floor. Everyone to enter these gates goes in backwards and unwillingly. One who rushes with courage—suddenly appears at the door of heaven. Double used here. Hell is caring no more to see what Life offers.	The Gate No one goes in. They sit outside and they hear and see: how interesting all is, how full of movement, design, poetry Life is. How full of *Heaven* Life is to the creature who sees it— nothing must be overlooked. Look at everything, see it— that is Heaven.

After everyone is in, scene changes to the Interior of Hell.

The guiding proposition is that "Hell is merely a repetition of Life, all in dark colours painted. Heaven is Life with its lights and shades etc."[7] Here Craig is opposing isolation to friendliness, agitation to tranquility, sadness and anger to joy and playfulness, noises and cries to song and music, and unproductiveness to creativity. As the spectacle unfolds before the audience, it becomes evident that Hell and Paradise are psychologically based notions and that our perceptions of the external world are purely subjective.

The contrast between Hell and Paradise is brought out by movement, color, sound, and sets of characters. The masque contains three major sequences: (1) the presentation of Hell and Paradise and the different attitudes to them as expressed by movement and gesture in the exposition scene; (2) the presentation of each town, Hell Town shown by general action and Paradise Town by a succession of short, unrelated scenes, depicting not a situation but a state of mind; and (3) the successive display of the gathering place in each town, the marketplace. Each of the Hell Town and Paradise Town scenes is a visual translation of the central idea that binds them all together. The Paradise scenes show "friendliness—humour—love—ease—peace" and the Hell scenes "hardness—seriousness—nervousness—fear."[8]

There is no major character, but Craig does introduce an allegorical figure, the Spirit of Hell Town that appears in the opening scene: "He is Hardness and mistrust personified. All is angular and he rolls two wheels on each side, which make much noise, and crushes things. He has no ears and no eyes."[9] This is a modernized and mechanized image of death, Lucifer, and snake at the same time. The other characters are deprived of all individuality, impersonal figures like the artist (the sculptor), the craftsman (the carpenter), or "a woman." The characters are engaged in different actions, physical movement reflecting a state of mind as well as social and economic conditions. In the scene inside Hell Town, for example, people "shun each other," "draw back against a wall or rush by each other"; "each one has something which he hides"; children play in the gutter while old hags throw coal at them, and the mob attacks a man. There were to be about twenty-five characters for Hell Town, among them old hags, children, mob, and the "finely dressed wretched man." The number of characters for Paradise Town is not indicated, but several specific characters mentioned are a little girl, a sculptor, a carpenter, and a woman with baby, as well as nondefined characters that perform various actions. Their movements are "placid" and quiet, they come and go in pairs, read, look at the sky, dance, play at competitive games (all are winners!), laugh, and sing—a picture of perfect harmony. In the marketplace of Paradise Town "all is given, not sold." The contrast between the two towns is also reflected in sounds: Hell Town has cries and noises, Paradise Town is full of laughter, music, and songs. And continuing the principle of contrasts, the costumes in Paradise Town are "of the simplest kind," while those of Hell Town would be a medley of variegated outfits.

For Hell Town, Craig first imagined a "strange town" of square, black-grey houses, then decided to harmonize the contrasts between the colors of the two towns, using one setting only and colored lights:

> Hell Town—Grey, brown, black, green and blue. but bad tones and no gaiety.
> Paradise Town—All perfect colours. As the old Munich. As Fra Angelico and the Italian paint towns. Is the same town as Hell but *beautiful* and colour.[10]

The image of Hell was built on Craig's impressions from his visit to Moscow in the winter 1905: "gloomy and sultry and suspicious like the Moscow feeling," a mob attacking a "finely dressed" but "wretched man." (Craig was in Moscow not long after the Bloody Sunday.)[11]

For the interior scenes, Craig planned to use flats, in a technique that amounts to a modernized version of the medieval wagon: "All these are flats from the beginning of the steps," he explained his design. "Ms [mansions] 1 2 3 4 built. And when their scenes inside are enacted, they are removed, and 5 6 7 8 are removed by being slided away below and 5 6 7 8 take the place of 1 2 3 4." Each mansion is a room: "Each room comes before the audience, as the audience cannot go to each room. And when a room and its occupants have been seen, the next is shown, and each brings the center of the town to the audience."[12] Two rooms were to be exposed at the same time, one on each side of the stage with the street in between, but action was evidently not simultaneous—that is, light would be focused on one room, then on the other, leaving half the stage always darker. With this system of sliding mansions, there was no need to lower the curtain with each change of scene (the screens were not yet invented).

The scenario of *Hell and Paradise* as it appears in the "Uber-Marions" notebooks is incomplete, and we do not know if it was intended to be a dumb show, a "silent drama," though voice is used here for song. The main importance of this piece for the modern critic lies in its having been designed by Craig to fulfill a definite purpose: "*to create a belief.*"[13] For this end, it would have used the man-made instrument, the über-marionette.

Voice and Drama

With the new use of voice as a physical expression that complements movement, the traditional play—and the playwright—became obsolete. The artist of the theatre now provided the action, the characters, the setting. Craig would compose different "motions" for the small figures of his stage model and experiment with voice, while he looked for a theatre of his own, where he could put his ideas to test. His theory of the ideal theatre was already shaped by the end of 1906.

≻ 10 ≺

Belief (I)

In retrospect, it seems that the modern theatre has benefited from Craig's predilection for secrecy, as bold technical innovations are more readily accepted than reforming moral or religious ideas. Thus, although it was ultimately rejected, the über-marionette was taken very seriously by critics and theatre people, but what Craig presented as Belief was interpreted as merely a poetical metaphor and did not get the attention it deserved. For me too, not long ago, Belief appeared to be a general and vague idea, embodying a multitude of spiritual values rather than a creed.[1] For Craig, however, Belief was as concrete as the über-marionette and the kinetic stage that were to be its vehicles. Once we understand the immediacy of Belief for Craig, much of his so-called obscure phraseology becomes clear. It is certain that if Craig had revealed his missionary fervor or disclosed all his mystical visions, he would have been regarded as so eccentric that the impact of his aesthetic reform would have been greatly diminished.

Although in Germany Craig occupied the position of an admired but feared outsider, he found moral support from not a few artists and art amateurs. His private life was not free of complications—Elena Meo, to whom he was deeply attached, had stayed in London; yet now he was in love with a sympathetic and stimulating and very creative dancer, who understood better than anyone his interest in movement. Instead of real work on new productions, there were only promises and endless discussions (the Duse production of *Rosmersholm* came late in 1906). He felt alternately puzzled and vulnerable, exalted and despairing, preoccupied by existential problems—a state to which his notes in the "Uber-Marions" notebooks bear ample proof. He had made the pursuit of art the goal and texture of his life, and here he was, with an idea that he believed in with all his might but with no tangible support for its realization. He oscillated between moments of great optimism, growing out of enthusiasm for his ideas and occasional glimmers of financial support, and annihilating despair.[2] All around him he found echoes of his own predicament as well as different successful or abortive attempts to find spiritual comfort, religious consolation, or philosophical and psychological solutions. Not long before, the conversion to Roman Catholicism of some of the most prominent of the English Aesthetes—like Beardsley and Wilde—had been compelled by a similar urge to believe, to find answers to metaphysical questions; Elena Meo was also a Roman Catholic and a fervent believer. In Germany, there was by this time a proliferation of writings on religious, philosophical, and psychological topics. Harnack's *Das Wesen des Christentums* had appeared in 1901 in its fifth edition (its English translation was published the same year and by 1904 had already reached its third edition); Freud's *Die Traumdeutung* had been published in 1900 and his *Zur Psychopathologie die Altagsleben* in 1901, William James's *Varieties of Religious Experience* in 1902, Rudolf Steiner's *Theosophie* in 1904, and Freud's *Drei Abhandlungen zur Sexualtheorie* in 1905. These were but a few of the influential writings that captivated the imagination of the artists and intellectuals in Germany during these years. Spiritualism, occultism, and so-called scientific approaches to religion were the fashion of the day. By 1906, Ernst Mach's *Die Analyse der Empfindungen und das Verhältnis des Physischen zum Psychischen* (1886), an attempt at a physical explanation of psychological phenomena, was in its fifth edition, and Georg Simmel's *Die Religion,* which established religion as a psychological need, was printed. Haeckel, who sought to reconcile science and religion, was becoming more and more popular—Isadora Duncan was one of his admirers. Besides the Protestant and Catholic social movements, the period saw a proliferation of religiocultic groups that preached either a return to an age-old occultism or various brands of a synthetic faith based on a jumble of alchemy and Indian beliefs. Messianic leaders attracted many of those whom positivism or the established faith had disappointed. Thomas Mann's *Beim Propheten,* published in 1904, exposed such a sham "spiritual leader" who, incidentally, was an artist. As Hauptmann later described in *Das Abenteuer meiner Jugend* in 1937, there was a feeling of spiritual void in the air, together with the expectation of a renaissance.

Craig was sensitive to this atmosphere. He was not a follower of

Haeckel, but he felt the metaphysical void and the urge to believe. A note in the "Uber-Marions" notebooks from 1905 says:

> The world lacks and needs a Belief. A childish one—one full of complicated customs and ceremonies. Much of the belief which possessed the Egyptians—which made them perform all the ceremonies—all so childish and lovely—of the dead and for the Gods—and for the Nile—and for all the rest of it. A Belief full of Beauty. That is what I will try to find for myself, and then for the world—passing it to them by means of my über-marionette.[3]

The idea continues in the essay "The Artists of the Theatre of the Future," where Craig claims that the future art "will be the first and final belief of the world." His position was not so far from that of Carlyle, Arnold, or Pater, but whereas they attempted to find in art a substitute for religious belief, Craig had a definite Belief in mind.

Craig was never a true aesthete, someone like Gabriel Nash in *The Tragic Muse,* Prince Amerigo in *The Golden Bowl,* or Gilbert Osmund in *The Portrait of a Lady,* or even like his own father, Godwin. By the time Craig decided to devote his time to wood engraving, as well as during his London productions, the aesthetic criterion or the "touchstone of taste" may have played an important role in his daily life, but it never shattered his belief in the educational and spiritual force of the theatre and of art. In Germany, the prevailing attitude toward the artist and his social role reinforced Craig's belief that artistic excellence should be the vehicle for spiritual value. Art was useful, for it had the power to restore joy, calmness, harmony.[4] It also imparted a feeling of continuity, as well as a feeling of peace and security that only a Belief could produce. To bring Belief to the world—this was the essential goal of art. As Pater affirmed in his "Appreciations," art should serve "to the enlargement of our sympathies with each other, or to the presentment of new or old truths about ourselves and our relation to the world as may ennoble and fortify us in our sojourn here."[5] The notion that art had a definite moral and religious value, beauty being subordinate to goodness and truth, was also that of Ruskin in *The Stones of Venice.* The view that art had a social role was common to most of the German artists and writers that Craig met, such as Van de Velde, Hauptmann, Josef Hoffmann, and Hofmannsthal. Georg Simmel's already popular *Philosophie des Geldes,* published in 1900, stated the commonly accepted view that the artist was entrusted with the catering to spiritual values; later on, in 1907, in "Der Dichter und diese Zeit," Hofmannsthal openly attributed a religious mission to poets. Thus, both his cultural background and his new surroundings encouraged Craig's sense of mission in 1905.

Favoring a historicist attitude and turning to study old civilizations,

Craig found the value of ancient Egyptian or Indian ceremonies to be not only aesthetic but also moral and social, as they provided a sense of cohesion and belonging, security and reassurance, which only a belief could provide. The theatre could combine these values while retaining the ceremonial aspect. In scenarios like *Hell and Paradise* and the *Tale of Troy,* Craig attempted to impart moral values and a belief in an optimistic attitude toward life.

Isadora's mystic attitude toward ancient Egypt served as an incentive for Craig. Isadora was fascinated by her relation—in name only—to the Egyptian goddess Isis, known for her magic, cunning, and knowledge. Francis Steegmuller reports the conversation—by written notes—between Isadora and Craig during their travel by train from Berlin to Dresden on 15 January 1905; when Isadora referred to herself as the Child of Isis and the Gift of Isis and remarked that Isis is the goddess of birth (Isis is often depicted as nursing the child Horus), Craig entered the game, drew "an Egyptian deity," and called upon Isis's lover—Osiris, her brother and husband—to protect him.[6] Isadora occasionally signed her letters "Isa Dora" (her birth certificate bears the name Dora Angela). In December 1904, probably soon after he met Isadora, Craig bought one of J. G. Wilkinson's books on ancient Egypt—either *Manners and Customs of the Ancient Egyptians,* in three volumes, or its shorter version *A Popular Account of the Ancient Egyptians.*[7] Besides that and the *History of Art in Ancient Egypt* by Georges Perrot and Charles Chipiez, which he passed on to Isadora, he probably also read E. A. W. Budge's *A History of Egypt* and *Gods of the Egyptians,* both of which Isadora is known to have read.[8] Craig found in ancient Egypt, as in ancient Greece, China, and India, models of institutionalized art that through rituals and ceremonies expressed a belief. It did not occur to him that he might be wrong, that it was modern man who had come to consider the codified forms of belief as Art.

As a rule, the formulation of Craig's concepts was stimulated and influenced by visual impressions that appealed to his imagination. He worked his way from visual images to abstract ideas. Now, by studying the past, the *ritual,* visual, aspect of the theatre became for him a "*natural*" feature, similar to the "natural" leading role of the stage director.[9] In the history of the ancient civilizations, Craig found support for his thesis that it was now incumbent upon the theatre to restore Belief to the world. Thus, a theatre for Belief, built on the ceremonial pattern, would be a preordained sequence of symbolic gestures intended to induce both the performers (that is, artist, manipulators, and other staff members including the "supers," athletes, and models) and the spectators into participating in a spiritual experience, conducive to a heightened sense of perception and perhaps also to Revelation—a Symbolist attitude discussed previously. The contents of this perception could be variously designated as God, the gods, the beyond. It was the apprehension of an overpowering presence, experienced by religious and profane mystics alike while in a state of heightened perception. The ideal theatre is therefore viewed by Craig as a ceremony, similar to the ancient mysteries. The hierophant of the Orphic mysteries, of the mysteries of Demeter at Eleusis, or of those of Isis and Osiris, had his analogue in Craig's ideal theatre: the director, the artist, the initiator. "For that is what the title of artist means: one who perceives more than his fellows, and who records more than he has seen," Craig wrote in "The Actor and the Uber-Marionette."[10] The artist is now the instructor; his deed—a preliminary act in view of the mystic communion—is part of the ritual; and the place where the ceremony unfolds takes on the distinctive features of a temple, a cathedral. The theatrical performance could thus become a profane mystery, the golden dream of Mallarmé, were it not for the Belief it would carry.[11]

To restore "Mystery" to the theatre—this was another reason Craig gave for his invention of the über-marionette, in his personal notes in the "Uber-Marions" notebooks. Although he did not specifically relate the theatrical performance of the ideal theatre to a mystery, at least not before 1908 (the year of his first vision), he did use the term *mystery* in connection with the über-marionette theatre. No doubt, one of the greatest merits of the term *mystery* is its own vagueness, and A. G. Lehmann was right to condemn the use of the term by the Symbolists, for they applied it with an uncritical zeal.[12]

As for Craig, he associated mystery both with form ("magical" procedures of the director, similar to those in Inigo Jones's masques), and with metaphysical contents. In the catalogue of his exhibition in Manchester in November 1912, that is, four years after his first vision, he says that mystery is contained not only in dark powers associated with evil, like darkness, lightning, and thunder, or the weird, but also in light and in "gaiety of feeling," when gaiety carries itself "with dignity." This was also his attitude in 1907. It was similar to that of Sérusier, who believed that art must hint at the mystery of all creation, landscape or soul, and reveal the great symbols of the universal language. It recalls also Gauguin, Sérusier's master, who so marvelously conveyed the sense of the mystery of Creation by using form and colors whose symbolism created an immediate bond between the artist and the beholder. Maeterlinck, whose main dramatic device was mystery—the unsolved metaphysical riddle—was the only contemporary playwright whose works Craig included in the repertoire of the über-marionette theatre. To Ellen Terry he wrote from Zurich in August 1905: "I am going to try and bring back mystery about all which concerns the theatre. It used to be one of its greatest attractions—and was so right."[13] The mystery of the artistry—the creation of form—would reflect that of Creation.

When an artist, who is not a writer by profession, chooses to explain himself in writing, should we consider his writing a piece of literature, that is, another artistic creation, and judge it as such? Or should we consider it a written comment, a factual statement? And is it important that the artist be able to "write well"? By the turn of the century, Craig considered writing a means of expression by which he could reach a larger number of people. He was not aspiring to a literary career but simply used writing as a means of furthering his work in the theatre; to "write well" would bring more people over to his idea.[14] Craig's critics and readers thought otherwise—judging by his later writings, such as *Books and Theatres* (1925) or *Ellen Terry and Her Secret Self* (1931)—and when whole passages in his two seminal essays from 1907 seemed incomprehensible, it was decided that Craig's prose was poetic and metaphorical. But for Craig, at this moment in his development as an artist, the images had a concrete reality; each one spoke of a belief, of an achievement in the past, and of a promise for the future. His "metaphors" are universal symbols; their "*correspondances,*" and the interrelated myths they evoke, convey the idea of a belief that, however mysterious it may be to us, was very clear to Craig. His discovery of the universal correspondences was illuminating; suddenly all made sense—his parents and his birth, scene and movement, nature and universe. The whole picture perhaps began as a dimly perceived vision, a state of feeling, but it did not vanish, and it returned again and again in what Craig called "illuminations" when he noted them down in the "Movement" notebook.[15] This was the discovery of a metaphysical sense of self as undeniable reality, a sense of self that modern man has lost but which Craig's two favorite poets, Blake and Whitman, possessed.

Craig found deep affinities in Blake and Whitman. Blake's credo, "I must Create a System or be enslav'd by another Mans," and the mythical world that he created, offered Craig a philosophical and artistic model for the creation of his own personal Belief. To the "unseen forces which dominate the action" [this was how Craig defined the supernatural in "The Ghosts in the Tragedies of Shakespeare" (1910)], Blake gave a visual form, integrating them in a coherent universe. Blake, working out of Paracelsus, Boehme, Fludd, and Agrippa, created a philosophical system that, far from preaching an adherence to moral or metaphysical statements, demanded only the poetical suspension of disbelief, taking imagination as the criterion of empirical reality. In other words, once one accepted the (imaginary) existence of Blake's system, one could accept the existence of the values it embodied. Blake was not a mere bedside poet for Craig but a living model. In his own way, Craig was attempting to create a symbolic system, a "belief," on the order of Blake's. Craig, as we have seen, noted in the "Uber-Marions" notebooks, "That is what I will try to find for myself, and then for the world." [16] What have been considered metaphors in his two 1907 essays are mythical symbols, pointing to correspondences that connect numbers, geometrical forms, rhythm, man and universe, man and woman; these symbols are also frequently used in occult sciences. The scales (taken as "the device of our new art"), the numerological system that Craig borrowed from music—like the simple meter of two and four and one and three or the distinction between masculine and feminine rhythms—and the square and the circle, the feminine and the masculine, were to be basic elements in a greater system, the elements of a new art of symbolic movement, which was intended to express and to be (form and contents are one) "the first and final belief of the world," as Craig wrote in "The Artists of the Theatre of the Future." [17] There is no evidence so far available to indicate that Craig belonged to any secret society, but the similarity between this aspect of his theory, namely the vision of Belief as embodied and conveyed by an art of symbolic movement, and contemporary religious experiments, like Rudolf Steiner's, is indeed striking. Nor is there any doubt that Craig considered himself a seer, who perceived those invisible things "seen through the eye and with the eye," as he wrote in the same essay.[18]

The "puzzling" key passage in "The Artists of the Theatre of the Future" has caught the attention of Lyons in his perceptive essay "Gordon Craig's Concept of the Actor." [19] Payne finds in it "a mysterious invocation of number magic and sexual cosmology" and recognizes, as Louis Jouvet and Catherine Valogne did, Craig's intention to erect "a new Church," a "new religion." [20] The passage reads as follows:

> The old divine unity, the divine square, the peerless circle of our nature has been ruthlessly broken by our moods, and no longer can instinct design the square or draw the circle on the grey wall before it . . . [pp. 48–49].
>
> . . . I am entirely conscious that [the movements attempted by my instrument] contain but the simplest of rhythms, the great movements will not yet be captured, no, not for thousands of years. But when they come, great health comes with them, for we shall be nearer balance than we have ever been before.
>
> I think that movement can be divided into two distinct parts, the movement of two and four which is the square, the movement of one and three which is the circle. There is ever that which is masculine in the square and

> ever that which is feminine in the circle. And it seems to me that before the female spirit gives herself up, and with the male goes in quest of this vast treasure, perfect movement will not be discovered; at least I like to suppose all this.
>
> And I like to suppose that this art which shall spring from movement will be the first and final belief of the world; and I like to dream that for the first time in the world men and women will achieve this thing together. [pp. 51–52]

And addressing the future artist, Craig says:

> You will not be a revolutionary against the Theatre, for you will have risen above the Theatre, and entered into something beyond it. [pp. 53]

Craig employs homologous symbols, drawn from different fields of thought. Like Blake, but also like Plato who believed that numbers are the soul of the world, Craig discovers mathematical relationships. He equates the (musical) rhythm of two and four with the (geometrical) square and with the (sexual) male figure. Likewise, he equates one and three with the circle and the female. Some of the rich symbolic content of these elements can best be shown graphically:

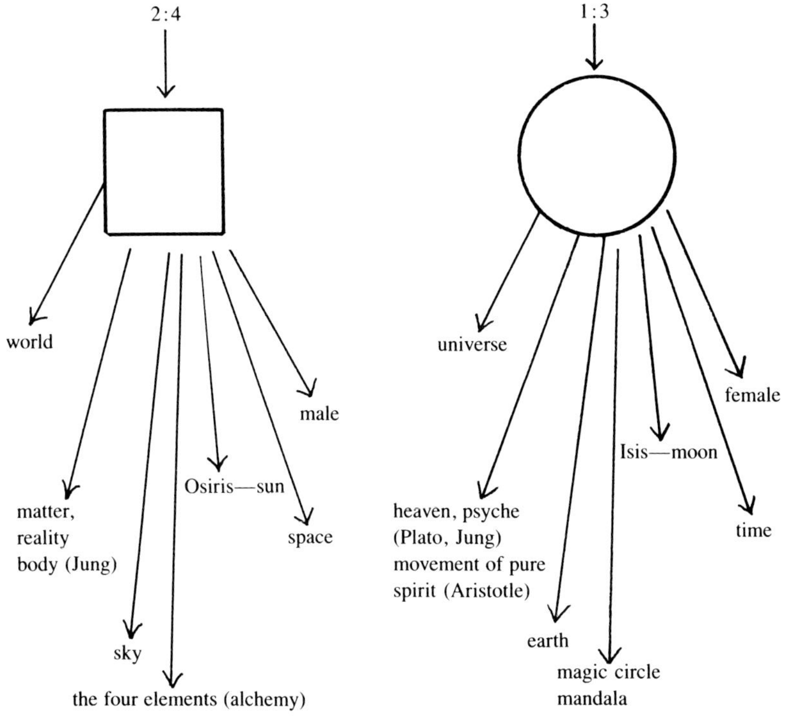

Craig affirms that the union of the male and the female "spirit"—possible only, according to him, by the submission of woman to man—can lead to a successful quest. Graphically, the union of the square with the circle is the well-known alchemical symbol of the concept of the squared circle, signifying wholeness or the union of opposites. The center of the squared circle is also the point of convergence of space, time, and eternity.[21] The quest for the "vast treasure" is a symbolic act, metaphysical as well as artistic. The "vast treasure" is connected by Craig to the "perfect movement"—achieved by the union of the rhythms, of male and female, heaven and earth, psyche and body, time and space—and the birth of the art "which shall spring from movement," the "first and final belief of the world." The "treasure" is one element in a complex constellation of images that, as Gilbert Durand brings out, are alike term for term in different fields of thought and signify the "substantial principle of things."[22] For the alchemist, this was the hidden substance, the stone—incidentally, the alchemist's work was also called "art." If we keep in mind that the circle is also an Aristotelian symbol representing the "movement of pure spirit," then the union of the circle with the square (man's artifact) is also the union of movement with scene, or Craig's ideal theatre, where little or no voice is used. On a private level, this union also represents the union of Craig's parents: Godwin, the architect, builder of scenes, with Ellen Terry, the actress, performer of movement—giving birth to Craig, the creator of the new art of theatre, made of scene and movement.

In addition to these symbols, Craig chose the scales, symbol of balance, as the device for the new art. The scales are also related to the image of death. In Christian iconography it is Saint Michael, the greatest of all angels, who is most often depicted with the scales, the scales of justice: he is the weigher of souls, the benevolent Angel of Death, who leads the righteous to Paradise. The image of a benevolent Death recurs in "The Actor and the Uber-Marionette" where Craig, impressed as he was by the ancient Egyptian art linked to the funerary rites, looked on death as a vitalizing force because it had inspired masterful works of art. He praised the expressivity of the Egyptian statues, inert figures that still exerted a beneficent emotional impact on their beholder and tried to assert Stillness and Death as positive forces of Life. The symbolism of death is closely linked to that of the moon (the agrarian-lunar cycle) and this brings us back to Isis and the Rites of Isis, where Craig discovered one of the models for his über-marionette:[23]

Belief (I)

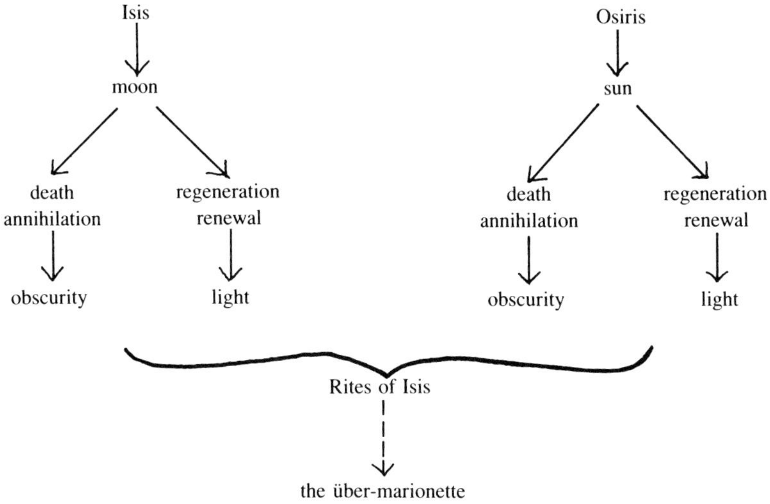

The Rites of Isis, with their reenactment of the death and regeneration of Osiris, celebrate death as a moment of *change,* not of annihilation. In the ideal theatre, the ceremony is a celebration of renewal and life or, in Craig's words in "The Actor and the Uber-Marionette," a "hurrah for existence."[24] (One must remember that by the turn of the century several religious groupings combined different elements of the ancient Egyptian or Greek religions and occult sciences with theatricals—MacGregor Mathers' *Rites of Isis* in Paris in 1899, for example, and Aleister Crowley's *Rites of Eleusis* in London in 1910. Rudolf Steiner, the founder of anthroposophy, wrote mystery plays, and from 1910 on he began to produce them with his believers. But the most famous contemporary artist whose interest in occult sciences shaped the greater part of his work was none other than Yeats [who was also the first to use Craig's screens on a stage]. This was a period when small cults proliferated and there was a renewed interest in the occult sciences, in Buddhist and Hindu beliefs, as well as a keen interest in the arts of hitherto remote civilizations of Africa and the Far East. There is no doubt that Craig was affected by this atmosphere.[25] A curious coincidence may be noted: the three stages established by Craig as leading the actor to the ideal state of artist of the theatre resemble the three degrees of the Masonic order: the entered apprentice, the fellow craft, and the Master Mason, the last being the stage of Revelation, when the secrets of the order are disclosed to the new master.)

Let us look again at some of the correspondences and examine the "union" of the elements, for it was this union that Craig was interested in:

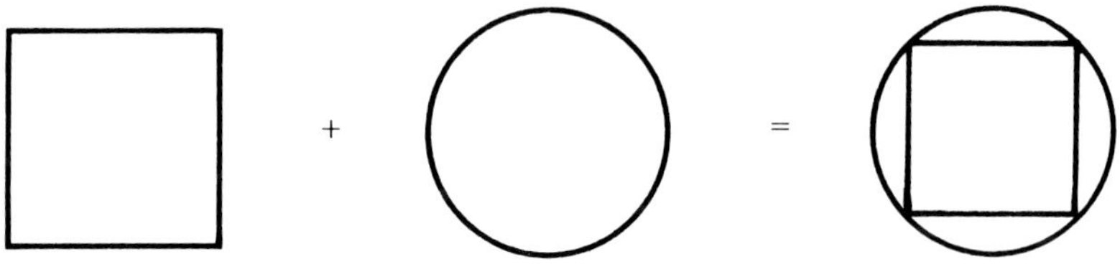

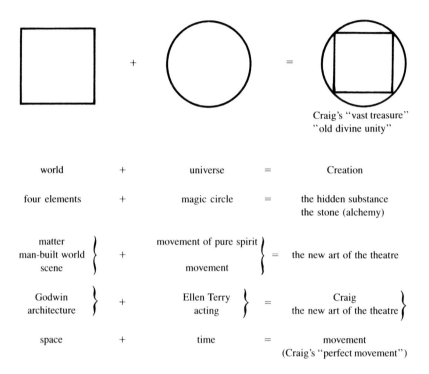

Craig's "vast treasure"
"old divine unity"

world	+	universe	=	Creation
four elements	+	magic circle	=	the hidden substance the stone (alchemy)
matter man-built world scene	+	movement of pure spirit movement	=	the new art of the theatre
Godwin architecture	+	Ellen Terry acting	=	Craig the new art of the theatre
space	+	time	=	movement (Craig's "perfect movement")

Thus, Craig "rediscovered" the macrocosm-microcosm analogy, the harmony of man and universe. On a second reading, the quoted passage from "The Artists of the Theatre of the Future" now seems less obscure.

It is interesting to observe the recurrence of the geometrical symbols in Craig's designs from the period under review, that is from 1905 to 1907. The square—and Craig named his parallelepipeds "cubes," as we have seen—and the circle (or rectangular shapes and curves) are used, for example, in a design for *Macbeth,* act 5, scene 1 (the sleepwalking scene), from 1906 (fig. 12). The stage is divided in two parts by a gigantic pillar; on the right, the straight lines and ascending steps, with a low vaulted door beneath; on the left, curves and a high-arched ceiling. Lady Macbeth is descending the steps, leaving the field of the straight lines (the male element) and moving toward the vaulted door beneath (the female element, this door—womb or cave—being a symbol of secrecy, dark powers, subconscious). Symbolically, Lady Macbeth is the link between the two realms, that of the square and that of the circle. Craig was aware of at least part of this symbolism when he prepared the design: "Her progress is a curve," he wrote, "she seems to come from the past into the present and go away into the future. That part from which she comes I have drawn in precise sharp lines; that part to which she goes is designed with vague and bending lines." [26] A recurrent pattern in Craig's designs is the mandala, which is associated by Jung with the realization of the self. The symmetrical arrangement of space around a central, symbolic element, such as in the forum scene in *Julius Caesar* (1905), has already been suggested by Denis Bablet as one of the characteristic features of the Craigian scene.[27] However, in most of his designs from 1905 to 1909 the mandala pattern is dominant: so it is, to name but a very few, in the woodcut entitled "Che peccato, or La Donna di Zena" (1905) and in the designs for *Caesar and Cleopatra,* act 1, scene 3 (1906), *Cupid and Psyche* (1906), *Macbeth,* act 1, scene 1 (1909), and *Macbeth,* act 2, scene 1 (1909), all published in *Towards a New Theatre* (1913). The same pattern can also be seen in the third mood of *The Steps* (1905), in the floor design. Moreover, the code of symbolic movement for the über-marionette was also based on the square and the circle (straight lines and curved lines).

Was Craig inspired by Vasari and Serlio and their own use of symbols? Vasari, whose *Lives of the Painters* Craig bought in 1906, drew occult and astrological symbols on the walls and ceilings of the Palazzo Vecchio in Florence, the city where Craig settled in 1907 and wrote the two essays. Serlio, whose designs inspired Craig's concept of the kinetic stage, was the disciple of Alberti, who introduced him to the "secret geometry." Craig read Alberti's *L'architettura* (1565), as well as Leonardo da Vinci's *Notebooks,* but most important, he also read Vitruvius' *Ten Books of Architecture,* which inspired the whole Italian Renaissance neoclassical movement. Vitruvius applied his anthropometric theory of proportion to architecture and asserted the supremacy of architecture among arts and sciences. The circle and the square, the two geometrical figures that, according to Vitruvius, perfectly encompass the figure of man, are basic to his theory of proportion. But if this theory established aesthetic norms, it also expressed a metaphysical attitude; as Frances A. Yates wrote, the image of man within the square and the circle was a "statement in symbolic geometry of man's relation to the cosmos." [28] Alberti and Leonardo developed the Vitruvian theory of proportion. According to Alberti, who elaborated its theoretical and methodical aspects, the proportions of the human body—visible incarnations of musical harmony—expressed the connection between the two realms, the celestial and the elemental, the spiritual and the corporeal, the round and

12. The sleepwalking scene from *Macbeth* (1906). From *Towards a New Theatre* (1913). Edward Gordon Craig Estate and Bibliothèque Nationale, Paris.

the square, or the macrocosm and the microcosm. The proportions of a building had to be based on those of the human body, whose proportions reflected those of the music of the spheres; thus, architecture came to embody ideal values. The Vitruvian ground plan of the theatre implied cosmological proportions, based as it was on four equilateral triangles within a circle—a circle identical with the figure of the Zodiac (the Renaissance astrologers used this figure to depict the musical harmony of the stars). Alberti went further than Vitruvius and emphasized the usefulness of the theatre, identifying it with the temple. Thus, art was not only based on "design" but was also the expression of a belief—an attitude that appealed to Craig. It is interesting to note that among Craig's various schemes for an über-marionette theatre building two schemes show a main cube-shaped structure, superposed by two smaller ones. Another scheme, clearly inspired by the Vitruvian plan for a theatre, shows a round, domed building, surrounded by a lower gallery with tall arched entrances. Still another scheme shows an octagonal structure, superposed by a smaller octagonal one, and enclosed on all sides by a lower octagonal gallery; its ground plan shows that the main building, housing the stage and the auditorium, must have been originally a circle: it still has a semicircular stage that occupies half the circle, and a semioctagonal auditorium (fig. 13).[29] Not only were the über-marionette theatre and the kinetic stage, the latter using the "cubes," the product of a careful design, according to the Italian Renaissance spirit, but they also possessed a magic appearance—like the Renaissance marvels or the "thaumaturgike." Thus, in his quest for sense and purpose, Craig took up a tradition handed down by Vitruvius to Alberti, Leonardo, and Serlio, a tradition also brought to life by the Symbolist quest for synthesis and correspondences. His annotations on Serlio's *Libro primo d'architettura* are enlightening. He discovered a similarity between one of Serlio's designs and the form of the protoplasm as it appears in Haeckel's books; that is, he found a correspondence between the form created by the artist's intuition and that of the living matter of plant and animal cells, discovered by science hundreds of years later. Craig also noted down Serlio's belief that the square is the perfect form, being based on the perfection of numbers: ten times ten. A plan of a theatre with the dimensions of a "perfect" stage, calculated according to the correspondence of numbers in time and space, appears in one of Craig's notebooks and can be dated as of 1907.[30]

What emerged for Craig was the discovery of a net of correspondences that gave sense and direction to his life and his work. Geometrical figures, numbers, musical proportions became signs in a newly (re)discovered code that connected and expressed the harmony between man and the universe, between Craig and his parents and the universe. His art bound together the arts in which each of his parents had excelled; it embodied such elements (the circle and the square, spirit and matter, acting and architecture, time and space) that ensured not only its ultimate victory but rendered it indisputably (or so it seemed to Craig) valid: it was the ultimate truth. Craig's belief in these correspondences was also confirmed by all those who turned to the study of the psyche, occult sciences, or ancient religions. On a subconscious level, he was trying to introduce

13. Scheme for a building for the Uber-Marionette International Theatre. From the "Uber-Marions" notebooks. Edward Gordon Craig Estate and Bibliothèque Nationale, Paris.

order and sense into his experience, to find justification in past and present events, and to negate the element of chance. Belief gave him the illusion of control over his life and strengthened his sense of mission (making him perhaps even more uncompromising than before). With all the ideas, projects, dreams, prospects, and expectations that came and went during the years 1904 to 1907, Belief was Craig's stronghold.

This Belief was syncretic; Craig never meant it to be restrictive. It was closer to a state of feeling than to a dogmatic religion—a state of feeling that Craig first experienced when he listened to Bach's *St. Matthew Passion,* a state of feeling that he sought to reproduce and convey through the rituals of his art. Like music, this state of feeling eluded a literal translation into discursive terms, but it could be conveyed by movement. The art that shall spring from movement, Craig said, will also be "the first and final belief of the world."[31] Art and Belief become so entangled in this future creation that they become inseparable; signifier and signified become one. This was already, as Craig himself announced, "something beyond" theatre, "above the Theatre."[32] Belief was a mystical vision of universal correspondences of which man—and Craig—was an integral part. "You will now reveal by means of movement the invisible things," Craig tells the future artist of the future theatre. The "invisible things" are perceived by special faculties, since they are "seen through the eye and not with the eye."[33] The artist, an initiator, is also an officiating priest, and like the highest priests of Re in Heliopolis, "the great seers," he too is a "seer." What is perceived will be disclosed "by the wonderful and divine power of Movement."[34] Craig's vision is of an art that is a ceremony in praise of supernatural, mysterious powers. This is not merely a theatre possessing ceremonial features but a novel creation, beyond theatre, a binding transcendental experience in which one reaches the divine, a mystical experience by which one attains not a knowledge of oneself (as M. M. Siniscalchi believes) but knowledge of Creation and the magic powers that animate it.[35] The performance *was* the Belief. Craig defined his ideal theatre as a "theatre of visions." Nor did he fail to emphasize in his "Note" for *Rosmersholm* that his aim was to show "*the value of the spirit*" (my emphasis), the "unseen forces." The performance embodies and conveys a vision; the spectacle is the vision. Craig did not believe in preaching: the suggestive images that he offered were designed to convey significance, including the mystery of Creation, and "inspire the people to fresh endeavour."[36]

The choice of repertoire for the über-marionette international theatre in Dresden reveals the same approach—included were Flaubert's *Temptation of St. Anthony,* along with *Everyman* and Bunyan's *Pilgrim's Prog-*

ress. Craig's mimo-dramas or masques, so far as one can learn from the existing scenarios and designs, are not explicitly didactic pieces but convey humanistic values. These pieces were supposed to affect the spectator by their use of melodramatic images: not only was the performer manipulated but so was the spectator. The spectacle of hunger in the *Masque of Hunger,* for example, was undoubtedly more eloquent and effective than any long tirade on the subject. Whether it was a ceremonial event, a succession of episodic scenes, or a spectacle built around a plot—like the *Tale of Troy,* for example—Craig offered a carefully designed performance aiming to affect and influence the spectator. The purpose of *Hell and Paradise* was, as we have seen, "to create a Belief": Craig stimulated the spectator's mind by drawing the spectator into witnessing an ordered world, a world not of rewarded virtue and chastised sin but of a self-created goodness. The spectacle was supposed to inspire a state of feeling that would generate a search for goodness, for "heaven in life," for "friendliness—humour—love—ease—peace."

A similar state of feeling was to be created by the kinetic stage. *Motion,* the four-page folder that Craig issued in 1907 in Florence, describes the movement of the architectonic bodies of the kinetic stage without mentioning the bodies (Craig used alternately the terms "movement" and "motion"): the outcome is a pervading sense of mystery and poetic beauty. In an explanatory paragraph Craig points to the union of three arts—architecture, music, and motion—out of which the ideal theatre will be born. The reason he gives for his choice of these specific arts is that their "impersonality" makes them best suited to serve the Religion of Truth—that is, a metaphysical purpose. This Religion of Truth is not destined for an elite but for the whole world; it will spread "from one end of the Earth unto the other." Here we have a theory of art similar in its beneficent effects on performer and audience alike to Appia's Living Art. Both Craig and Appia shared a mystical attitude toward movement and theatre, but whereas Appia believed in man as a source of creativity and celebrated the human performer of movement and the communion of men in art, Craig viewed movement as a symbolic manifestation of the divine and eternal power of Life and chose a man-made instrument to perform it. In the ceremony that celebrates Life, man is not an officiant. Instead of man, Craig first chose man's symbols, the über-marionette, the mask. The kinetic stage without the figure would ultimately exclude man's image altogether, and his role would be limited to that of onlooker, an onlooker who would be submerged and altered by the spectacle.

There is no doubt that Craig intended the kinetic stage to inspire people to a "new endeavour." Indeed, in *Motion,* Craig affirms that it would perform movement for the sake of movement. But the draft for this piece, as it appears in the "Movement" notebook, includes this crossed-out passage: "I can only make signals to you, signs which at once proclaim my—I am tonguetied—and alone. Though if I could speak you would—if I could sing—if my throat were loosed—For the nature of that which I have made and which appear here is different." In spite of Craig's wish to disclose as little as possible about his invention and the Belief, the following passage was left intact (and may indeed only look "poetical"): "I can only ask you for your gracious and affectionate attention—for your silence—and for your permissive eyes to travel with what is before you, the stage designs. Ascend and descend with these forms—to mount upon them fold and unfold with these shapes. Cleave the Darkness with the Light—or faint and ascend with the mists—In silence and without desire for words, move—incessantly move—even as all things since the Beginning have moved—advancing from the First False Dawn until the dusk of this the Last Hour."[37] The artist/initiator invites the reader/beholder to undertake a series of actions whose purpose is discovery; the spiritual experience that translates a cosmic feeling is referred to in explicit symbolic terms, Light and Darkness, although these are at the same time accurate technical terms, because light is indicated in the stage designs by diagonal lines; the beholder performs the steps leading to his discovery—a ritual—by movement (movement of eyes, of spirit); the revelation cannot be translated into discursive terms, and Craig's designs are only "signals" and "signs."

It was not long after he wrote *Motion* that Craig made this entry in the "Movement" notebook:

<table><tr><td>That is what I would</td><td>translate
recreate</td><td>by the</td><td>means
symbols</td><td>of this new art—</td></tr></table>

The new Light—the new Day—Night—earth Life—the old Love.[38]

The mysteries of Creation: in the theatre-temple, it is the drama of the entire Creation that is now recreated.

After Craig became aware of the mystical nature of his visions, he ceased to publish them, and their theistic import was never disclosed while he lived. It was only in 1970, four years after Craig's death, that two of his "illuminations" were made public by Arnold Rood.[39] In 1908, the year of his first "illumination," Craig knew that the stage of Interpretation was far from being implemented in the theatre and that the stage of Revelation was even further away. He was moved by a messianic utopianism, believing with many other artists in what Roy Pascal calls "the universality of the spirit and of art as its most tangible expression."[40] The artist-redeemer suffered because "the old divine unity, the divine square, the peerless circle of our nature has been ruthlessly broken by our moods, and no longer can instinct design the square or draw the circle on the grey wall before it," as he wrote in "The Artists of the Theatre of the Future."[41] And so he dreamed of the day when the Religion of Truth would restore the world to an ideal, pre-Fall state of "friendliness—humour—love—ease—peace," affirming the triumph of Life. "A Belief full of Beauty." No more a quest, but a Revelation.

≻ *Part III* ≺

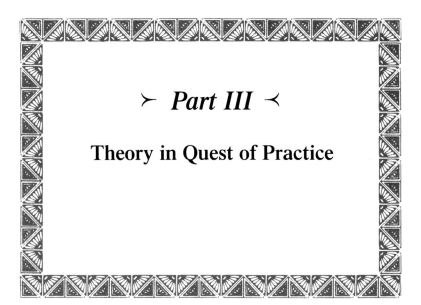

Theory in Quest of Practice

≻ 11 ≺

The Uber-Marionette International Theatre

The three years that followed Craig's departure from England established him as a dominant figure in the theatre world. His travels and his exhibitions, as well as his abortive but numerous projects, brought him fame as a "reformer." Though he was disappointed in his hopes of getting a theatre of his own where he could have complete control over his productions, he promulgated his views in published essays and in his designs. Duse's *Rosmersholm,* in which Craig imposed his own interpretation of the drama by means of his unusual settings, did nothing to launch him as a stage director.

Craig also had in mind a School for the Art of the Theatre and he hoped to accomplish now what could not have been done earlier in London. He had written to Martin Shaw in 1904: "I feel so strongly about the school that I am of all people *the* one person to create such a place & from it the theatre. I can tell you that I've just finished *re*writing 'the School Introduction & Scheme': & have got some shape into it." And he added: "What I mean by the THEATRE—but I mean something which has not been seen yet & has not been dreamed of except by me— . . . You see, I can't explain, I can only *do* it."[1] The school was to be opened under the auspices of an International Art Theatre Society. In his "Notes and Plans" for the school and the Art Theatre Society, compiled between 1904 and 1906, Craig mentions twelve theatres to be built in twelve different countries or cities; these theatres would have been the first seeds from which the new art of the theatre would simultaneously grow and develop. Such a colossal enterprise was of public interest, Craig argued in his notes, because the theatre was an educational and spiritual force.[2] This grandiose project fell through, though Craig continued to think about a school on a more modest scale.

By the beginning of 1907, Craig had decided to devote all his efforts to one project only, the Uber-Marionette International Theatre. The original project for this theatre took shape in 1905. An international committee of writers, artists, and architects, with Kessler as its president, was to sponsor it. Kessler, having in mind the German system of theatre patronage or support by enrolled members, suggested establishing the theatre as a stock company and issuing a prospectus "setting out expenses," with shares of £100, £50, and £5, to be offered by specially appointed agents in Berlin, London, and New York.[3] To this end, he interested several businessmen in the project, and they formed a provisional committee. The home city of the theatre was to be Dresden, which had a long and respectable tradition of cultural life. Craig, for all his inclination to secrecy, mentions Dresden many times in the "Uber-Marions" notebooks as the city where the theatre was to be built and opened in May 1906. His code name for the chief investor or the representative of the group of businessmen and potential backers was "the Dresdenman." Craig sent a copy of *The Art of the Theatre* to this "Dresdenman" as soon as it was published.[4]

The Uber-Marionette International Theatre was a venture that apparently did not pose any threat to the established, regular theatre and also seemed to have all the novelty that could make it a commercially successful enterprise. (The threat to the actor materialized only with the publication of his essay "The Actor and the Uber-Marionette" in 1908.) The fact that it had the moral support of a group of aesthetes was probably not as important for the businessmen as the fact that it was headed by a flamboyant personality, the son of England's most famous actress. Moreover, Craig had already established himself as an innovative artist and had been introduced by Isadora Duncan into artistic, intellectual, and fashionable circles all over Europe. The Uber-Marionette International Theatre could after all have been a very interesting financial investment, if only its principal actor—the über-marionette—had been ready in time for public exposure.

The project was prepared by Craig in minute detail, for it was to be the sign and signal of the third stage of the theatre, that of Creation and Revelation, but he could not seem to complete a satisfactory über-marionette in time. The idea of the project remained with Craig in spite of setbacks—the withdrawal of the businessmen, estrangement from Isadora, and the eventual loss of her financial support. Craig dedicated the best of his mature years to this project. Gradually, hopes of fulfillment faded, and before the First World War, Craig's interests were in his school and a smaller theatre at the Arena Goldoni in Florence—both of which were intended to pave the way for the über-marionette. But in 1905, when the idea of the über-marionette was fresh and the newly invented instrument was Craig's main concern, the project was real and possible. Craig, in a letter in October 1905 to Martin Shaw, who had suggested a new common production in London, explained that all his efforts were now directed toward one goal, the über-marionette theatre, and he proposed that Shaw should take over the musical direction of the new theatre.[5]

Craig's plan was to create a traveling theatre that would either have its own building in different cities all over the world or would use its own portable wooden construction. He even considered the possibility of traveling with only the figures, the sets, the costumes, and some of the technical staff. Although Craig spoke of entrusting the building of the theatre to Alfred Messel, he prepared several tentative plans of the building and its surroundings and also built a model. He made detailed plans of the stage with its adaptable proscenium and electric bridges and all its equipment. He also drew up lists of properties and costumes, even indicating style and fabric. The electrical equipment would have used the latest technical innovations. A detailed list of the artistic, technical, and administrative staff was made, and Craig also estimated the cost of productions, supplies, fittings, insurance, and travel expenses. All these plans certainly do not look like those of an impractical man.

The theatre was to open in Dresden in May 1906, and Craig should have started the preparations for three productions by December 1905.[6] Craig had several possible repertoires in mind. A first list included three revivals of London productions (*The Masque of Love, Dido and Aeneas,* and *Bethlehem*), *The Temptation of St. Anthony, The Intruder* or *Intérieur, Everyman,* and a mystery play. A second list added Purcell's *Fairy Queen.* A third list proposed three groups of productions: (*a*) *Faust, Part II, Macbeth, The Temptation of St. Anthony, Everyman, Hippolytus* or *The Bacchae, Oedipus Rex, Bethlehem* or a "religious play"; (*b*) operatic works: *Dido and Aeneas, The Masque of Love, The Pilgrim's Progress;* (*c*) dramatized tales taken from *The Arabian Nights,* Boccaccio, Greek mythology, or the dramatization of a *cause célèbre, The Case of the Artist vs. the Critic (Whistler vs. Ruskin).* All of the proposed productions belonged to a genre that Craig considered "poetic drama." The emphasis was on metaphysical subjects expressed through music and movement.

It is not clear why Craig did not proceed with these preparations; instead, in December 1905 he went to Amsterdam, and during the first months of 1906 he was on tour with Isadora and Martin Shaw. Still to be discovered are the details of why the whole scheme collapsed in March 1906, after Craig had a meeting with the businessmen. It is very probable that in spite of his overconfidence in the über-marionette, Craig failed to find a suitable puppet in time and became aware that he had to make experimental ones first.

In 1907 Craig still believed that his experiments with his newly invented instrument for movement would soon be finished and that it would not be long before he would be able to open the Uber-Marionette International Theatre. In 1906 he had been temporarily distracted by work on *Rosmersholm,* and after the final unpleasant meeting with Duse in Nice in February 1907, he went to Florence, where he met Martin Shaw. More and more, Florence seemed to him the ideal place to settle down, and that May he returned, this time to stay. Florence, with its mild weather and moderate cost of living, offered Craig a new promise of freedom for concentrated work, away from the social and financial obligations of Berlin, and away from Isadora, whom he now considered an emotional burden and an obstacle to his artistic development. Florence was well off the circuit of Isadora's tours, yet not isolated. Though he had no intention of severing all ties with Isadora, he wanted to put an end to his hectic life and devote all his time to his project. The Dresden affair was a missed opportunity that had caught him unprepared. Now, thanks to Isadora's promise of financial support, he had a second chance to see the über-marionette theatre come to life, if only he kept working at it. Craig thought he might tour with Isadora, alternating his über-marionette productions with her dance recitals—both bringing to the world their new art of movement. He had tried to get a contract drawn up before leaving Heidelberg and coming to Florence, but without success. As a close examination both of Isadora's schedule between 1904 and 1907 and of the terms of the contract shows, this contract would not have imposed more duties on her than she actually had, but Isadora's sister Elizabeth, who directed her school, opposed it as a legal bond that might have deprived the school of Isadora's support.[7] Nor was Craig even certain of Isadora's good will after they quarreled in Florence in September 1907. She continued to send him money at least until the end of the year, but their estrangement ended the project of the Uber-Marionette International Theatre.

Henceforth, Craig had to count on his own resources to finance his experiments, though Ellen Terry helped to cover Craig's living expenses and those of his family as long as she lived. As his friend William Rothenstein recognized, "people are very prejudiced against him and what he cares for."[8]

≻ 12 ≺

Experiments

Within a month of taking up residence in Florence, Craig had acquired a small staff of craftsmen and was at work on a stage model. By December 1907, the stage model was finished and figures had been made according to Craig's designs. Craig summarized his progress in a letter to Martin Shaw:

> I am not awfully rich as I have stopped playing impresario for a bit (for 6 months) & turned to my work. first time for 3 years. And I've had a good 6 months. made 24 etchings—built a theatre in a new villa. . . . 6 feet opening, 12 feet full length, 8 feet deep, and 12 feet high. 3 prosceniums & altogether a daisy. Scene—(not scenes) & light are being added. Figures made. about 30. more follow. and although there is nothing wonderful about it, it is the best there is in Europe. I send you a Note on Scene, it will explain some of what I am making to take the place of scenery. I follow the nobler of the old masters in making this attempt—they said scenery was a farce—& it is one I enjoyed but one must march forwards—head high & the old banner in tight hand.
>
> The Theatre took 3 months to build—wood and canvas. Very neat Italian workers—& a Californian as my assistant—6 workers in all—
>
> . . . Miss Duncan came but has gone on tour—has to for her school which she is enlarging. Oh lor! I have no one who helps finance this affair but it seems less necessary than I had thought. It's a spurt of the old independent Purcell time—only alone—alone—alas! Well, you have your path and it ought to be full of flowers.
>
> I shall try to take my theatre first to Munchen—second to Paris. I have

> just issued a portfolio of etchings—only 30 sets—£16. "If you know anyone"—old song.
>
> . . . I am having one of the hardest but best times in my life. My work is on me strong!!!
>
> . . . I may be heard of again as a scene designer soon but I rather wish to avoid that ditch if possible.[1]

The "nobler of the old masters" whom Craig had followed was Serlio. Serlio's importance for Craig lay not only in the technical details he provided, which inspired Craig's vision of a kinetic stage and indirectly that of "scene" or the screens, but also in his spiritual approach to his art. As one of Alberti's disciples, Serlio also believed in the sacredness and symbolism of numbers and the "right proportions" that link man with the universe. Serlio looked on architecture not as a craft but as a sacred art; geometry, the pure creation of the spirit, was the source of beauty, a "divine demonstration"—and this was also Craig's definition of it in the first issue of *The Mask,* published in 1908. By following the old master and initiator, Craig was connecting his invention to the wider spheres of universal creation. In Florence, Craig had also learned the technique of etching from Stephen Haweis, and this newly discovered medium seemed to him the most appropriate for conveying his vision of a new stage that, according to his conviction, marked the fifth phase in the development of the stage since its early beginnings.[2]

The architectonic bodies that Craig imagined for his kinetic stage took on—at first for the sake of his experiments—the more practical form of *screens.* These were easily manipulated screens of different sizes, widths, and lengths, usable alone or in combinations—double-jointed folding screens, painted in monochrome. The screens made possible the unfolding of the performance without the usual interruptions for scene changes, and they also allowed the creation of multiple locales, including curves, with one set only. "The Thousand Scenes in one Scene," as Craig called them, were all the more flexible because they were of a neutral color that could be changed simply by colored lights. The screens seemed best suited for the poetic drama. Craig applied for a patent on the screens in England in 1910, then in France, Italy, Germany, and the United States. They were used for the first time on a full-size stage on 12 January 1911 at the Abbey Theatre in Dublin; the plays were Lady Gregory's the *Deliverer* and *The Hour Glass* by Craig's old friend and supporter, W. B. Yeats.[3] During the years that followed, Craig devoted much of his time to the problems of lighting, since light alone could endow the scene with life, movement, and character. He also experimented with natural light. The most sophisticated of his stage models, Model A, was completed in 1921, and it used screens, props, and an elaborate lighting system. The proportions of the stage models built by Craig up to the start of the war were very different from those in his designs: the height of the opening of the stage was lower and its width greater. The stage was expanded horizontally instead of vertically; this way, it became more manageable and allowed the figures and the screens to be manipulated more easily.

Craig's experiments with different puppets began soon after he arrived in Florence. Several months later, when he was interviewed by Francis Cotton of the *Washington Post,* Craig demonstrated what Cotton describes as "a very impressive creature, evidently inspired by an Egyptian bas relief. It was quite half the size of life and appeared to be striding formidably along its platform." Its movements struck Cotton as very skillful:

> On pulling a series of strings many accomplishments declared themselves—a skinny arm was extended as if to summon an imaginary ghost, then the finger opened quickly as if to grasp a victory and finally the left hand felt for the hip as if to swing the scabbard within reach before the clash of the charges. And these were beautiful, rhythmical gestures, such as hardly an actor of our day commands.
>
> Mr. Craig explained that the torso moved, and also the missing head, but that the whole thing was too complicated and had ceased to interest him. In the main the new puppets will have no individual gestures, though, of course, they may be moved readily about the stage.[4]

Craig was only beginning his long search for a suitable figure for the über-marionette theatre. Besides the round figure, he also used flat figures of all sizes, made of thin boards and defined by their draped costume; he used these figures on the stage model that he showed to Cotton. In order to give the impression of space and depth, especially for the crowd scenes, Craig reduced the size of the figures or used "shadows"—a technique that he discusses in the "Über-Marions" notebooks. The short performances that Cotton saw used no spoken text; he noted, however, that for *Romeo and Juliet* "an argument will be read as a concession to the unimaginative, after which no word will be spoken." Everything depended on the expressive power of movement, form, and light: "Each [of the figures] had a bold and expressive silhouette—a characteristic pose that the puppet holds for an entire act. They were boldly and simply scored with the chisel—affording splendid lines of delineating shadow when the puppet is swept by the strong side light."[5] Cotton was also impressed by Craig's use of light from projectors (though without completely discarding the footlights) and by his different devices for color and chiaroscuro.

Unlike the stage models he built, many of the puppets that Craig designed and had made are still in existence in different collections, such as two round puppets—two Roman actors—and several flat figures made of cardboard and wood, which he made in 1907.[6] They came in different sizes, made of cardboard, wood, metal, or plaster, with costumes made of fabric, paper, or metal. These were articulated puppets, with few fixed movements of the limbs, manipulated by strings underneath. Puppets for the stage models were scaled down to fit; the proportions of the puppet to the screens of the stage models were generally 1 : 6, sometimes 1 : 12 (incidentally, 6 was one of Vitruvius's perfect numbers). After several years of experimentation and study of the puppets in his own collection and those made according to his designs, Craig came to prefer flat figures, usually made of cardboard, with only one or two movable limbs; these figures, later known as the "black figures" because Craig used them for his prints, were very easily manipulated, yet, like the mask, very expressive.

It was in 1908, while Craig was working on his experiments with the stage models and the figures, that Stanislavsky, acting on Isadora's suggestion, invited Craig to mount a production at the Moscow Art Theatre. *Hamlet* was decided on. The story of this now-famous production has been presented in its various aspects by Edward Craig, Bablet, Marotti, Claudine Amiard-Chevrel, and Christopher Innes, and by Laurence Senelick, who has become the expert on this subject. According to Amiard-Chevrel, who has dwelt on the atmosphere and the "inner politics" at the Moscow Art Theatre during the period preceding Craig's arrival in Moscow, Craig's invitation from Stanislavsky came at a time when the latter's position in the theatre was precarious; moreover, he was then preoccupied by what would later become his "system" of acting.[7] Craig's success or failure was to be regarded by the board of directors, and especially by Nemirovich-Danchenko, as Stanislavsky's personal merit or fault; Stanislavsky's own future as a director of the theatre was at stake. Thus, quite apart from the importance of the production as an artistic venture, for Stanislavsky it was a personal venture, which had to be a success.

In his letter to Stanislavsky of 10 July 1908, Craig introduced himself as the Artist par excellence: for him, Art was a game, he said, and he invited the actors of the Moscow Art Theatre to play the game with him.[8] For all those involved, this was certainly a "hide and seek" game. Craig kept coming and going, and his ideas changed frequently; he was the type of director, not uncommon nowadays, who expected the actor to invent along the lines he provided, and would then proceed to cut the actor's creation and polish and fashion the final product. Craig expected the actors of the Moscow Art Theatre to embody his ideal of a creative actor; unfortunately for all concerned, they were only good performers, who, furthermore, had been trained in an altogether different style of acting, more akin to Craig's hated Realism than to his own. Craig's interest in *Hamlet* was, of course, not simply professional: on a personal level, this production was another subconscious attempt to exorcise his demons. And on the professional level, this was not only another interpretation of a literary play—a challenge in itself—but also an interesting experiment, an opportunity to test some new ideas concerning movement and voice and examine their implications as they were performed by figures and by living performers. The production of *Hamlet* gave Craig the opportunity to work "under the conditions which are today offered us," as he wrote—which meant that, as in London in 1903, he was to direct professional (and not so great) actors. It was this encounter that led him to a more thorough evaluation of the different means by which the existing actor might turn his body into an instrument for movement. For *Hamlet,* Craig had to find new elements that would complete and enrich his theory. The production itself was an experiment, this time with living figures. Unfortunately, Craig did not dedicate all his efforts to this task. He made a clear-cut distinction between his research, which included the experiments using man-made instruments for movement, and the work on the production, where Craig used the actor. Not only did his work in Florence prevent him from becoming more deeply involved in the Moscow experiment—*The Mask* was already being issued and this also kept him away—but it also provided him with a most welcome ivory tower where he could escape all the inconveniences, skirmishes, and wearisome details that are generally part of the director's experience before each new production.

The production of *Hamlet* took the better part of four years, owing to the rivalry between Stanislavsky and Nemirovich-Danchenko, Stanislavsky's illness during the summer of 1910, the professional training of the actors, and, not least, Craig's delays. Craig had expected to have pliable actors and complete control over the production. Stanislavsky wanted, more than anything, a successful production—meaning, that is, a production that would immediately please the public. Stanislavsky always thought—and this is made quite clear in his autobiography, *My Life in Art*—that a favorable reaction affirmed the value of his work; an adverse reaction would lead him to doubt the validity of his principles and system, because his touchstone was a psychological "truth" that he believed he shared with the larger public. Craig could not have been more different: he believed that the taste of the public had to be shaped, and he did not hesitate to impose his own artistic standards. Thus Stanislavsky was forever fearful of going too far; he kept trying to moderate Craig's "demands," temper his enthusiasm, override his suggestions, and thwart his ideas, warning him that he might "repulse" the public.[9]

At the beginning of his work in Moscow, Craig feigned modesty, though he had high hopes for this production. In a conversation with one of the actors of the Moscow Art Theatre, Ivan Mosqvin, which he reported in his diary, he said:

> I added that I wanted to find a new land for a new fresh purpose—for a new race—for the true race of the actor; and if this true race is ever to appear it must appear as a new race of beings, not as "actor"—not as "artist" even—Even as the idea of becoming a priest was that of becoming a new and greater, finer being than all others. So the actor of the future.
>
> And my tribute to the theatre will be *to have begun the search for this new land* in which the new actor may live and give birth to his power. Scenery and such things take up 3/4 of the time, 3/4 of the recourses of each theatre. The actor cannot develop. His mind is obliged to shift with every shifting of the scenery—and what a variety of artificial, hypocritical places he has to shift his nature to dwell in. The Shakespearean scenery, the modern realistic scenery, the Romantic scenery, the bad scenery—the painted heart of an artificial panorama. He is asked *to believe in* all this at once. He is asked to develop his art under these shifting and gross conditions. His art is something he is never permitted to reach to. He is imprisoned in a stranger's land, Shakespeare, Moliere & Tchekov—his jailors.[10]

As if conventional scenery were the real impediment to the emergence of the actor "à la Craig"! In this futile attempt to please the actor, Craig went so far as to claim that his only contribution to the modern theatre was the creation of a new environment, the screens, meant to facilitate the actor's "art"—an art whose existence Craig had publicly denied (his two essays on the actor had already appeared in *The Mask*). No wonder that the Moscow actors often found him inconsistent. Nonetheless, Craig's basic attitude to the actor is made clear: he does not consider it his task to teach the actor a system of acting.

Craig's so-called belief in the actor's "art" was also belied by his own "game": He brought along his own stage models with screens and figures and had a scale model of the actual stage built in Moscow. He explained his idea in detail, showed the movements and blocking by first working with the stage models and the figures. Then the actors were expected not only to copy these movements but to elaborate on them, to "invent," and Craig would correct and shape their invention. He certainly did not believe that acting should be motivated by the actor's emotional and psychological impulse.

In order to develop his vision of movement, Craig had to measure his views on acting against well-defined principles of psychological truth and reality. By observing Stanislavsky's system at work, Craig found himself also dealing with psychology, only this time it was not the psychology of the character but that of the actor. He arrived, not unexpectedly, at some conclusions that only reinforced his aesthetic approach. Taking up William Archer's idea, he wrote in his diary: "The actor hates the natural. That is why he plays the Role of the stage. He loves the disguise, the mask."[11] Not only did Craig possess a keen sense of observation, but he was himself an actor and he loved masks and disguises. He made a clear distinction between real (lived-through) experience and aesthetic experience, the latter being based on a fictitious element. Therefore, he believed, the aesthetic convention the "game" of the theatre was based on had to be recognized for what it was: a convention. To be "natural" in acting was a fake (the dupe being the public, not the actor).

Few of Craig's ideas seemed to suit the actors' and Stanislavsky's expectations. Wilde had written: "In point of fact, there is no such thing as Shakespeare's Hamlet. If Hamlet has something of the definiteness of a work of art, he has also all the obscurity that belongs to life. There are as many Hamlets as there are melancholies."[12] Craig made his melancholy Hamlet's. The key to Craig's interpretation was his belief that all the events at the Court were seen through the eyes of Hamlet and have to be rendered as such: a private vision that distorts reality. Craig got nowhere in his attempts to develop this vision, either because of Stanislavsky's subtle opposition, the technical impediments, or the actors' inability to carry out his wishes. For example, he wanted to use a marionette as Hamlet's double and also proposed the use of tiny marionettes representing Rosencrantz and Guildenstern—for parody and distancing. This was evidently not carried out; nor did Stanislavsky accept Craig's idea of presenting the Ghost as a hallucination.[13] The only scene that bore Craig's stamp was the court scene, where a golden cloth cloak, the cloak of corruption, enveloped the King, the Queen, and their subjects—here again Craig turned the actor into an organic, but symbolic, element of the scenery, as he had done in *Acis and Galatea*. Even the screens could not be moved as easily and smoothly as they had been at the Abbey Theatre, and the curtain had to be lowered for each change of scene.

What Craig aimed at, and what would have been achieved not only by the acting but also by the movable screens, was a *symbolic rhythm* from the beginning to the end of the performance. This rhythm should have been a reflection of Hamlet's state of mind and would have changed accordingly; for example, it would have become swifter when he felt that people or events were too swift, and slower when he felt that they were slow. This meant a distortion of the shape and duration of everyday, or "natural," movement. As we have seen, one of Isadora's achievements that Craig admired was her interpretation of time; this often differed from that of the composer whose music she used and was the result of her own notions of order, frequency, and duration. By manipulating time—that is, the duration imposed by music—she was expressing her own interpretation of experience, an experience suggested by music. Craig planned to do the same thing in his production of *Hamlet.* He wanted to convey his own interpretation of Hamlet's ordeal not by a realistic production but through a special use of movement, unobstructed by changes of scene, and voice—that is, by manipulating time and, indirectly, creating mood. He believed that this could be accomplished by speeding up the delivery and by few and simple movements. (He intended, in addition, to use background music to inspire the actors while they were working on the preparation of their roles, believing that adequate music could convey to the actor both meaning and rhythm, but Stanislavsky wanted the music to come "from within.") As Craig explained in a letter to Haldane MacFall, Hamlet was a strong man who achieved what he set out to do, a man whose spirit is "courage." Therefore, speech should speed "like lightning," then slow down and finally pause before an action (Craig even made a little sketch indicating the progression of speech before an action, slowing down, "then—hit." He also noted that this technique could actually help the audience by preventing the weariness that a long text invariably causes.)[14] Nothing of this was carried out by Stanislavsky, who supervised the rehearsals and actually shaped the acting style.

By May 1909 Craig had thrown up the struggle and had given Stanislavsky carte blanche to do with the actors as he wished—while he was away. The rest of the collaboration was punctuated by unpleasant misunderstandings, many of them concerning Craig's fees and expenses. Craig felt betrayed, and his reputation as "hard to work with" grew stronger. Stanislavsky's *Hamlet,* with Craig's screens, lighting, and costumes, and with some of Craig's ideas but without his coherent vision, opened in Moscow on 5 January 1912.

Florence was a retreat that was open to all winds. What had been Craig's chief reason for staying there—his experiments—had by 1909 become only one of many activities. Besides his trips to Moscow, he continued to write for The *Mask,* he made a new stage model for the screens and new figures, and as always, he planned new projects for impossible productions.[15] Craig always lost patience with serious commitments, and now, with *Hamlet* more or less out of his hands, he felt that he was wasting precious time. He wrote in his diary on 18 September 1909: "I want time to study the theatre. I do not want to waste time producing plays. For that is vanity—expensive—unsatisfying—*comic.*

I know *something* about my art after 20 years study—I want to know more—I want to know enough to be of use to those who can do more. I want to leave behind me the seeds of the art—for it does not yet exist—and such seeds are not to be discovered in a moment." [16] His desire to uncover the secrets of what he believed to be a long-lost art and restore it to its greatness and his belief in the theatre as the source of spiritual salvation to man had been present in his mind when he first went to Moscow in 1908: "If I loved anything but a theatre which must obliterate the theatre, I would stay here for ever and do my dull best—but I must do my gambling *worst*—must risk all and again all to drag the soul of the theatre out of its cursed body and force it of all trials and trappings—their—theirs—others!!" [17] But Craig was forever restless, and whether in Moscow or Florence, he was always sure that he was working in the worst conditions: in Moscow he lacked moral support, and in Florence financial support. Writing was thus more and more not simply a way for Craig to formulate and propagate his views but also a kind of evasion of the difficulties he encountered in his experimental work. It was not long before he came to be known mostly as a theorist, while Reinhardt, who borrowed his ideas, came to be known as the practical man. Craig himself realized this. Thus, soon after he had agreed to produce *Hamlet* in Moscow—apparently in spite of his intention not to "waste time producing plays"—he announced in *The Mask* his readiness to work in the existing theatre in order to "raise the standard of the work" and for the purpose of "bettering the artificiality of the theatre." [18]

Though *Hamlet* still took much of his time and his efforts in 1910 and 1911, Craig's experiments in Florence continued. To Ellen Terry he wrote: "We have made a marionette here in Florence which is perhaps the best in Europe. It is large—it is touching, it moves us—we hold the strings. It is not surprising but it is tender and proud in its whole bearing. I am very contented with it. Now we will make further experiments. The Arena [Goldoni] begins to look fresh and beautiful. Everyone works well and is happy. That is much." [19] Craig's experiments were, however, far from being conclusive. He was trying to discover in the different uses of materials (puppets, elements of scene, and lighting) not only expressivity but also a recurring pattern that might indicate the existence of a law of expressivity and thereby lay the foundations of the art of the theatre. By 1911 he thought he had made enough progress regarding movement and scene but not voice: "Movement. Scene. Voice. The Drama is made of that. The first two I have mastered and I know the principles of each. The voice now. The improvisers who speak according to *rules*—noble *rules*—sound and *sense*, who move according to the same rules, action and expression. These improvisations of action, scene and voice—then to be recorded on paper. Ecco!—drama. fresh born instead of dry and old."[20]

This enthusiasm was premature and the experiments went on. The rules he searched for were to serve the actor during the stage of Interpretation, indicating the lines along which action could be carried out in a newly created drama—with no need of a playwright—as in the commedia dell'arte. But despite the intensity of his vision, Craig's experiments lacked assiduity, direction, and method. Preoccupied as he was by his other activities—projects for future productions, articles for *The Mask,* and *Hamlet*—he carried out his experiments, including small-scale productions with figures and the stage models, not systematically but by fits of inspiration. What Craig lacked was not so much self-discipline as a suitable framework, a framework that could be provided by a team and a school of his own, and he was well aware of it. Indeed, when Jacques Rouché, the director of the Théâtre des Arts in Paris, in 1910 asked him to produce *Hamlet* in Paris, Craig refused; he would rather have turned Rouché's theatre into a school first.[21]

In 1912 in London, Elena Meo, after many weeks of unabated effort pursuing various possibilities, got a solid promise of financial support for a School for the Art of the Theatre from Lord Howard de Walden. Craig declared the school open at the Arena Goldoni, in Florence, on 27 February 1913, Ellen Terry's birthday. There were thirteen students and the curriculum was ambitious. The subjects of study, as enumerated by Ernest Marriott, one of the students, were: "Gymnastics, Music, Voice training, Scene designing and painting, Costume designing and making, Modelling, Fencing, Dancing, Mimodrama, Improvisation, Lighting Theory, History of the Theatre, Marionette designing, making and performing, Stage model making—all of which are part and parcel of *Stage* Managing."[22] As Craig had written in 1911, the school was a "School of Experiment" that would help the students to develop their creative faculty; moreover, he conceived the school as a sort of "think tank," which could provide the manager of a theatre with a mise en scène for the play he wanted to produce.[23] As Edward Craig points out, the students studied movement, dance, mime, light, screens, marionettes, and masks. "Studied" in the sense of experimenting, for they worked with stage models, screens, figures, and masks and even built an eight-foot-high figure.[24] They also built a model for the *St. Matthew Passion,* embodying several locales.

The school provided Craig with a rare opportunity for testing his ideas on movement, scene, and voice by carrying out several simultaneous experiments, helped as he was by a group of enthusiastic and gifted young people. Unfortunately, the war put an end to this experimentation, and the school closed on 5 August 1914, never to reopen. The Arena Goldoni was requisitioned in December 1916, and Craig left for Rome, then settled down in 1917 in Rapallo, near Genoa.

≻ 13 ≺

On the Actor and the Uber-Marionette

Craig's writing went hand in hand with his experiments. His "Letter to Ellen Terry," written shortly after "The Artists of the Theatre of the Future" and "The Actor and the Uber-Marionette," on 18 March 1907, and published a year later in *The Mask,* focuses on the problem of acting without bringing the über-marionette into discussion.[1] Here Craig claims again that acting can never be taught, since it is a gift from nature to a very few "great" actors; they alone are able to improvise on an idea by using movement, scene, and voice. The appropriate acting style should be symbolic, not realistic, for only the symbolic can best create and communicate a vision, or so Craig believed. But not only Realism is dismissed here: so is the playwright and his contribution to the theatrical creation, the written text of the play. The purpose of his "Letter to Ellen Terry" was not only to expose the rarity of "good" acting but also to explain the urgent need to reform the theatre. Two obstacles barred Craig from freely proceeding with this reform: the actor's "personality" (or, more precisely, the actor's belief in his own creative powers) and the growing influence of Realism in acting.

Craig's fight against Realism had begun long before, with his London productions, his stage designs, his book *The Art of the Theatre,* his work on Duse's *Rosmersholm* and his "Note" in the program of this play. He was fighting a dragon whose feats he sometimes admired because he could not deny their sensual appeal. Now he decided to attack this dragon on an international scale. As Craig wrote, for a reform to be effective it must be undertaken simultaneously in several parts of the world.[2] This he intended to achieve by reaching a growing number of potential supporters through his organ, *The Mask,* which began to appear in 1908. According to the "Uber-Marions" notebooks, Craig conceived the idea of issuing a theatre journal on 7 August 1905, in Zurich, during a short respite from his skirmishes with his critics in Berlin. "No one likes to be attacked by a wild animal," he wrote. No one likes to be attacked by a tame bull even—No one likes to be attacked by a fellow man." He went on to elaborate this idea in a short tale about Craig the Artist, whose ideas were attacked by a blind worm. It is this piece of therapeutic writing in which Craig took visible pleasure that led, by a process of association, to the idea of issuing a theatre journal, to be called "The Mask." By 1905 there were two such journals in Berlin, *Das Theater,* first issued in 1903, and *Die Schaubühne,* which began to appear in 1905. Craig intended his journal to reach an international audience and to be of a high standard, rather along the lines of *The Studio:* "a Book to interpret and Instruct, and Fascinate, not an advertisement sheet." The journal was to be addressed to artists, actors, musicians, playwrights, and amateurs.

The Mask, as it was to be called, did not appear in Berlin in 1905, as Craig planned, but three years later, in Florence. Despite financial problems it survived until 1929. Under the cover of *The Mask* and of his many pseudonyms, used in order to create the illusion of a journal that was not the mouthpiece of one person but of a community of artists, Craig in turn attacked.[3] Verbal expression, discarded by Craig in the theatre, now became a persuasive weapon. The journal also expressed Craig's growing interest in the history of the arts of the spectacle: the past suddenly became, in Craig's hands, a powerful ally. The impressive argumentative power of past achievements, carefully brought to light by the editor John Semar—none other than Craig—was implicitly used to add weight to Craig's own arguments. Besides, the past and present conditions of the theatrical enterprise—the moral, social, economic, political, and religious context, as well as acting styles and the actor's personality—were part of Craig's research material. For Craig was searching for recurrent patterns that would explain the emergence of great works of art; he emphasized the need to discover such "laws," since they were "thc truths which are the basis of all things."[4] One pattern that he singled out very early in his search was Belief, the emotional power that could not only hold a community together but also inspire brilliant achievements in art. Historical evidence, even if arbitrarily selected, both inspired and supported Craig's ideas.

In 1908 Craig launched his campaign against Realism in *The Mask* under the guise of an "international symposium" on "Realism and the

Actor." Like William Archer, who had based his *Masks or Faces* in 1888 on a questionnaire submitted to actors, or like Jules Huret's *Enquête sur l'évolution littéraire* in 1891, Craig interviewed many of the leading contemporary artists. His purpose was to bring a heightened awareness of the dangerous expansion of Realism and, at the same time, to close the ranks of the Idealist camp, but he also wanted to get a commonly accepted definition of Realism in acting. Once defined, the dragon seemed easier to fight. These were the three questions Craig posed: (*a*) "Do you consider Realism in acting to be a frank representation of human nature?" (*b*) "In your opinion should the Actor be allowed the same liberty in his expression of the Passions, as is permitted to the Writer or the Painter?" (*c*) "Do you think that Realism appeals to the General Public or only to a limited section of Playgoers?"

The way these questions were formulated says much about Craig's own views on the subject: his conception of the actor as an instrument in the hands of the director; his belief that the subject matter of the theatre should be more restricted than that of literature or painting; and his not quite overtly expressed hope that perhaps, after all, Realism might appeal only to a few. Craig's answer to these questions in his essay "Realism and the Actor" (1908) presents Realism in acting as a "frank" representation of human nature, a "frankness" that displays the ugly and the brutal.[5] To the Realists in the theatre, Craig opposes the Idealists, who, though perhaps not so "frank," are nevertheless "clear-sighted" and concerned with such values as Beauty and Truth—meaning aesthetic standards and a transcendental perception of Truth. He affirms that the theatre is a special medium that does not allow the same crude Realism in the portrayal of the Passions as painting and literature do, implying that the fictive but nevertheless living occurrences onstage can offend or corrupt the spectator, reenactment having a stronger affective impact. As for the public's favoring Realism, Craig attributes it to a special appeal to the baser common instincts. Adopting a definite Idealist attitude, Craig offers an impassioned argument, as seen in this November 1908 selection from his daybook:

> If the Realists in the Theatre wish to reveal the soul's secrets, should they not first become possessed of a nobler material than their own poor bodies through which to tell these secrets of the soul?
>
> What does the body know of the soul? What will the body say in favour of the soul—ever something too biased towards materialism to be called spiritual.
>
> Only music and architecture are entirely true to the true spiritual world for only these two possess spiritual languages—languages of the soul—languages as unintelligible as they are satisfying. The theatre to be listened to must first

> become unintelligible. *Flux alone illumines that which is still dark.* What folly—what cruelty—inhumanity to demand of the Body the revelation of its enemy.[6]

Craig's suggestion at this time of an "unintelligible" language for the theatre is noteworthy. If, as we have seen, he had thought to create a "language" by the moving "cubes" of the kinetic stage, here as of 17 November 1908, he suggests applying this same concept to the movements of the "Body"—in effect an actor or, perhaps, even an inanimate figure. Craig now saw this as his *abstract theatrical code of movement,* untranslatable into discursive terms and excluding all mimetic elements, yet as expressive as music or architecture. The code had only to be discovered, as he had written in the "Uber-Marions" notebooks.

Craig encountered the problems of such a code when he tried to convey in *Hamlet* an impression by altogether different techniques than in real life; thus, he proposed the use of suggestive movement and the emphasis on the musicality of voice (sound), "to add colour"—not sense—to the impression. As Craig had not yet discovered the ideal code of movement, he hoped to find it among the actor's "inventions." As in a research laboratory, he expected to find the "rules" of abstract but expressive movement by watching the reactions of the living organism under scrutiny, after he had put it in a suitable environment—the "new land," the screens—and stimulated it by providing the general lines along which the actor had to "invent" movement. The rules would have helped the formation of a code to be used not only by the actor but also by the über-marionette. However, no such rules were discovered, probably due both to the realistic style of training actors and Craig's contradictory approach: he expected the actor's personality to invent the code, yet at the same time he denied the right of personality to exist on the stage. One cannot help wondering what great feats of improvisation Craig witnessed at the Moscow rehearsals to prompt him to write the following in his diary on 3 February 1909: "I wish to remove *the word* with its dogma but to leave *sound*—or the voiced *beauty* of the soul. I wish to remove *the actor* with his *personality* but to leave *the chorus of masked figures.* I wish to remove *the pictorial scene* but to leave in its place the *architectonic scene.*"[7]

Because he believed in the educational force of the theatre, Craig had to create a language that could easily be decoded by the audience, yet this language had to be formed according to definite aesthetic criteria—such as the exclusion of mimetic elements—which could prevent this decoding. This made Craig's task impossible. Moreover, his conviction that theatre had to restore Belief implied, as long as the kinetic stage was only an imaginary possibility, the use of the figure as an instrument, and the figure introduces, *nolens volens,* by its very form, the mimetic element. By keeping sound or the musicality of voice, depersonalized figures, and a pliable, neutral scene, Craig came nearer to his ideal art of the theatre. He believed that art is "the expression of spiritual life. And artists are but the instruments of the Gods."[8] The actor's personality interfered with the director's task, that is, with the artist's mission; moreover, it could easily destroy whatever symbolism the character was endowed with. True art had to present, in Symons' words, the "pattern of a pattern." The über-marionette, or the figure (and for that matter the kinetic stage) was to turn the theatre into a true art. To those who claimed that art is the expression of "real" life, he answered: "Life and something living in art. Yes. Yes. But remember that there are two qualities of life, human and divine, material and spiritual & that if the human can be expressed by the human body, the divine cannot be expressed but only through some channel which is entirely cleansed of all dross."[9] This entry in his daybook was made in Paris on 22 January 1909, two months after his first "illumination." In September 1937 he added: "sounds like a sermon," but in October 1939, when he went back to the text of the old daybook, he wrote: "Yes—but happens to be more or less true."

Craig carried on his attack on Realism in acting. In one of his articles written during 1909 he discussed the concept of naturalness in acting, going to great lengths to demonstrate that artificiality was the natural state of the theatre, wherein the mask and the marionette, as well as dancing and pantomime, were integral.[10] He praised the convincing power of the mask and recommended it to the actor instead of makeup. The mask Craig proposed was not a copy of, or a return to, the ancient models but a modern creation, expressing the modern mind. Masks were also being made and experimented with at the Arena Goldoni. His work in Moscow, far from mellowing his position, had reinforced his faith in his own creations for expressive movement. In his "Notes for a Short Address to the Actors of the Moscow Art Theatre" (1909)—an address that was never delivered—he disclosed his frustration at the actors' inability to carry out his suggestions and concluded: "I made [then] one more design for an über-marionette."[11] He opposed another approach to Stanislavsky's method of acting, suggesting that the actor try to create "through the senses, not through the brain, for when we begin to think about the tragic or the comic we shall neither weep nor laugh." This is why he wanted to use background music, which would literally have "moved" the actor as he worked on his part. Furthermore, Craig argued, the director must appeal to the actor's "common sense."[12]

On the Actor and the Über-Marionette

In spite of Craig's attempts to experiment with the actor, his concept of a highly conventionalized theatre did not change. He wrote in November 1909:

> The theatre does not hold/contain an art, it contains something which poses as an art. The thing must be removed from the theatre before the theatre can be in a condition fit to hold that which is made by the artists. That which has to go is once more written down & the order in which its parts have to go are indicated. The thing—The artificial—and as assisting towards artificiality, the human material.

The order—	1. The woman or actress	(Boys)
	2. The human face & form	(masks)
	3. The artificial time & light	(day)
	4. The Play	(Ceremony)
	5. The spoken word	(song, written words)
	6. Man	

> Finally what remains—Light—shadow—motion through unpersonal mediums—and silence.[13]

The "unpersonal mediums," über-marionette and kinetic stage, together or apart, would ultimately perform the Ceremony, the artist's praise of Creation and his expression of Belief. This vision, however, remained secret.

During 1910 Craig was granted a patent for the screens in England. He was continuing his experiments and his writing, according now more and more attention to the "practical" aspects of theatre, to its "business," and trying to remind his critics that he had never ceased to be a practical man. Unwisely perhaps, he continued his criticism of theatre managers as part of his complaint that commercialism was preventing the theatre from becoming an art. In the second dialogue on "The Art of the Theatre," he praised the system by which the Moscow Art Theatre was organized, its shareholders having agreed to wait ten years before receiving any returns on their investment. Craig also proposed in this article the foundation of a School for the Art of the Theatre supported by the state. Another target for his criticism was actresses. Women began to be employed in the theatre for reasons of economy, he explained—because they could be paid less than men. Their employment was therefore not only the sign of an increased commercialism but a threat both to the artistic quality of the production and to effective theatre management. Craig reproached the actresses for their frivolous attitude toward their work, their temperament, and their lack of discipline. This is why, he concluded, they should be banished from the stage.[14] This attitude toward women was also held by Mondrian, who was a theosophist. To the female element, who represented the static, preserving, and obstructing factor—the matter, which he expressed by the horizontal line—Mondrian opposed the kinetic, creative, and progressing male element, the spirit, symbolized by the vertical line.[15] Craig's similar attitude is characteristic of his whole dualistic Weltanschauung. His kinetic stage,with the moving, elongated bodies, can easily be interpreted as having the same referent as Mondrian's vertical line.

Craig's encounter with Stanislavsky's method of directing proved to be very stimulating, as it helped him define his own conception of the actor more clearly. He wrote in his diary: "After two years experience of this Moscow theatre I find in it a man who has an even worse opinion of the actor than I have, Stanislavsky. He uses them as one uses bookbinding tools or needles and threads. Can he *make* an actor do this or that—if yes, then he considers him a good actor. It was this I feared. This point of view I have always tried to steer clear of. It is a practical one and valuable but quite inhuman. See 'Actor and UM.'"[16] By now, Craig had discovered two apparently dissimilar models—the Noh and the improvisation of the commedia dell'arte—and from 1910 on there were more and more articles on these subjects in *The Mask*. The restricted code of movement, the preference given to the physical expression over the verbal, and the actor's complete control of his instrument—his body—within these two acting styles appealed to Craig. Furthermore, they were both tangible proofs that the actor could become what Craig envisioned. On 2 October 1910, Craig wrote in his daybook: "Acting is a means of *expression*. Expression, the formulated emotion created by the action of all the senses. Modern 'acting acting' [Stanislavsky's system] is not created—it is imitated. That's why it can be taught."[17] Still, Craig's ideal restricted code of movement had to be found, "created," before it could be passed on.

Finally, Craig proposed his own "method"—not of producing or acting in a play but "of working out a scenario":

A method of working out a scenario: A) fable or story
B) rough map of *situations*

1) scenes and figures on a model stage
2) the actors watch
3) " " manipulate the figures
4) " " on the stage improvise
5) Improvisation taken down and transferred to model stage when the actors *speak* their improvisation
6) a few rehearsals
7) the performance is never *finished* even on the last night for additions are made by improvisation
[the] director's task is to cut out the unnecessary.[18]

By this method, the artist—the director—could convey to the actor the movement that he envisioned: this is the basic movement (manner and rhythm), the principles of which would guide the actor in his improvisation. No written text is used, neither is there a psychological approach to the part. The figure is now used as a mediator between the director and the actor. After watching the director demonstrate his "design" by the use of the figures on the model stage, the actor himself manipulates the figure that represents his character. In doing so, he acquires a new perspective on his body: his body becomes now a separate entity, an instrument. All physical and affective ties to the figure/body are, thus, severed. The actor is expected to have the same control of his body as of the figure he has manipulated. He is also expected to improvise, not through the figure but directly on the stage, because Craig never relinquished his belief that the (ideal) actor has to invent the symbols he would use in movement. The technique—the preparation of the role—is cerebral, compositional. After the movement improvised by the actor has been "shaped" by the director, it is transferred to the figure. Now, voice must be coordinated by the actor with the movement of the figure. This procedure treats movement and voice as independent, expressive means and helps, through distantiation, to achieve a better control of voice and body. Rehearsals follow. Nothing is left to chance, however: Craig is well aware that the contact with the audience may and will lead to further improvisations, all of which will be "shaped," in their turn, by the director. The new element in this development of Craig's theory is that, unlike the fixed performance he had in mind when he was writing his essays and the "Uber-Marions" notebooks, in 1905, 1906, and 1907, the performance is now a *living* work of art, developing and changing with each performance. This was also the method Craig used at his school in 1913 and the method he proposed to work by in 1915 at Oberlin College in the United States.[19]

Craig's campaign against Realism weakened for a time, as Diaghilev's Russian Ballet became his new target: it embodied a kind of artificiality that he considered as dangerous as Realism. In a series of articles in *The Mask,* published during 1911, 1912, and 1913 under various pseudonyms, Craig launched a virulent attack against what he considered a modern evil, an aesthetic fraud, and the epitome of vulgarity. He accused thc Russian Ballet of stealing Isadora's ideas and was more than happy in 1913 to publish Nijinsky's acknowledgment that Isadora did indeed inspire Fokine. Though Craig recognized Nijinsky's and Pavlova's feats of virtuosity, he condemned the "cult of the body" of the Russian Ballet, a cult that was spreading into the theatre. Craig was never enticed by fashionable spectacles and never spared those he considered a threat to the theatre the sting of his irony—such as Bakst, for example, or the group of painters who contributed to the Russian Ballet's productions. Craig claimed that they lacked the knowledge of theatrical matters necessary for the creation of a theatrical environment. The Russian Ballet ran counter to everything that Craig held most important: movement that did not go against the natural limitations of the human body, simplicity, self-expression of the artist. He condemned the Russian Ballet as merely "sensual" and its performances as a pretense of art.

Nor was Jaques-Dalcroze spared, although Craig conceded that he was nearer to Isadora's ideal than any of her imitators. But what Craig condemned in eurythmics was the suppression of individual personality—the very thing that he wanted to deprive the actor of, no matter how little the director "shaped" his improvisation. However, Craig's attitude mellowed with time, and he was later to recognize Jaques-Dalcroze's contribution to the development of modern dance.

The formal recognition of Craig as one of the world's leading theatre artists came with the public dinner given in his honor in London on 16 July 1911, when he was acclaimed by outstanding writers, painters, musicians, and theatre people. Several months after the public dinner, in September, an exhibition of his drawings and stage models opened at the Leicester Galleries in London. In the meantime, an English Advisory Committee had been formed to gather funds for Craig's School for the Art of the Theatre. In December, when his collection of essays *On the Art of the Theatre* appeared, he was in Moscow, attending to the last preparations for *Hamlet.*[20] Craig returned to London in February 1912, then went to Paris, where he stayed several months. There he met many of his old friends, among them Kessler, Yvette Guilbert, Henry van de Velde, Maillol, and Chaliapin. Plans for a production with Jacques Rouché were still alive, and he also devoted some enthusiastic attention to a possible production of the *St. Matthew Passion,* to be backed by the Countess Grehfühle.[21]

The essay "The Actor and the Uber-Marionette" included in *On the Art of the Theatre,* together with the note added to "The Art of the Theatre" (first dialogue) expressing Craig's belief in the victory of the über-marionette and the unspoken drama, had stirred up adverse reactions. The timing was unfortunate: after the testimonial dinner in London, the success of *Hamlet,* and the prospect of new productions—with actors!—in Paris, there was now also a new hope for a school. Was Craig so buoyed up by this atmosphere of success that he feared the consequences if he did not retract a little? Or was his article "Gentlemen, the Marionette!" which was published in the October 1912 issue of *The*

Mask—an issue devoted to the marionette—only another example of his toying with the public? In this article, written in Paris earlier that year, Craig seems to say (perhaps he is deliberately vague) that the über-marionette is only a metaphor, a model for the ideal actor, and he denies that he ever wished to replace the actor by a figure moved "by real metal or silken threads" instead of by divine inspiration. Indeed, he says, he never believed in the "mechanical nor in the material."[22] But Craig's remarks in a letter to his mother written on 23 March 1912, while he was preparing the material for the publication of *Towards a New Theatre,* may be the clue to his real intentions and the meaning behind this obfuscation: "My book shall come out—that is less difficult, I believe—though they shy at the übermarionette. So strange too . . . as if 10,000 übermarionettes would alter the earth or the stage to the extent feared by all—even if to the extent *desired* by all."[23]

In fact, Craig's experiments with the figures continued. In September 1912, another exhibition of Craig's designs and models opened in London and was later moved to Manchester, Liverpool, Dublin, and Leeds. *Towards a New Theatre,* a collection of stage designs done between 1906 and 1910, appeared the same year. In the notes that accompany the plates, Craig underlines the two functions of the scene, namely, to express movement and to serve the movement of the performer. The note to a "Study of Movement" (1906) discusses the need for "symbolical gestures which suggest action" or the movement of another instrument that conveys meaning.[24] Craig's wish to turn the actor into a "superior puppet" that uses a mask is made explicit in another note.[25]

But in spite of his professed use of the actor, it was still the marionette theatre that Craig preferred, and in 1913 he even contemplated the possibility of producing several marionette plays in London.[26] In his article "The Modern Theatre and Another" (1913) Craig demonstrated that rather than the modern theatre it is the marionette theatre, presenting the silent "Drama of Wisdom," that can bring peace and repose to the spectator. In his notes from 25 February 1914 in his diary, Craig discussed the possibility of a religious theatre that would be a theatre of marionettes.[27] These notes were written shortly after Craig met Appia for the first time.[28]

The outbreak of war in 1914 brought an end to the school in Florence. Though Craig tried to carry on with his work as best he could, his students were gone and his funds withdrawn. Craig turned to writing, and in 1915 began to prepare material for another book, to be called "The Theatre, the New Movement, and the Newer One."[29] Ten years had passed since he announced his theory on theatre. Now he published in *The Mask* a new series of articles in which he abandoned his old preoccupation with the ideal evolution of theatre as an art in favor of a more realistic position. This is not to say that he abandoned his previous standards, but he was obviously trying to allow for historical truths and probabilities. He tried to incorporate in his theory those factors whose existence in the past could not be overlooked and whose existence in the future could not be prevented, like economic and social factors. Craig's distinction between a *durable* and a *perishable* theatre now reflected his old dualistic outlook and his ambivalent attitude toward the actor, but it also allowed a bigger part to the actor's interpretation or, in Craig's words, to improvisation. The durable theatre was a religious experience where a ceremony representing a religious, silent drama was acted out in a sacred edifice. But whether the actor could perform in this theatre was not yet certain: "Do not fear that I am going to spring an Uber-Marionette into the midst of [the actors]. If he arrives it will be no case of my bringing him there, but because no one can prevent him from coming."[30] Craig now simply demanded that the Western actor achieve the same high standards of expressive movement as the Eastern actor; otherwise there would be no choice but "to fashion something to represent man."[31]

The über-marionette was threatening to replace the actor in the durable theatre, but fortunately for the actor, there was the perishable theatre, where Craig made him a king—for he took care not to emphasize again the role of the artist, the director. In the perishable theatre, improvisation on light subjects was to replace the written play. Craig had in mind the well-planned and well-executed improvisation of the commedia dell'arte, prepared under the supervision of the director. The perishable and the durable theatres were intended for the future, and each would fill a separate function: the perishable, to amuse and/or instruct; the durable, to create the one ceremony that would inspire men to a fresh endeavor, to a new beginning, all over the world.

As for the existing theatre, Craig now gave aesthetic legitimacy to two styles, Idealism and Realism, wishing all the while for the speedy disappearance of the latter.[32] His new argument against Realism was one calculated to please the actor: Realism, Craig suggested, turned actors into slaves, forcing them to use "pretense," to imitate—that is, it was debasing for the actor to have to follow strict conventions. On the other hand, Craig explained that the actor's need to "pretend" was the result of his lack of belief in the value of his work (Craig refrained from using the term "art").[33] But perhaps the ordinary actor would have preferred to be a slave and a pretender instead of being "marionettized, masked, impersonal," as Craig suggested in a letter to Sheldon Cheney in December 1915.[34]

On the Actor and the Über-Marionette

Though Craig's basic attitude toward the actor did not change, several new elements were added to his theory of movement and voice. It was now the musicality of voice that Craig emphasized, using it in order to create mood and even convey meaning, as in the speeding up of delivery he suggested for *Hamlet*. As for movement, Craig's concept of the ideal movement—an abstract code of movement—did not change, nor did he change his mind about the actor's role in the theatrical creation. Nonetheless, from 1910 on, Craig devoted more of his efforts to the improvement of the ordinary actor, and he now searched for various means that could enhance the actor's creativity, proposing to teach the actor movement by using the figure as a model and as a tool. He also suggested using background music in order to convey meaning to the actor and stimulate his powers of invention. These procedures are closely linked to Craig's conviction that the actor must work, in stage terms, "from the outside in" and not "from the inside out," that is, the actor's interpretation is a direct result of his sense of observation and his ability to translate his perceptions into a symbolic pattern of movement. The actor was to create a role along the lines provided by the director through the figure. By watching the figure on the stage model and then manipulating it, the actor would acquire the right creative perspective as well as gain control of his tools (body and voice). Craig demanded that the actor approach the fiction character he created in a detached manner, as Henry Irving did, or like a painter who covers the canvas with forms and colors, the painting constituting a separate physical entity. In other words, Craig asked of the actor a kind of detachment that would have ensured not a critical rendering of the character, as Brecht would suggest, but design and control in the creation of the character by movement and voice.

Craig's decision to demonstrate the practical side of his concept led him to forgo any further comments on the actor's steps toward becoming an artist of the theatre. Instead, he accorded the actor an important role in the perishable theatre, a theatre where the ordinary actor had a future—with Craig's blessing and instructions, of course.

And the über-marionette? As we have seen, Craig's 1912 retraction of his expressed wish to replace the actor with a figure was a strategic move to attract new productions. Unfortunately, it did not work. But Craig did obtain his school, where he continued, not unexpectedly, his experiments and even made an eight-foot-high über-marionette. The movement he proposed in 1915 was the same movement that he tried to create in his London productions, that he advocated in his numerous articles, and that he proposed to the Moscow Art Theatre, along with masks and the symbolic use of voice. This was an ideal symbolic movement initiated, controlled, and shaped by the director, a movement that was never created.

Nor did Craig's preference for "unpersonal mediums" change. In fact, the "marionettized" actor and the über-marionette, as well as the kinetic stage, can be seen as part of a larger trend to depersonalize art. Thus, for example, Marcel Duchamp created his first ready-made in 1914. A year later, De Chirico created his *pittura metafisica*. A year after that, in 1916, the Dada movement was founded in Zurich.

14

Belief (II)

Craig's first "illumination"—this is how he referred to his mystical experiences as soon as he became aware of their nature—occurred on 17 November 1908 in Moscow. Stanislavsky spared no effort to make Craig feel at home at the Moscow Art Theatre. Here he was, a stranger among strangers but also an artist coming to create a piece of art—another brick in the universal temple of the theatre. Was it the cold sky of Moscow and the sudden appearance of the sun in the midst of a gray, snowy winter day that caused the vision? "Three years ago, in Moscow, in the cold north land, it seemed to me that Light was beginning and end," he would write in 1911.[1] As it had happened before, in 1906, when Craig had the vision of the kinetic stage, again he now seemed to grasp intuitively the secret of Creation. He experienced an epiphany. In a kind of mystical flash, he apprehended not only the interrelation of all living things but also the great forces—the "unseen forces"—that inform the universe. He had looked on movement as the symbol of life and believed that the existence of God could be demonstrated through motion, but now he perceived the force that made motion and life: light and its source, the sun. This was a sudden comprehension of what he would henceforth hold as an absolute truth. Craig's description, entitled "LIGHT," is enigmatic, yet precise:

> All is clear suddenly—
> The only secret mysterious profound truth
> is the simple Light.

and the Heart of that—the Sun—

Where I sought for motion
I was meaning Light.

*

The Sun is our only God—
In Movement our ceremony
and the priests—the rays—waves—
vibrations. atoms
of Light itself—

*

Without Light Sun—Light
All would be Hell,
Sun purifies, yet warms
everything—comforts and creates.

The Sun is the God
of Movement and Life. Growth

*

our Love for that God
need never cease.
We show our love for him in our ceremonies to his glory.[2]

Craig put this vision—as well as his later illuminations—in writing in the "Movement" notebook, discovered by Arnold Rood. But rather than containing Craig's secret thinking about movement, the notebook holds his thinking about the Belief he had envisioned three years before; movement was only the symbolic instrument for the performance and the revelation of the Belief.[3]

Craig himself did not reveal his vision, but his short article "God Save the King" (1909), which was first printed in *The Mask* in 1909 and later as a dedication of *On the Art of the Theatre,* bears proof to his mystical approach to the sun, the summit of all Creation, the "symbol of the Divine."[4]

Soon after the illumination, Craig decided to learn more about the cult of the sun: "What does Moses say of the Sun? What Dante? What Socrates—Job—Jesus—the Greek poets. The Sicilians. The Romans. What the Indians, the Chinese, the Japanese, the Egyptians, the Babylonians, the Persians. The dwellers in the snow and cold darklands—and the savage tribes."[5] Then he added a memorandum:

Obtain every book on the Sun, on Light.
REWRITE THEM
Look at every picture of the Sun and of Light. The Ancients wrote and drew understandingly of both. The Artists—attempt to destroy these works of the demons calling themselves Scientists, these dry unbelieving blind beings.[6]

For a moment, he believed that his newly acquired, intuitive knowledge, an artist's privilege, enabled him to reinterpret all that was ever written on the subject. For the present, Craig focused not on the philosophical but on the performative aspect of the cult of the sun: "We can perform more wonderful and more moving ceremonies in [the sun's] honour than any other people. We perform these only in the Day. To the moon, the symbol of Death, ceremonies are also due and willingly performed. These are performed only at night." He already saw the colors and moods of these ceremonies:

The Sun symbolizes Joy— yellow silence
The Moon sadness— Blue speech.[7]

He visualized two different ceremonies, one for men and one for women:

A ceremony. (I would make it compulsory that daily—at home—this ceremony should be performed. Morning and evening.)

Sun on water, colour, form.
Sun in darkness and in light.
The Beam against the ripple.
The Reflection—
A ceremony for men.

The moon. A reflect light.
a solemn—smaller ceremony.
Perhaps performed by women—certainly for women.

The ceremony of the 365 days and nights. The processions of wild flowers—thoughts—trees—animals—rocks—streams—birds—frogs—winds—colours—grasses—metals—elements—

Not the sign of a real man in such processions or the act of a man—

For what does man need but a rest from regarding himself—that has made him in love with himself and now he lies like Narcissus all the day looking at a grey reflection in a dark glass.[8]

Not only do these ceremonies lead to the reunion of man and woman with nature; they also bring about the reunion of man and woman and the symbolic orders of the universe to which each of them belongs: the male—sun—light; the female—moon—darkness. Thus, a new and vital element was now added to Craig's belief in universal correspondences: knowledge, understanding, or "illumination."

Craig's second illumination occurred on 5 November 1911 in London. In this illumination, he visualized the cycle of life (creation, life and death, and reincarnation), intimations of which he had already had in 1905 and 1906, when he was reading about ancient Egypt. Now he understood the formal expression of Light and Creation through movement. He drew a sketch of the different directions of movement, each direction symbolizing another moment in Creation. The third illumination occurred in Italy, on 8 May 1913, soon after the school was established. This was a conception of God as symbolized by light and the sun, and a vision of a ceremony with *chants* "in Praise of the God of all things—the Creator of Light and Motion—the symbol of our Art."[9] Craig, in transcribing this vision, added a prayer.

The illuminations reinforced Craig's belief in his mission. Like Blake, to whom he dedicated *On the Art of the Theatre,* he now considered art as both a religious activity and a religious product. Shortly after his first illumination, he wrote to his friend William Rothenstein that he felt impelled to leave Moscow—where he had been so enthusiastically welcomed—and dedicate himself to a loftier task than that of interpreting a play and working on productions.[10] In January 1912, two months after his second illumination, he expressed in his diary the wish that the theatre may unite men, whatever their belief may be.[11] His God was a universal God, whose main manifestations were through Light and Movement, and whose symbol was the sun, the supreme force of life. The illuminations inspired Craig's idea of a durable theatre—the theatre that according to his theory would be built during the third phase, that of Creation and Revelation. In the durable theatre, a drama of universal interest, a drama of silence, would be performed. Thus, theatre became an act of worship, an act of belief, a collective religious experience. The ceremony would be performed in daylight, Craig wrote, but he nevertheless continued his experiments with lighting.

Craig kept his belief and his illuminations secret. In 1914, after meeting Appia in Zurich, he wrote in the "Movement" notebook, where he had described his illuminations: "Appia and the others (although only he counts and the others count not at all), are on the wrong track. They are leaning upon the *habitual supports:* Music, Dancing and the other arts (*the human* person in movement) and though they take these very far, and perfect them, yet because they try to *unite* them and desire to fit them into the Theatre's System, they must fail. *For they are on a wrong track.* I am on the right track and it is not without great danger."[12]

Was he again afraid that the "enemy" might steal his ideas? Quite possibly, for he believed that he was approaching his goal. He had discovered the "Law of Balance which is the heart of perfect Beauty," a discovery that had not only an aesthetic but also a metaphysical relevance now, for it revealed the existence of a divine pattern in Creation. His sense of mission was reinforced, since he was convinced that "art is the expression of spiritual life and artists are but the instrument of the Gods."[13] He had discarded the "human person," and in its stead was a man-made instrument—a "channel" that was entirely "cleansed of all dross" and through which the spiritual could now be expressed. Craig was also preparing his production of the *St. Matthew Passion,* his first ceremony created in praise of a universal God, wherein the new art of movement would have unfolded for the first time.

The war came. The school, which had come into existence after more than ten years of efforts and represented the hope and the promise of a new art of the theatre, was closed, and several of its students were killed in the war. In January 1916, in a moment of depression, Craig wrote to Rothenstein: "I begin to turn from everything Eastern. India. Poo! China. rubbish. Why, even the dear old man Blake is not our best guide—So I feel anyhow. Therefore for two years I have been watching a certain English master—(dead)—quite a baffling one—still sound—very manly—mainly that—The result is I can at this hour do little or nothing—" [14] The English master was Byron, in whose poetry he now took refuge. Craig returned to his marionettes when he settled down in 1917 in Rapallo, but the illuminations never returned.

Craig's Belief, a deliberate act reinforced by the illuminations, never lost its impetus.

≻ 15 ≺

"Bending to the Wind"

The war interrupted what had been for Craig, in spite of all the aborted projects, a fruitful period, as it contained the first steps toward the implementation of his idea of movement, namely, experiments and the opening of his school. With the school closed, the students gone, and Lord Howard de Walden's support suspended because of the war, Craig's experiments with movement and with new kinds of articulated puppets were slowed down.[1] In 1915 he received a visit from Jacques Copeau, who spent a month in Florence, trying to learn the master's craft. Craig's ideas on scene were becoming part of the contemporary scenography. The concept of the director as the only artist in the theatre was gaining converts, as was the idea of a conventionalized, "artificial" theatre. Compared with the new artistic movements in theatre (Futurism, Dada, and what was soon known as Expressionism) that moved toward a disconcertingly fragmented and distorted representation of reality, Craig's ideas on scene and the mise en scène—but not on movement—were moderate enough to be borrowed more and more.

After the war, it was impossible to reopen the school, as no funds were available, but *The Mask* survived until 1929. Craig continued working with marionettes and stage models, planning productions that were never to see the light, writing articles and books, holding exhibitions, and keeping up an extensive correspondence. He became the Sage of the modern theatre, not a practitioner. His writings and his exhibitions attracted a worldwide audience, inspiring a new generation of directors and scenographers. He never gave up hope that England would give him a theatre and a school, but neither did he stop searching for a theatre and a school elsewhere—be it in Mussolini's Italy, in the United States, or with Habimah in the late 1930s in Palestine—a theatre and a school that were intended to implement his ideal theatre. Up to the Second World War, Craig continued his sustained though fruitless efforts toward this end. In the absence of any real opportunity to work in the theatre, Craig used writing to express his views. He now concentrated on the "fringe of the idea," namely, on the need to improve acting in the existing theatre. Aware that he had alienated the actor, his soldier, Craig hoped that he might still obtain the actor's allegiance. He also tried to find suitable arguments to convince potential backers, especially the English government, of the importance, effectiveness, and practicality of his ideas. He never really abandoned his idea (practical or not) of a new art of movement performed by a man-made instrument, but now his desire to be practical made him take steps that may appear incomprehensible.

After 1918, Craig turned more and more to the study of the history of the theatre and the theatrical genres, and it was not long before he became an authority on the subject. This interest in the past was not a sort of escapism, as it may appear at first glance, but grew out of his search for constants, for aesthetic patterns and rules. From his studies, Craig found that Realism in theatre production was a recent concept and not a theatrical tradition. Craig also discovered that the theatre was always sponsored, a historical fact that he used as an argument when he tried now to convince the state (England, of course) to support his theatre. He found more support for his belief in the commedia dell'arte as an example of good acting and for his idea of reviving that sort of improvisation in place of modern acting techniques. Finally, by examining the past, Craig found that the theatre of the past had left behind only a few relics, sacred and precious *objets d'art:* these were the extant theatre buildings and the rigid acting codes of the Eastern theatre. The durable theatre was supposed to build new edifices that would be real *objets d'art.* Craig also continued to take an active interest in contemporary arts, eager to judge the latest developments. Whether it was Cubism or Futurism, opera or cinema, he never missed the opportunity to emphasize and praise those works that supported his theorics and pan those that did not.

Craig spent most of 1917 and 1918 on experiments on the forerunner of the über-marionette, the marionette, but he missed the human contact and the stimulation provided by the school. In a letter to William Rothenstein in August 1917 asking him to send him material on marionettes in Europe, Burma, and Java, Craig remarked: "I am as devotedly attentive to the marionette as I was, and seem to think I shall ever be—and seriously—although just for the moment their silliness and dollishness is often uppermost—having considered rather too long their *profundity*—and without an audience to correct the necessary poison—."[2] He was also working on plans for a new magazine entirely dedicated to the marionette, its history and drama, its technical features and its future. Not long before the first issue appeared in April 1918, he wrote Rothenstein somewhat philosophically: "We all work . . . live our work—keep to what we can comprehend—within those frontiers . . . and I prepare and make figures to fill the stageworld which I once wasted so much time regarding as a rather empty place. Again . . . you know."[3] Only twelve issues of *The Marionnette* were published, all within a year of the first one. Craig filled them with several of the marionette plays that he had begun writing in 1914 as amusement pieces for his children. These plays or "motions" (not mimo-dramas but spoken dramas) were to be part of a larger circle, the *Drama for Fools*.[4]

In response to Rothenstein's criticism of the marionette and Craig's preoccupation with it—"This is not playing the game," Rothenstein had written him—Craig explained:

> I am more interested in the work I'm at because you know how great pleasure or pain works—well this is good deal of pain—I labour—have done these last 3 or 4 years to produce a tiny bit of a Drama which shall move, and as I know nothing about the business, you can guess how unpleasant I feel. . . . I was brought up to realize things in a Theatre have to be done on a big scale & so there is not much fear of my falling into the Little Theatre trap. . . . It must be all on a great scale or less than little—a peep show. . . . I was the best in my line—but my line was obviously a line which needed something—I am suspending a marionette from the end of it—If that is wrong, perhaps if I add something more to the doll, it will all come right. A Drama—made for it—wait, as the good Mr. Asquith said once, & see. I say it in as decent a tone as an appeal can be put. . . . Again, I love the whole idea of Puppets. I see—big lands of them. I fear entering—If I enter I go on with any old specimen—the great gods would make me speechless & turn me to stone—I have 3 of these here. They are marvels—more strange than most things wonderful. You seeing them would understand why I join the ordinary 2 1/2^{d} species & serve them at present.
>
> The great marionettes are far & away some of the most extraordinary things on earth—[5]

In another draft of the same letter (there were six of them), Craig tried to define the phase he was in by words and a sketch:

> Don't you find your work becomes more difficult?—& yet do you not dare each new step?

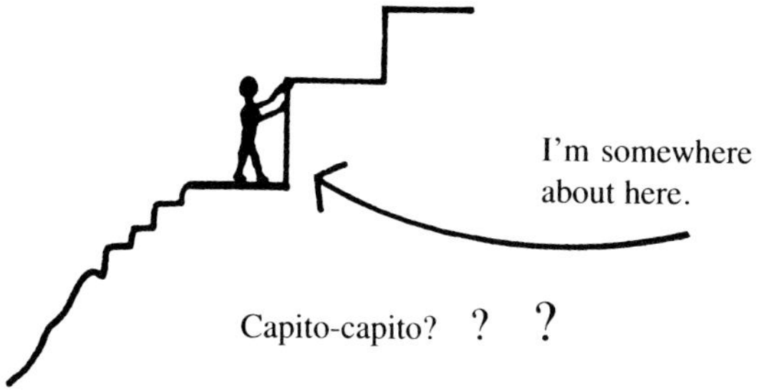
I'm somewhere
about here.
Capito-capito? ? ?

> If you don't capito—you are nothing but an old Londoner obsessed by fogs & fashions.

With a rare psychological insight, he explained in the same draft: "This communing with rag & bone reduces things a good deal to the size I naturally like them to be. No longer a vast Theatre & a multitude all breathing, gazing & longing in harmony, & so causing my dead body to rise and tread the stage & then the air & live two long lives of an afternoon—So, good horse, let us jog on to the next reality—& wait till night if you wish to dream a dream of wings. Cellar talk with a shapeless burattini, worth still as much as a golden image of Kewana."[6] Craig was playing his own game, alone and in control. In an article in *The Marionnette* signed under the pseudonym Jacques Fox-Laurier, he ridiculed Depero's futuristic marionettes, and in his aesthetic credo, published in *The Mask* and in *The Marionnette* in 1919, he reaffirmed his belief in the marionette. The über-marionette was conspicuous by its absence among the other theatre elements that Craig professed to believe in.[7] Craig explained its (temporary) disappearance in a footnote to his article "The Marionette Drama. Some Notes for an Introduction to 'The Drama for Fools' by Tom Fool."[8] Here Craig affirmed that the über-marionette would come *after* the marionette was accepted and established. This acceptance was the enormous step that Craig now faced; the next would have been the introduction of the über-marionette itself.

In February 1921, a special issue of *The Chapbook,* an English magazine, was issued. It was entitled *Puppets and Poets* and was written entirely by Craig. After a short history of the puppet, Craig compared its expressivity with that of the actor and concluded that the puppet could teach the actor. He expressed his hope that in the long run the actor would turn to the puppet and use it as an instrument for interpretation of drama. Thus, the idea of the actor turned into an artist and manipulating a man-made instrument returned in a modified version.

That same year, in the preface to the first English edition of *The Theatre Advancing* (an American edition had come out in 1919), Craig publicly stated his case for a theatre of his own in England. With a sweeping arrogance, he brushed aside whatever contradictions his theory might have, claiming that "a paradox covers the whole truth." The burden of his argument was that though he had many followers who were applying his ideas in the theatre, he was still without a theatre in his own country. Although seen as publicly critical of the English theatre people who refused to see him as their leader, Craig was privately hurt by their attitude.[9]

But Craig was not isolating himself and working only on the marionette; he was also adapting his ideas on scene to "the conditions which are today offered us." For example, in a note for the catalogue of his exhibition in Amsterdam in 1922, he proposed that the theatre should be an empty place, with a scene and an auditorium built each time according to the type of drama produced.[10] Likewise, in *Scene,* the collection of stage designs that he published in 1923, he specified that the function of the stage was to serve the actor, and emphasized the use of light in acting. Craig had always accorded an important place to electricity in the technical management of the stage and was always looking for new ways of using it to add movement and expressivity to the stage. The spectacle of traveling light on the "cubes" of the kinetic stage seemed to him to create a new expressive language, like music—enabling the kinetic stage to fulfill its function.[11] Movement and light were to create on the kinetic stage a vision similar to that of his "illuminations" in its effect on the audience.

It is of interest that at the same time Craig was looking for his "unintelligible" language in theatre, similar experiments in music were being conducted by Schoenberg, for example, who was then writing his athematic and atonal compositions; but while Craig was still carrying on his experiments in the early 1920s, Schoenberg had already systematized his invention and devised the twelve-tone technique.

This was also the period of various experiments in theatrical movement, all of which bear witness to Craig's influence. Craig's refusal of a psychological approach in the preparation of the role, as well as his separation of movement from voice, each to be shaped independently by the director, inspired Meyerhold's biomechanics. Meyerhold's actor became a pliable tool for expression. The same attitude toward the actor guided Jessner, for example, in his Expressionist mise en scène of *Richard III* at the Staatliches Schauspielhaus in Berlin in 1920. Here, movement and voice were used the same way that Craig used the mask, that is, by singling out a dominant and symbolic feature and exaggerating it, thereby enhancing its power to convince. But this acting style, unlike that envisioned by Craig, was characterized by great mobility. Interesting experiments in nonmimetic movement were carried out by the Bauhaus at Weimar and at Dessau. Oskar Schlemmer, for example, searched for a new code of movement inspired by modern technology, a sort of "mathematics in motion, the mechanics of joints and swivels, and the exactitudes of rhythmics and gymnastics."[12] Consequently, the human body was not negated but transformed by padded or architectonic costumes. Movement was ordered and controlled by the artist and director—according to the rules of form, color, and direction established by Kandinsky's theory of correspondences—and by means of the restricting costumes. In the *Triadic Ballet,* for example, first performed at the Landestheater in Stuttgart in September 1922, movement was expressed by pure geometrical lines and figures. Large, flat, geometrical figures were manipulated by actors in the *Mechanical Ballet* performed at the Stadttheater in Jena in August 1923. In these experiments, the actor was depersonalized, his role relegated to that of a worker.

It was in 1923 that Craig's son Edward Craig found the technical solution to the manipulation of the kinetic stage by remote control, but when Craig learned that Edward had dared discuss his idea with a young student of hydraulics, he flew into a rage, which was followed by anguished fears that the "enemy" might steal his idea. The model of the kinetic stage was hidden away, "never to be seen again."[13]

Not only was the kinetic stage hidden away, so was the über-marionette! In the 1924 preface to the new edition of *On the Art of the Theatre,* Craig made what is considered his retraction: "I no more want to see the living actors replaced by things of wood than the great Italian actress of our day [Duse] wants all the actors to die. . . . The Uber-marionette is the actor plus fire, minus egoism: the fire of the gods and demons, without the smoke and steam of mortality."[14] Was his retraction of 1912 lacking conviction? Not his statement of 1924: the über-marionette was never anything but a metaphor. Few of his readers in 1924 knew about Craig's old project of an über-marionette international theatre in Dresden or about his subsequent experiments in Florence. Many accepted the statement at its face value, many did not. Did Craig indeed consider the actor capable of becoming an über-marionette, capable of an inventive spirit and perfect self-control? Experience had taught him that this was not completely impossible, because he could recall the idealized image of Irving the actor. The man of vision was now setting an ideal for the actor to aspire to. In fact, according to Craig's theory, the actor-über-marionette would inevitably be on the path predicted and prepared by Craig: he would become an artist of the theatre who would reach the point where he would find and use a man-made instrument for movement instead of using his own body. Anyhow, Craig was loyal to his word, as witnessed by the chapter on "Books and Actors" in *Books and Theatres* (published in 1925), which was full of good advice to the ordinary actor. To become a good actor, though not a great one, the actor should experiment, use his brains and imagination, and learn about the theatre and its history as much as possible by reading—by reading Craig's books too, of course.

An opportunity to work again with ordinary actors, some of whom never read Craig's books, came with the production of Ibsen's *Pretenders* in 1926 at the Danish Royal Theatre in Copenhagen. At the invitation of Johannes Poulsen, one of its outstanding actors and directors, who admired Craig, the Danish theatre invited Craig to produce the play and design the scenery and costumes. Unlike other proposals, Craig accepted this one, largely because the terms of the invitation were not restrictive and binding. The play opened on 14 November 1926 and had sixteen performances in all. It was far from being a success with the larger public or with the critics; the latter claimed that Craig failed to express the Nordic and medieval tone of Ibsen's play.[15] As was usual with Craig, and according to his theory, he sought to convey his personal interpretation of the drama (though the critics condemned it as being "Irish"). He believed not in an accurate historical reproduction but in the creation of a symbolic image that would stimulate the imagination. He viewed the play as a conflict between two powers, the autocratic Skule, with whom he identified, and Haakon, the enemy, the "organizer."[16] As Frederick and Lise-Lone Marker point out in their study of this production, Craig's approach to the composition of scene (scenery, lighting, and costumes) lacked stylistic consistency.[17] He did not use screens but a set of platforms, panels, and parallelepipeds. What is striking but nevertheless characteristic of Craig's designs made after the war is the fact that these designs were only variations on old themes: he sought inspiration in old designs from 1904 and 1906.[18] Craig devised the whole scheme of lighting, but his designs for costumes were not used after all. He also devised the incidental music (including choral singing), in order to express the central theme of a scene, create mood, and impose a certain rhythm to the action. As for movement and voice, when he first arrived in Copenhagen, Craig intended to work with the actors and guide them, teaching them first of all how to speak.[19] Instead, he backed down and left this task to Poulsen, who directed the rehearsals; the artist watched and made notes that he later passed on to Poulsen. These notes referred to gestures and movements, pace, blocking, and the coordination of movement and voice with scene. Most of Craig's instructions were followed. Thus, as Frederick and Lise-Lone Marker so aptly point out, Craig's role with regard to movement and voice was that of an advisor. It was not until

1930 that the designs Craig prepared for the 1926 production were published.[20] In 1928, Craig prepared the stage designs for Douglas Ross's production of *Macbeth* at the Knickerbocker Theatre in New York, again seeking inspiration in old designs.

In 1929 Craig made an attempt to accommodate his apparently contradictory views on the actors and formulate them into an aesthetic theory—this time again, he had high hopes for a possible production with Poulsen. Six years earlier, Craig had started making notes for a "manual" for the theatre, to be called "An Easy Book on the Theatre." This book was never finished, but Craig worked on it from time to time until 1930 and had made a detailed outline. The first part would have discussed theatres ("the place"), the curtain, and the public (with the specification: "Never consider it"). The second part would have dealt with scenes ("the view"), namely, views and plans, machines, and his own scenes and stage models. The third—lighting. The fourth—figures; this part focused on movement and treated such topics as single figures ("in repose, feeling, in action, doing"); groups of figures ("as background, as foreground"); and crowds (as a person, as a mass), all manipulated to music or without. Acting, dancing, and singing as well as costume, makeup, and masks were also to be discussed here. The fifth part was to be devoted to marionettes—not to be confused with the figures, that is, the über-marionettes; the sixth, to "the whole show at work"; the seventh, to drama (plays, playwrights, and librettisti); another part to theories on theatre; and the last one to the stage director. In 1929, Craig wrote, but never completed, a few notes for the chapter on the actor—intended for the fourth part of the project.

These notes are particularly relevant because they try to solve once and for all what was, and still is, considered a contradiction in Craig's attitude toward the actor. He was accused, Craig wrote, of fostering the idea of an ideal theatre where, in his words, all chance of accident is eliminated, "man no longer the actor." But, he says, on the other hand "I would seem to say: the finest and best theatre is that where the actor improvises—where all is chance—all hot and spontaneous." Indeed, Craig recognized, even praised two "extremes" in acting: Sarah Bernhardt's "volcanic improvisation," the expression of the "earthly" and Henry Irving's "cold perfection of a man," the expression of the spiritual. As Craig now explained, improvisation was only a "*necessary trial,*" a stage in the actor's development on his way to becoming an artist of the theatre.[21]

Craig's book on Henry Irving, published in 1930, discusses not only the famous actor's personality but his acting and the preparation for his roles. By presenting Irving as the actor-über-marionette, Craig brings to note a system of acting. He describes the brilliant way in which Irving used his body, overcoming a bad walk and poor diction and says that Irving is an example of how an actor can use whatever natural physical gifts he has and compensate for lack of others. He emphasizes Irving's use of symbolic gesture, immobility (*stasis*), and slow movement. Within the limits of his instrument (that is, his body), Irving found an endless variety of expressive gestures, proceeding by the combination, elimination, and stylization of movements. In this way, the artist creates what we now call a kinesymbolic art, where even the absence of movement—*stasis*—is expressive. Irving took his inspiration from nature, and then by a process of contemplation, meditation, reflection, selection, and stylization, he arrived at expression. Isadora created movement in the same way. Images suggested by nature were at the core of their expressive movement. This is a method by which the actor works "from outside in." Sir Laurence Olivier, for example, has said that in the death scene in his film *Richard III,* he was inspired by the convulsions of a dying reptile: a fascinating, compelling, yet cruel image that arouses repulsion and disgust—these were exactly the feelings that Olivier's acting inspired in the audience.[22] This was also Irving's method. Craig tries hard to make a case for Irving as a would-be believer in the über-marionette but leaves us only with an impression: "Irving's regret was that in his theatre they [puppets] had to be made of flesh and blood: he never expressed this, but he never failed to feel it."[23]

A similar process of expression in acting was followed by the Expressionist theatre, but in order to ensure the proper response from the audience, gesture and movement were exaggerated. Craig's reaction to this style of acting was enthusiastic, as was his praise of Habimah's productions in 1931. He saw *The Dybbuk* ("perfect") at least twice, *The Golem* ("remarkable") three times, *David's Crown* ("brilliant") once, and also *Twelfth Night* once ("poor").[24] But these were rare cases of what he considered good acting. On 16 December 1934 he wrote in his diary: "It is as I knew in 1907—as I read all about Russian theatre today 1934—the marionette must claim the theatre from the actor—for the actor refuses to become *super-marionette.*"[25] By now he was sixty-three, but he had received new promises of productions in Vienna and in Moscow: from now on, there would be no mention of the über-marionette in Craig's diaries, but his views on acting did not change. For example, his 1935 notes for "On Creating a Theatre," another book he intended to write, include the same recommendations for the actors in *Hamlet* as in 1909: the same speed of delivery, the use of *stasis,* and slow movements.[26]

Though Craig's preference for symbolic movement was as strong as ever, he appreciated Meyerhold's work with the actors and the results of his method, because it broke free from Stanislavsky's "psychologism."

He wrote to Meyerhold in 1935: "You seem to have released the Russian actor from a strait-waistcoat. Now he breathes and smiles and dances. If he thinks, he no longer troubles the spectator with all that—if he has worked hard, we spectators are never reminded of that."[27] Craig seemed to find in Meyerhold a fellow artist who shared with him the same preoccupation with movement; Meyerhold tested Stanislavsky's method, the commedia dell' arte improvisation, and the biomechanics and finally adopted a stylized movement according to each type of drama produced—all the while controlling the depersonalized and often-masked actor. Craig wrote to Meyerhold with sad irony:

> As you know, I am a nice-scenographer—"très jolis décors, quelquefois tragiques." . . . more important still, you like them—ça je le vois! But the ideas for Theatre—these serious ideas, these reasons—which really may be good—these you cannot know of: and they are so contradictory that I myself have been very busy for some years trying to divide the sheep and the goats, the chicken and the turkeys and so on—and the elephants. And when my Ark—my Noah's Ark is ready to float, there will be only two people whom I shall not be able to find a reason for or be in any way obliging to. Those will be the man and the woman. That will be the tragic thing: and it would have been so fine to have been able to speak your language with you, so that you might have helped to pass through this difficult problem. It is really a problem which has troubled me for many years: and when I see you and your wife [Zinaida Raikh] on the stage, then I say to myself "the problem is solved" . . . and yet I have my doubts.
>
> You understand, don't you, Meyerhold . . . you have thought of all this yourself, too, and it has puzzled you.
>
> If the Book of Genesis is to be believed, this problem of man and woman on the larger scale was one which puzzled le bon Dieu. I don't know whether he has solved it to this day.[28]

For Craig, the problem remained unsolved, for, as he said, the actor refused to be a super-marionette: the ideal in which he had believed thirty years earlier was still unshattered.

In 1936 Craig left Italy and went to France, where he would spend the rest of his life. He left behind the stage model. His experiments were never to be renewed, though he would never give up the hope of a school. He remained committed to his idea of an ideal theatre using "unpersonal mediums." In 1944 he still considered "The Actor and the Uber-Marionette" his best essay, as shown by his note on an old draft of a letter to his friend Jan C. de Vos.[29] And in 1951, while contemplating a reproduction of one of Piero della Francesca's paintings, Craig jotted down instructions for some future painter of über-marionettes.[30]

The *Index,* written by Craig in 1955, when he was eighty-three, contains an interesting passage that illuminates Craig's sometimes opportunistic attitude toward all those—artists and critics, patrons and powers to be—whom he expected to help him reform the theatre:

> For although I have swayed in the wind for more than eighty years of life, by *bending to the wind* I have prevailed for fifty-two years with my dream for the Theatre.
>
> . . . The bending I refer to here is *the kind which knows how* to avoid a break. And in my work, which I realised *would take long to do,* a hundred storms would come upon me. *I would not permit a break*—bending, one is to be endured, and so I bent with the wind.[31]

This is why the kinetic theatre was kept out of sight, the idea of the über-marionette was put in the wings, and the Belief was never disclosed.

Craig died eleven years later, in 1966.

Afterword

"Bending to the wind," unwilling to intimidate or alienate the actor, Craig was preparing the ground for the realization of his new art of the theatre. His detractors were many, and Lee Simonson was certainly not the fiercest among them.[1] Nevertheless, the list of those for whom Craig was a master is very long: Meyerhold, Tairov, Vakhtangov, Reinhardt, Jessner, Schiller, Côpeau, Baty, Jouvet, Decroux, Artaud, Barrault, Robert Edmond Jones, Peter Brook, Svoboda, and Strehler passed on his teachings to new generations of artists, such as Patrice Chéreau or Peter Hall. Craig's work sanctioned the idea of an artificial theatre that initiates a new dialectical relationship between empirical reality and artistic truth, a relationship based not on the illusory reproduction of empirical facts but on the expression of an intuitive or intellectual comprehension. Craig's once revolutionary concept of a simplified, architectonic, and suggestive scene, a concept that Appia shared, has been part of our contemporary theatre for a long time. His screens have never become outdated and his designs were used in recent years, for example, by Richard Peduzzi for Chéreau's productions, such as *La Dispute* (1973), *The Ring of the Nibelung* (1976), *Peer Gynt* (1981), and *La Fausse Suivante* (1985), and by Yannis Kokkos for Antoine Vitez' production of *Hamlet* (1983) and *Le Prince Travesti* (1983). The cult of the actor has been replaced during the past few decades by that of the director, and although Craig's concept of the director as a multi-faceted artist has remained only a vision, his concept of the actor as an instrument has inspired directors of such varied orientations as Richard Foreman, Chéreau, Robert Wilson, and Tadeusz Kantor. Not so long ago, marionettized actors were used by the Bread and Puppet Theatre, and life-size marionettes were used together with actors by Tadeusz Kantor in *The Dead Class*. The mask is used not infrequently on the contemporary stage. But the marionette theatre is still a minor genre, as it was fifty years ago, and the kinetic stage has never been brought into being. Thus, many of Craig's ideas have been put into practice, but the theatre he envisioned has never been created.

Neither did the emergence of the actor as an artist à la Craig take place. Tools in the hands of a director or free to compose their characters, actors today still "impersonate" and few are able to "interpret." Nor can we say that Craig helped the actor reach the phase of interpretation. He did not discover the rules that lay at the basis of his ideal art of movement. And he did not find the right puppet for the über-marionette theatre.

Craig aspired to build a fictitious world by means of movement, scene, and voice—a world where magic and religion would merge.[2] Figures, props, and scene were to be real *objets d'art,* which would continue to exist long after the performance ceased.[3] These *objets d'art* were supposed to present neither "real" nor "ideal," but "true," life. But the main problem that Craig encountered was the expression of Truth, a moral perception, not by these *objets d'art,* but by movement: through the molding of an unstable, flowing, temporal medium, sensually apprehended. Craig proceeded first to the simplification and stylization of everyday, routine movement, discarding mimetic gestures and adopting geometric, symbolic forms; his second step was to sever the traditional ties of movement to linguistic utterance—yet keeping some linguistic utterance in improvisation. While the elimination of the written text reduced significance, it also clarified it: Craig did not intend any place for entropy in this world. He considered the production a metaphor, made up of the organized interaction of symbolic elements. Defining the symbol as the "visible sign of an idea," he claimed that symbolism was "the very essence of the Theatre."[4] Suggestive and symbolic movement replaced realistic acting, then the über-marionette replaced the actor. In his search for symbolic movement, Craig modified performative movement. His treatment of movement involved manipulation of its shape (simplification and stylization of routine movement), frequency, and speed. He preferred suggestive, nonmimetic forms—excluding deictic, intentional, and attitudinal gestures—and reduced their frequency, thereby enhancing expressivity. He also manipulated duration, devising slow or swift movement and actions; rhythm thus became symbolic. By reducing the number of gestures and by using *stasis,* Craig dematerialized the dramatic subject; symbolization led to its actualization. In addition, the systematic use of nonrealistic, uncommon, symbolic means and techniques had a stronger impact on the audience, a subliminal impact.[4] Craig aimed at creating a transcendental experience; not an aesthetic experience for its own sake, as Wilde would claim, but one that would "restore Belief," permeating everyday life.

No doubt, Craig's self-imposed martyrdom was not without its charm. While he suffered from being kept at a safe distance by the majority of the theatre people in England as elsewhere, he took pride in being not only one of the "Impossibles," an *artiste maudit,* but also a Sage.[5] He never stopped being an actor who loved masks and cherished some of the images created and projected by the "enemy," though he was helpless—or perhaps too disdainful—to fight the rest. What was Craig's "Secret Self"? This question still awaits an answer. But the main reason for Craig's being "misunderstood" was his attitude toward the actor, an attitude that confused followers and opponents alike. Indeed, Craig praised different levels of creation and expression in movement: an ideal, abstract movement performed by a man-made instrument; the symbolic interpretation of the gifted actor, master of his mind and body; and the mimetic projection of a powerful personality. One's need to believe in Craig's sanction of the actor as a creative artist is certainly not a good reason for taking Craig's retractions—as alluring as they might be—at their face value. Craig's greatness lies elsewhere. Even when he chose to establish Irving as a model for the creative actor, Craig still regarded the über-marionette as the ideal performer, always to be trusted. Had he "bent" less to the "wind," there would also have been, no doubt, fewer misunderstandings concerning Craig's views.

But the main charge against Craig is his failure to complete a formulation of a coherent theory of movement, which would have certainly made clear once and for all his attitude toward the actor. The factors that prevented Craig from completing his theory are not only complex but also interwoven. Some are psychological, some aesthetic; some are related to the medium itself (movement), and some are purely circumstantial. For example, it is possible that Craig's attitude toward Irving was a major obstacle not only in his career as an actor but also in his various attempts to systemize his innovations in movement. Thus it is important to recall Craig's biographical notes, written for the catalogue of his exhibition that opened in Vienna on 1 October 1905: "18 years old—accept office. The progression of E[dward] G[ordon] C[raig]. Theatre—as actor. All the parts. Felt, not *perceived,* that beyond Irving one could not go. Saw no way. Stopped acting. Then came the beginning of perception. Saw dreams. Attempted to realize them on paper in paint, ink, line & colour. Impossible—."[6] Irving's dominant personality made Craig aware of his limitations as an actor (though he was considered a good one), of his inability to go "beyond" Irving, that is, to compete with and overshadow him. By then, Craig only "felt" this "beyond," perception came later. How to realize this perception, this vision, by means of his own body, he ignored. His attempts in stylized movement in his London productions were only improvements—inspired by French Symbolism—on Irving's style. Irving remained the model for the existing actor—a model whose method, not product, Craig sought to understand, if not to duplicate. The existing actor was expected to invent, like Irving, a pattern of symbols, namely, to interiorize images perceived in daily life and convey them through symbols. Craig himself was unable to teach this process, but no act of artistic creation can be programmed or taught. If Craig-Hamlet was unable to break away from the spell of Irving's acting and his Claudius was not killed after all, his Ghost was nevertheless revenged, if only partially, for Craig did develop a new and coherent theory of a kinesymbolic, architectonic scene.

An obstacle of a different nature was the complexity and insubstantiality of the medium itself. Movement is a *process* that is visually perceived, first in its relation to space, then to time. Indeed, this very insubstantiality, as well as the indisputable physical impact of movement on the beholder, led Craig to consider movement as the most appropriate medium for conveying spiritual values. The shaping of movement involves solving interrelated problems concerning space, time, and dramatic function. The director must determine not only the form and orientation of movement but also its position within the physiological context and its position and conspicuousness within the larger context, or syntax, of the stage. Factors such as duration, tempo, timing, rhythm, and frequency are essential. Finally, the director has to coordinate movement with voice, sound (music and sound effects), settings, props, and lighting. As it was, Craig provided only basic principles and guidelines but not a formulated solution to these problems. He proceeded to define his ideal movement by elimination, by instructing "what not to do." He rejected the stereotypes of pantomime and recommended, without entering into details, the use of suggestive and symbolic forms, as well as a symbolic manipulation of duration. He assumed he could discover the basic *rules* by which the rich complexity of movement could be ordered, so that each production would no longer get an ad hoc treatment—as in Craig's own London productions. Rules could facilitate the change of form and duration and ensure the aesthetic value and the impact of movement. The rules were supposed to bring order and control into the insubstantiality of the medium, while they would also assure its expressivity. However, the complexity of the medium is so great that it is unlikely that *universal* rules, such as Craig searched for, can ever be discovered.[7]

Nor could Craig's short-lived experiments lead to the discovery of these rules. Craig's attitude in carrying out these experiments was self-contradictory: he considered the artist a "seer" and the work of art an intuitively comprehended "revelation." Yet he now expected to reach his goal through a series of experiments that he carried out in a pseudoscientific spirit, for he lacked both method and assiduity. Besides, the instrument he used for this purpose was unsuitable, for the puppet has only a limited range of movement; as we have seen, this limited range of movement appealed to Craig because it offered an already simplified, restricted, stylized, and nonrealistic movement. In addition, the puppet was a constant reminder of the actor's flexibility and of Craig's own inability to work with actors for a long period. Thus, contrary to Craig's expectations, and without his being aware, the puppet proved to be a psychological and technical hindrance. Experiments carried out with actors, as well as practical work in the theatre, could have evolved a more coherent theory of movement: the fact is that Craig's main innovations concerning movement were made during his work on the London productions and on *Hamlet* in Moscow. Practice would have put Craig in close contact with other fellow artists, a contact that had proved so beneficial for him in the past. Work with a group of dedicated people, such as those at his short-lived school, could have kept Craig's creative powers alert, for even bad improvisation, such as he had often witnessed in Moscow, could be stimulating to him, stirring up a process of assimilation, selection, rejection, transformation, or invention of images.

Craig's limited practice in working in the regular theatre brings up the issue of his "practicality." Since those who worked with him and were sympathetic to his ideas claim that he was a practical man of the theatre, the question to be raised is why the image of the impractical Craig was born and why it still survives. The answer lies with those who created it and whom Craig called the "enemy": those who opposed his ideas but were unable to fight them on aesthetic grounds, those who considered these ideas subversive because they threatened their very existence as "artists of the theatre," and even those who interpreted the über-marionette as a metaphor because of their own need to believe in the creative actor. Yet it is easy to understand how this image prevailed. In his work with the actors Craig was often searching and experimenting before arriving at a final, set expression—a method far more confusing than a system of acting that dictates what to do instead of "what not to do." Nor were the innovative screens an easy tool for the unimaginative actor, director, or designer. Unfortunately for Craig, it was this image that a whole community of theatre people identified with. Craig never resigned himself to being only a theorist, but his readiness to accept the existing conditions is questionable, since he always imposed his own conditions: to compromise meant to deny the very things he held sacred in art. Consequently, it is not surprising that his lack of practical work directly rebounded on his theory of movement and that he never had the chance to test his ideas on acting and improvisation.

Finally, Craig's ideal theatre, using a man-made instrument for movement, never came into being, not because it was impractical, but because it was based on a concept that overlooked one of the major functions of theatre. Not only is theatre an answer, religious or not, to a transcendental urge, it also fulfills a basic psychological and social need. It gratifies the need to present or witness a fictitious event, in common: this is a collective experience—bringing together the performers and the audience, be that audience one or many—ratified by social and cultural conventions. The theatrical experience gratifies not the actor's need to pretend, as Craig claimed, but his need to transgress—by means of his pretending—the limits of his socially recognized self, within the limits of social and cultural conventions, for a definite span of time. It also gratifies the spectator's need to witness (by sensual perception) a fictitious event (the presentation of real experience) performed by real people and to become emotionally and intellectually involved—that is, respond to the event or to the manner of its presentation—in the (often erroneous) belief that this act would have no direct repercussion on his life. The spectator's involvement can also be caused by his very participation in the act of witnessing, by the awareness of belonging to a larger social body that endorses this "make-believe," the presentation of a fictitious event. The sanction of the event by society is vital, because it is also the sanction of the special bond between the actor and the spectator, a bond created by means of a delegation of power: the actor is (also) the spectator's extension, and the actor's (fictive) transgression becomes that of the spectator. Such an unmediated bond of complicity and communion can never exist in the über-marionette theatre, only in a theatre where the performer is a living human body. The advent of the über-marionette and for that matter of the kinetic stage, alters the relationship between the stage and the audience. The new art, which may or may not "restore Belief to the world," can never create such a communal experience of authorized transgression nor have the same emotional and physical impact.

Craig sowed, as he said, the "seeds" of a new art of movement.[8] The scions of these seeds were engrafted on the living tree of the theatre, as were those sown by Appia, Isadora Duncan, Stanislavsky, Brecht, and Artaud, and as will be those sown today by Merce Cunningham, Richard Foreman, Robert Wilson, and Pina Bausch. Thus, one day, the theatre will perhaps, in Craig's words, "unite men" and "restore Belief to the world," a belief in "friendliness—humour—love—ease—peace."

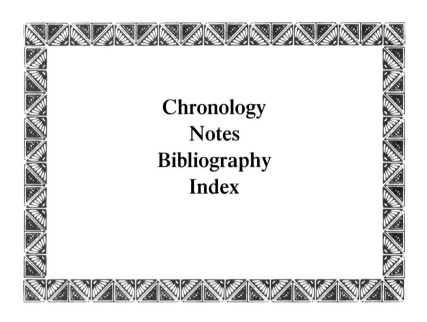

Chronology
Notes
Bibliography
Index

Chronology

1872	Edward Gordon Craig born to Ellen Terry and Edward William Godwin at Stevenage, England, January 16.
1889	First acting role, at the Lyceum.
1897	Last acting role.
1898	*The Page* (1898–1901).
1899	*Gordon Craig's Book of Penny Toys.*
1900	*Bookplates.* Productions: *Dido and Aeneas.*
1901	Productions: *The Masque of Love.* Exhibition in London.
1902	Productions: *Acis and Galatea, Bethlehem.* Exhibition in London.
1903	Productions: *The Vikings at Helgeland, Much Ado about Nothing.* Exhibitions in London.
1904	Berlin. Isadora Duncan. Exhibitions in London, Weimar, Berlin.
1905	*The Art of the Theatre.* The über-marionette project. Exhibitions in London, Berlin, Dresden, Weimar, Dusseldorf, Cologne, Munich, Vienna.
1906	*Isadora Duncan. Sechs Bewegungsstudien.* The kinetic stage. Scene for Duse's *Rosmersholm,* Florence. Exhibitions in London, Rotterdam, Florence.
1907	Florence, *Motion.* Experiments with the über-marionette and the stage model. The screens. Writes "The Artists of the Theatre of the Future" and "The Actor and the Uber-Marionette." Exhibition in London.
1908	Publishes a portfolio of etchings. *The Mask* (1908–29). Publication of the two articles, written the previous year, in *The Mask.* Begins work on *Hamlet* in Moscow. Exhibitions in London and Florence.

Chronology

1909 Experiments with screens on the stage model.
1910 Patent for the screens. Publishes another portfolio of etchings.
1911 *On the Art of the Theatre*. Exhibitions in New York and London.
1912 *Hamlet,* Moscow. Exhibitions in London and Manchester.
1913 *Towards a New Theatre. A Living Theatre*. The School for the Art of the Theatre, Florence. Exhibitions in Liverpool, Dublin, Leeds, Warsaw, Mannheim, and Cambridge, Mass.
1914 World War I. Exhibitions in London and Zurich.
1915 Exhibitions in London.
1916 Marionette plays. Exhibition in Florence.
1917 Rapallo.
1918 *The Marionnette* (twelve issues). Publishes five motions for marionettes.
1919 *The Theatre Advancing*. Exhibitions in London.
1920 Exhibition in London.
1921 *Puppets and Poets*. Exhibitions in Oxford and London.
1922 Exhibitions in Amsterdam, London, Manchester, Glasgow, Bradford.
1923 *Scene*. Exhibitions in London, Florence, Haarlem.
1924 *Woodcuts and Some Words*. Exhibitions in London and Wembley.
1925 *Books and Theatres, Nothing, or the Bookplate*. Exhibition in London.
1926 Produces *The Pretenders,* with Johannes and Adam Poulsen, Copenhagen. Exhibitions in Manchester and The Hague.
1927 Exhibitions in Brooklyn, Amsterdam, Magdeburg.
1928 Designs for *Macbeth*. Exhibitions in London, New York, Whitechapel.
1929 *Hamlet,* Cranach Press, Weimar, with designs by Craig. Last issue of *The Mask*. Exhibition in Barcelona.
1930 *Henry Irving, A Production—The Pretenders*. Exhibition in Berlin.
1931 *Ellen Terry and Her Secret Self.*
1934 Exhibition in New York.
1938 Exhibition in London.
1948 Exhibition in London.
1949 Exhibition in London.
1955 Exhibitions in Paris and Vienna.
1957 *Index to the Story of My Days*. Exhibition in London.
1960 Exhibition in Paris.
1961 Exhibitions in Paris, Nottingham, Boston.
1962 Exhibitions in Florence, Rome, London, New York, Paris.

Chronology

1963	Exhibitions in Oakdale, Long Island; Flushing, New York; Venice.
1964	Exhibitions in London.
1965	Exhibition in Einhoven.
1966	Exhibitions in Paris and London.
1966	Death of Edward Gordon Craig at Vence, France, July 29.

Notes

Preface

1. Charles R. Lyons, "Gordon Craig's Concept of the Actor," in *Total Theatre,* ed. E. T. Kirby (New York: Dutton, 1969), pp. 59, 63.
2. Dietrich Kreidt, "Kunsttheorie der Inszenierung: Zur Kritik der Konzeptionen Adolphe Appias und Edward Gordon Craigs," Diss. Freien Universität Berlin, 1968, pp. 126–30, 139–40.
3. Arnold Rood, " 'After the Practise the Theory': Gordon Craig and Movement," *Theatre Research,* 11, Nos. 2–3 (1971), 84.
4. Harry C. Payne, "Rituals of Balance and Silence: The Ideal Theatre of Gordon Craig," *Bulletin of Research in the Humanities,* 82, No. 4 (Winter 1979), 426.

1. Father and Master

1. In 1876 Godwin advised John Coleman and Samuel Phelps on the settings and costumes chosen for the production of *Henry V.* In 1880 he designed the costumes for Miss Bateman's production of *Othello* and in 1881 the settings and costumes for W. G. Wills' *Juana,* produced by Mrs. Squire Bancroft. For Tennyson's *The Cup,* produced the same year by Henry Irving at the Lyceum, he designed Ellen Terry's costume and the cup. In 1882 he attended to the mise en scène of *Queen and Cardinal,* by W. S. Raleigh, at the Haymarket Theatre and helped Hermann Vezin to produce *The Cynic,* by Herman Merivale. Godwin designed the settings and costumes for Robert Buchanan's *Storm Beaten* in 1883, produced at the Adelphi Theatre, as well as the costumes for *The Merchant of Venice* produced by Hermann Vezin, and the settings and costumes for two productions of Wilson Barrett: *Claudian,* by W. G. Wills, in 1883, and *Hamlet,* in 1884. At the request of Lady Archibald Campbell, a well-known Aesthete and painter, he produced in

1884 an open-air performance of *As You Like It,* with a group of amateurs coming from fashionable society and Aesthete circles. In 1885 he produced another open-air performance with "The Pastoral Players," as this group came to be known: this was *The Faithful Shepherdesse,* by Fletcher. In 1886, not long before he died, Godwin produced *Helena in Troas,* by John Todhunter, at Hengler's Circus, *Fair Rosamund,* adapted from Tennyson's *Beckett,* and *The Fool's Revenge,* adapted from Hugo's *Le Roi s'amuse.* See John Stokes, *Resistible Theatres* (London: Paul Elek Books, 1972), pp. 31–68, and Dudley Harbron, *The Conscious Stone* (1949; rpt. New York: Benjamin Blom, 1971), pp. 103–15, 121, 145–46, 167–83.

2. Enid Rose, *Gordon Craig and the Theatre: A Record and an Interpretation* (1931; rpt. New York: Haskell House Publishers, 1973), p. 4.
3. Denis Bablet, *Edward Gordon Craig* (Paris: L'Arche, 1962), p. 16.
4. Paul M. Talley, "Architecture as Craig's Interim Symbol: Ruskin and Other Influences," *Educational Theatre Journal,* 19, No. 1 (March 1967), 53–54.
5. Michael Peter Loeffler, *Gordon Craig und die "Purcell Operatic Society": Ein Früher Versuch zur Uberwindung des Bühnenrealismus* (Bern: Theaterkultur-Verlag, 1971), p. 20.
6. Payne, p. 441.
7. Ellen Terry referred to the incident in a letter that Edward Craig discovered after his father's death. The letter is printed in full in his *Gordon Craig: The Story of His Life* (London: Victor Gollancz, 1968), pp. 47–48.
8. Edward Craig says that Edy "hated her father for ever afterwards." Could this have been because she rather resented his failure to take her away?
9. Edith Craig and Christopher St. John, eds., *Ellen Terry's Memoirs* (1933; rpt. Westport, Conn.: Greenwood Press, 1970), p. 83.
10. Ibid., p. 39.
11. Edward Craig, *Gordon Craig,* p. 73.
12. *Index to the Story of My Days: Some Memoirs of Edward Gordon Craig, 1872–1907.* (London: Hulton Press, 1957), p. 48; hereafter cited as *Index.* See also Edward Craig, *Gordon Craig,* pp. 52, 333.
13. *Index,* p. 163.
14. Ibid., p. 58.
15. For the letter, see Edward Craig, *Gordon Craig,* p. 73.
16. *Index,* p. 128.
17. Ibid., pp. 162, 246–48.
18. A photograph of Craig in the role of Edward IV appears in the French edition of the *Index.* See *Ma vie d'homme de théâtre,* trans. Charles Chassé (Paris: Arthaud, 1962), p. 121.
19. Ellen Terry was not in the cast. After the opening night she left for a short holiday on the Continent. See Christopher St. John, ed., *Ellen Terry and Bernard Shaw: A Correspondence* (New York: G. P. Putnam's Sons, 1932), p. 104.
20. The dates indicated in the *Index* are inaccurate. On 26 December 1896 Ellen Terry was not in London but in Monte Carlo. See ibid.

21. *Index*, p. 182.
22. On Irving's state of drunkenness that night see also Madeleine Bingham, *Henry Irving: The Greatest Victorian Actor* (New York: Stein and Day, 1978), pp. 272–73. This thesis is rejected by Laurence Irving. See his *Henry Irving: The Actor and His World* (London: Faber and Faber, 1951), pp. 596–98.
23. Christopher St. John, ed., *Ellen Terry and Bernard Shaw*, p. 105.
24. *Index*, pp. 72, 76.
25. Ibid., p. 193.
26. See Antoine Compagnon, *Nous, Michel de Montaigne* (Paris: Seuil, 1981), pp. 170–92.
27. *Index*, p. 221. See also his scrapbook "E. W. G[odwin]. 1875. Stage 1897. 1900. 1901. 1902. 1903." This scrapbook is now in the Collection Craig at the Bibliothèque Nationale in Paris; hereafter cited as Paris.
28. Edward Craig quotes the entry in full. See his *Gordon Craig*, pp. 141–42.
29. Correspondence with Martin Shaw, Gordon Craig Collection, Humanities Research Center, University of Texas at Austin; hereafter cited as Austin.
30. *Henry Irving* (London: J. M. Dent and Sons, 1930), pp. 93, 143. See also *Index*, pp. 49, 51.
31. *Index*, p. 14.
32. See also Talley, p. 54.

2. *Setting the Stage*

1. Craig believed that she recommended him to read Ruskin only because of Godwin's admiration for this artist (*Index*, p. 105).
2. Ibid., p. 66.
3. Ibid., p. 120. In 1899 his mother gave him a much-prized gift—Rossetti's scrapbook, with drawings by the artist and many newspaper clippings (etchings and drawings of medieval costumes, arms and ships, crowd scenes, and various ceremonies) that Rossetti later used for his paintings. This scrapbook is now in the Collection Craig at the Bibliothèque Nationale in Paris.
4. *Index*, pp. 99, 100, 173. On Loeb's influence on Craig, see Ferruccio Marotti, *Edward Gordon Craig* (Bologna: Cappelli, 1961), p. 25.
5. Emile Zola, *The Experimental Novel and Other Essays* (New York: Cassell Publishing, 1894), p. 109.
6. Edward Craig, *Gordon Craig*, p. 82
7. According to Edward Craig, he acted in twenty-four plays. See ibid., p. 390. See also Craig's "Notebook of a Young Actor. 1896. 1890–92. 1936," Paris.
8 Edward Craig, "Gordon Craig and Hubert von Herkomer," *Theatre Research*, 10, No. 1 (1969), 7–16. See also Stokes, *Resistible Theatres*, pp. 69–110.
9. William Rothenstein, *Men and Memories: A History of the Arts 1872–1922, Being the Recollections of William Rothenstein* (New York: Tudor Publishing, n.d.), I, 277.
10. *Ellen Terry and Her Secret Self* (London: Sampson, Low, Marston, 1931), p. 74.

3. The Symbolist Theatre

1. Stéphane Mallarmé, *Divagations* (Paris: Eugène Fasquelle, 1897), p. 142.
2. Haskell M. Block, *Mallarmé and the Symbolist Drama* (Detroit: Wayne State University Press, 1963), p. 92.
3. Pierre Valin, "Le Symbole au Théâtre," *L'Ermitage*, 3 January 1892, pp. 28–29.
4. François Coulon, "De l'Action dans le Drame symbolique," *La Plume*, No. 87, 1 December 1892, pp. 499–500.
5. Camille Mauclair, "Notes sur un essai de dramaturgie symboliste," *La Revue Indépendante*, March 1892, pp. 307, 309, 314.
6. Charles Morice, *La Littérature de tout à l'heure* (Paris: Perrin, 1889), pp. 34, 366.
7. "La synthèse rend à l'esprit sa patrie, réunit l'héritage, rappelle l'Art à la Vérité et aussi à la Beauté. La synthèse de l'art, c'est: LE REVE JOYEUX DE LA VERITE BELLE" (ibid., p. 359). Emphasis in the original (my translation).
8. "La suggestion peut ce que ne pourrait l'expression. La suggestion est le langage des correspondances et des affinités de l'âme et de la nature. Au lieu d'*exprimer* des choses leur reflet, elle pénètre en elles et devient leur propre voix. La suggestion n'est jamais indifférente et, d'essence, est toujours nouvelle car c'est le caché, l'inexpliqué et l'*inexprimable* des choses qu'elle dit" ibid., pp. 378–79. Emphasis in the original (my translation).
9. See James L. Kugel, *The Techniques of Strangeness in Symbolist Poetry* (New Haven, Yale University Press, 1971), pp. 28–31.
10. "La mise-en-scène dépend nécessairement du système dramatique adopté, et puisque symbole il y a, elle en est le signe et le symbole même. . . . La parole crée le décor comme le reste. . . . *Le décor doit être une pure fiction ornementale qui complète l'illusion par des analogies de couleur et de lignes avec le drame*. . . . Le plus souvent, il suffira d'un fond et de quelques draperies mobiles, pour donner l'impression de l'infinie multiplicité du temps et du lieu. . . . [Ainsi] le théâtre sera ce qu'il doit être: un *prétexte* au rêve" (Pierre Quillard, "De l'Inutilité absolue de la Mise-en-scène exacte," *La Revue d'Art Dramatique*, 22, April–June 1891, p. 180). Emphasis in the original (my translation).
11. Jarry's *Ubu Roi* at the Théâtre de l'Oeuvre on 10 December 1896, is an example here. Arthur Symons and W. B. Yeats were among the audience on this memorable evening.
12. *Index*, p. 150.
13. "Uber-Marions. Berlin. 1905. 1906.", UM-B, p. 15[v], Paris. Throughout, I shall use Craig's own short titles for the notebooks, UM-A and UM-B, and his pagination.
14. Jacques Robichez, *Le Symbolisme au théâtre: Lugné-Poe et les débuts de L'Oeuvre* (Paris: L'Arche, 1957), p. 75. See also Anatole France, "The Marionettes of M. Signoret," *The Mask*, 5, No. 2 (October 1912), 98–103.

15. Agnès Humbert, *Les Nabis et leur époque, 1888–1900* (Geneva: Pierre Cailler, 1954), pp. 108–9.
16. Rothenstein, I, 276.
17. Ibid., p. 275.

4. The London Productions

1. See Edward Craig, *Gordon Craig,* p. 114.
2. Edward Craig, "Gordon Craig and Hubert von Herkomer," pp. 11–13.
3. See his notes for the catalogue of his exhibition in Vienna in October 1905 ("Uber-Marions," UM-B, p. 14[v]).
4. Reproduced in the *Index,* p. 208.
5. Max Beerbohm, "'Much Ado' and Mr. Craig's Setting," *Saturday Review,* 30 May 1903; reprinted in *More Theatres, 1898–1903* (London: Rupert Hart Davis, 1969), p. 574.
6. Edith Craig and Christopher St. John, eds., *Ellen Terry's Memoirs,* p. 267.
7. "Notebook. 1897," Department of Special Collections, University Research Library, University of California at Los Angeles; hereafter cited as UCLA.
8. Text and design by Craig reproduced in T. S. Eliot, "Gordon Craig's Socratic Dialogues," *Drama,* No. 36 (Spring 1955), p. 19.
9. Arthur Symons, "A New Art of the Stage," in *Studies in Seven Arts* (London: Constable, 1906), p. 350.
10. Edward Craig, *Gordon Craig,* p. 129.
11. Symons, p. 138.
12. Edward Craig, *Gordon Craig,* pp. 153–54, 172–73.
13. Letter to Ellen Terry, 3 June 1903. See Christopher St. John, p. 294.

5. Foundations

1. *Index,* p. 213.
2. "Book Reviews," *The Mask,* 1, No. 8 (October 1908), 161.
3. Letter to Ellen Terry of August 1905 from Zurich, UCLA.
4. Letter to Martin Shaw, quoted by Edward Craig, *Gordon Craig,* p. 184.
5. *Henry Irving,* p. 175.
6. Oscar Wilde, "Pen and Pencil," in *Complete Works* (London: Collins, 1973), pp. 997, 1030.
7. Ellen Terry told Bernard Shaw, in her letter of 13 October 1896, that "Ted caught socialism long ago." See Christopher St. John, p. 75.
8. Edward Craig, *Gordon Craig,* p. 168.
9. Ibid., p. 173.
10. "Notes and Plans for the School of the Art of the Theatre and the International Art Theatre Society. 1904–1906," Austin.
11. See Edith Craig and Christopher St. John, eds., *Ellen Terry's Memoirs,* p. 256.
12. Wilde, "The Critic as Artist," in *Complete Works,* p. 1026.

13. Ibid., p. 1017.
14. Ibid., p. 1033 (my emphasis).
15. "Sketchbook 1896–1899," UCLA.

6. Assertions and Self-assertion

1. *Index,* p. 251. The chronology published by Janet Leeper mentions July 1903 as the date of Craig's visit to Weimar. See Janet Leeper, *Edward Gordon Craig: Designs for the Theatre* (Harmondsworth: Penguin Books, 1948), p. 35.
2. Isadora Duncan, *My Life* (1927; rpt. New York: Liveright, 1955), p. 184.
3. See Edward Craig, *Gordon Craig,* pp. 180–83.
4. Gerhard Masur, *Imperial Berlin* (London: Routledge and Kegan Paul, 1971), p. 245.
5. Roy Pascal, *From Naturalism to Expressionism: German Literature and Society, 1880–1918.* (New York: Basic Books, 1973), pp. 277–314.
6. Sheldon Cheney, *The New Movement in the Theatre* (1914; rpt. Westport, Conn.: Greenwood Press, 1971), p. 103.
7. Hugo von Hofmannsthal, *Hugo von Hofmannsthal, Harry Graf Kessler: Briefwechsel, 1898–1929,* ed. Hilde Burger (Frankfurt am Main: Insel Verlag, 1968), pp. 55–102.
8. *Isadora Duncan: Sechs Bewegungsstudien von Edward Gordon Craig* (Leipzig: Insel Verlag, 1906). The Isadora Portfolio, as this publication came to be known, included six designs of Isadora and a poem.
9. See also Herman K. Doswald, "Edward Gordon Craig and Hugo von Hofmannsthal," *Theatre Research International,* 1, No. 2 (Fall 1975), 134–41.
10. Bablet, *Edward Gordon Craig,* pp. 108–9; J. L. Styan, *Max Reinhardt* (Cambridge, Cambridge University Press, 1982), pp. 43–53; Paul Stefanek, "Max Reinhardt und die Londoner Szene," in *Max Reinhardt in Europa,* eds. Edda Leisler and Gisela Prossnitz (Salzburg: Otto Müller, 1973), pp. 77–116; Frank E. Washburn-Freund, "The Evolution of Reinhardt," in *Max Reinhardt and His Theatre,* ed. Oliver M. Sayler (New York: Brentano's, 1926), pp. 44–56; Arthur Hopkins, Reply to "An International Symposium on Reinhardt," ibid., p. 339. See also Gottfried Reinhardt, *The Genius: A Memoir of Max Reinhardt* (New York: Alfred A. Knopf, 1979), pp. 70–71.
11. "Theatre–Shows and Motions," 1905, 1908–9, Austin.
12. Edward Craig suggests that Craig borrowed this form from Leoni di Sommi. See his *Gordon Craig,* p. 209.
13. Correspondence with Ellen Terry, UCLA.
14. See Loeffler, p. 119, N. 17.
15. *On the Art of the Theatre* (1911; rpt. London: Heinemann, 1968), p. 145.
16. Ibid., p. 168 (my emphasis).
17. Ibid., p. 147.
18. Ibid., p. 138.

19. Correspondence with Martin Shaw, Austin. This letter, from Dresden, was written if not during the very days when Craig was working on *The Art of the Theatre* then about a fortnight later. Craig was in Dresden briefly for the opening of his exhibition on 1 May and, according to the *Index* (p. 274), returned there on the fifteenth after finishing the essay. He was back in Berlin on the twentieth.
20. Correspondence with Ellen Terry, UCLA.
21. "'Stars,' Mr. Frohman, and the Theatre of the Future," *Saturday Review,* 3 November 1906, pp. 548–49.

7. Movement

1. Francis Steegmuller, ed., *"Your Isadora": The Love Story of Isadora Duncan and Gordon Craig Told through Letters and Diaries* (New York: Random House, 1974), pp. 87, 93, 234–35, 241, 248–49, 267, 269–70, 282–83.
2. See ibid., pp. 47, 93, 102.
3. Ibid., p. 170.
4. Two-thirds of the immigrants came now from the Austro-Hungarian empire and from the Russian empire; the rest came from Italy, Greece, Germany, Norway, Sweden, and Ireland.
5. Isadora Duncan, *The Art of the Dance,* ed. Sheldon Cheney (1928; rpt. New York: Theatre Art Books, 1969), p. 56.
6. Steegmuller, p. 47.
7. Duncan, *The Art of the Dance,* pp. 90–91. See also Steegmuller, p. 91.
8. Steegmuller, pp. 42–43.
9. Duncan, *The Art of the Dance,* p. 110.
10. Ibid., p. 190.
11. John Martin, "Isadora Duncan and Basic Dance," in *Isadora Duncan,* ed. Paul Magriel (New York: Holt, 1947), pp. 1–17.
12. Susan Langer, *Feeling and Form* (New York: Charles Scribner's Sons, 1953), pp. 183–84.
13. Carl van Vechten, "Duncan Concerts in New York" and "The New Isadora," in *Isadora Duncan,* ed. Paul Magriel, pp. 19–25, 27–33.
14. See Paul Magriel, ed., *Isadora Duncan,* p. 59.
15. Duncan, *My Life,* p. 168.
16. Steegmuller, p. 176.
17. Duncan, *The Art of the Dance,* p. 30.
18. Duncan, *My Life,* pp. 340–41.
19. Steegmuller, p. 91. Steegmuller believes that her essay "The Dance and Nature" was written during this period.
20. Ibid., pp. 170–71, 172–73, 175. Her preoccupation was also closely related to the difficulties she was experiencing at that moment: a weak physical condition, bad orchestras, and the urgent need to renew her repertoire.
21. Martin Fallas Shaw, *Up to Now* (London: Oxford University Press, 1929), p. 59.

22. Harry Kessler, *The Diaries of a Cosmopolitan: Count Harry Kessler, 1918–1937,* ed. Charles Kessler (London: Weidenfeld and Nicholson, 1971), p. 328.
23. Steegmuller, p. 79.
24. Reproduced in Steegmuller, n.p.
25. Correspondence with Martin Shaw, Austin.
26. Letter of February 1905, ibid.
27. Francis Cotton, "Gordon Craig's Scheme to Abolish Both Actors and Playwrights," *Washington Post,* 1 December 1907.
28. *On the Art of the Theatre,* p. 53.
29. "Uber-Marions," UM-B, p. 18^r.
30. Laurence Irving tells about the one actor in Irving's company who ever dared and asked Irving to let the moon rays fall also on him—in other words, to let him also stand in the light, as the plot demanded. This actor was none other than William Terris, who befriended Craig while he was a young, inexperienced actor at the Lyceum. See Laurence Irving, *Henry Irving,* pp. 362–63.
31. "Uber-Marions," UM-B, ft. p. 18^r. Pierre Bugard's psychoanalytic study of the actor would have greatly pleased Craig, for it confirms his thesis that acting is not an art. See Pierre Bugard, *Le Comédien et son double: Psychologie du comédien* (Paris: Stock, 1970).
32. Letter of 2 August 1905 from Zurich, correspondence with Ellen Terry, Austin.
33. Henry Irving, *The Drama: Addresses* (1892; rpt. New York: Benjamin Blom, 1969), pp. 56–57.
34. "Uber-Marions," UM-B, p. 15^v.
35. Ibid., UM-A, pp. 9^r, 9^v, 10^r (my emphasis).
36. *On the Art of the Theatre,* p. 11.
37. Ibid., p. 174.
38. Ibid., p. 11. On the artist's interiorization of images perceived in nature, see Mikel Dufrenne, *Phénoménologie de l'expérience esthétique* (Paris: Presses Universitaires de France, 1967), pp. 195, 405, 631.
39. *On the Art of the Theatre,* p. 35.
40. Ibid., p. 37.
41. See John Heilpern, *Conference of the Birds* (New York: Bobbs-Merrill, 1978), p. 18.
42. *On the Art of the Theatre,* p. 13.
43. Masks were used, for example, for *The Masque of Love,* where most of them had been made by Craig himself. See Edward Craig, *Gordon Craig,* p. 148.
44. "Uber-Marions," UM-A, p. $3b^v$.
45. Paul Ricoeur, *La Métaphore vive* (Paris: Seuil, 1975), pp. 310–21, 374–99.
46. Correspondence with Ellen Terry, UCLA.
47. Payne, p. 426.
48. "Confessions. 1901. 1902. 1903," Austin.
49. This book has been pointed out by Jean Jacquot. See his "Craig, Yeats et le

théâtre d'Orient," in *Les Théâtres d'Asie,* ed. Jean Jacquot (Paris: Centre National de la Recherche Scientifique, 1968), pp. 271–83.

50. Arthur Symons, *Plays, Acting, and Music: A Book of Theory* (London: Duckworth, 1903), pp. 3–8. See also his "Word on Puppets," *The Mask,* 5, No. 2 (October 1912), 103.
51. See Craig's "Note" on *Rosmersholm,* published in the program in December 1906.
52. Edward Craig, *Gordon Craig,* p. 210. Teschner's name was misprinted here as "Jessner" (private communication of Edward Craig to the author).
53. See Franz Hadamowsky, *Richard Teschner und sein Figurenspiegel* (Wien: Eduard Wancura, 1956), and Arthur Roessler, *Richard Teschner* (Wien: Gerlach und Wielding, 1947).
54. Erwin Panofsky, *L'Oeuvre d'art et ses significations: Essais sur les "arts visuels"* (Paris: Gallimard, 1969), p. 63.
55. In a letter to Martin Shaw that can be dated as of 1905 or 1906, Craig wrote that he was reading daily about Egypt (correspondence with Martin Shaw, Austin). See also Edward Craig, *Gordon Craig,* p. 226.
56. "Uber-Marions," UM-B, p. 4^{v}.
57. Correspondence with Ellen Terry, Austin.
58. Correspondence with Martin Shaw, Austin.
59. "Uber-Marions," UM-B, p. 17^{r}.
60. Ibid., p. 18^{r} (Craig's emphasis).
61. Ibid., UM-B, p. 17^{r}.
62. Ibid.
63. Ibid., UM-A, p. 5^{v}.
64. Ibid., p. 10^{v}.
65. Ibid., UM-B, p. 17^{v}. See also his notebook "The Theatre. Costume. Action. 1901. 1905," Paris.
66. "Uber-Marions," UM-B, p. 4^{v}.
67. See the interview with Francis Cotton, "Gordon Craig's Scheme to Abolish Both Actors and Playwrights," *Washington Post,* 1 December 1907, p. 4.
68. "Uber-Marions," UM-A, pp. 24^{v}–25^{r} (Craig's emphasis).
69. Ibid., p. 12^{v}.
70. Nina Auerbach, *Woman and the Demon: The Life of a Victorian Myth* (Cambridge, Mass.: Harvard University Press, 1982), p. 100.
71. *On the Art of the Theatre,* p. 86.
72. Arthur Symons, *Studies in Seven Arts,* p. 352.
73. " 'Stars,' Mr. Frohman and the Theatre of the Future," *Saturday Review,* 3 November 1906, pp. 548–49.
74. "Uber-Marions," UM-B, p. 21^{r}.

8. Scene and the Kinetic Stage

1. See letter to William Rothenstein, written after the opening night of *The Vikings.* Quoted by Rothenstein, II, 54.

2. Arthur Symons, *Studies in Seven Arts,* pp. 349–50.
3. Ibid., pp. 353–54.
4. Talley, p. 52–60.
5. Catherine Valogne, *Gordon Craig* (Paris: Presses Littéraires de France, 1953), p. 27; Denis Bablet, *Esthétique générale du décor de théâtre de 1870 à 1914* (Paris: Centre National de la Recherche Scientifique, 1965), p. 303.
6. *A History of Art in Ancient Egypt* (London: Chapman and Hall, 1883), p. 325.
7. "Sketchbook 1896–1899," UCLA.
8. Gordon Craig Collection, Austrian National Library, Vienna.
9. The design was reproduced in the *Index,* p. 241, and in *Towards a New Theatre* (1913; rpt. New York: Benjamin Blom, 1969), p. 23. Edward Craig describes how Craig got this idea for shadows. See his *Gordon Craig,* p. 152.
10. Ferruccio Marotti, "Stage Management of Gordon Craig. Problems of Documentation," in *Regie in Dokumentation, Forschung und Lehre,* ed. Margret Dietrich (Salzburg: Otto Müller, 1974), p. 46.
11. Talley, pp. 52–53.
12. *On the Art of the Theatre,* p. 50.
13. Marotti, *Edward Gordon Craig,* p. 149.
14. Victor Zuckerhandl, *Sound and Symbol: Music and the External World* (Princeton: Princeton University Press, 1969), p. 68.
15. Ibid., pp. 376–77.
16. Edward Craig, *Gordon Craig,* p. 317.
17. *Motion* served also as a preface to the first portfolio of etchings in 1908 and was printed in *The Mask* the same year (*The Mask,* 1, No. 10 [December 1908], 185–86).
18. T. S. Eliot, "Gordon Craig's Socratic Dialogues," p. 18.
19. Gilbert Durand, *Les Structures anthropologiques de l'imaginaire: Introduction à l'archétypologie générale* (Paris: Presses Universitaires de France, 1963), p. 138.

9. Voice and Drama

1. Craig printed this reconstruction as an appendix to his *Henry Irving.*
2. "Uber-Marions," UM-B, p. 16^{r}.
3. In the *Index,* Craig recalled the performance of *L'Enfant prodigue* by a French troupe, seen in the company of Ellen Terry and Henry Irving in July 1891. *Index,* p. 127.
4. Correspondence with Martin Shaw, Austin (Craig's emphasis).
5. Ibid.
6. "Uber-Marions," UM-B, p. 38^{r} (Craig's emphasis).
7. Ibid., UM-A, p. 26^{r}.
8. Ibid., p. 18^{r}.
9. Ibid., p. 25^{v}.
10. Ibid., p. 26^{v} (Craig's emphasis).

11. Ibid., pp. 25^{v}, 26^{r}.
12. Ibid., p. 27^{r}.
13. Ibid., p. 26^{r} (my emphasis).

10. Belief (I)

1. See my article "Gordon Craig, the Uber-marionette, and the Dresden Theatre," *Theatre Research International,* 5, No. 3 (Autumn 1980), 180.
2. This is visible in his letters to Ellen Terry and Martin Shaw written during 1905 and 1906, as well as in the "Uber-Marions" notebooks. On 13 March 1905, for example, he wrote an enthusiastic letter to Shaw about an "immense affair"—his forthcoming über-marionette theatre; in May, the tone of his letters was subdued. It was during this period that he wrote in the "Uber-Marions" notebooks: "You speak of your idea of the über-marionette–You don't find the response you expected" (UM-A, p. 8^{v}). An entry of 15 July mentions the intolerance of the "cliques" by which he was surrounded (UM-A, p. 12^{v}). On 7 August he sent another enthusiastic letter to Shaw, and not long afterward he sent from Zurich a similar one to Ellen Terry. The same day, in his notebooks, he expressed his disgust for his critics and devised an appropriate means for attack and self-defense: a theatre journal, to be called "The Mask." The notes on the journal are followed by the sketch of a theatre building and by a short defense of the stillness of the über-marionette, followed in its turn by the vision of "Hell and Paradise," a mimo-drama intended to "create a Belief" (UM-A, pp. 21^{r}–28^{r}).
3. "Uber-Marions," UM-B, p. 3^{v}.
4. These are Craig's words. See his introductory poem to the Isadora Portfolio.
5. Walter Pater, *Works* (London: Macmillan, 1910), p. 38.
6. Steegmuller, pp. 56, 59.
7. Referred to in the *Index,* p. 266, as "Life of the Egyptians."
8. Steegmuller, pp. 137, 141, 152–55.
9. See letter to Martin Shaw, in ibid., p. 100.
10. *On the Art of the Theatre,* p. 86.
11. Stéphane Mallarmé, "Solennité," in *Divagations,* p. 234. On the mystical aspect of Symbolism, see also Guy Michaud, *Message poétique du symbolisme* (Paris: Nizet, 1966), pp. 222–25; A. G. Lehmann, *The Symbolist Aesthetic in France, 1885–1895* (Oxford: Basil Blackwell, 1968), pp. 50–55; Philippe Jullian, *Dreamers of Decadence: Symbolist Painters of the 1890s* (London: Phaidon, 1971), pp. 71–85.
12. Lehmann, p. 54.
13. Correspondence with Ellen Terry, Austin.
14. Edward Craig, *Gordon Craig,* p. 168.
15. Gordon Craig Collection, UCLA.
16. "Uber-Marions," UM-B, p. 3^{v}.
17. *On the Art of the Theatre,* p. 52.
18. Ibid., p. 46.

19. Lyons, pp. 63–64.
20. Payne, pp. 428, 431; Valogne, p. 57.
21. Gérard de Champeaux et Dom Sébastien Sterckx, *Introduction au monde des symboles* (Paris: Zodiaque, 1966), p. 31; Mircea Eliade, *Images et symboles. Essais sur le symbolisme magico-religieux* (Paris: Gallimard, 1952), pp. 66–72.
22. Gilbert Durand, *Les Structures anthropologiques de l'imaginaire,* p. 280.
23. *On the Art of the Theatre,* pp. 83–84.
24. Ibid., p. 92.
25. There is no evidence as yet that Craig read Madame H. P. Blavatsky's *Isis Unveiled: A Master Key to the Mysteries of Ancient and Modern Science and Theology* (1877) or her *Secret Doctrine* (1888).
26. "Catalogue of an Exhibition of Drawings and Models for *Hamlet, Macbeth,* and Other Plays, by Edward Gordon Craig," City of Manchester Art Gallery, November 1912, pp. 32–33.
27. Denis Bablet, *Esthétique Générale,* pp. 304–7.
28. Frances A. Yates, *Theatre of the World* (Chicago: University of Chicago Press, 1969), p. 132.
29. "Uber-Marions," UM-B, pp. 9^{r}, 9^{v}, 11^{r}, 12^{r}.
30. "Mss. 1907–08. 1915–16. 1945," Paris.
31. *On the Art of the Theatre,* p. 52.
32. Ibid., p. 53.
33. Ibid., p. 46.
34. Ibid.
35. Marina Maymone Siniscalchi, "Edward Gordon Craig: The Drama for Marionettes," *Theatre Research International,* 5, No. 2 (Spring 1980), 127.
36. *Towards a New Theatre,* p. 86.
37. "Movement," pp. 4^{r}, 4^{v}, UCLA. We follow Craig's graphic arrangement and punctuation.
38. Ibid., p. 5^{r}.
39. Arnold Rood presented parts of the "Movement" manuscript, which includes the illuminations, at the Third Annual Gordon Craig Memorial Lecture delivered in Venice on 12 September 1970. See his "'After the Practise the Theory': Gordon Craig and Movement," pp. 96–101.
40. Roy Pascal, *From Naturalism to Expressionism,* p. 306.
41. *On the Art of the Theatre,* pp. 48–49.

11. The Uber-Marionette International Theatre

1. Correspondence with Martin Shaw, Austin.
2. "Notes and Plans for the School of the Art of the Theatre and the International Art Theatre Society. 1904–1906," Austin.
3. "Uber-Marions," UM-A, p. 18^{v}. See also my article "Gordon Craig, the Uber-Marionette, and the Dresden Theatre."

4. "Uber-Marions," UM-34[r].
5. Letter of October 1905 to Martin Shaw, Austin.
6. However, in November 1905 Craig spent a fortnight in Dresden, then went to Amsterdam in December. During the first months of 1906 he was traveling with Isadora in various parts of Europe.
7. Steegmuller, pp. 227–32, 283.
8. Letter of 8 December 1907 of William Rothenstein to Mary Berenson, in *Max and Will: Max Beerbohm and William Rothenstein, their friendship and letters, 1893 to 1945,* ed. Mary M. Lago and Karl Beckson (Cambridge, Mass.: Harvard University Press, 1975), p. 48.

12. Experiments

1. This letter was later wrongly dated as of 1908. Correspondence with Martin Shaw, Austin. The Californian assistant was the painter Michael Carr. The project of a tour to Munich and Paris did not materialize.
2. The first phase was that of the classical (Greek and Roman) theatre, with its open-air performances and architectural scene; the second—the medieval religious theatre, with the drama being performed in churches (Craig excludes as marginal the performances of the morality and mystery plays that took place outside the church); the third—the Italian commedia dell'arte, where the scene was still architectural (a street, a "wing of palace"); the fourth—the indoor performance, on a stage generally built of wood and using painted scenery and, later on, realistic sets. The fifth phase opened with Craig's invention of the new architectural scene, which used mobile screens. Craig expounded this theory in *Scene* (1923; rpt. New York: Benjamin Blom, 1968).
3. See James W. Flannery, "W. B. Yeats, Gordon Craig and the Visual Arts of the Theatre," in *Yeats and the Theatre,* ed. Robert O'Driscoll and Lorna Reynolds (London: Macmillan, 1975), pp. 82–108, and Karen Dorn, "Dialogue into Movement: W. B. Yeats's Theatre Collaboration with Gordon Craig," ibid., pp. 109–36.
4. Francis Cotton, "Gordon Craig's Scheme to Abolish Both Actors and Playwrights."
5. Ibid.
6. Gordon Craig Collection, UCLA.
7. Claudine Amiard-Chevrel, *Le Théâtre Artistique de Moscou (1898–1917)* (Paris: Centre National de la Recherche Scientifique, 1979), pp. 152–53.
8. Laurence Senelick, *Gordon Craig's Moscow 'Hamlet': A Reconstruction* (Westport, Conn.: Greenwood Press, 1982), p. 17.
9. Laurence Senelick, "The Craig-Stanislavsky 'Hamlet' at the Moscow Art Theatre," *Theatre Quarterly,* 6, No. 22 (Summer 1976), 73.
10. Daybook I (November 1908–March 1910), p. 19, Austin (Craig's emphasis).
11. Ibid., p. 71.

12. Wilde, "The Critic as Artist," in *Complete Works,* p. 1034.
13. See Craig's article "The Ghosts in the Tragedies of Shakespeare" (1910), in *On the Art of the Theatre,* pp. 264–80.
14. Undated letter, correspondence with Haldane MacFall, Paris.
15. See, for example, Orville K. Larson, "Robert Edmond Jones, Gordon Craig and Mabel Dodge," *Theatre Research International,* 3, No. 2 (February 1978), 126–33.
16. Daybook I, p. 151 (Craig's emphasis).
17. Letter from Moscow to William Rothenstein that can be dated as of November or December 1908, correspondence with William Rothenstein, Paris.
18. "Foreign Notes. Florence," *The Mask,* 1, No. 11 (January 1909), 222.
19. Undated letter of 1911, correspondence with Ellen Terry, Austin.
20. Note made on 26 February 1911 in Paris, Daybook II (March 1910–December 1911), p. 189, Austin.
21. See René Piot's letter to Jacques Rouché, quoted in Rose-Marie Moudouès, "Jacques Rouché et Edward Gordon Craig," *Revue d'Histoire du Théâtre,* 10, No. 3 (1958), 313–14.
22. Ernest Marriott, "The School at Florence," *The Mask,* 6, No. 1 (July 1913), 46.
23. See his article "Thoroughness in the Theatre" (1911) in *The Theatre Advancing* (1919; rpt. New York: Benjamin Blom, 1963), pp. 216–28.
24. Edward Craig, *Gordon Craig,* p. 292. See also Arnold Rood, "E. Gordon Craig, Director, School for the Art of the Theatre," *Theatre Research International,* 8, No. 2 (Summer 1983), 1–17.

13. On the Actor and the Uber-Marionette

1. "Letter to Ellen Terry" (18 March 1907), *The Mask,* 1, No. 6 (August 1908), 109–11.
2. "Some Evil Tendencies of the Modern Theatre" (1908), in *On the Art of the Theatre,* p. 95.
3. "Uber-Marions," UM-A, pp. 21^r–24^r. These are (some of?) the pseudonyms used by Craig in *The Mask,* listed alphabetically: AB (used also by Dorothy Nevile Lees, or "D. N. L.," his secretary), ABC, William Addicote, G. B. Ambrose, Anonymous, Lilian Antler (also by D. N. L.), the Author of "Films," J. Somers Bacon, John Balance (also by D. N. L.), John H. Benton, Charles Borrow, Britannicus, John Bull, Edwin J. Burlin, Henry Gay Calvin, Allen Carric, Chi lo sa, Chi sa, CGE, CGS, Georges Devoto, Diddled, Mabel Dobson, Edward Edwardovitch, François M. Florian, Adolf Furst, Antonio Galli, Hadrian Jazz Gavotte, E. Gordon, Fanny Hepworth, Franz Hoffer, Jan van Holt, G. H. (George Hown?), Ivan Ivanovitch, IM, T. Kempees, Jan Klassen, Heinrich Klinkenstein, Carlo Lacchio, J. Moser Lewis, Lois Lincoln (also by D. N. L.), Stanislas Lodochowskowski, William McDougal, Ma che, Louis Madrid, William Marchpane, Giovanni

Mezzogiorno, N. or M, George Norman, O. P., Julius Oliver, Drury Pervil, Henry Phips, Giulo Pirro, Everard Plumbline, Philip Polfreman, Samuel Prim, QED, John S. Rankin, Benjamin Rossen, O. Salamini, Rudolf Schmerz, John Semar (also by D. N. L.), C. G. Smith, John Brown Smith, V. Surgen, Marcel de Tours, Conrad Tower, Scotson Umbridge, Felix Urban, R. T. Vade, Edwin Witherspoon, XYZ, Yoo No Hoo, You No Hoo, Yu No Whoo, Z. A. See Marotti, *Edward Gordon Craig,* p. 97; Bablet, *Edward Gordon Craig,* p. 144; Ifan Kyrle Fletcher and Arnold Rood, *Edward Gordon Craig: A Bibliography* (London: Society for Theatre Research 1967), p. 62; Lorelei Guidry, *Index and Introduction to The Mask* (New York: Benjamin Blom, 1968).

4. *On the Art of the Theatre,* p. 96.
5. Ibid., p. 286.
6. Daybook I, p. 11 (Craig's emphasis).
7. Ibid., p. 77 (Craig's emphasis). See also his notebook "Masques. G. C. 1908," p. 5, Paris.
8. Daybook I, p. 11.
9. Ibid., p. 87.
10. "Open Air Theatre" (1909), in *On the Art of the Theatre,* p. 289.
11. *The Mask,* 7, No. 2 (May 1915), 115.
12. "Psychology and the Drama," *The Mask,* 1, Nos. 10–12 (April 1910), 163–64.
13. Entry of 6 November 1909, Daybook I, p. 183.
14. "Sada Yacco" (1910), in *On the Art of the Theatre,* p. 265.
15. See Peter Gay, *Art and Act: On Causes in History—Manet, Gropius, Mondrian* (New York: Harper and Row, 1976), pp. 222–23.
16. Daybook II, p. 27 (Craig's emphasis).
17. Ibid., p. 117 (Craig's emphasis). (See also his notebook "Commedia dell'arte," 1910, 1911, Paris.)
18. Entry of 11 November 1910, ibid., pp. 132–33 (Craig's emphasis).
19. See letter of 10 December 1915 to Sheldon Cheney, correspondence with Sheldon Cheney, Paris.
20. See Laurence Senelick, *Gordon Craig's Moscow 'Hamlet,'* p. 152. On the influence of the production, see ibid., pp. 174–90.
21. Edward Craig, *Gordon Craig,* pp. 277–80.
22. "Gentlemen, the Marionette!" in *The Theatre Advancing,* pp. 110–11.
23. Correspondence with Ellen Terry, UCLA (Craig's emphasis).
24. *Towards a New Theatre,* p. 48.
25. Ibid., p. 33.
26. Letter of 3 November 1913 to Elsie Fogerty, correspondence with Elsie Fogerty, Paris.
27. Daybook III (December 1911–18), p. 157, Austin.
28. Craig's claim that he never heard about Appia while he was in Germany is indeed very puzzling. As their correspondence shows, both Kessler and

Hofmannsthal knew Appia and his work. See, for example, Hoffmannsthal's letter of 6 October 1903 to Kessler, in *Hugo von Hofmannsthal, Harry Graf Kessler: Briefwechsel, 1898–1929,* p. 55.

29. This book was never completed. Gordon Craig Collection, Austin.
30. "A Durable Theatre" (1915), in *The Theatre Advancing,* pp. 19–20.
31. Ibid.
32. "Rearrangements" (1915), ibid., pp. 205–9.
33. "Belief and Make-Believe: A Footnote to 'The Actor and the Uber-Marionette'" (1915), ibid., pp. 63–67.
34. Letter of 10 December 1915, correspondence with Sheldon Cheney, Paris.

14. Belief (II)

1. "Movement," p. 10^{r}..
2. Ibid., pp. 6^{r}–5^{v}. The close examination of the handwriting, hand pressure, and flow of ink or lead marks shows that Craig often used to write first on the recto of a new page. He continued sometimes on the opposite page (the verso of the previous one), if he had left it empty.
3. For a view that the "Movement" notebook is "the repository of Craig's unshared thinking about movement," see Rood, "'After the Practise the Theory': Gordon Craig and Movement," p. 95.
4. *The Mask,* 2, Nos. 1–3 (July 1909), 2; *On the Art of the Theatre,* p. xxii
5. "Movement," p. 6^{v}.
6. Ibid., p. 7^{r}.
7. Ibid., p. 5^{v}.
8. Ibid., pp. 7^{v}–8^{r}.
9. Ibid., p. 28^{r}.
10. Letter from Moscow to William Rothenstein, which can be dated as of November or December 1908, correspondence with William Rothenstein, Paris.
11. Daybook III, p. 15.
12. "Movement," p. 32^{r} (Craig's emphasis).
13. Entry of 3 February 1909, Daybook I, p. 77.
14. Letter of 19 January 1916 to William Rothenstein, correspondence with William Rothenstein, Paris.

15. "Bending to the Wind"

1. See his "Notebook 13. Florence. April–May–June 1915," Paris.
2. Letter of 27 August 1917, correspondence with William Rothenstein, Paris.
3. Letter written in early 1918 from San Ambrogio, ibid.
4. See also Siniscalchi, "Edward Gordon Craig: The Drama for Marionettes," pp. 131–36.
5. Letter of 13 July 1918, draft A., correspondence with William Rothenstein, Paris.

6. Letter of 13 July 1918, draft D, ibid. In Indian mythology, Kewana, or Cyavana, was an old sage.
7. Jacques Fox-Laurier, "A Marionnette in Rome," *The Marionnette,* 1, No. 4 (June 1918), 116–25.
8. *The Marionnette,* 1, No. 1 (April 1918), 6.
9. See his letter of 16 November 1921 to Rothenstein, correspondence with William Rothenstein, Paris.
10. See Denis Bablet, "La remise en scène du lieu théâtral au vingtième siècle," in *Le Lieu théâtral dans la société moderne,* ed. Denis Bablet and Jean Jacquot (Paris: Centre National de la Recherche Scientifique, 1969), p. 22.
11. *Scene,* p. 25.
12. Oskar Schlemmer, "Theater (Bühne)," in *Theater of the Bauhaus,* ed. Walter Gropius (Middletown, Conn.: Wesleyan University Press, 1961), p. 95.
13. Edward Craig, *Gordon Craig,* p. 317.
14. *On the Art of the Theatre,* pp. ix–x.
15. Frederick J. Marker and Lise-Lone Marker, *Edward Gordon Craig and 'The Pretenders': A Production Revisited* (Carbondale,: Southern Illinois University Press, 1981), pp. 15–16.
16. Ibid., p. 52.
17. Ibid., p. 47.
18. Ibid., pp. 68, 76.
19. Ibid., p. 25.
20. *A Production, Being Thirty-Two Collotype Plates of Designs prepared or realized for 'The Pretenders' of Henrik Ibsen and produced at the Royal Theatre, Copenhagen, 1926* (London: Oxford University Press, 1930).
21. "An Easy Book on the Theatre," Austin.
22. CBS interview, "60 Minutes," 2 January 1983.
23. *Henry Irving,* p. 111.
24. Entry of 6 January 1931, Daybook V (1930–33), Austin.
25. Daybook VII (November 1933–March 1935), p. 83, Austin (Craig's emphasis).
26. "On Creating a Theatre. 1934–1935," Austin.
27. Letter of 6 April 1935 from Moscow, correspondence with Meyerhold, Paris.
28. Letter of 14 May 1935, ibid.
29. See Steegmuller, p. 291.
30. Jottings from 1951 on Iris Bucher's *Piero della Francesca Fresken* (Stuttgart: Deutsche Verlage Anstalt, 1949), Private Collection of Professor Norman Philbrick, Stanford Exhibition, October 1985.
31. *Index,* p. 236 (my emphasis).

Afterword

1. Lee Simonson's virulent attack on Craig was published in 1932. See Lee Simonson, *The Stage is Set* (1932; rpt. New York: Theatre Arts Books, 1963). For a more recent refutation of Craig's work see the psychoanalytic

interpretation of Frederick Brown in his *Theatre and Revolution: The Culture of the French Stage* (New York: Viking Press, 1980), pp. 211–26.

2. See "On Learning Magic" (1914), in *The Theatre Advancing,* pp. 230–35.
3. "Uber-Marions," UM-B, p. 7^{r}.
4. "Symbolism" (1910), in *On the Art of the Theatre,* p. 293.
5. *Index,* pp. 246–48.
6. "Uber-Marions," UM-B, p. 14^{r} (Craig's emphasis).
7. In a public appeal, published in *The Mask* and signed by "John Semar," Craig wrote: "I believe . . . that a great college is the first necessity; such a college to have branches in all the European and American states so that men (not women, by the way) may be trained all over the Earth, who will, after many years, unite the great capitals of Europe and America by means of an art which has in it the seeds of a universal language. . . . the language of symbolic movement" ("To Mr. Andrew Carnegie," *The Mask,* 1, Nos. 3–4 [May–June 1908], 74.
8. Entry of 18 September 1909, Daybook I, p. 151.

Bibliography

Because of space limitations, this is a selected list of works on the topics examined. Other works, not included here, appear in the notes.

Manuscript Collections

Bibliothèque Nationale, Paris. Gordon Craig Collection.
Edward A. Craig Library, Long Crendon, England. Gordon Craig Collection.
Houghton Library and the Theatre Collection, Harvard University, Cambridge, Massachusetts.
Humanities Research Center, University of Texas at Austin, Texas. Gordon Craig Collection.
Osterreichische Nationalbibliothek, Theatersammlung, Vienna.
Philbrick Library, Los Altos Hills, California. Gordon Craig Collection, as exhibited at Stanford University, October 1985.
Arnold Rood Library, New York, Gordon Craig Collection.
University Research Library, Department of Special Collections, University of California at Los Angeles.
Victoria and Albert Museum, London. Department of Prints and Drawings and the Enthoven Collection.

Works by Edward Gordon Craig

Notebooks and Typescripts

"Sketchbook 1896–1906." UCLA.
"Notebook. 1897." UCLA.
"Confessions. 1901. 1902. 1903." Austin.
"M[asques]." 1903. Paris.
"Notes and Plans for the School of the Art of the Theatre and the International Art Theatre Society. 1904–1906." Austin.

Bibliography

"The Isadora Duncan Notebooks." 1904–1944. Austin.
"Uber-Marions. Berlin. 1905. 1906." Paris.
"Theatre—Shows and Motions." 1905, 1908–9. Austin.
"Stockholm. Book A. Berlin 1906." UCLA.
"Movement." 1907–55. UCLA.
"Mss. 1907–08., 1915–16." Paris.
Daybooks. 1908–43, Austin; 1948–64, Paris.
"The Allasio Notebook." 1911, 1912, 1913. Austin.
"Minute Book of the 'Society of the Theatre.'" 1912. UCLA.
"The Theatre. The New Movement and the Newer One." 1915. Austin.
"The Drama for Fools." 1921. Austin.
"Scene." First draft, 1921. Second draft, 1921. Austin.
"An Easy Book on the Theatre." 1923–30. Austin.
"Tritons and Minnows." 1932–33. Austin.
"On Creating a Theatre." 1934–45. Austin.
"Art and the Nation." N.d. Austin.

Correspondence

Letters to Sheldon Cheney (Paris), Jacques Copeau (Paris), John Cournos (Harvard), Elsie Fogerty (Paris), Haldane MacFall (Paris, Austin), Meyerhold (Paris), William Rothenstein (Paris, Austin, Harvard), Martin Shaw (Austin), Ellen Terry (Paris, Austin, UCLA).
Bablet, Denis, ed. "Correspondence inédite entre Adolphe Appia et Edward Gordon Craig (1914–1924)." Diss. Sorbonne, 1965.

Annotated Books

Alberti, Leon Battista. *L'architettura.* Monte Regale: Torrentino, 1565 (Paris).
Bucher, Iris. *Piero della Francesca Fresken.* Stuttgart: Deutsche Verlage Anstalt, 1949 (Philbrick Library).
Harbron, Dudley. *The Conscious Stone: The Life of Edward William Godwin.* London: Latimer House, 1949 (Paris).
Serlio, Sebastiano. *Libro primo d'architettura.* Venetia: Sessa, 1560 (Paris).

Published Works

"'Stars': Mr. Frohman, and the Theatre of the Future." *Saturday Review,* 3 November 1906, pp. 548–49.
Isadora Duncan: Sechs Bewegungsstudien von Edward Gordon Craig. Leipzig: Insel Verlag, 1906.
"Letter to Eleonora Duse." *Washington Post,* 1 December 1907.
The Mask: A Journal of the Art of the Theatre. Florence, 1908–29.
On the Art of the Theatre. 1911; rpt. London: Heinemann, 1968.
Towards a New Theatre. London: J. M. Dent and Sons, 1913.
The Marionnette. Florence, 1918–19.
The Theatre Advancing. 1919; rpt. New York: Benjamin Blom, 1963.
Puppets and Poets, (*The Chapbook,* No. 20 [February 1921]).

Scene. London: Oxford University Press, 1923.
Woodcuts and Some Words. London: J. M. Dent and Sons, 1924.
Books and Theatres. London: J. M. Dent and Sons, 1925.
Henry Irving. London: J. M. Dent and Sons, 1930.
A Production being thirty-two collotype plates of designs projected or realised for "The Pretenders" of Henrik Ibsen and produced at the Royal Theatre Copenhagen 1926 by Edward Gordon Craig. London: Oxford University Press, 1930.
Ellen Terry and Her Secet Self. London: Sampson, Low, Marston, 1931.
Fourteen Notes. On eight pages from "The Story of the Theatre" by Glenn Hughes with some fourteen notes by Edward Gordon Craig. Seattle: University of Washington Book Store, 1931.
Index to the Story of My Days: Some Memoirs of Edward Gordon Craig, 1872–1907. London: Hulton Press, 1957.
Ma vie d'homme de théâtre. Trans. Charles Chassé. Paris: Arthaud, 1962.
Gordon Craig's Paris Diary, 1932–1933. Ed., with a prologue, Colin Franklin. North Hills, Pa.: Bird and Bull Press, 1982.
Craig on Theatre. Ed. J. Michael Walton. London: Methuen, 1983.

Works on Edward Gordon Craig

Arnott, Brian. *Towards a New Theatre: Edward Gordon Craig and Hamlet*. Ottawa: National Gallery of Canada, 1975.
Barshay, Bernard. "Gordon Craig's Theories of Acting." *Theatre Annual*, 1947, pp. 55–63.
Bablet, Denis. *Edward Gordon Craig*. Paris: L'Arche, 1962.
———. "Edward Gordon Craig and Scenography." *Theatre Research*, 11, No. 1 (1971), 7–22.
Brook, Peter. "The Influence of Gordon Craig in Theory and Practice." *Drama*, No. 37 (Summer 1955), pp. 32–36.
Clark, Georgina. "Gordon Craig and the Paradox of Shakespeare." *Maske und Kothurn*, 28th year, No. 2 (1982), 113–19.
Copeau, Jacques. "Visites à Gordon Craig, Jaques-Dalcroze et Adolphe Appia (1915)." *Revue d'Histoire du Théâtre*, 15 (1963), 357–74.
Cotton, Francis. "Gordon Craig's Scheme to Abolish Both Actors and Playwrights." *Washington Post*, 1 December 1907.
Craig, Edward. *Gordon Craig: The Story of His Life*. London: Victor Gollancz, 1968.
———. "Gordon Craig and Hubert von Herkomer." *Theatre Research*, 10, No. 1 (1969), 7–16.
———. "Gordon Craig and Bach's *St. Matthew Passion*." *Theatre Notebook*, 26, No. 4 (Summer 1972), 147–51.
———. "Edward Gordon Craig's Hamlet." *Private Library*, 2d ser., 10, No. 1 (Spring 1977), 35–48.
———. *Edward Gordon Craig: The Last Eight Years*. Andoversford: Whittington Press, 1983.

Bibliography

Dorn, Karen. "Dialogue into Movement: W. B. Yeats's Theatre Collaboration with Gordon Craig." In *Yeats and the Theatre,* Ed. Robert O'Driscoll and Lorna Reynolds. London: Macmillan, 1975, pp. 109–36.

Doswald, Herman K. "Edward Gordon Craig and Hugo von Hofmannsthal." *Theatre Research International,* 1, No. 2 (Fall 1975), 134–41.

Eliot, Thomas Stearn. "Gordon Craig's Socratic Dialogues." *Drama,* No. 36 (Spring 1955), pp. 16–21.

Eynat, Irène. "Gordon Craig, the Uber-Marionette, and the Dresden Theatre." *Theatre Research International,* 5, No. 3 (Autumn 1980), 171–93.

Flannery, James W. "W. B. Yeats, Gordon Craig and the Visual Arts of the Theatre." In *Yeats and the Theatre,* Ed. Robert O'Driscoll and Lorna Reynolds. London: Macmillan, 1975, pp. 82–108.

Fletcher, Ifan Kyrle, and Arnold Rood. *Edward Gordon Craig. A Bibliography.* London: Society for Theatre Research, 1967.

Franklin, Colin. *Fond of Printing: Gordon Craig as Typographer and Illustrator.* London: Hurtwood, 1980.

Grossman, Harvey. "Gordon Craig and the Actor." *Chrysalis,* 6, Nos. 7–8 (1953), 3–14.

Guidry, Lorelei. *Index and Introduction to "The Mask."* New York: Benjamin Blom, 1968.

Herstand, Theodore. "Edward Gordon Craig on the Nature of the Artists." *Educational Theatre Journal,* 18, No. 1 (March 1966), 7–11.

Hewitt, Barnard. "Gordon Craig and Post-Impressionism." *Quarterly Journal of Speech,* 30, No. 1 (January–February 1944), 75–80.

Innes, Christopher. *Edward Gordon Craig.* Cambridge: Cambridge University Press, 1983.

Jacquot, Jean. "Craig, Yeats et le théâtre d'Orient." In *Les théâtres d'Asie.* Ed. Jean Jacquot. Paris: Centre National de la Recherche Scientifique, 1968, pp. 271–83.

Kreidt, Dietrich. "Kunsttheorie der Inszenierung: Zur Kritik der ästhetischen Konzeptionen Adolphe Appias und Edward Gordon Craigs." Diss. Freien Universität Berlin, 1968.

Larson, Orville K. "Robert Edmond Jones, Gordon Craig, and Mabel Dodge." *Theatre Research International,* 3, No. 2 (February 1978), 126–33.

Laver, James. "Gordon Craig and the English Theatre." *Drama,* No. 13 (May 1949), pp. 24–28.

Lee, Sang-Kyong. "Edward Gordon Craig und das japanische Theater." *Deutsche Vierteljarsschrift für Literaturwissenschaft,* 55, No. 2 (July 1981), 216–37.

Leeper, Janet. *Edward Gordon Craig. Designs for the Theatre.* Harmondsworth: Penguin Books, 1948.

Lees, Dorothy Nevile. "Notes on Work with Gordon Craig and *The Mask* in Florence: From the Beginning of 1907 Onwards." TS, Gordon Craig Collection, Humanities Research Center, University of Texas at Austin, Texas.

Loeffler, Michael Peter. *Gordon Craig und die "Purcell Operatic Society": Ein früher Versuch zur Uberwindung des Bühnenrealismus*. Bern: Theaterkultur-Verlag, 1971.

Lyons, Charles R. "Gordon Craig's Concept of the Actor." In *Total Theatre*. Ed. E. T. Kirby. New York: Dutton and Co., 1969, pp. 58–77.

Magnus, Maurice. "Gordon Craig and His Art, 1907." TS, Gordon Craig Collection, Humanities Research Center, University of Texas at Austin, Texas.

Marker, Frederick J., and Lise-Lone Marker. *Edward Gordon Craig and "The Pretenders": A Production Revisited*. Carbondale: Southern Illinois University Press, 1981.

Marotti, Ferruccio. *Edward Gordon Craig*. Bologna: Capelli, 1961.

———. *Amleto o dell'Oxymoron: Studi e note sull'estetica della scena moderna*. Roma: Mario Bulzoni, 1966.

———. "Stage Management of Gordon Craig: Problems of Documentation." In *Regie in Dokumentation: Forschung und Lehre*. Ed. Margret Dietrich. Salzburg: Otto Müller, 1974, pp. 43–46.

Mariott, Ernest. "The School at Florence." *The Mask*, 6, No. 1 (July 1913), 46.

Moudouès, Rose-Marie. "Jacques Rouché et Edward Gordon Craig." *Revue de la Société d'Histoire du Théâtre*, 10, No. 3 (1958), 313–19.

Myers, Norman. "Early Recognition of Gordon Craig in American Periodicals." *Educational Theatre Journal*, 22, No. 1 (March 1970), 78–86.

Nash, George. *Edward Gordon Craig, 1872–1966*. London: Victoria and Albert Museum, 1967.

Newman, Lindsay Mary. *Gordon Craig Archives: International Survey*. London: Malkin Press, 1976.

Osanai, Kaoru. "Gordon Craig's Production of *Hamlet* at the Moscow Art Theatre." *Educational Theatre Journal*, 20, No. 4 (1968), pp. 586–93.

Payne, Harry C. "Rituals of Balance and Silence: The Ideal Theatre of Gordon Craig." *Bulletin of Research in the Humanities*, 82, No. 4 (Winter 1979), 424–49.

Rood, Arnold. "'After the Practise the Theory': Gordon Craig and Movement." *Theatre Research*, 11, Nos. 2–3 (1971), 81–101.

———, ed. *Gordon Craig on Movement and Dance*. New York: Dance Horizons, 1977.

———. "E. Gordon Craig, Director, School for the Art of the Theatre." *Theatre Research International*, 8, No. 1 (Spring 1983), 1–17.

Rose, Enid. *Gordon Craig and the Theatre: A Record and an Interpretation*. 1931; rpt. New York: Haskell House Publishers, 1973.

Senelick, Laurence. "The Craig-Stanislavsky 'Hamlet' at the Moscow Art Theatre." *Theatre Quarterly*, 6, No. 22 (Summer 1976), 56–122.

———. "Moscow and Monodrama: The Meaning of the Craig-Stanislavsky 'Hamlet.'" *Theatre Research International*, 6, No. 2 (Spring 1981), 109–24.

———. *Gordon Craig's Moscow "Hamlet"; A Reconstruction*. Westport, Conn.: Greenwood Press, 1982.

Siniscalchi, Maria Maymone. "Edward Gordon Craig: The Drama for Marionettes." *Theatre Research International*, 5, No. 2 (Spring 1980), 122–37.

Steegmuller, Francis, ed. *"Your Isadora": The Love Story of Isadora Duncan and Gordon Craig Told through Letters and Diaries.* New York: Random House, 1974.
Talley, Paul M. "Architecture as Craig's Interim Symbol: Ruskin and Other Influences." *Educational Theatre Journal,* 19, No. 1 (March 1967), 52–60.
Valogne, Catherine. *Gordon Craig.* Paris: Presses Littéraires de France, 1953.

Other Works

Amiard-Chevrel, Claudine. *Le Théâtre Artistique de Moscou (1898–1917).* Paris: Centre National de la Recherche Scientifique, 1979.
Appia, Adolphe. *L'Oeuvre d'art vivant.* Paris: Atar, 1921.
———. *Designs for Stage Settings and Scenery.* Zurich: Art Institut, Orell-Fussli, 1929.
———. *La Musique et la mise-en-scène.* Bern: Theaterkultur-Verlag, 1963.
Archer, William. *Masks or Faces? A Study in the Psychology of Acting.* London: Longmans, Green, 1880.
Ariès, Philippe. *Western Attitudes toward Death: From the Middle Ages to the Present.* Baltimore: Johns Hopkins University Press, 1974.
Auerbach, Nina. *Woman and the Demon: The Life of a Victorian Myth.* Cambridge, Mass.: Harvard University Press, 1982.
Bablet, Denis. *Esthétique générale du décor de théâtre de 1870 à 1914.* Paris: Centre National de la Recherche Scientifique, 1965.
———. "La Remise en scène du lieu théâtral au vingtième siècle." In *Le Lieu théâtral dans la société moderne.* Ed. Denis Bablet and Jean Jacquot. Paris: Centre National de la Recherche Scientifique, 1969, pp. 13–25.
Beerbohm, Max. *Around Theatres.* 1926; rpt. London: Rupert Hart Davis, 1953.
———. *More Theatres, 1898–1903.* London: Rupert Hart Davis, 1969.
Bensky, Roger-Daniel. *Recherches sur les structures et la symbolique de la marionnette.* Paris: Nizet, 1971.
Block, Haskell M. *Mallarmé and the Symbolist Drama.* Detroit: Wayne State University Press, 1963.
Boon, James A. *From Symbolism to Structuralism: Lévi-Strauss in a Literary Tradition.* New York: Harper and Row, 1973.
Bouleau, Charles. *The Painter's Secret Geometry: A Study of Composition in Art.* New York: Harcourt, Brace and World, 1963.
Brown, Frederick. *Theatre and Revolution: The Culture of the French Stage.* New York: Viking Press, 1980.
Brown, J. F. "Aleister Crowley's *Rites of Eleusis.*" *Drama Review,* 22, No. 2 (T78) (June 1978), 3–26.
Bugard, Pierre. *Le Comédien et son double: Psychologie du comédien.* Paris: Stock, 1970.
Chamberlin, J. E. *Ripe Was the Drowsy Hour: The Age of Oscar Wilde.* New York: Seabury Press, 1977.

Bibliography

Champeaux, Gérard de, and Dom Sébastien Sterck. *Introduction au monde des symboles.* Paris: Zodiaque, 1966.

Compagnon, Antoine. *Nous, Michel de Montaigne.* Paris: Seuil, 1980.

Coulon, François. "De l'action dans le drame symbolique." *La Plume,* No. 87 (1 December 1892), 499–500.

Craig, Edith, and Christopher St. John, eds. *Ellen Terry's Memoirs.* 1933; rpt. Westport, Conn.: Greenwood Press, 1970.

Creese, Robb. "Anthroposophical Performance." *Drama Review,* 22, No. 2 (T78) (June 1978), 45–74.

Dale, Peter Allan. *The Victorian Critic and the Idea of History: Carlyle, Arnold, and Pater.* Cambridge, Mass.: Harvard University Press, 1977.

Damrosch, Leopold, Jr. *Symbol and Truth in Blake's Myth.* Princeton: Princeton University Press, 1980.

Deak, Frantisek. "Symbolist Staging at Théâtre d'Art." *Drama Review,* 20, No. 3 (T71) (September 1976), 117–22.

Decroux, Etienne. *Paroles sur le mime.* Paris: Gallimard, 1963.

Dufrenne, Mikel. *Phénoménologie de l'expérience esthétique.* Paris: Presses Universitaires de France, 1967.

———. Le Poétique. Paris: Presses Universitaires de France, 1973.

Duncan, Isadora. *My Life.* New York: Liveright, 1927.

———. *The Art of the Dance.* Ed. Sheldon Cheney. 1928; rpt. New York: Theatre Art Books, 1969.

———. *Isadora Speaks,* Ed. Franklin Rosemont. San Francisco: City Lights Books, 1981.

Durand, Gilbert. *Les Structures anthropologiques de l'imaginaire: Introduction à l'archétypologie générale.* Paris: Presses Universitaires de France, 1963.

———. *L'Imagination symbolique.* Paris: Presses Universitaires de France, 1964.

Elam, Keir. *The Semiotics of Theatre and Drama.* London: Methuen, 1980.

Eliade, Mircea. *Images et symboles: Essais sur le symbolisme magico-religieux.* Paris: Gallimard, 1952.

Eynat, Irène. "Adolphe Appia: De la Communication au Jeu." *Maske und Kothurn,* 22d year, Nos. 3–4 (1976), 238–52.

Gay, Peter. *Art and Act: On Causes in History—Manet, Gropius, Mondrian.* New York: Harper and Row, 1976.

Gettings, Fred. *The Occult in Art.* New York: Rizzoli, 1979.

Hofmannsthal, Hugo von. *Hugo von Hofmannsthal, Harry Graf Kessler: Briefwechsel, 1898–1929.* Ed. Hilde Burger. Frankfurt-am-Main: Insel Verlag, 1968.

John, S. Beynon. "Actor as Puppet: Variations on a Nineteenth-Century Theatrical Ideal." In *Bernhardt and the Theatre of Her Time.* Ed. Eric Salmon. Westport, Conn.: Greenwood Press, 1984.

Kessler, Harry Klemens Ulrich, Graf von. *The Diaries of a Cosmopolitan: Count Harry Kessler, 1918–1937.* Ed. Charles Kessler. London: Weidenfeld and Nicolson, 1971.

Kugel, James L. *The Techniques of Strangeness in Symbolist Poetry.* New Haven: Yale University Press, 1971.
Lehmann, A. G. *The Symbolist Aesthetic in France, 1885–1895.* Oxford: Basil Blackwell, 1968.
Magriel, Paul, ed. *Isadora Duncan.* New York: Holt, 1947.
Mallarmé, Stéphane. *Divagations.* Paris: Eugène Fasquelle, 1897.
Masur, Gerhard. *Imperial Berlin.* London: Routledge and Kegan Paul, 1971.
Mauclair, Camille. "Notes sur un essai de dramaturgie symboliste." *La Revue Indépendante,* March 1892, pp. 305–17.
Morice, Charles. *Demain: Questions d'esthétique.* Paris: Perrin, 1888.
———. *La Littérature de tout à l'heure.* Paris: Perrin, 1889.
Nadel, Myron Howard, and Constance Nadel Miller, eds. *The Dance Experience: Readings in Dance Appreciation.* New York: Universe Books, 1978.
Panofsky, Erwin. *L'Oeuvre d'art et ses significations: Essais sur les "arts visuels."* Paris: Gallimard, 1969.
Pascal, Roy. *From Naturalism to Expressionism: German Literature and Society, 1880–1918.* New York: Basic Books, 1973.
Perrot, Georges, and Charles Chipiez. *A History of Art in Ancient Egypt.* London: Chapman and Hall, 1883.
Pischel, Richard. *The Home of the Puppet-Play.* Trans. Mildred C. Tawney. London: Luzac, 1902.
Quillard, Pierre. "De l'Inutilité absolue de la mise-en-scène exacte." *La Revue d'Art Dramatique,* 22 (April–June 1891), 180–83.
Ricoeur, Paul. *La Métaphore vive.* Paris: Seuil, 1975.
Roach, Joseph R., Jr. "G. H. Lewes and Performance Theory: Towards a 'Science of Acting.'" *Theatre Journal,* 32, No. 3 (October 1980), 312–28.
Roessler, Arthur. *Richard Teschner.* Wien: Gerlach und Wielding, 1947.
Rothenstein, William. *Men and Memories: A History of the Arts 1872–1922, Being the Recollections of William Rothenstein.* New York: Tudor Publishing Co., n.d..
St. John Christopher, ed. *Ellen Terry and Bernard Shaw: A Correspondence.* New York: G. P. Putnam's Sons, 1932.
Schlemmer, Oskar. "Theater (Bühne)." In *Theater of the Bauhaus.* Ed. Walter Gropius. Middletown, Conn.: Wesleyan University Press, 1961.
Schorske, Carl E. *Fin-de-siècle Vienna: Politics and Culture.* New York: Random House, 1981.
Shaw, Martin Fallas. *Up to Now.* London: Oxford University Press, 1929.
Simonson, Lee. *The Stage Is Set.* 1932; rpt. New York: Theatre Art Books, 1963.
Stanislavsky, Constantin. *My Life in Art.* Boston: Little, Brown, 1938.
Stokes, John. *Resistible Theatres: Enterprise and Experiment in the Late Nineteenth Century.* London: Paul Elek Books, 1972.
Symons, Arthur. *The Symbolist Movement in Literature.* London: Heinemann, 1899.
———. *Plays, Acting and Music: A Book of Theory.* London: Duckworth, 1903.

———. *Studies in Seven Arts.* London: Constable, 1906.
———. "Word on Puppets." *The Mask,* 5, No. 2 (October 1912), 103.
Terry, Ellen. *The Story of My Life.* 1908; rpt. New York: Schocken, 1982.
Valin, Pierre. "Le symbole au théâtre." *L'Ermitage,* 3 January 1892, pp. 28–29.
Veinstein, André. *La Mise-en-scène théâtrale et sa condition esthétique.* Paris: Flammarion, 1955.
Wilde, Oscar. *Complete Works.* London: Collins, 1973.
Zuckerhandl, Victor. *Sound and Symbol: Music and the External World.* Princeton: Princeton University Press, 1969.

Index

Index

Index

Index

Index

Index

Index

Index

Index

Irene Eynat-Confino received her Ph.D. degree from the Sorbonne, Paris. She has contributed articles on modern theatre to various publications, including *Theatre Research International* and *Maske und Kothurn*. She has taught theatre history and criticism at Tel-Aviv University and is currently working on the meaning of the fantastic in modern Western theatre.